## THE KILLING ZONE

The president's agonized voice cut him off again. "Get those people out of there," he shouted. "Now!"

There was a general scramble for the door. In a moment, the president sat alone, the soft slur of the speaker drifting in the air. Very slowly, he leaned forward, putting the butts of his palms into his eye sockets.

He looked like a man who had just glimpsed a vision of hell.

*Other Avon Books by*
**Charles Ryan**

CODE BLACK

# CHARLES RYAN

# TRACK
## OF THE
# BENGAL

AVON BOOKS ◆ NEW YORK

This is a work of fiction. Names, characters, places, and incidents either are the product of the author's imagination or are used fictitiously. Any resemblance to actual events, locales, organizations, or persons, living or dead, is entirely coincidental and beyond the intent of either the author or the publisher.

AVON BOOKS, INC.
1350 Avenue of the Americas
New York, New York 10019

Copyright © 1999 by Charles Ryan
Published by arrangement with the author
Visit our website at **http://www.AvonBooks.com**
Library of Congress Catalog Card Number: 98-93301
ISBN: 0-380-79132-3

First Avon Books Printing: January 1999

AVON TRADEMARK REG. U.S. PAT. OFF. AND IN OTHER COUNTRIES, MARCA REGISTRADA, HECHO EN U.S.A.

Printed in the U.S.A.

WCD 10 9 8 7 6 5 4 3 2 1

*Things that are known alike;*
  *which are not wholesome*
*To those which would not know them,*
  *and yet must*
*Perforce be their acquaintance.*

*King Henry VIII*
William Shakespeare

*And as soon as that packet was out on the sea . . .*
*'Twas dev'lish hard treatment of every degree . . .*

"Blow the Man Down"
Sea chantey

*To Mike and Charlie,*
*sons of the heart . . .*

NEGEV DESERT, ISRAEL
AUGUST 15

THE STRIKE TEAM WAITED THREE WEEKS FOR THE MESsage.

There were seven men in the team. Their desert battle fatigues and *jamadani* turbans were sweat-stained, their faces masked by scraggly, dust-covered beards. Each was heavily armed—Heckler and Koch MP5K nine-millimeter assault pistols, sawed-off twelve-gauge Remington pump shotguns. One man carried an RPG-7 portable rocket launcher.

They were Kurdish guerrillas called *Persh Megras* from the Zagros Mountains of northern Iraq. All were veterans of elite terrorist training camps in Turkey, Yemen and Bab Aziza, Libya.

They'd come from the Egyptian Sinai, crossing the frontier into Israel east of El Kuntilla, moving only at night aboard KLX-650 Kawasaki off-road motorcycles fitted with oversized tanks, extra cans of gasoline and saddle packets of C-4 explosive.

Their leader was a Bakhtari Kurd named Mashhad Jadid. Thirty, slender and wiry as a ballet dancer with thick black hair swept straight back into a *dabbah*, an assassin's knot,

1

he was a man consumed with a dark restlessness and had the eyes of a viper. Descended from Kur warrior clans, he was known for his skill with the knife.

It was early afternoon of the twenty-second day. The men were sprawled in the shady mouth of an ancient copper mine in the Arava Se'la Mountains in the southern Negev. They were eating their noon meal, paper-thin *tiroq* crackers and goat jerky. The cave stank of bat guano and the acid odor of feldspar dust.

Occasionally, a small British PVS 5400 radio on Jadid's belt would beep, then crackle with voice transmissions in Hebrew or Arabic. The radio was programmed to guard 7390.5 kilohertz, an amateur frequency often used by Bedouin contraband runners.

A half mile downslope was a narrow road. Its asphalt surface fumed heat waves. This was the cutoff from Route 40 out of Beersheba and led to the ruins of Kadesh Shivun six miles farther south. In the second century, a Roman garrison had been posted there to guard the caravan trail north from the Red Sea. Now the Roman ruins served another purpose. Beneath the tumbled walls and truncated watchtower was a honeycomb of tunnels that housed a secret arms cache and a contingent of crack Israeli paratroopers. But no sign of life showed above the ruins.

Since the Negev is not a sand desert, its barren wastes are composed of upthrust scrag and low folds of limestone and chalk instead of dunes. These are webbed with deep wadis and erosion craters.

When the guerrillas first arrived, Jadid had chosen his kill zone at a point where two wadis paralleled the road. Over two nights, under the cold, blue-white desert moon, they'd buried their Kawasakis in shallow pits and camouflaged them with sand-colored tarps and stones. Then they strung C-4 charges with radio-impulse fuses across the road. . . .

Their meal completed, the men faced Mecca and prostrated themselves in prayer. Then they withdrew deeper into the cave and lay down to sleep.

All but Jadid. He paced agitatedly, now and then scanning the desert with binoculars. The land lay vast and empty and dun-colored. Mirages formed lakes of dancing water, and tiny dust devils whirled for a moment before disappearing. Everything hummed with heat and distance.

The radio beeped.

Jadid reached down and flicked up the volume. Several loud transmitter clicks sounded, little popping snaps. These were immediately followed by a series of long whistles.

The men sat up to listen.

The whistles stopped. A burst of static swept past like the pelting of heavy raindrops. Then, very rapidly, came groups of three letters in Morse code, each linked to a marker ID:

CQ-KLK . . . CQ-JDJ . . . CQ-ZIZ . . .
CQ-AMM . . . CQ-XXX

Again the riffle of static and a repeat of the letter groups. "Up, up!" Jadid yelled in Kurdish. "It comes."

Before the code sequence was completed a second time, the guerrillas were moving. . . .

They left one at a time, disappearing over the lip of the cave and drop-sliding along crevices in the rock face, hunched, holding to cover.

Jadid was the last to leave. He glassed the north for a moment, then swung the binoculars to his right. The coast town of Eilat and the Gulf of Aqaba lay to the east, thirty miles away.

He swept the horizon slowly. A thin, dark line was etched along the horizon like a penciled shadow. He smiled. It was a dust storm. Often, in the afternoon, such storms blew off the gulf.

By the time he reached the kill zone, his second-in-command, Zub Hadiv, had already ordered the men to unearth their motorcycles. Jadid dropped to his knees where his own was hidden and began to dig, hauling off the tarp and pulling the machine upright, gypsum dust powdering the metal.

Then he gathered the men around him. Their faces were sweat limned, their eyes sparkling with excitement. "The message indicates that there will be three units," he told them. "What we seek is in the middle vehicle. Be careful with it."

Quickly he reviewed their assault plan. Then he went to each man in turn. Speaking his name, Jadid took the man's face between his hands and kissed his mouth. *"Newroz an Inshallah,"* he whispered. This day which God wills.

Afterward, the guerrillas moved off to take up their assigned positions beside the road: four to the left, two to the right. Before crossing, Hadiv paused beside Jadid to assemble his rocket launcher.

He grinned broadly. He was a handsome young man with feminine eyes. He jerked his head toward the dust storm. "Look, Allah sends us help."

Jadid nodded, checked his watch. It was 2:45. He estimated that the storm would be on them within twenty minutes. But would it remain long enough? If they could mount the assault while they were still in its midst, everything would be hidden from the periscopes of the Kadesh Shivun garrison. It would even interfere with the convoy's radios so they couldn't sound an alert. That would give the strike team more time to escape back into the hills.

Hadiv scurried away, the barrel of the launcher gleaming dully in the harsh sunlight.

Jadid pulled up his desert goggles and adjusted them snugly against his face. Then he took off his *jamadani* and rewound it, using the long cloth to cover both his face and head. The other men did the same.

He stretched out against the ground, the binoculars propped so that he could look eastward across the approaching storm front. It now appeared at least five hundred feet high, a gray-brown moving mass like a cliff face that boiled and churned. In front of it, high up, vultures made lazy-eights, gaining altitude.

Jadid closed his eyes and played out the coming strike in his mind. His thoughts moved with great speed. He could smell the strong, acrid odor of his own body's musk seeping up through the turban cloth. He opened his eyes. Lifting his assault pistol, he chambered a round. The weapon's breach bolt made a sharp, metallic snap.

Ten minutes passed.

They could hear the storm clearly now, a low rumbling moan. A gentle countering breeze started, blowing toward the front. It was furnace hot and flicked off little tongues of gypsum dust. A covey of desert sparrows, fleeing the storm, came suddenly hurtling along the wadi, their wings burring the air.

The roaring grew ever louder as the dust storm came on, crossing hillocks and craters like the downward surge of volcanic ash moving at fifty miles an hour. Then it had them.

The air instantly seemed to ossify, the pressure hurting Jadid's ears. Pebbles and small rocks went whipping past, ricocheting off the road. The thickness of the wind clogged up his face cloth, choking him.

Nearly all light vanished in the first slamming rush of the storm. Then, gradually, the darkness thinned into a dim, whirling dusk.

He pressed himself as tightly as he could against the ground and waited.

The Israeli RAM V-11 armored car appeared through the dust two hundred yards away. Its headlights glowed, two orange disks. It looked stubby and sat on high, thick rubber wheels.

On the open deck behind the driver's seat its twin 0.5-inch machine guns were swung around and canted to keep dust from the muzzles. The two gunners were hunkered down, covered over with plastic coverlets that flapped furiously.

Directly behind the APC came a tall, sand-colored van, rocking in the wind. Behind it, nearly against its bumper, was a second RAM V-11. The three vehicles moved rapidly. The driver in the lead APC craned his neck, squinting through the little windshield in order to keep from going over the side of the road into a wadi.

Jadid stiffened, felt the adrenaline surge through his veins like a frost. He slipped the small pulse detonator from his pocket. The man closest to him turned and peered at him, then turned back.

The Israeli convoy came on. Fifty yards . . . twenty . . .

The APC's front wheels crossed the first C-4 charge. Jadid jammed down the detonator button. There was a muffled explosion from beneath the vehicle. The earth shook, and chunks of asphalt and limestone went zinging overhead.

The force of the explosion lifted the front wheels of the APC off the ground. Then it slammed back down, skidding sideways, momentarily out of control.

The van, unable to stop, smashed into the side of the armored car. The jolt of the collision knocked one of the gunners out onto the road. The other gunner was trying desperately to extricate himself from his plastic cover, one arm flailing to jack back the bolt of his machine gun.

The APC's left front wheel slid over the second C-4 charge. Then the third. Jadid detonated them simultaneously. This time the whole vehicle was hurled upward twenty feet. It twisted before landing upside down. The gunner was trapped beneath his weapon's swing frame.

The other APC had fish-tailed to a stop. But its gunners managed to charge their weapons and were now swinging the barrels up and around. Thirty feet away, the soldier who had fallen to the road from the first vehicle staggered dazedly to his feet. He was instantly cut down in a raking fusillade.

A low rush seemed to hollow out the storm for a moment from across the road as Hadiv fired his rocket launcher. A flash of light burst from just behind the driver's seat of the second APC as the armor-piercing missile went through its plating.

An instant later came a rending explosion. The armored car burst into flames. The body of one of the gunners, legless, went flying almost lazily into the air.

By then, four soldiers from the van had tumbled out the back. They began to fire their automatic weapons blindly, sweeping the wadi on Jadid's side. The bullets tore huge divots from the rock. Their tracer rounds sketched green fire lines through the dust.

The Kurds opened up with all their firepower, filling the wind with the rattle of the Heckler and Kochs and the heavier booms of shotguns hurling double-ought buckshot. Three of the van soldiers went down instantly. A second later, the other fell over backward and lay struggling to get back up.

Bellowing, the *Persh Megras* rose out of the wadis and swarmed onto the road. Jadid headed for the first vehicle. A man was trying to crawl through the smashed windshield. He had a pistol. Jadid shot him in the head, then raced past toward the van. The others were prowling amid the wreckage, killing survivors.

The flames from the burning armored car roared in the wind. Jadid leapt into the back of the van. Inside were benches along both sides. The floor was littered with peanut husks. In the center was a small metal box bolted to the floor.

Beyond it, sprawled against the driver's wall, lay a paratrooper. There was a wide gash across his forehead beneath his wine-colored beret. His face was bloody, his skull bared. His eyes were half open.

Jadid moved around the box, grabbed the man's hair through the beret and jerked his face up. With a swift, graceful movement, he unsheathed his boot knife and slashed it across the trooper's exposed throat. Blood gushed from the wound. The man stared up at him with a strange, puzzled look.

Jadid moved away and knelt to examine the metal box. It had two bars across the front, forming an *X*. The ends were bolted to the top with heavy locks reeved through the bolt heads.

Quickly he took some C-4 gel from his leg pocket, pressed balls of it around each bolt head and inserted the fuses. Then he ducked back through the rear door. The heat from the burning APC was powerful. He heard a man screaming inside, a wild, animal-like shrieking. A moment later, it stopped.

The explosion blew black smoke and peanut husks through the van doorway. Jadid waited a second, then went back in. The air smelled like acrylic paint. Both bolt heads had been sheared off. He pulled away the crossbars and opened the box.

The inside was filled with styrofoam packing, some of it scorched by the seeping blast of the C-4. He tore it out and threw it aside. Below the styrofoam was a small, polished metal canister about the size of a tea pitcher. It had red Russian stenciling on it.

Jadid's heart pounded as he lifted the canister. It weighed about fifteen pounds. He rolled it in his hands. One side of it had a milled-out depression with a rubber-sealed hole in the center. The metal felt as cold as a chunk of ice.

Cradling it gently, he left the van just as one of the guerrillas came around the corner. "*Khan* Mashhad!" he yelled over the wind. "Zub is down."

Hadiv was lying in the bottom of the wadi. A huge hole had been blown through his fatigue shirt. Underneath, his intestines were visible, twisted bluish coils like pieces of a snake's body. He'd been hit by one of the twelve-gauge blasts.

Jadid bent close to hear his words. He was in deep shock, the words meaningless. Jadid began to weep. He ran his fingers over Hadiv's face. It felt cold, clammy.

After a moment, he lifted him and set him on his knees with his face toward Mecca. Hadiv slumped forward. Jadid picked up the rocket launcher. He slipped a round from Zub's belt, fitted it into the breach of the weapon and locked the ignition wire. He knew he had to destroy any possibility that the Israelis could identify Hadiv.

He bent and whispered something into Hadiv's ear, then turned and walked back up onto the road. From fifty yards away, he fired the rocket into his companion. It blew his body apart.

One minute later, the remaining *Persh Megras,* motorcycles screaming under the wind, disappeared into the whirling dust.

JACK ASHDOWN WAS STILL HALF DRUNK WHEN HE FOUND the *Bengal*'s berth.

A hundred yards up the dock, he paused to survey the ship. It was moored beside two gigantic dry-dock cranes that rose like brilliantly lighted buildings against the night sky.

He immediately recognized the vessel's lines: the full scantling hull of welded plating with a raked stem and cruiser stern; the forward deck's signature "cookie cutter" sheer; the utilitarian blunt rise of her midhouse. She was a Liberty, E-class C-1 cargo ship. Thousands just like her had come off the ways during World War II.

The hull was still painted wartime gray. But it and her upstructures carried dark rust stains. The plating was dented and gouged from minor collisions over her fifty-plus years of service.

Even as far off as he was, he spotted the heat scouring around the starboard hawsepipe. The metal was tempered and discolored, which meant that fire had once run wild in the ship's forward hold and upper deck—had probably brittled up her steel, he thought.

Slowly he scanned until his gaze reached the stern. There was an empty thirty-seven-millimeter gun pit still mounted over the afterhouse. The house itself was a box of rust.

He hissed with disgust. The ship was a beat-up old barge—not the best choice for his first time to walk steel deck after six years. He started toward her again.

Ashdown was a youthful-looking forty-five-year-old: big-shouldered, with muscular lines and tanned skin and a shock of brown, sun-streaked hair. He wore salt-stiff shorts, a T-shirt and beat-up Adidas deck shoes, and he carried a camo battle jacket slung over his shoulder.

The jacket was the same one he'd worn as a lieutenant with the First Cavalry Division in Nam. It and his wallet were the only things he'd managed to save before his thirty-foot sloop, *C J*, had gone to the bottom in the Singapore Strait eight days earlier.

He reached the accommodation ladder and climbed up. It swayed, squeaking on its davits. He stopped before stepping aboard. There was no standing watch, he noted.

But now, up close, he could smell the ship. Its essence sifted through the richer harbor redolence of oily water and diesel fumes—a sour stench of old iron and vermined ballast water and deck machinery grease long since turned to shellac.

Men were working somewhere forward. He heard the hiss of welders' torches, muffled hammering. The sounds, interspersed with bursts of Malay chatter, drifted back under the weather alleyway overhang. Yet they seemed peripheral, not part of the ship. It sat silent, cold.

He made a fist and knocked it sharply against one of the deck stanchions. A droplet of blood formed. He smeared it onto the bulwark. An ancient sailor's custom: give some of your blood to a new ship, and she'd bring you home safely.

He stepped aboard.

Turning aft, he climbed the ladder to the boat deck, then went up to the starboard wing on the bridge deck. He lit a cigarette and gazed down through the braced booms and masts of the forward derricks.

The working party he'd heard was putting new canvas onto the hatch boards on number-three hold. The men were all Malaysian. They wore T-shirts with National Football League logos. The flickering, blue-white light and hot sizzle from the welders' torches flashed out of the number-one hold.

He surveyed the entire foward area. On each side of the fo'c'sle deck were two round antiaircraft gun pits, cement-coated for protection against bullets. Like the thirty-seven-millimeter pit astern, they too had not held weapons for a long time. Instead, small, red-painted barrels were strapped inside.

Farther back, the deck was congested with standing machinery, derrick booms, stacks of dunnage and several tall, mushroom ventilators that resembled nuns with their heads bowed. Acetylene lines and electrical cords snaked everywhere. Near both derrick masts were twin lifting winches. Their gypsy heads and spooled cables were brown with rust.

Finally, he flicked his cigarette over the side and pushed open the wooden door that led into the bridge. The room was small, no more than twenty feet across. He stepped inside and instantly caught the suddenly familiar odor of old wood and brass and pennant cloth.

In the middle of the bridge stood the wheel box and helm. Directly in front of it was the tarnished brass half cone of the binnacle. Beside the helm rose the annunciator or engine-order telegraph. Its handle was worn, the order plate yellowed with age.

Slowly he walked around looking at things, idly touching surfaces. He paused to peer through the three small windows in the forward bulkhead. He tested the wheel. The wooden spokes were bungeed. He clicked the radio mike, fingered the pennants in their rack on the after wall.

Jack had spent twelve years at sea aboard merchantmen. After the army, he'd attended the Merchant Marine Academy in Vallejo, California, and came out a third mate. Within six years, he was a first officer. Another two would have brought him his captain's papers.

His last cruise had been as First aboard the Sea-Land container ship *Charleston Iron* in 1992. It had carried military cargo to the Persian Gulf for Desert Storm.

*That was also the year Carol and Jamie died. . . .*

He shook off the memory and pushed through the inboard door into the passageway. The bulkheads were painted a faded seafoam green, the deck covered with chipped brown linoleum. A faint red line ran down the middle. Music drifted in from somewhere, rapid blues runs by B. B. King.

The chart room was just off the bridge. Beside it was a cabin with a small brass plate on the lintel that said MASTER'S SUITE. He knocked lightly, twice. There was no answer.

He went on around the stack shaft to the port side of the ship. The first compartment he came to was the radio room, from which the music was issuing.

He looked in. A black man was working on a power panel. He whistled softly to himself and tapped his right foot in time with the music.

"Hey, partner," Jack said. "The captain aboard?"

The black turned. He had close-cropped hair, wraparound, metallic-coated dark glasses and a Filipino *balagong* shirt. He gave Jack a quick up-down.

"Yeah, he floatin' about somewheres," he said. "Who're you?"

"Second Mate."

"Oh, yeah, right." The man flashed him a smile. It was warm and full of beautiful teeth. He leaned out, offered his hand. "Keyshawn Collins," he said.

"Jack Ashdown." They shook.

Collins sat back. "Damn, it's good to hear straight American for a change. Where you all from in the States?"

"San Francisco, originally."

"Fine city. Me, I'm from Dee-troit. And damn if I can't wait to get my poor black ass back there."

"Beached in Singapore?"

Keyshawn chuckled. "Yeah, you got that right." He explained. He was an ex-marine who'd been posted at the American embassy in Thailand. When his enlistment ended, he married a honky-tonk girl from Bangkok and stayed in-country.

"You know, runnin' some transactions?" he said. "Then I screwed up and lost my juice. Overstepped my bounds, you might say. Pretty quick I'm jacked out, my old lady runs off and I'm standin' with my dick in diddy-wah-diddy."

"And the Singapore constabulary figured you ought to be somewhere else."

"Oh, yeah. Unreasonable motherfuckers."

"Who you ship with before?"

"Nobody. Shit, the only boats I ever been on was LCUs during assault exercises. An' them suckers made me puke my guts out."

Jack frowned. "You're not licensed?"

The music tape clicked off. Before answering, Collins flipped it over, started it through again. "Sweet Little Angel."

"I don't have no maritime ticket, if that's what you talkin' about. But in the Corps, my MOS was a twenty-eight thirty-one. You know, radio tech, multichannel rating. I told the old man straight out, and he say that's good enough for him."

Jesus, Jack thought. A scow of a ship and now an unlicensed radio officer.

Collins sucked spittle through his teeth and nodded at the panel he was working on. "But I gotta tell you, man. This radio gear is some old shit. Fuckin' vacuum tubes and transformers, for Chris' sake."

Jack talked with Collins for a while longer, then wandered around the rest of the ship. He finally ended up at the engine-room door in the after part of the midhouse. He looked down into the semidarkness. The space was cavernous and consisted of three levels. A main blower was running somewhere. He could hear men talking.

He slipped down the ladder to the first grating. Machinery and piping were crammed everywhere. The pipes were wrapped in heat packing that was grimy with oil. The bulkheads and floor plates were old and heat scoured, and the air, stifling hot, smelled strongly of hot metal and babbitt and Bunker C crude.

Directly under the grating was the huge engine block with its triple cylinder heads and rings of pressure bolts and safety valves. In contrast to everything else, the entire block had been freshly coated with silver lead paint, the valve stacks with red and black.

A deep, booming hammering started. A man cursed, his voice hollow-sounding from down in the main shaft pit. The hammering stopped for a few seconds, then started again.

Jack descended to the second grating and peered through the slender, polished shafts of the connecting rods. He couldn't see anyone. But the foot of a five-ton jack was visible near the thrust collars at the main journal.

He went all the way down to the machinery floor and paused beside the throttle station. Forward of it was the firing alley. The two main boilers were on the port side. Across from them were pressure gauge boards and a high-voltage panel with rows of copper U switches.

"Aye, *you!*" someone yelled. "What the bloody hell are you doin' down here?"

A small, sweaty man scooted out from around the bull gear housing. He was thin and wiry, and looked to be in his sixties. He had a gray brush mustache and a red, weatherbeaten face, and he wore oily shorts and a shapeless, sweat-stained Aussie bush hat.

"I'm looking for the captain," Jack answered.

"Well, he ain't here, mate," the man snapped. His

speech carried an Australian slur. He studied Jack. "Who are you, the Second?"

"Yes. Jack Ashdown."

The man nodded and moved to the throttle desk. He had the quick, darting moves of an elf. He yanked open a metal box resting beside the desk. It was half full of gasoline and cans of Foster's beer.

He withdrew two of the latter, uncoupled a hose line beside the desk and blew high-pressure air over the cans for a few seconds. He tossed one to Ashdown.

Jack cracked the top and took a long pull. The beer was surprisingly cold.

The man introduced himself. His name was Jeremiah Pepper, Chief Engineer, from Toolaray, Australia. He leaned against the desk and looked at Jack's salt-encrusted clothes. "You look like you been swimmin'."

"I lost my boat off Port Dickson last week."

"Your boat?"

"A thirty-foot sloop. I got rammed by a tanker."

One of Pepper's eyebrows lifted. "Lord Jesus, a bleedin' canvasback. How much triple-expansion steam time have you logged?"

"Six months on a coastal."

Pepper snorted and took a drink.

Jack scanned the engine space. "She's beat-up, ain't she?"

"Aye," Pepper answered. "But she's still good an' solid. I shipped on these old twenty-five hunderts in the Second War. They can be bullheaded sometimes, but they'll stick."

"How's the old man?"

Pepper's eyes narrowed. They were deep blue with a webbing of tiny wrinkles at the edges. "That's to be seen. He's a bloody Mick. Him *and* his First." He shook his head. "Never much cared for Micks. Skiters, the whole lot of 'em."

"Ashdown," a sharp voice suddenly bellowed from the engine-room door. "You down there?"

"Yeah," Jack called back.

"Well, get your scumber arse up here. Cap'n wants to see you."

Pepper looked up. "In your boot, ya bugger," he growled quietly. To Jack he said, "That's the First now. Boyle's his name." He gave him a sidelong glance. "Watch out for him, mate. He's a snarkey bastard with a temper on him like flame to high octane."

Jack finished the rest of his beer and set the empty can on the throttle desk. "Thanks, Chief."

He turned and went up.

Boyle was shorter than he but carried heavily muscled shoulders and arms covered with tattoos. His hair was burred and blond, his beard short. He would have made a decent Viking.

He stood braced at the top of the ladder, his thumbs hooked into the top of a heavy seaman's belt. A short leather whip was clipped to it. He stared at Ashdown with black, dead eyes, then snapped his head, upward and went out the door.

The captain's name was Sean O'Mallaugh. He sat at his desk with his seaboots up on one corner and silently watched Jack. A bottle of whiskey was tucked between his legs.

Ashdown went through the protocol, his sea experience, rating, department experience. Then he laid his First Mate's card on the desk along with the Singapore commissioner's slip.

O'Mallaugh ignored both items. He had beetling eyebrows, a high forehead and a thick black mustache. The skin of his face and forearms was sun-reddened like a farmer's, and his black coveralls and gray work shirt made him look even more rural.

Jack waited. His eyes furtively took in the cabin. It was untidy and held a boar-den odor. A cat-o'-nine-tails whip with metal rings in the leather knotting hung on the outboard bulkhead. Beside it was an Irish long sword, thick, dirty-bladed and easily five feet long from hilt haft to tip.

Finally, O'Mallaugh pushed himself forward and shoved several papers across the desk. Jack glanced at them. They were the voyage contract and shipping articles required by international law.

He quickly noted that the *Bengal* was registered under the Cameroon flag and categoried for free transit. That meant she was a tramp, with no definite ports of call, going wherever there was a cargo consignment.

"What's our first port, sir?" he asked.

"Colombo, Sri Lanka. We pick up an owner's rep there." O'Mallaugh's brogue was heavy.

Jack signed, then pushed the papers back.

The captain took a drink and lowered the bottle. "Tell me, Ashd'n, how many typhoons have ye been in?"

"Three."

"Make you shit your trousers, did they?"

"They were hairy enough."

"But you managed to keep yoursef decent enough?"

"Yes."

O'Mallaugh nodded. "Good. All right, get yoursef settled in. Your cabin's starbood the Chief's on boat deck."

"Thank you, sir."

Back out in the passageway, Collins's tape was still sending B. B. King riffs around the curve of the stack.

MAGGIE WOULD HAVE LIKED THIS WEATHER, DUFF GREEN thought. She had always preferred the gray chill of the moorlands of Yorkshire over any other place on earth. This, at least, was a gentle sweetness to her homecoming, and he was glad for it, even though it had come of its own.

There was only a handful of people at the graveside: old friends from Maggie's school days, a maiden aunt now as frail as a wisp of dying heather. It was very cold, and the rain made small pockets in the newly unearthed soil, then slipped in tiny streams into the grave.

The cemetery stood on a slight incline a few yards from a twelfth-century church, separated from it by a stand of ancient yews. Far downslope, below Wass village, stood the ruins of Byland Abbey. Little was left of the structure save its facade and the tumbled, moss-covered arches of the north wall, misty in the distance.

The parson, tall and gangly as Ichabod Crane, was nearing the end of his service. Duff closed his eyes as he felt the pain in his upper abdomen grip down suddenly. For a

moment, it was as· if he could feel the contours of the thing
down there in his flesh—separate existence.

It faded slowly. He opened his eyes again. Water slipped
from his thick, gray-streaked brown hair and dripped off
his eyebrows. He ignored it.

The parson closed his book. He came to Duff and murmured a few words of condolence. The others followed,
each mourner pausing beside the grave to drop a handful
of soil onto the coffin. The maiden aunt moved slowly,
assisted by a young blond girl in a shawl. A few minutes
later, the tiny entourage of cars left, following the hearse.

Duff walked down to the grave and squatted. The grave
diggers stood off, leaning on their shovels and smoking,
their cigarettes cupped in their hands. The air smelled of
rain and fecund earth and roses.

He gazed at the coffin. It was made of brass with silver
handles. The dirt clods had already begun to melt into little
rivulets of brown water. He picked up a clod and dropped
it. It made a dull, hollow sound on the top of the casket.

"I'm sorry, Maggie," he said softly. "You deserved better from me."

He stood and moved away.

The man was standing among the yews. Dressed in a
black overcoat and hat, he was slender with pale, sharp
features and a pointed chin.

Duff stopped and looked silently at him.

The man came down and stood with his hands in his
coat pockets. "I'm terribly sorry, Duff," he said quietly.
He looked back at the grave, shaking his head. "Bloody
wicked, this."

The man's name was Nigel Leigh-Simmons. He was station chief for MI-6 in Israel. He fell in step as Green continued down the hill to his rented car. A boy on a bicycle
passed on the road, a small transistor under his jacket. It
was playing punk rock music.

At the car, Leigh-Simmons said, "I need to talk with
you."

Silently Duff opened the door and slid behind the wheel.

He started the engine and waited until the other got in, then drove slowly away from the church.

It was market day in the village. In the square, vans and RVs were parked in a cluster with awnings and hastily fashioned pipe stalls covered with umbrellas and spread with clothes and food and produce. Several green-and-white tourist buses were parked across the street.

Duff stopped beside a pub. Called the Abbey Heifer, it had a pewter carriage lantern above the sign and leaded bay windows partially obscured by climbing roses.

Inside it was smoky, noisy and crowded. The bar was made of some ancient wood, one portion under repair and covered with a sheet of presswood. There were stacks of produce boxes near a doorway that led to the kitchen.

They waited for an empty booth and finally got one near the front window. Several American tourists were playing darts next to them. They drank draught beer and laughed in raucous bursts.

The barman came up, wiping his hands on his apron. He had a thick scar on his chin. "Whot's your fancy, gents?" he asked.

Duff ordered whiskey, straight up; Leigh-Simmons, a pint of bitter. The barman brought the drinks and went away. Green immediately downed his drink, waited to catch the barman's eye and held up his fingers for two more.

Leigh-Simmons took off his hat, shook the rain droplets from it and laid it on the table. He ran his hands over his hair. His hands were as slender as a pianist's, his hair black and combed straight back.

He eyed his companion closely. After the barman had gone away the second time, he said, "You look ill, old man."

Duff downed the second whiskey, turned and looked out through the window. He was perhaps fifty, with a wide face and gray, winter-sky eyes that, when peering from under his eyebrows, looked oddly catlike but, one suspected, could go steely in anger. There had been weight loss in his

features. It accented his cheekbones and formed deep
creases at the ends of his well-formed lips. His skin was
slightly tanned but beneath was a yellow pallor.

"How serious is it?" Leigh-Simmons pressed.

Green's gaze swung back. He put his hands on the table,
softly, gently. "Why are you here, Nigel?" he asked.

Leigh-Simmons tented his delicate fingers. "To offer
you an assignment."

"Why?"

"I need your expertise."

"Does Control know about this offer?"

"Absolutely not. This is and will remain strictly between
you and me."

For twenty-two years, Duff Green had been an MI-6 operative. Assigned to the service's Special Operations Bureau C, he was an expert in antiterrorism, first in Ireland,
then in the Middle East.

Three years before, he had been quietly expunged from
the service and ordered into retirement. His suspected but
unproven involvement in the assassination of a high-
ranking member of the *Jama'at-i Islami* party in Lebanon
had badly embarrassed the British government. In truth, the
official had also been a field commander of the secret Iraqi
terror organization called *Ikut al Iraqiyah,* Fist of Iraq.

It had taken those three years for the Ikut to take its
revenge—with a quick, unseen needle of Rison poison into
his wife's thigh in a church outside the small Spanish coast
town of Marbella, where he and Maggie owned a vineyard.

The village doctor ascribed the death to a heart attack.
Duff knew better. Maggie had never been sick a day in her
life. And he had seen the tiny, nearly invisible signs of the
castor bean poison on the corpse.

Leigh-Simmons took a sip of his bitter and wiped a forefinger across his upper lip. "This assignment could be—
advantageous to you."

"In what way?"

"Maggie's death wasn't natural, was it?"

"No."

"I thought not." Leigh-Simmons hissed. "Damned Ikut vermin." He was silent for a moment, then said, "I think I know you well enough, Duff. It's to be a death for a death, correct?"

Nigel did, indeed, know him. From the moment Duff had seen his wife's body in the deadhouse in Marbella, so fragile and alone in a tiny white room with a window like a cross, he had sworn revenge. Its obligation rose from the code by which he had lived half his life. But this time something else was added: a profound awareness that in a very real sense he had been a conspirator in Maggie's death.

"Tell me about this assignment," he said.

The Americans whooped suddenly. One of the party did a silly dance. Leigh-Simmons turned and watched a moment, then came back.

He leaned in closer. "A fortnight ago, an armed Israeli convoy was attacked in the Negev, on the road to the munitions cache at Kadesh Shivun. A total wipe—all troopers dead." His eyes widened slightly for emphasis. "More importantly, something—we don't know *what* exactly—was taken by the assault team."

Duff listened, his eyes steady, a finger toying gently with his jawline.

"Mossad, of course, is livid. Their Department of Security has gone to top-priority alert—all stations call, the works. And they're keeping the entire cock-up solidly under wraps. Fortunately, our CGHQ managed to pick up a military signal about the attack.

"Now, we've drawn certain assumptions. Since the convoy was unusually small, merely two V-11s and a carriage van, it was obviously intended to be inconspicuous. That means unusual cargo. Second, it came from the Beersheba Desert Research Institute. *That* strongly hints at assumption number three."

"The cargo was nuclear."

"Precisely." Leigh-Simmons shook his head. "This could prove to be a very dangerous situation, Duff."

"Any claims of responsibility?"

"If the Israelis have received any yet, we don't know about it. As I said, everything is being kept tight as a drum. But *we* suspect a new Iraqi terrorist group that's been active lately; calls itself the KIE—*Kanun ittani Elhamar*, Red January. It's in remembrance for the start of the Gulf War. They've already kidnapped and murdered an American electronics expert in Haifa and set off a bus bomb in Eilat."

Duff downed his drink. The liquor was doing nothing for him. "Has Control approached Mossad directly?" he asked.

"Can't. We'd compromise our intercept capability."

For the first time, Duff smiled. It was wistfully cynical. "And so you want me to play at tracker hound."

"Exactly. We *must* know what those terrorists nicked off with." Leigh-Simmons withdrew a long brown envelope from his coat pocket. He laid it on the table. "Most of what you'll need is here—three thousand pounds, travel tickets, false passports and cover portfolios. You'll cross over via Rome and Cairo."

He studied Duff silently for a moment. "Understand that you'll be in place naked, strictly on your own—no assets, couriers or safe houses. All contacts will be solely with me. My X-sites and alternates in Haifa and Jerusalem are also listed along with my personal cyphers. Your code name will be Canaan."

Duff tilted his head. "Sticking your neck out a bit, aren't you?"

"Certainly. Still, any—extraneous business you might conduct in your travels as a private citizen would, of course, be of no official interest to me or the organization."

Green looked out the window again. The rain had momentarily stopped. He saw a pretty girl hurry past, her umbrella and boots bright yellow.

"What do you know about Maggie's killing?" he asked softly, still gazing out.

"Not much, really. Some whispers were about that a two-man Ikut hit team was on the continent two months ago. Seems to have surfaced twice in Italy." He inhaled deeply and sighed. "No one in the system caught the connection to you that they might have. It was backlogged as low-priority material, actually. Damned sloppy of us. I'm sorry."

"What was their port of entry?"

"We think Naples."

Duff's head swung back, his eyes going hard. "Klein?"

"Quite possibly."

Heinrich Klein was a German living in Egypt. His father had been among the many high-ranking Nazi SS officers who had fled Europe after World War II. Now at fifty, the younger Klein was owner of a pharmaceutical company in Cairo and was strongly suspected of running an underground network for terrorists, supplying weapons and false passports, and maintaining safe houses in Europe and South America.

The man was meticulously careful. No national security police or antiterrorist organization had ever been able to clearly connect him to anything. Still, Naples always seemed to be a favorite jumping-off spot into Europe for his particular clients.

Again Leigh-Simmons appraised Green narrowly. "I must say, old man, now that I see you, I wonder if you're up to going back into harness."

Duff looked at him for a long moment. Then he reached out, picked up the envelope and shoved it into the pocket of his anorak. Wordlessly, he rose, turned and went out.

The rain was back, sweeping down the street. It hissed on the cobbles and drummed on the market stall umbrellas. He started toward his car. And the pain, coming with a quick snake-strike of nausea, hit him. He gritted his teeth and held it off. Gradually, resisting, he forced it away.

For the last three months, Duff Green had been slowly dying of liver cancer.

THE *BENGAL* WAS AT LAST COMING ALIVE.

For two days they had provisioned her, completed the repairing and finally made up steam to move her the half mile to the fueling dock. The Malaysian crew sang loud *sepak raga* songs as they hauled in the hawsers.

The slow, even throb of her engine made the deck tremble. Her single screw, sitting high, slashed ponderously at the brown-green estuary water as she glided slowly past the warehouses and the bank fishermen to her fueling station at Pier F2. Since the ship would be running in ballast, her deep tanks took the first Bunker C crude. It was as thick as hot tar and stank of sulphur.

The crew roster was twenty percent below full complement, with no Third Mate or Second Assistant Engineer. The ABs and black gang had also been cut in half. All were Malaysians, except for the young, hippy-looking German First Assistant named Claud Vogel.

But the men seemed experienced and under control. Crews shipped in Asiatic ports were often drug users, opium and hash. These were alert, worked quickly and efficiently, and could take commands in English.

The bosun, a small Malay named Tun, was short and husky with a thunder in his voice. He always wore a San

Francisco Giants baseball cap and chewed betel nut leaves, which made his gums look bloody.

No one got much sleep during this period, least of all Captain O'Mallaugh. He drank whiskey continuously but the only effect it seemed to have was a deepening sullenness and an occasional look in his eyes that was like a melancholy, only uglier.

The harbor inspectors came aboard, gave the ship a perfunctory search for contraband and then went away. Afterward, the ship's shore agent came aboard to check on the crew and sign-off manifests. He was a rotund Chinese with broad buttocks in a gray Mandalay silk suit. With him was a shy Vietnamese paddy girl who looked about fourteen. He called her his *jinyu*, or niece.

Finally at 12:03 A.M., September 2, O'Mallaugh ordered Pepper to make up steam for departure.

## 4:00 A.M.

Jack, in command of the forward deck party, paced beside the windlass. A breeze had worked up since midnight. Now it came briskly in across the outer channel, smelling of open ocean.

Along the dock, the fueling gantries were covered with lights. They resembled carnival rides and made the estuary water, rippled by the wind, shimmer and dance.

To the south, the brilliant glow of central Singapore was etched against the darker night beyond. Closer in, the residential area of Jurong Town sat dark in the predawn, silent save for the occasional primeval roar of a crocodile that drifted up from the Bird Park.

Jack felt good. There was always an anticipatory excitement whenever a ship made secure for sea—the last-minute closing of hatches, the tying down of loose objects. A sealing of itself against the vastness it was about to enter.

He leaned against the bow bulwark, an old World War II walkie-talkie tucked under his arm. For a moment, he

felt out of time. He glanced down at the deck, pressed it
with his shoes. It had been a while, ever since . . .

A bolt of old sorrow came, so sharp it made him actually
draw away from the bulwark as if it had suddenly burned
his flesh. The pain was clothed in its familiar image, burst-
ing anew across his mind:

*His wife, Carol, lying under a white sheet in a room
filled with hoses and electronic gear that pinged softly, releasing fragile bubbles of sound into the air. The sheet
looked flat, made her contourless, as if somehow the lines
and curves of her had been partially drawn into the bed.*

She had been in a level-four coma ever since she and
their daughter, Jamie, were in a head-on outside Alpine,
Texas, just a mile from their house. Jamie had been killed
instantly.

It took Jack a week to get home from the Persian Gulf.
Carol's hospital was new and had long, bright corridors
where sounds didn't carry. Two doctors met him. They
were very solemn. They said his wife was already brain-
dead. Only the machines were keeping her alive.

He sat with her for two days, holding her hand. It felt
so cold, as if she had lingered too long in the snow. The
doctors came and tried to talk to him, pointing out that
decisions had to be made. He refused to speak to them. Yet
the nurses said that sometimes in the night they could hear
him murmuring softly to her.

At last, he came out of the room and told the doctors to
shut down the machines. He signed all their papers. Two
days later, during a thunderstorm, he buried his family in
a small cemetery that overlooked a meadow of bluebonnets.
Then he got drunk and stayed that way for three months.

When he finally sobered up, he was in San Francisco.
He couldn't remember how he'd gotten there, and only
vaguely recalled that he'd won owner's papers for a battered thirty-foot sloop in a crap game in a Tenderloin bar.

The boat was berthed in a shabby slip in the Alameda
basin. With the money he had left, he refitted and provisioned her and renamed her *CJ*. Two days later, he crossed

under the Golden Gate and swung the sloop's bow southward. . . .

At 4:15, the harbor pilot arrived, a gangly Englishman in white ducks and a gold-leafed commodore's cap.

"Good morning, good morning," he greeted Jack brusquely as he clambered up the Jacob's ladder. For a moment he paused, faced the stern and, in proper navy fashion, snapped off a salute to the ensign. Then he hurried off to the bridge.

Two tugs came in soon after, plowing up the estuary, their diesels rumbling. They looked clean and washed down, the high deckhouses sheeny-polished under running lights.

Jack's walkie-talkie crackled intermittently with interference as the pilot talked with the tug captains, setting their vessels into position.

Finally, Boyle's voice came on: "Stand by to single up, fore an' aft."

Jack acknowledged. He quickly positioned his men and signaled the dockhands. Two minutes later, the lines were let go. The ship's engines throbbed powerfully as she backed, her stern moving away from the dock. One tug slipped in quickly as she swung broadside to the estuary current.

With their diesels roaring and fading, the two tugs got the *Bengal* turned and headed down the estuary. She passed the refitting docks, going smoothly now, her bow wave rebounding off the banks into her hull and giving a tiny roll to the deck.

They cleared the estuary roadstead. The colored lights of the oil refineries of Pulau Ayer Island lay off the port beam. Far beyond the glow of Singapore, the eastern sky was beginning to gray up with dawn, faintly feathered with orange streaks.

Soon one tug fell off the starboard quarter. The other came in close, slightly nudging the *Bengal* into the outer channel. Then it, too, dropped back. A moment later, both vessels swung sharp 180s, and their running lights soon merged into the background glare of the main harbor.

Two miles beyond the outer channel buoy, they stopped to drop the harbor pilot. Hove to, the little pilot boat bobbed wildly in the ocean swell. But as soon as the Englishman was aboard, it turned and gunned up, throwing spray off its chines.

Slowly, sluggishly, the *Bengal* began picking up speed again. Jack could feel the heavy rhythm of the engine increasing revolutions, the pulse of it coming up through the deck plating. Below, he caught the old familiar sound of a bow cleaving water.

The walkie-talkie crackled. "Bridge to bow," Boyle called. "Stow your lines. An', Ashd'n, keep your foking eyes open for fisher boats."

Jack's men were already stowing the hawsers down into the lockers beneath the windlass. He walked around, checking. The lines were wet and made the deck slippery. A solid wave of air washed over them now as the ship climbed to steaming speed.

He glanced aft. The outline of the midhouse was beginning to emerge from darkness, gradually silhouetting itself against the lightening grayness in the sky. Higher up, the ship's lights were sharp and prickly with brightness.

Jack felt the bow swing a few degrees to the left as O'Mallaugh shaped up the course. Then the *Bengal* straightened, rolling easily as she responded to the southern swell, and headed for the open sea.

Mashhad Jadid tried desperately to hold off his orgasm.

He was in a dark room in a house in the Sri Lankan seaport town of Colombo. It sat along Galle Face Green, a seashore promenade. The man who owned the house was his cousin Ghanem, who owned a textile shop in the Pettah district. He had six children and a Tamil wife called Chandrika.

Outside the house, the light was gray-yellow. The sun had not yet topped the high central massif of the Bulutota Range to the east. As Jadid pumped furiously into his woman, he watched through the window for the first explosive spark of sunlight, holding himself back so that he could time it to his own spending.

Below him, in silent submission, lay his cousin Nufissa. She was nineteen, a teacher in a Muslim school in the highland town of Kandy. Jadid had repeatedly coupled with her throughout the night. Her body bore the marks of his passion—bruises around her dark nipples, grip marks upon her buttocks.

She would bear Jadid's offspring. Her coming to him had been scheduled for her most fertile time. Although she had never met him, she could not refuse to have his child. He was a *hashishiyun*, an assassin. That automatically rendered him the right to plant his seed in her. Her refusal would have brought beatings from her father and brothers and a total ostracism within her clan.

Jadid had already impregnated two other women after the attack in the Negev. Both were also cousins, one in Gur, the other in Bombay. There would be no chance that his seed would lie fallow. He deserved heirs to glory in his memory.

The first shaft of white light from the sun's rim burst above the mountain. Jadid closed his eyes and let himself go, his explosion violent and throbbing with ecstasy as he thrust as deeply as he could into Nufissa. She whimpered softly with pain. He vaguely felt her tiny fingers claw at his shoulder. Then, panting, he withdrew and fell onto his back beside her.

He closed his eyes. His body felt expended, the tissue of it suddenly softened. For a moment, he drifted in the luxuriousness of it. Disparate images slipped through his mind. Minute sounds came and went like unseen mites in the atmosphere. All were clothed in green, the color of Paradise.

Then, as he remembered, the fear came again—suddenly, rearing up out of the tinctured silence. Jadid braced himself. The softness of his body disappeared, replaced by a spasm of muscle. He felt Nufissa slip gently from the bed and go off in the cool, still-gray shadows of the room.

He trembled. His eyes darted from object to object in an attempt to dissuade the panic. Dresser, nightstand, closet. The long, white, ritual *galabia* that had been prepared for him hung near the door. It had been softened with clove oil and sprinkled with cinnamon. He inhaled the air. It smelled of coffee and coconut-oil pomade and the thick external scent of frangipani.

Slowly his mind regained control.

Nufissa and the rest of the household left him alone. He could hear them dressing, moving about the house trying to be silent. The children whispered with urgent curiosity.

At last, he rose and dressed in the *galabia*, then pulled on a head covering called a *kaffiyeh*. He bound it tightly with a black cord. Now, clothed like his ancestors, he prostrated himself to perform the dawn prayer.

Afterward, he summoned Nufissa. She came immediately, as if she had been waiting just outside the door. She carried a silver tray bearing three dishes and a tiny copper cup. She was dressed in a striped silk gown that covered all but her hands and face.

She served him bitter coffee and sheep cheese and goat's liver with rice. It was his first food in forty-eight hours, and he ate hungrily. Nufissa watched him silently. When he finished, she took the utensils away. The house fell silent again save for the cries of crows in the plumeria trees and the far-off, chuffing pant of a cane train pulling a grade.

Jadid again dropped to his knees. The time had come for him to perform the final part of his ritual. He laid a sheathed, curved knife on the floor before him. Then he annointed himself with date oil—forehead, center of chest, penis. Once more he prostrated himself.

He prayed that Allah would keep him constant. That he would enter into the eternal verdantness of Paradise clothed in the iridescence of martyrdom. That the last word on his lips would be of his God. He prayed so intensely that he wept.

At last, he straightened and swiftly took the knife from

its sheath. The blade was as slender as a reed. He lifted the hem of his *galabia*, reached down and took his scrotum in his left hand. With a quick flick of the knife tip, he sliced into the skin.

It bled profusely. He cupped his hand, and the blood pooled in his palm. He lifted it to his mouth and drank, feeling the warmth of it, the saltiness in the back of his throat.

He stanched the flow of blood with his gown until it stopped. It left a large fan of red on the cloth. Then he returned the knife to its sheath and relaxed back on his legs. His heart was pounding.

It was done, the final act. The completion of a circle, his blood unto his blood. Now he was a full-fledged *hashishi-yun al katil nafsahu.*

A suicide assassin.

## STRAITS OF FLORIDA
## SEPTEMBER 4

THE HELICOPTER HOVERED FIFTY FEET ABOVE A SMALL schooner.

The chopper, trembling in the wind, was a Russian Helix Ka-27. It possessed a compact body with two contra-rotating rotors and three tail fins like those of a regular aircraft. It was white with a red banner strip and the ID numbers and initials of the Cuban navy's Western Flotilla.

Twenty minutes earlier, its crew had picked up a Mayday from the schooner, which was now hove to seventy-four miles west of Bahia Honda, Cuba. The vessel, called the *Evergreen*, was captained by an Englishman from Roseau, Dominica. One of his crewmen had a burst appendix.

It was mid-afternoon. The sea was choppy, with wind speeds around thirty knots. Just below the helo's struts, the masts of the schooner jacked back and forth as the boat rolled in a moderate seaway.

The helicopter commander was Cuban First Lieutenant Ana Castile. Her copilot was a handsome, jovial ensign named Jesse Perez. Intermittently, their intercom crackled as the winch operator, Seaman Tony Escalera, called po-sitioning reports. Escalera had already deployed a rescue basket. Ana could feel its weight through the controls as it swung at the end of its cable.

"To the right," Escalera called in Spanish. "Close in now . . . ten feet to the right . . . forward two feet. Watch out!"

A sudden down-gust of wind rocked the helo, and Ana felt the aircraft drop sharply. She shoved the throttles forward. The twin Isotov TV3-117 turboshaft engines lifted the Helix up and away.

The VHF receiver clicked and the schooner's captain came on. "Bloody hell, man, you nearly took off our after mast."

Perez keyed. "Kilo Charlie, just checking to see if you are alert, *amigo*."

Ana gave him a wink.

Stopping the ascent at 150 feet, she neutralized and then began another slow lowering. From that height, she could now see the schooner. Its crewmen were standing on the stern, waving.

"Come left two feet," Escalera started again as she began another approach. "Five feet forward . . . three. Lower ten feet. Hold there. The steadying line just crossed the stern."

Perez keyed again. "Kilo Charlie, can you reach the line?"

"Affirmative."

"Remember to ground it before touching the basket. You copy?"

The steadying line helped guide the basket to the deck. But it also carried a grounding wire. Since rotating blades created heavy charges of static electricity, anyone touching the rescue basket without a ground could instantly be electrocuted.

"We have it," the captain answered.

"Hold it in tight, Lieutenant," Escalera said. "I'm setting the basket down now."

Ana waited. The chopper vibrated rhythmically. Another

gust struck the chopper broadside, making it rock slightly, but it held position.

At last, Escalera came on again. "Basket secured. Lift away."

Ana put on power and pitched backward slightly. She felt the weight of the basket instantly come on. Slowly they rose, the whine of the winch a small, slurry sound in the engine roar.

Three minutes later, the winchman notified her that the injured crewman was aboard.

The captain called up, "Thank you, chaps. Splendid job. Do take care of my lad, will you? Kilo Charlie Golf, two-one-eight, clear."

Ana swung the Helix northeast and headed for the Cuban naval base at Mariel. Twenty-six minutes later, they picked up the base beacon.

Ana Castile had taken her first plane ride when she was six years old—with Fidel Castro, in a brand-new two-seater, single-engine Orolov T-11, a personal gift to El Líder from Khrushchev.

Ana's father, Enrique Cebuela, had been an intimate of Castro then. A one-time sugar plantation overseer in Puerta Padre, he had joined Fidel's tiny guerrilla army and fought with it in the Sierra Maestra Mountains during the fifties. After Castro's sweeping victory, he was appointed minister for sugar production.

With Ana, Fidel flew the small aircraft with abandon—loops and barrel rolls and even an Immelmann, pulling Gs. Ana squealed with delight, sitting next to the man she thought was the greatest in the world. She would always remember how his green fatigues smelled of cigar smoke and good man-sweat, and how he laughed and ruffled her auburn hair.

At eighteen, she married a Cuban hero, Major Antonio Santamaria Castile, a handsome, dashing veteran of the fighting in Angola and Ethiopia. Three years later, they had a daughter, Pilar. Then, in the summer of 1993, Antonio was killed in a freak boating accident while fishing off the Isla de la Juventura.

Over the years, many changes had come to Cuba under Castro. Eventually, those changes touched Ana's father. Like everyone in Cuba, he was stunned by the executions of eight patriots in 1989. Among them had been General Arnaldo Ochoa Sanchez and Colonel Tony De La Guardia, both charged with corruption and drug smuggling. Enrique had been close to the men; they were *compañeros* from the mountain days.

In the wide purge that followed the executions, numerous military and government leaders were jailed or dismissed. Enrique—mostly because of his son-in-law's prestige—was merely forced into retirement. But he no longer possessed power or contacts. In an instant, he'd become an *hombre de papel,* a paper man.

When Soviet Russia finally crumbled in the early nineties, the reverberations in Cuba were horrendous. Without Russian aid, the nation immediately began a decline into economic disaster. Everything became scarce, even food.

Gradually, the stagnation deepened. Protests began to form, but the regime instantly tightened its hold. Freethinking and antigovernment activity were brutally dealt with. Everything was censored; people watched. Old freedoms disappeared.

A man with a deep sense of national pride, Enrique grew more and more bitter. Still, he kept his silence. He'd given too much of his life to the Revolution, to El Comandante. His heart told him his Cuba was dying; his loyalty accepted the inevitable.

Now he lived with his daughter, a dark, brooding presence who drank too much rum and inwardly railed against the insanity that devoured his beloved country.

It was an hour after sunset when Ana pulled her battered Chevy '58 coupe to the front of her home in Old Havana. It was on Obispo Street, a narrow thoroughfare lined with old, Moorish-styled, two-story houses with peeling white or beige paint. Most had blue balconies, metal-strapped windows and tile roofs.

Ana slid from the car and crossed the sidewalk to her front door. Even in her green flight suit, she was a strikingly beautiful, graceful woman in her early thirties.

Her long auburn hair, pulled back into a bun, exposed the full symmetry of her face. It possessed a rich, sensuous mouth and deep brown eyes that carried a soft hint of laughter. Her skin seemed forever summer-tanned from the whisper of mulatto blood in her ancestry.

Inside, the house was cool and dark and smelled of rum and leather polish. She knew her daughter would already have left for her nightly tennis session. Leaving the light off, she went into the parlor.

The room was sparsely furnished with rattan pieces, a black-and-white television set and an ancient upright piano. Soft voices came from the patio. Curious, she looked out the back door.

The patio was small, with two mango trees and Spanish dagger and oleander plants. An alley separated the yard from an unfinished five-story building.

Her father was talking to a man in the shadows, a fat man with a goatee and thick, powerful arms. She couldn't hear what was said. Finally, the man shook Enrique's hand and slipped through the gate into the alley.

Later, changed into a T-shirt and shorts, she prepared supper. Her father came into the kitchen to mix himself another rum-and-water. She studied him.

"Who was he, Papa?"

Enrique turned and looked at her. "What?"

"The man in the garden."

"Ah, you saw him."

"Yes."

Enrique shrugged. He was large, with thick, curly gray hair, black eyebrows and tired, puffy eyes. "An old friend from Puerta Padre—Gustavo del Pino. Tavo was in the city, so he came to tell me his wife had died."

"I don't recognize the name."

"You weren't even born when I knew him."

"Why so secretive? Sneaking out the back way?"

Again Enrique shrugged. He avoided her eyes.

She shook her head slowly. "Watch out, Papa. You know they're always watching."

A look of cold anger came into her father's eyes. "Ach, let the bastards watch," he snapped, and left the kitchen.


CAIRO, EGYPT
SEPTEMBER 5

The inside of the rental car was already stifling hot, although it was only eight in the morning. Duff Green closed his eyes and worked his neck around in a circle, listening to the soft crack of his vertebrae.

He was parked on the promenade beside the main gate of the Gezira Sporting Club. The entrance had a high stone archway with a bronze crest at the apex. Built by the British in 1882, it was located on the Nile's Gezira Island in central Cairo.

Green had been there since dawn. He'd also spent all of yesterday there. Waiting for Heinrich Klein.

Off to the right, behind a high wire fence, stretched the club's exquisitely kept polo fields. A pair of grooms was currently exercising a string of polo ponies.

Across the promenade ran the east bank of the island. It was lined with rowboats and *feluccas* in which whole families lived under tarps and makeshift coverings of palm leaves.

Now and then, boat children dressed in filthy loincloths approached Duff's car. Without guile, they offered to sell him papyrus bookmarks or Nile stones or black hashish.

He lit a cigarette and rested his head back against the seat. His body felt stilled, almost natural. The cancer had strange ways. Often it would become quiescent like this. But at other times, it struck savagely, as it had at Cairo International when he'd first arrived two days before. He had just made it to a rest room where he violently vomited a dark bile.

A breeze riffled up off the Nile. It smelled of pesticides and sulfurous smog and that distinctive, fecund sourness of the river itself. A triple-decked cruise ship passed and slipped under the 6 October Bridge. On its prow was a giant statue of the falcon Horus painted in gold.

A moment later, Green stiffened.

A black, chauffeured Mercedes had just swung through the club's entrance. Seated in the back was Klein. His shock of gray-white hair looked almost luminous through the tinted windows. The car went up the palm-lined drive and disappeared down among the club's stone stables.

According to MI-6 files, Klein was an avid horse breeder and polo player, completely addicted to the game. He was, in fact, one of the senior board members of the sporting club. Duff knew that sooner or later he'd show up there.

The British Intelligence files also showed something else—the German's other proclivity. Duff intended to use *that* addiction to allow himself to get close to Klein.

For the next two hours, he watched him out on the polo field as Klein and four other riders worked out. The German was extremely good. He played the leader's number-three position and rode his animal with a swift, graceful control.

Finally, around noon, the Mercedes reappeared down the long drive. The chauffeur took it across the Tahrir Bridge to the West Bank and turned south. Duff followed as closely as he could in the throng of buses and cars.

They went through El Giza, Green once almost losing the vehicle near the Zoological Gardens. He picked it up again as it swung onto Pyramids Road. Soon after, it turned into the parking lot of a private restaurant called the Burdkan.

Duff parked along the street beside it. The Burdkan was a low building faced with white marble. It had an open-air eating area that overlooked the boulevard and encompassed miniature orange trees and a crystalline blue pool. The waiters were dressed in white dinner jackets.

Klein joined three Arabs at a table under the orange trees. The men were dressed in red *kaffiyeh* headpieces and long white gowns, and drank from large bottles of Coca Cola. A belly dancer in filmy blue-and-silver pantaloons swayed and undulated among the tables, her jewelry jingling. Whenever she passed near the Arabs, they put money into her waistband.

It wasn't until mid-afternoon that Klein left the restaurant. Again Duff trailed the Mercedes as it crossed the Geziret Bridge and went down into the *sug* of Old Cairo.

This was a labyrinth of dark, claustrophobic alleys of ancient stone. Crippled beggars rolled themselves about on wheels, and black-draped women sold produce from aluminum trays. The Mercedes turned onto a street of drug cafés where old men in striped *galabias* smoked hashish pipes and played lethargic games of chess.

At last it stopped before a doorway cut into the stone of the alley. A man in a filthy coat with a monstrous leg from elephantiasis sold roasted watermelon seeds beside the door. His coal-fire roaster made a haze of gray smoke. Klein got out and went past him and up a narrow flight of stairs.

Duff parked beyond the Mercedes beside a snake charmer's stall. He opened the glove compartment and took out a nine-millimeter Beretta with a silencer. He'd brought the weapon through Egyptian Customs easily since he carried forged documents that identified him as a Swiss diplomat.

He waited ten minutes, then got out and locked the door. He walked back past the Mercedes. The driver was reading a copy of the daily *Al-Ahram* and didn't look up as he went by. When he reached the stairs up which Klein had gone, he quickly stepped onto them and went up to a second floor.

It was formed into several apartments, and the air was thick with the stench of raw sewage and rot. He went down the line of apartments, listening at each door. The doors were made of laburnum wood on which pornographic Arabic graffiti had been gouged.

At the third door, he heard a man moan. Again—a soft, ecstatic wail. A woman cursed in the Masri dialect. Then came the sound of something snapping, like the breaking of a twig.

Duff pushed against the door. It was unlocked. He entered.

The single room was in near darkness. The only light came through latticework on the opposite wall. It was faint and smoky. The room smelled of olive oil, the sharp odor of hashish and the musky scent of vagina.

He stood a moment, letting his eyes accustom themselves to the dimness. Objects slowly took shape. To his right was a large bed with a delicately carved headboard and a canopy of dark silk. Hanging on the left wall were various whips and spurs and oddly formed leather harnesses.

In the center of the room rose a metal frame with twin arms. Klein, facing toward the light, was handcuffed between the arms, his limbs spread wide. Beside the frame was a three-foot-high hashish pipe. The German wore only his jodhpurs and knee-high black riding boots. He panted audibly.

Behind him stood a woman with a short leather whip in her right hand. She was completely naked, her head shaved. The dark flesh of her glistened with oil. She stood with the help of a crutch under her left armpit. Her left leg was missing from the midpoint of the thigh.

As Duff watched, she hissed an obscenity and lashed the whip across Klein's back, the tiny leather thongs of the whip snapping. He moaned.

Green came up lightly behind the woman. He lifted the Beretta and put the silencer against her head, in back of her ear. She instantly froze.

"Do not move," he said in Arabic. "Do exactly as I say or you will die."

Klein's head lifted. *"He! Aish e?"* he said.

Duff led the woman to the bed and shoved her face down

onto it. Her buttocks quivered. He tapped his finger lightly on her shaved head. "Remain silent."

Klein was trying to turn his head to see, but the cuffs prevented it. *"Minhu' di, Tante Zuzu?"*

Duff walked around the frame and stood in front of the German. The man's long gray-white hair, sweat-drenched, hung down across his forehead. He had a rough-hewn face, a thick nose and gray eyes. The front of his jodhpurs was wet with semen.

Green looked at him silently.

*"Min ite?"* Klein growled.

Duff slashed the Beretta across the point of the man's chin. Klein's head snapped to the side. When it came back, slowly, the skin marked, he stared balefully at Green.

"Speak English," Duff said.

"Who the hell are you?" Klein's English was flawless.

"I want information."

Klein's eyes narrowed for a moment. Then his lip curled with distaste. "I know you. You're that MI-6 ass that got himself cashiered."

"Ever hear of Maggie Green?"

"Who the bloody hell is Maggie Green?"

"My wife. You helped kill her."

*"Das ist Unsinn,"* Klein snapped in German.

"Who were the men who hit her?"

"I know nothing of that."

Duff lifted the gun and placed the tip of the silencer against Klein's left eye. "Again. Who were the men who hit her? You have ten seconds."

For a fleeting moment, Klein's visible eye darted away, then came back. "I tell you, I know nothing of this."

"Five seconds."

Again the eye darted. "All right. Perhaps I may have heard certain things."

"Who?"

"Two men. Syrians."

"Their names?"

"I only know one. Akhram Hibril."

"Where is he?"

"He could be anywhere."

"Where?"

"Damascus. His home is Damascus."

The woman on the bed sighed. From somewhere in the outer alley came the soft whisper of the snake charmer's flute, the cry of a child, the echo of a camel's growl. In the room, the smoke drifted like ghosts against the light.

Duff pulled the trigger.

COLOMBO, SRI LANKA
SEPTEMBER 5

THE *BENGAL* ARRIVED AT COLOMBO IN THE EARLY EVE-
ning.

It was raining lightly. In the harbor and along the town's
seashore promenade, a Buddhist *vassa* festival was in full
swing. Throngs of people were gathered to watch the last
of the day's canoe races. The canoes were long and slender
and decorated with colored lights and dragon heads.

Captain O'Mallaugh had the conn. He brought the ship
in close along the roadstead, fifty yards from surfers out
near the breakwater. Just outside the main channel, they
dropped anchor in fifteen fathoms of water beside several
other commercial ships. All the captains had chosen to remain outside the harbor during the festivities rather than
risk a collision or fire.

As dark came on, a tremendous fusillade of fireworks
erupted along the inner harbor. Tiny, fiercely burning spirit
boats began drifting out on the outgoing tide, and elephants
strung with lights lumbered along the promenade to the
raucous sound of cymbals and screeching pipes.

Jack watched from the starboard wing. He felt quiet, at
ease. It was good to be aboard a ship again, like the re-

turning from a long illness. He had also discovered, with pleasant surprise, that the *Bengal* was a decent ship after all, quick to answer the helm and stable in a seaway.

During the crossing from Singapore, they'd run into occasional rain squalls from the southwest monsoon and had to buck a drift up into the Bay of Bengal. The sea was gray and leaden-glassy, with a long sweeping swell running northeast.

Yet the ship, with its wide, flat bottom and bilge rolling chocks, had cut smoothly through the cross swell. She heeled in gentle, even swings and recovered nicely. But since they were riding in ballast, she pitched a little whenever a particularly large swell crossed through her bow.

For Ashdown, this was the first free time he'd had since leaving Singapore. O'Mallaugh had everyone standing staggered watches. Jack had spent most of his time overseeing working parties on deck or taking the bridge watch between Boyle and the captain. He grabbed sleep whenever he could.

For the most part, the sleep was quick and sound, down deep. Sometimes he dreamt, but these dreams were disconnected montages of images that drifted through his unconsciousness like scenes viewed from a slow-moving train.

Only one drew him precipitously from sleep with sweat on his forehead, his heart pounding. It was the replay of that night with the tanker out in the Singapore Strait. That particular incident had exposed something in him.

Through the six years following his family's death, Jack had deliberately, self-destructively tempted fate. The consequences didn't matter. He drank too much, got into too many barroom brawls and repeatedly threw himself into activities of extreme high risk.

He smuggled guns, dodging through gauntlets of Aussie patrol corvettes and Indonesian pirates. He ferried illegal refugees out of Thailand, drugs from Chinese sea labs and whores out of the brothels of Honiara. He hunted sharks with scuba gear and drunkenly challenged storms that roared into the Passthrough.

The constant danger was like a fire. It cauterized the guilt that had infected him as he sat at his wife's bedside. He was there now that he was not needed; he'd been half a world away when he was.

But there was a strange irony to it, too. Somewhere along the line, the continual challenges had dissolved normal human fear—the kind he'd known in Nam, terror that hung on the edge of sheer panic. But that was what gave danger meaning. Now it was gone. He no longer *cared* whether he lived or died.

Until the night of the tanker.

It was just after midnight, twenty miles off Kuala Lumpur in the strait. He first spotted the tanker approaching from the south—a great hulking blackness with its running lights floating high above the sea and the sound of its bow like escaping steam coming to him against the wind.

He'd been running south from the Nicobar Islands, headed for Singapore to replenish stores, his sloop running clean on a southeast wind. He watched the tanker come up and suddenly, on an impulse, he swung the *CJ*'s head onto a long port reach and made for a close-in crossing of her bow.

Nearer the vessel came as he heeled his boat down as close to the wind as he could get her, timing the crossing point. The distance diminished quickly. A quarter mile . . . three hundred yards . . . two hundred . . .

The tanker's bow watch angrily flashed a light at him, the beam dancing on the dark ocean. Then the tanker blew its horn, the deep bass sound of it rushing up into the night so close that he heard the horn's baffles clicking.

Still the huge ship came on, looming like a dark, moving cliff. The bow wave was nearly fifteen feet high and sizzled like a waterfall. He was fifty yards from the crossing point when a violent gust of air, driven forward by the moving mass of the ship, struck him. It instantly hurled his sloop completely over to starboard, actually lifting her hull out of the water.

For a wild, black, chaotic moment, Jack was slammed against the deck as he and the sloop went under. He could hear the heavy churn of the tanker's screws, the throbbing of her turbines. With so much mass moving through the ocean, he felt a deep tidal surge of displaced water roll into him.

With it came a jolt of pure adrenaline. Frantically he shoved with all his might and speared out into free water, away from the *CJ*. He began a thrashing swim directly off the tanker's bow. Another surge of water struck him. This drove him forward like a dolphin just beneath a wave.

Finally the outthrow of water calmed for a few seconds. Then, powerfully, it reversed itself. It began to suck at his body as the stern approached and the gouging propellers pulled surrounding ocean back and into their ponderously turning blades.

He fought it, a terrible river current in a total liquid blackness. The heavy shushing of the screw blades neared, growing in volume. He began to lose traction in the sea and went tumbling, somersaulting in a maelstrom of agitated water.

For one terrible agony of vision, he saw himself going into the blades, huge as houses, coming round and round in their slow, inexorable, deadly weight. There was a moment of complete disorientation. His head banged violently into his knee. His arms strained against the powerful current.

Then suddenly he was free, still going over and over but slowing, the counterpane of the ocean rolling and churning white in the faint, receding stern lights of the tanker. Like a petal caught in the curling after-surge of a river, he at last drifted into calm water that rose and fell with the even rhythm of open ocean.

At dawn, he was picked up by a Singapore fishing boat. But the incident left a disquieting question. Why had the capacity to fear returned?

*   *   *

Jack was standing the eight-to-twelve bridge watch when Collins poked his head through the door.

"Taxi-boat requesting approach to discharge a passenger, Jack," he said. "They got a owner representative aboard."

"All right. Tell them to come up on the starboard side, midships."

"You got it."

Jack sent the helmsman, a tall, raw-boned Malaysian AB named Datuk, to the starboard wing to watch for the boat. Then he keyed the walkie-talkie and ordered the bosun to run down the Jacob's ladder and bring the passenger to the bridge.

He stepped back to the captain's door and knocked.

"Come."

He went in. "The owner's rep's coming aboard in a few minutes, Captain."

O'Mallaugh was in his shorts at his desk. He had a hairy barrel chest. The room smelled of musk and whiskey. A song was playing on a small shortwave radio/tape recorder. Soft bagpipes.

He nodded. "Bring him up and thin stow his gear in the steward's cabin."

"Yes, sir."

"Order Pepper to make up steam and rig for sea. You'll take 'er out. Set up for two-three-zero."

"Right."

Returning to the bridge, he relayed the command to Pepper. Since they hadn't gone cold iron on the boilers, Jeremiah informed him that he'd have steam in less than an hour. Jack told Tun to get Boyle and stand by for lifting the anchors. He posted lookouts on the bow and stern.

For the next few minutes, he worked in the chart room, going over the harbor map for Colombo and working out the easiest exit from the roadstead. Then he plotted the course and called to Collins for the latest eighteen-hour weather.

Datuk notified him that the taxi-boat had discharged its passenger and was pulling off. From the chart room, Jack saw a slender, dark-haired man with a tight knot at the nape of his neck come around the stack bulkhead a few moments later. He carried a small handbag. Behind him, one of the crew had his suitcase.

Jack stepped into the passageway and officially welcomed the man aboard. The owner's rep said nothing. He had sharp, almost gaunt features and bright, staring black eyes. He was ushered into the captain's cabin.

At 9:45, Jack ordered the anchors taken in. Boyle was working the forward crew. The ship's hull rumbled softly as the chains came in.

Then Boyle barked out for the final clearing off, and Jack put the *Bengal* into motion, ringing down speed changes to the engine room as the ship pulled herself out of inertia and moved slowly past the other anchored ships toward the north entrance to the roadstead.

By 10:30, they were clear and steaming in open ocean.

At eleven o'clock Boyle came up to the bridge. He stood around scowling. So far, the First had left Jack alone, except for long, insolent glares each time he passed. He always seemed in a foul mood.

Ashdown saw that the crew openly feared the Irishman, with his aura of swaggering menace and that simmering rage just behind his blue eyes. He insulted the men and cursed them. Although Jack had never seen it himself, word was that Boyle occasionally struck them with his fists or the small whip he carried on his belt.

Now he lounged against the bridge door like a cocky dicky boy outside a Belfast pub. Outside, the night was clear, windless. But a strong current was running out of the southeast, and Jack had to adjust the ship's heading continually to compensate, quietly giving Datuk wheel changes.

The Malaysian was slightly slow in steadying up each time. As a result, they'd drift a few degrees past the proper heading and then had to ease back.

Boyle watched Datuk do it twice. The third time, like a lion exploding from brush, he leapt across the bridge and cuffed the man sharply across the back of the head with his open palm.

"Steady it up correctly, ya bloody heathen bastard," he bellowed.

Datuk's head snapped forward. He twisted and stared narrowly at the First Mate, his eyes smoldering.

Boyle's own eyebrows lifted. "Ah, look at me like 'at, will you." He struck Datuk twice across the face—quick, hard blows. The helmsman took the impacts but his hands lifted away from the wheel. It immediately began to fall off to the right.

Jack, near the forward window, quickly stepped in and grabbed Boyle's arm. "Hold it," he growled. To Datuk: "Bring her back to two-two-nine. Make it quick."

Boyle turned slowly and looked at Ashdown, a sudden, dancing fire in his eyes. "Whot's that you say, mate?"

"There'll be none of that shit on my watch."

Boyle reached up and gripped Jack's wrist. His fingers were very strong as he pulled Ashdown's hand away and shoved it aside. He chuckled devilishly, deep in his throat.

"So we've got a bloody saint 'ere, have we? Maybe you'd like a bit of that *shit* yoursef', aye?"

"I have Two-Two-Nine, sir," Datuk called.

For a fleeting moment, Jack thought Boyle would swing on him. He braced, moving his left shoulder in to take the blow.

"Get off the bridge," he said slowly.

"Ah, no, mate, not yet," Boyle leered. "First you and me, we've got to settle an appointment."

Jack nodded. "You say where and when."

"The after pit when you come off watch."

"I'll be there."

Boyle went out, still chuckling.

At 11:50, Captain O'Mallaugh came to take the bridge. He said nothing while Jack ran through the litany of relief. When Datuk relinquished the wheel to the new helmsman, he looked back at Ashdown before silently departing.

In his cabin, Jack tore strips of cloth from the bedsheet and bound his hands. Before he finished, Collins came to the door.

He smiled with glee. "So, you gon' whip his ass, man?"

"We'll see."

"Watch out for that dude, baby. He the kind of motherfucker pull a shiv on you." He reached into his back pocket and pulled out a large switchblade. He flicked it open, the blade snapping out clean, the thin oil on it catching light. "Here, just in case."

Jack shook his head.

Keyshawn frowned. "Yo, you crazy, man." He went away, shaking his head.

Boyle came right at him the moment he climbed into the gun pit. The pit was twenty feet wide, a steel bowl, with steps going all around. The center was flat where the thirty-seven-millimeter cannon had been anchored. The steel was rough with rust, and there were pools of rusty water under the steps.

Boyle came in with his powerful arms flailing. His shoulder drove into Jack's midsection, slightly off, Jack turning to the side to take the blow as he saw the man emerge out of the dimness. The night was lit only by the after lights, the high mast lights far up and the clear, diffused illumination of the stars.

They wrestled for a moment and then went down against the steps. Jack felt the edge of the upper step gouge into his back, numbing it for a moment. Then he twisted Boyle off a little and began to punch at him, outside crosses with both hands.

Boyle broke off and came to his feet; Jack came up, too, swiftly, catlike, his heart racing and the blood running hot in his temples. They squared off, hands up in fighting stance, circling in the restricted space.

Boyle, growling, came in again, swinging a wide roundhouse. Jack stepped to the side and jabbed twice, then moved away. Again Boyle came in, flailing. Jack held his shoulders up, smothering the blows. His flesh went numb where the man's fists struck.

For a second, Boyle was silhouetted against the high lights. Jack threw two swift right jabs and followed with a cutting left cross, his hand quick. It struck Boyle's head, jerking it to the side. Instantly, Jack stepped in, planted his feet and threw a triple combination. Right to the face, a left cross, then a shoulder-high, body-weighted right to the head.

Boyle staggered a moment and tried to close, wrapping his arms around Ashdown. He was panting heavily, and wetness dripped off his goatee, smearing across Jack's neck.

They drew apart again. Jack could feel his breath coming heavily, burning in his throat. Boyle murmured something. His right hand jerked up, and there was something in it. The thing caught the faint light like a tiny shaft of moon-glow.

The sight of the knife made Jack's heart jump. In reflex, he dodged back, and then the blade came around in a wide arc, slicing through the air, with him sucking in and retreating. His foot struck the lower step. He went down on one side, falling onto his buttocks.

Boyle, yelling, came in, hurling his body at him. Jack felt the full weight of the man, heard the soft tang of the blade as it hit the step. He twisted to the right, trying to dislodge himself, and heard the blade contact metal again.

Rage poured through him. He bodily lifted Boyle away and came up, kneeling, and then to his feet as the First came up, too, and they closed.

Jack jammed his knee into Boyle's groin and felt him stall for a single, fleeting moment. In that moment, Jack got him around the waist, turned his body and swept his leg back, lifting Boyle into the air, feeling his weight, and then Boyle was falling, the knife clattering away. He struck the deck, the air going out of him, and he lay gasping.

Without volition, the simple act coming as an extension

of battle, Jack shoved a knee into Boyle's chest, and, locking his fingers together, he smashed them down into Boyle's nose. Blood spewed onto the bandages on his hands.

He threw the knife far out over the sea and then climbed down out of the pit, with Boyle still gagging and spitting mushily in the night under the steady, throbbing pound of the *Bengal*'s engine.

By the time he reached the boat deck, his body began to ache, the pain fusing up out of his cooling flesh. He climbed the inner stairway.

Beside the top of the stairs to the bridge deck was the steward's cabin. The door was ajar, and the owner's rep was staring through the crack—dark, smoldering eyes like a snake watching from shadow. A moment later, he quietly closed the door.

Jack continued on toward his own cabin. Then, suddenly curious, he stepped into the empty officers' mess. On the back of the doorway was posted the list of lifeboat assignments. He ran his finger down the list, stopped at the steward's cabin and read the owner's rep's name.

Mashhad Jadid.

# 00:06

OTHMAR ABU ISFAHAN LIVED IN THE PENTHOUSE OF A
high-rise building in downtown Damascus, off Choukri
Kouwatli Avenue near the university. The splendid, modern
living area of glass and white-leather furniture had windows
that offered a panoramic view of the Old City's covered
market.

Yet the rooms were overlaid with his desert heritage—
ornate brass artifacts, a *kat* water pipe, and brightly colored
camel rugs and silken cushions on the marble floors.

Now he leaned back in his desk chair and benignly studied Duff Green through yellow-tinted glasses. He lifted a
delicate hand, offering the Englishman a chair. Duff sat
down.

Isfahan studied him a moment longer. "You look—
worn, my friend," he said in Arabic.

"A bit," Duff answered in the same language.

"What has befallen you since you left the Middle East?"

"You already know."

"Ah?" Isfahan lifted an eyebrow. He was a jowly man,
partially bald, with gray hair and mustache. Now he wore
a striped gray shirt with a button-down collar. It gave him

55

the summery look of a vacationing Israeli businessman. Actually, he was a Zoroastrian Iranian from Baghdad who smuggled drugs and guns across the Caspian Mountains under the guise of an importer.

"Don't be coy, man," Duff said. "It ill suits you."

Isfahan sighed. "Yes, my friend, I do know. And I am sorry for your loss. You realize, of course, that I could not intervene on your behalf. It would have been dishonorable."

Duff nodded. He understood Arabic ways.

He had arrived in Damascus from Cairo an hour earlier and come straight to the Iranian. Ten years before, while tracking a Lebanese terrorist, he had accidentally stumbled into an assassination attempt on Isfahan's only son, Ishmael. From a rival smuggler clan, the hit was set to go down in a brothel in Hims, but amid flying bullets, Duff had impulsively extricated Ishmael safely. Both Iranians would never forget his act of bravery.

"I have also heard of the death of *ilkhawaja* Klein," Isfahan said. He shook his head. "A rather messy affair. But no great loss. He was *mush mustakim*. A very dishonest man."

Duff made no comment.

"I suspect there is a connection with your return?"

"Yes."

"Understandable. But now you come to me. Why?"

"Assistance."

Isfahan remained silent, composed.

"Do you know where Akhram Hibril is?"

After a moment: "Yes. But you know my honor prevents me from telling you."

"I don't want you to tell me. I merely want you to deliver a challenge."

"Mm?"

"I claim the ancient right of blood revenge. *Mukatali mufrad*. Single combat."

The Iranian nodded. A faint smile touched his lips. "A marvelous stroke."

"Will he meet me?"

"He must. What weapons?"

"Handguns."

"I'll arrange it."

"When?"

"Immediately."

"Where?"

Isfahan thought a moment. "The oasis of Al Kismiyah. At sundown this day."

Duff rose. "Thank you, friend."

"May God go with you," Isfahan said.

The desert lay in barren, golden splendor under the dying rays of the sun. To the west, the sky held a penumbral crimson. It shimmered in the last of the day's heat, looking like a vast, pulsing fire far off, etching the date palms of the Al Kismiyah with wisps of blood.

A hundred yards away, Duff sat on a rock, the Beretta resting lightly on his knee. He faced toward the sunset. He had chosen that deliberately. Anyone coming at him from the old Aleppo road would be strongly silhouetted against the distant horizon.

There was a deep stillness in the air, as if the earth itself were closing down into sleep. There was only the murmuring chitter of desert grouse, the occasional screel of a hawk, both sounds instantly swallowed by the silence.

The oasis was fifty miles east of Damascus, beyond the agricultural belt. On the way out, Duff had passed the sprawling Palestinian refugee camp of Jaramanah. And then there were wheat fields, the grain newly harvested and piled into tentlike stacks. Beyond the oasis lay open desert all the way to the Euphrates.

He checked his weapon. He was sweating heavily. The sweat smelled foul, like sour armpit odor. He inhaled and let the air slip quietly through his lips. He felt his heart. It beat softly, almost gently. There was no apprehension in him.

A tiny spiral of dust appeared westward at the junction

of the highway and the oasis road. It lifted into the air like
a thin genie. Two minutes later, a royal green Egyptian
Hilal sedan stopped at the edge of the palms. Isfahan, alone,
got out and stood with his arms crossed. Nothing was said.

They waited. The golden sheen of the desert deepened
to the color of old brass. Across the horizon, the crimson
threads dissolved slowly into indigo.

The sound of the motorcycle was like a bee caught in a
bottle. The tone of it rose and fell. And then it was there,
the rider skidding to a stop beside Isfahan's automobile. He
was dressed in a turban and a long white *fuuta*, like a desert
sheik. The blackness of his short beard and mustache were
dark against the cloth. In his belt was a curved, jeweled
knife.

Duff stood up.

The rider, Akhram Hibril, dismounted and walked toward him, striding, the folds of the *fuuta* fluttering around
his legs. He stopped fifty yards away.

The two men looked silently at each other. Then Hibril
began to shout, screaming insults as he walked back and
forth, gesturing wildly, whipping himself into a frenzy. He
cursed Duff. His wife. His ancestry.

Then he proclaimed his own ancestry—ancient warriors
who had risen like winds from the desert. He told of how
brave he was, how all the land would tremble to witness
his courage and fierceness.

He paused. His hand suddenly swept down and up again,
and there was a gun in it. He fired, three times, rapidly.
The explosions blew holes in the silence that also was
quickly closed by the vastness.

Duff heard, felt the bullets whip past him. A tearing of
cloth. He lifted his arm. Out there, the white *fuuta* made a
brilliant patch against the indigo. He fixed the now-naked
muzzle of the Beretta on the center of the patch.

Hibril fired again, three more rapid rounds. One struck
the rock Duff had been sitting on, then went shrieking
away. There was a sudden burning pain in Duff's shoulder,
as if a white-hot iron had passed through his flesh. For a

second, his eyes teared with the pain, Hibril's gown blurring slightly.

He fired. Again. And again. The smell of cordite came sharply up to him, the empty casings flinging out and back softly into the sand. He heard triple impacts, thuddings.

Hibril was flung backward and down. But he came up again, to a knee, firing wildly. Bullets zipped through the air. Then he fell down again, rolling from side to side.

Duff lowered the Beretta and walked slowly to the downed man. He stood over him. Hibril's face was contorted, his eyes clamped closed. There was blood all over the front of his *fuuta*. He grunted like a man lifting a great weight.

Duff bent and pulled Hibril's knife from its scabbard. He put the tip of the blade against the man's chest. With all his weight, he shoved down. The blade went in, struck bone, slipped sideways and then all the way in, the curve of it going into Hibril's heart.

The assassin lifted slightly at the plunge, his hands grasping the haft. His eyes shot open, wild and dark, with fierceness in them—and then surprise and then nothing.

Under the overhead light of the rental car, Duff examined his wound. The bullet had gone through the muscle between neck and shoulder. It throbbed, and blood ran down his chest, soaking his shirt. He formed a compress of his handkerchief and held it tightly against the wound.

Isfahan walked over and stood beside the vehicle, paying no attention to Hibril's corpse lying out there with the knife still in it. He silently watched the Englishman. The desert night was coming swiftly now, stars appearing like pinpricks in the sky's mantle. The air grew cool.

At last he said, "Now you are avenged, my friend. You can go home in peace."

"Not quite."

The Iranian shook his head. "I fear you are too late for the other."

Duff's eyes narrowed. "He's already dead?"

"I was told the Mossad killed him." He shrugged. "Perhaps it is true, perhaps not."

"Who was he?"

The Iranian sighed. "If I assume the news is true, then I break no honor. His name was Toufiq Nidali."

Duff started to speak, then jerked his head up suddenly. He had seen lights in the oasis. Isfahan turned to look. The beams of small flashlights showed among the date palms and wild *kat* brush, then came the soft tinkle of a bell.

A moment later, the lights emerged from the brush. In their glow, the men saw two young boys wrapped in ragged coats. They were herding several black goats.

The Iranian turned back. "Shepherds," he said. "Pay them no heed. Undoubtedly, they'll steal the dead one's motorcycle after we leave."

Duff checked the wound. It had stopped bleeding. He put the compress back and pulled on his shirt. "Where did Mossad kill him?" he asked.

"Jerusalem."

The two boys played their lights out on the desert. The beams found Hibril's body, paused there a moment, then moved on. A goat baaed in the darkness, and the bell tinkled like a broken chime.

Isfahan turned and started back to his car. He stopped, thoughtful for a moment, then came back. "Tell me, do you still have contact with MI-6 since your disgrace?"

"One."

"They are searching for something the Israeli recently lost, are they not?" He pronounced Israeli with the accent on the last syllable.

"Yes."

Isfahan snorted. "A terrible evil, that. One I do not condone."

Duff got out of the car. For a moment, he felt dizzy. He put his hand on the door. "You know where it is?"

"No."

"But you know *what* it is?"

"Perhaps."

"Tell me."

Isfahan laughed. "You know I cannot."

"Yes."

"But perhaps a *khayal,* a hint. Consider Moshnabad Bahra."

Lake Moshnabad.

Duff instantly recognized the reference. When he was still with British Intelligence, a wild rumor had circulated throughout the Mideast. It claimed that a Russian aircraft had crashed into Lake Moshnabad, on the Iran-Afghan frontier, in 1989. Bound for Afghanistan, the plane was said to have carried two new bombs which the Soviets, desperate to end their war there, had considered using.

Called Red Bombs, they were supposed to be extremely "dirty" nuclear devices manufactured from red mercury. No definite trace of these bombs had ever been found, however, neither in the Middle East nor in Russian research or military archives.

Still, the rumors persisted. It was even said that the Iraqis had actually obtained one from desert tribesmen who discovered it floating in the lake near Asiye. But searches by international inspection teams after Desert Storm discovered no evidence of such a bomb.

Duff stared at the Iranian. "My God," he said in English. "The Red Bombs?"

Isfahan's face was impassive. "I have said nothing." He turned and walked away. A few yards off, he stopped, turning. "One bit of advice, my friend. It is often very foolish to assume the obvious."

Then he strode to his car and drove off into the night.

PORT TAMATAVE, MADAGASCAR
SEPTEMBER 11

"God dammit, Tun," Jack Ashdown yelled across hold number two at the bosun, who was operating the port winch. "Stop that fucking swing. Haul down on the fairlead."

Tun finally got the load adjusted, the winch cables thwanging with tension and the load itself hanging quietly now out there at the end of its cargo fall. The strapped metal pallet was piled with fifteen-foot timbers of *keawe* wood.

The timber was from the high forests of the island's Ankaratra Range, a type of wood similiar to balsa. The *Bengal* was loading from a barge a half mile offshore near the small port of Tamatave, on the eastern shore of Madagascar. The port was primarily a rice depot and had only two loading berths set up for conduit delivery.

Thickly forested mountains rose a quarter mile beyond the town, which consisted of thatched, red dung-brick houses. In between were rice paddies and clove and vanilla plantations. The offshore breeze was cool and smelled heady with ylang-ylang blossoms and coffee and cloves.

Ashdown directed Tun, easing the timber load delicately

down into the hold. Below, the barge crew stacked the timber platforms first in the bottom and then in the tweendecks spaces, with the ship's crew supervising and then strapping the loads down with cables. The timbers banged hollowly against bulkheads, and the wood seeped drops of sap that stank of turpentine.

The *Bengal* had made good time from Sri Lanka, running a slightly northerly track to take advantage of the northeast trades. The weather was clear; the sea, a deep, iridescent blue under the sun.

Since their fight, Boyle had generally avoided Jack. He skulked around with his broken nose taped and one cheek the color of liver. Whenever they relieved each other on the bridge, Boyle snarled out the status reports, his turquoise eyes sparking with unconcealed animosity.

It was plain that his normal level of rage had gone up several clicks. Now when he bullied the crewmen, he hissed at them like a cornered snake. Although he didn't do it in Jack's presence, it was obvious that he was still physically taking out much of his frustration on them.

Immediately after they had let go their anchor, Boyle had taken a bum boat and gone ashore to arrange the barge load with the local agent. He hadn't yet returned.

Jeremiah Pepper sidled up beside Jack, who stood near the number-five hold. "How's it goin', mate?" he asked.

"We've about got her, Chief. Ballast all dumped?"

Jeremiah nodded. "Aye. An' I've shifted oil, too." He looked down into the hold and watched the stevedores for a moment. "You know that them Malagashee is Polynesians? Same as them abos in New Zealand and the Societies."

"Oh?"

"Aye." In the sun, Pepper looked shriveled and gray-whiskered.

"I was hitched to a Poly sheila onest. Big as a bloody house. Damned near ate me out of hearth an' lot." He chuckled and shook his head wistfully. "But a damn game lady, she was. Screwed like a bleedin' diesel locomotive.''

Jack had gotten to know Jeremiah quite well since Singapore. After his victory over Boyle, the Aussie had taken a particular liking to him. The diminutive Chief Engineer was a dynamo who seemed to live on no sleep and Foster's beer. But Ashdown quickly learned that the man knew his steam engines. He had the golden touch and engine man's ear for running machinery.

During World War II, Jeremiah had first gone to sea in the Australian navy, he told Jack, aboard high-speed L-boats hunting German lighters in the Mediterranean. Later, he transferred to corvettes and then to Liberties hauling material for MacArthur's push up through the Pacific.

After service, he made a living afloat wherever he could—like Jack, dealing in things legal and illegal. For a time, he'd owned an ancient PT boat—with the hottest pair of Hall-Scott engines around—and he ran things across the western Pacific and up through the Celebes.

One night he'd been shelled by a Filipino patrol boat while he was hauling a load of contraband Laotian parrots. The birds all flew away, but his PT went to the bottom and he spent the next five years in a prison in Zamboanga. . . .

Pepper sighed. ''When you get 'er buttoned up, come below. I'll stand ya a plow in the froth.''

''Sounds good,'' Jack said.

In the darkness of the captain's cabin, the Irish pipes wailed a *Farewell to Lough Neaghe*. The mournful skirl partly covered the distant whine of the after loading winch and the hollow thunder of the timbers in the holds.

O'Mallaugh, bottle in hand, stared fixedly into the dimness as if he could see the sound of the pipes in their melancholy curlings. Now and then he swore.

Time was racing irretrievably away from him. Soon his part of the bargain would be manifest. And his soul would fly, sundered, to whatever heaven there was for a hero of his country.

Except that no one would ever really know of his bravery. Nor would there be a part of him left to lay beneath the sweet grass. Sometimes the fear and regret of that was so great, he cried out to have this burden pass from him. Like Christ on the cross.

But it wouldn't, he knew. The People, the Libyans, were already fulfilling their part of the agreement. He'd always called them that, ever since he first attended their guerrilla camps at Tokra and Az Zauiah. They called themselves that, too. People of the Desert.

Sean O'Mallaugh was a member of the Provisional Arm of the IRA, had been since those tumultuous days of 1973—Bloody Friday, with British paratroopers in their blue berets killing his countrymen. Soon afterward, his brother, Liam, was murdered by B-Specials of the Protestant UDF.

Liam was a milk farmer out on the border country of Lough Erne. The Specials came in the night and cut off all the teats of his cows. When Liam came to investigate the bawling, the men took him. They held him down on the steps of his own house and dropped chunks of cement onto his outstretched legs from the roof. His bones shattered right through the skin. Then they shot him four times in the head as his wife, Moira, and their twin sons watched.

Sean was at sea at the time. He'd shipped out of Derry at fourteen, strapping as he was. By twenty-five, he carried captain's papers. But Liam's death and Bloody Friday changed all that. He became a Provo, battled those same paratroopers in Creggan and the Bogside and carried out vicious border raids. He set off bombs in Manchester and Carrybridge and the big one at Canary Wharf in the London docksides.

During the mid-seventies, he spent time in Libyan guerrilla training camps, honing weaponry skills. But the Provos' headquarters in Belfast quickly realized he was much more valuable as a captain. So they used him, instead, to smuggle arms and explosives out of Portugal and Cyprus.

In 1987, he was arrested by Interpol agents and imprisoned in France for five years. When he got out, he returned to Derry and was appointed Provos Officer of Armoury, utilizing underground networks out of Italy, Spain and the Mideast to obtain weapons.

On Christmas Day in 1996, he was approached by an agent of Gadhafi's secret police. The Libyans had come up with a wild, daring operation. For his participation in it, they were willing to supply the Provos with twenty million dollars in Russian and Czech arms. . . .

The intercom buzzed. He reached up and flicked the switch. "Whot?"

It was Jack. "There's a Tamatave constable requesting to come aboard, Captain. Says he needs to speak with you."

"Grant him permission." He shut down the tape recorder and leaned around to pull back the porthole curtain.

Several minutes later, a short, fat man entered, dressed in a dirty white uniform and a red-and-blue pith helmet. He introduced himself as Sergeant Philibert Tsiranana.

"I believe I am having distressing news for you, *mon capitaine,*" he said with a heavy French accent. He withdrew a paper sack from his tunic and put it on the desk. "Is this being from one of your crews?"

O'Mallaugh opened the sack. Inside was a wallet. He looked into it. It was Boyle's. He glanced up quickly. "Whot's this about?"

Tsiranana shook his head sadly. "A most unpleasant situation. The man who carries this document holder was killed an hour ago."

O'Mallaugh did not move. Only his eyes went flat. "How?"

The sergeant sighed. "This man was most intoxicated. He proceeded to enter a native cafe, the Chat Botte. He became most abusive when told he could not." He shrugged. "There was a . . . *une lutte* . . . how you say? Fisticuffs? Unfortunately, this man was stabbed many times."

O'Mallaugh put the wallet back into the sack and tossed it across the desk. "It doesn't belong to any of my men."

"Ah?" Tsiranana said. "But a beachman claims it was from this ship he was coming."

"He was wrong."

The constable picked up the wallet, studied it perplexedly. "What to do now? I believe I must impound your ship for further investigations."

"Like hell you will! You put one man aboard and I'll bloody well blow 'is focking head off."

"But the investigations . . ."

"Away with you, sergeant," O'Mallaugh roared.

The constable went away shaking his head. "Most distressing," he murmured.

At 5:03 in the afternoon, the captain ordered steam up. He also instructed Pepper to charge the deck fire mains. To Jack, who was now in-duty First Mate, he said, "If any constabul'ry try to board when we pull hook, give the bastards the hoses."

"What if they fire on us?"

"Then we'll fair fire back. No bleedin' A-rab'll stand deck on this ship."

"Aye, sir."

At last everything was snugged down, the timber holds canvased and batten-barred. O'Mallaugh took the conn, scowling and alert. He posted Jack on the starboard wing with the bridge doors open. Down on the main deck, the whole crew was mustered, a man posted at each fire-main hose with Tun handling the anchor ground tackle.

A few minutes after eight, O'Mallaugh rang down for engine stand-by. Then he called to Ashdown, "Charge the windlass an' stand to your tackle for heave up."

Jack relayed the order to Tun. It was instantly carried out.

"Any sign of boarding boats?" O'Mallaugh shouted to Jack.

"No, sir."

"Heave up."

Jack relayed.

The chains came rumbling up through the hawsepipes,
the windlass whining and the heavy links shifting up on
the forward deck. Before they went down the spill pipes
into the chain locker, the men hosed the salt away.

"Anchor clear and onboard," Tun reported.

The captain rang down for forty revolutions. The *Bengal*'s props dug water, the deck jarring slightly, and then
they were moving away from the anchorage.

The evening sky was still lit as the houses of Tamatave
slid past slowly. Many were on stilts over the water. Their
lanterns cast yellow lights out onto the slightly choppy bay.

No one tried to board.


At eight o'clock, Jack relieved O'Mallaugh. By then the
ship was twenty miles at sea. He went over his plot, took
a position bearing off the Mananjary Light and then wrote
up the rough log.

The bridge doors were still open, and the night sea air
rolled in over the wing barrier. It felt humid and warm.
Jack sniffed at it, smelled rain. He'd already detected a
slight roll in the ship, a bit of pitch. Obviously, a storm
was making up to the southeast.

He called the radio room. "Collins, what's the latest
weather?"

"She comin' in now, First."

"Bring it up when you've got it."

Five minutes later, Collins came onto the bridge and
handed him the yellow weather sheet. "She's flat whippin'
up out there, man," Keyshawn said. "A tropical depression
to the northeast. About two hundred fifty miles from us at
thirty degrees latitude. Damn winds is already runnin' about
sixty knots."

Jack nodded. "We'll probably catch the edge."

"Shit," Collins said disgustedly. "I was just gettin' my
stomach into shape. Now we got a blow makin' up. My
goddamn gut's gonna let go all over again."

Jack gave him a sly grin. "A blow making up? Damn,
you're starting to sound like an old salt, Keyshawn."

Collins snorted. "Shit, you run with the motherfuckers, you start talkin' like the motherfuckers."

At 10:30, a dark figure skittered across the forward deck, went up the ladder to the fo'c'sle, passed the gun pit and ducked down beside the starboard windlass. It was Jadid, carrying his satchel.

He paused, feeling the roll of the ship, the pitch of the bow. The movements were exaggerated by his forward position. A wave of nausea struck him, bringing dizziness. He clung stupidly to the windlass housing.

He'd been seasick ever since Colombo and had remained in his cabin the whole time, vomiting or curled in his bunk between bouts of restless sleep. The captain sent his food in, but he ate little of it.

Only once did O'Mallaugh come to see him, standing silently over Jadid's bunk like a dark angel. He handed over a sheet of paper and a flashlight and then went away. On the paper was a crudely drawn map of the forward deck with an X marking the small hatch to the forepeak.

Jadid at last braced himself and moved forward. In the dim glow from the stars and the ship's running lights, he saw the lookout standing at the bow. He was whistling softly, tapping his flashlight on the plating.

Jadid slipped forward and went into the space between the windlass and the wildcat drum. He felt for a hatch in the deck plating, found it. It had a dog fitting. It was tight, but he finally got it loosened.

He lifted the hatch. The seals made a sucking sound, and then came the soft squeak of the hinges. A deep stench of old metal and sour water drifted up. Quickly he climbed down into it and closed the hatch.

He took out his flashlight and flicked it on. The steel plating of the ladder shaft was rusted and streaked with orange slime. He went down.

He passed through a small rope locker, rolls of deck line on shelves, then a carpenter's shop with piles of dunnage roped to the bulkhead and a workbench and tools fitted into wall brackets.

At last he reached the lowest space. It was small and tight, and there was a tank fitted directly into the point junction of the bow with its piping and wheel valves. Everything was painted with red lead that had flaked, and chips of paint coated the deck. An officer's cap sat on top of the tank, the cloth rotted and torn.

Jadid could really feel the solid lift and plunge of the ship here, and he actually heard the water sloughing past on the other side of the hull plates. The throb of the engine came up off the deck and made the piping and cross members creak.

Another rush of nausea hit. He bent over and vomited between his feet, spewing out a yellow bile that burned his throat and stank like acid. He finished, slumping weakly.

Finally, he forced himself to move again. He opened his satchel and took out a bundle of straw. He quickly undid the straw, exposing the metal canister from the Israeli convoy. Again he noticed the heavy weight of the metal and its coldness, as if he had just taken it from refrigeration.

He peered around the tank piping, down near its foundation. A small angle iron crossed the tank strut and was bolted to a second iron that seated a drain sump plug. He pushed the canister in under the tank, wedging it between the sump plug and the bottom angle iron. He bound it to the iron with a strip of cloth.

Another wave of nausea. He waited, feeling it churning just below his chest. It faded. Inhaling deeply, gathering strength, he started back up the ladder as the *Bengal* lifted and then dropped, the sea beyond the plate hissing like the suck of a fire.

## 00:08

HAVANA, CUBA
SEPTEMBER 11

THE PEBBLE ZIPPED THROUGH THE OPEN PATIO DOORWAY and struck the corner of Enrique Cebuela's rocking chair with a tiny thunk. He looked down at it. *Ay, que es eso?* He leaned down and picked it up. It was folded into a piece of tissue paper.

Enrique had been watching Mexican soap operas—all the sexy *mexicanas* and their handsome *amantes*. It kept him from being bored. It was now early afternoon.

He unfolded the tissue. There was a short note written in tiny red letters. It said:

*Urgent*
*Colon—8A—Santeria*
*Very dangerous*
*Tavo*

His blood made a flush in his head. He hurriedly pushed to his feet and moved to the doorway to peer out. The patio garden was afternoon-still, only a bee busily fussing among the oleander blossoms. He looked over the gate hedge to

71

the alley and the empty building beyond. No one was out there.

He studied the pebble, thinking: they must have used a slingshot. He reread the note. Colon cemetery. He knew immediately what it and 8A meant. Everybody did, ever since 1989. That was the code for executed General Arnaldo Ochoa: *ocho* for eight, and an *A* added. Of course, Ochoa's grave at the cemetery.

Five minutes later, he boarded an *el micro* headed for Colon. Furtive now, his nerves tingling, he watched the other passengers and glanced back through the dirty window to see who might be following.

The cemetery had a huge ceremonial archway with a statue of the Virgin. Inside were avenues lined with jacaranda trees and blocks of graves—giant sepulchres with sculptured angels and saints and monuments that looked like tiny churches.

Enrique walked along the cemetery's C street. On the next street was a white hearse with a line of mourners following, everyone dressed in black. Closer in, several women placed flowers in the cement fingers of a statue of Our Lady of Sorrows.

He wandered around with studied aimlessness, watching. The air was scented from the jacaranda blossoms and newly mown grass. He paused here, there, seeming to meditate at a grave site, his eyes darting to the other wanderers among the graves.

There was no sign of del Pino.

He had lied to Ana about del Pino. He wasn't an old friend from the mountains; instead, Enrique had actually met him a year before, at the fish market. They'd accidentally bumped into each other. Del Pino, huge and lumbering and jolly, had apologized and started an idle conversation about the scarcity of good *jaqueton* and German brown mountain trout.

He invited Enrique to share a beer. They sat out in the sun and talked further, still only about old fishing trips and those that got away, the fat man laughing and making fun of himself.

Two weeks later, Enrique ran into del Pino again. Once more they drank beer and exchanged thoughts. Only this time, Enrique's natural bitterness began to seep out. He commented on how utterly fouled up everything was.

Del Pino agreed. He grinned in the sunlight, his big forehead touched with perspiration. He said, shrugging, "But there is nothing to be done, no?"

The meetings developed into a regular thing. There was more mutual complaining and a growing tone of clandestine intimacy. Then, one morning after Ana and Pilar had left for the day, del Pino showed up at Enrique's home. He came in through the garden, seeming distracted, nervous. He worked around things, avoiding direct statements.

Finally, Enrique challenged him. "Tavo, you came here to say something. So, say it."

Del Pino's eyes narrowed. "Can I truly trust you, *amigo*?"

"Tell me and see."

"I'm with Alpha 66." Alpha 66 was a counterrevolutionary group of exiled Cubans in Miami.

"Ah," Enrique said. "Ah." He walked around the room for a little while, absorbing that fact. At last he turned. "Why do you openly tell me this?"

"Because I think you can be one of us. We need you— your knowledge of Fidel, his weaknesses." He paused. "And also your experience in guerrilla fighting."

Enrique's expression stiffened. "Has it gone that far?"

"Not yet. Someday. Perhaps soon."

"Others have failed."

"We won't."

Enrique refused to become involved. He feared the consequences to his family, Ana and Pilar and many others, sisters and cousins in the midland. To actually raise arms against Fidel? Unthinkable.

Yet he kept del Pino's secret.

Tavo continued coming to the house, always when Enrique was alone—slipping past the neighborhood watches, pleading, wheedling, trying to sway him. If Enrique wouldn't join, then he might at least defect to the U.S. Alpha 66 would arrange it. Once there, he could openly speak out against the regime.

Still Enrique refused.

Then Tavo laid in the bomb. He told Enrique that his son-in-law, Major Castile, had been talking with Alpha 66, actually drawing up plans to get himself and his family across to Miami.

Tavo paused a moment, then continued. "That's why he was murdered. On direct orders from the Ministry of Defense."

Enrique stared at him, stunned. "How can you say this thing?"

"Because it's true. It was my own cousin who set the bomb on his boat."

*"Jesus Cristo!"*

"My cousin was a strong-arm with MINFAR. Six months after the explosion, he was imprisoned on a morals charge. They said he had sold his sister into white slavery. An outrageous lie. Within a week he was dead, killed right inside Guanajay prison."

Del Pino leaned forward. "But before he died, he smuggled word to me of what had really happened, what MINFAR had ordered him to do."

At that moment, Enrique's bitterness turned to rage.

Gradually he worked his way to cemetery street K. Here, the grave sites were unkept, the grass tall and weedy. This was Colon's potter's field. He went down into it.

Drifting idly, he approached a particular white tombstone, number 46672, the grave of General Ochoa. He stopped a ways off and studied the site.

There was a small plaque on the marker. It read A NINE DE SU FAMILIA. *Nine*, Ochoa's family nickname. Even in death, the regime had not permitted his real name to be written.

Enrique looked in the grass beside the marker for a message, anything. There was nothing.

He heard a soft cooing. Two Santeria priestesses had approached from the left. They wore long white gowns and turbans and colorful beads around their necks. They seemed to float like ghosts among the graves, murmuring prayers. They did not look at him.

He recalled the note. Santeria, it had said. Was he to speak to these? Follow them? He hung back until the two women headed toward the entrance. As they passed through, he hurried after them.

They went four blocks to the north, into an area of old four-story blue buildings with clothes drying on the balconies and broken windows. In the street, young girls in sexy summer dresses giggled at young men in undershirts who worked on delapidated Eisenhower-era vehicles.

The two women went through a white door in one of the buildings. Enrique stopped beside a Sailor's Store across the street. He gave the area a thorough scan. His heart was pounding. Still, nothing seemed out of the ordinary.

He finally crossed the street and knocked on the white door. One of the priestesses opened it instantly. She jerked her head for him to enter. He stepped in.

The priestess led him down a dark corridor, past two old men playing the guitar in a small room. Beyond was a candlelit room with an altar. On its top were porcelain figurines, African masks made of coconut shells, and tiny model cars. There were also statuettes of Santeria gods like Shango and Obatala and Oshun. A man was prostrated before the altar, praying.

At the end of the corridor, the woman disappeared into a side hallway. To Enrique's left, a man stood in a shadowed doorway. It was del Pino. He took his arm and pulled Enrique inside.

There was very little light here, too. The room was close, smelled of sour mangos and Tavo's musky sweat. A tiny window, draped with gunnysacking, gave onto an alley.

"Tavo, what is this about?" Enrique demanded. "This crazy note business and—"

Del Pino cut him off. "You were about to be arrested."

Enrique's heart turned over in his chest. "What? Why?"

"Three of our people were picked up two days ago." Del Pino spoke quietly but rapidly, breathlessly. "They talked, told names. Including mine and yours."

"But I've done nothing."

"It won't matter now. To them, you are part of it."

Enrique stared at him. "How do I know you're telling me the truth?"

Tavo moved to the window. He motioned Enrique over and slid the gunnysack aside a bit. "See for yourself."

Three men stood on the corner of the alley. They wore baggy shirts, but the bulky outlines of their pistols were clear beneath the material. They had the restless insolence of policemen, standing out there smoking and waiting.

Enrique hissed. GRU agents, the secret police.

"They already have your house staked out," Tavo said. "One of those followed you from Colon."

Enrique put his head down, his thoughts racing, plunging ahead at what was coming. What of Ana, Pilar?

"Come with me," Tavo said. "We'll go to the mountains. We can get you out."

"But my family . . ."

"We'll get them out, too." Del Pino gripped his arm again, squeezed it to emphasize his words. "You have no choice now, *mi amigo*."

They went down a narrow stairway to the basement. It was very dark, and there were stagnant pools of water on the cement. Rats chirped in the darkness.

Tavo was fooling with metal, scraping something. There was a sudden stench of wet dirt and decay. "Here, down here," he whispered.

Enrique put his hands out, felt a metal plate, ran his fingers around. A cement culvert, piping. It was some sort of drain.

"We'll wait here till night," del Pino said. "Then we'll slip out of Havana."

Enrique climbed down, feeling sudden claustrophobia. He hunkered down, trying to dispel the fear. Tavo closed the metal lid. He could hear his breathing.

"What about the people here? They'll arrest them."

Tavo laughed, a deep chortle from his chest. "No, they will be safe. Even El Comandante doesn't fuck with Santeria priestesses."

They waited.


The agent wore dark glasses and toyed with a golden pen, a Parker, with cross-hatching of silver. He had a tight, angry face and nice hair, curled at the neck. But he spoke very softly and courteously.

"Please forgive this interruption of your duties, Lieutenant Castile," he said. "This won't take long. Sit, please."

Ana sat down. She was nervous but hid it. She glanced at the other man who was moving around the office of the Mariel air base commander.

She had been called away from the flight line at three in the afternoon. At first, she feared that something had happened to her daughter, then her father. A medical problem, an accident.

But the moment she saw the two men in their white, short-sleeved shirts and dark glasses sitting in the commandant's office, she knew. GRU agents.

"You are, of course, a loyal soldier of the Revolution," the agent said. "Yes?"

"Yes."

The man nodded. "And you wish to protect it and our supreme leader. Yes?"

"Of course."

Again the man nodded. He twirled the pen slowly between his fingers. He had long, slender fingers. He glanced up sharply. "Where is your father?"

Ana's heart went solid. "At home," she finally managed.

"Unfortunately, that is not so."

"What's happened?"

"If he were to go anywhere, where would it be?"

"I don't understand."

The second agent came and stood beside her. She could smell his aftershave lotion—woody with the tang of gingers.

The man at the desk took three photographs from his shirt pocket. He sat staring at them as if debating whether to show them to her or not. At last he did, one at a time.

"Do you recognize this man?" he asked. He held up the first photo. It showed a thin man in a bathing suit beside a dock, with small sailboats in the background.

Ana looked at it, shook her head. "No."

Another photo. A man in the jungle, moving through brush, the photo slightly blurred from his movement. "This one?"

"No."

Another. Ana stiffened, quickly caught herself. This one was of the man her father had told her was Gustavo del Pino. She tried not to show it in her eyes. She shook her head. "No."

The GRU agent nodded and replaced the photos in his pocket. "Is your father a loyal citizen of Cuba?"

"Yes," Ana answered sharply. "He's a patriot, a fighter at El Líder's side. You already know that. Why are you asking me these foolish questions?"

The man ignored that. He went on for the next thirty minutes, asking more questions, toying with his pen. They were pointed inquiries about how her father felt about the regime, the state of the nation.

Then he would suddenly switch, commenting on inane things: the exhilaration of flying, the soft smell of the ocean that wafted in through the open window.

Inwardly, Ana was in turmoil. It was obvious that her father was in serious trouble. At least they didn't know where he was. That meant he had fled. To where? How? With this del Pino? And what of Pilar? Of herself?

At last, the two agents left her. She rose and quartered the room. Gradually, her distress began to turn to anger. What was this persecution of her father, her family? They were all good Cubans. That had been proven throughout their entire lives.

The agents came back and began questioning her again. She challenged them, demanded to be told why this nonsense was being carried on. They waited for her to finish, then went right on as if she had not spoken at all.

It was almost six in the evening before they finally dismissed her. The silent agent walked with her out to the entrance of the building. He watched her cross the tarmac to the pilots' wardroom.

Pilar was pouting, in her Pioneer uniform with her tennis racket and books, when Ana pulled up in front of her school. The girl climbed in, giving her a look.

"You're late," she said testily.

"No hug?"

Pilar leaned over and gave her a halfhearted squeeze. She was a pretty fourteen-year-old with long, straight brown hair and dark eyes and a mouth that could tremble in hurt or curve downward in pout. But it could also open in a smile so clean and bright with those dark eyes twinkling excitement that it always made Ana's heart ache with love.

"Why were you late?" Pilar demanded now.

"An emergency."

Pilar's head swung around. "What?"

"A fishing boat."

"Tell me."

Ana did, making up something, all the time watching her daughter, enthralled at the story, the brightness now in those eyes. But her heart was like a heavy stone.

At home, she came gently into the house, listening. It was quiet, the silence like the heavy stillness before a storm. Pilar hustled past her, into the living room.

"Papa?" the girl called. "Papa, you here?" She listened, then turned. "Where is he?"

"Probably visiting."

"But he never does."

"Today he is," Ana snapped and was immediately sorry. She put her arm around the girl. "Take your things in, *dulce*. I'll start dinner."

Pilar went off. Ana felt a wave of fear wash over her. To dispel it, she moved to the window beside the front door and looked out. In the deepening shadows, two little girls in Flintstones T-shirts played in front of the adjoining house. An old woman sat on the stoop with a young man who wore a faded leather jacket and played a guitar.

A blue Moskvich car came slowly up the street. She saw two men in it, their heads turning slowly as it passed. White *guayabera* shirts, dark glasses. The man in the passenger seat was the silent agent from Mariel.

*Dear God,* Ana thought.

JACK WATCHED THE STORM COME AT THEM FROM OUT OF the night, and his spirits lifted with the wind.

By ten o'clock, the barometer had fallen to 29.82 inches, ten-hundredths below normal. The wind registered a steady twenty knots with gusts to thirty, and there was a long-reaching cross swell, peaks at fifteen feet, running out of the south-southeast.

In it, the *Bengal* took the swells on her port bow, lifting her head evenly and then dropping down into the trough. Water flew over the bow bulwarks and foamed back across the foredeck. Her roll was mild, mostly to starboard, from which she recovered smartly.

In the sky, there were still stars to the north. The dark waves came in smoothly, looming up without crests, their faces not yet confused but polished and shimmering in the starlight.

Ashdown was dressed in a yellow foul-weather jacket he'd found under the bunk in Boyle's cabin. It had been wrapped around an old sawed-off Mannlicher twelve-gauge shotgun with six cartridges taped to the stock.

Most of the time he conned from the port wing, standing out there with his legs taking up the pitch and roll of the deck, feeling the wind whipping over the barrier with the powerful smell of open ocean and storm and distance in it.

81

O'Mallaugh had chosen to remain in his cabin, merely instructing Jack to keep him apprised of the situation. Collins had twice come to the bridge to bring Jack the latest weather reports. He was monitoring radio broadcasts from the weather center at Capetown and Radio Port Louis on the island of Mauritius, eight hundred miles due east of their position.

He looked haggard and oddly thin-faced. "Jee-sus God in Heaven," he groaned. "I think I just puked up my fuckin' asshole."

Jack grinned at him. "Go chew some ice, Keyshawn. Sometimes that helps."

Collins grabbed at his stomach, a stricken look on his face. "Oh, shit, here she come again." He lunged away.

The weather reports indicated that the tropical depression had developed into a moderate cyclone heading northeast. It was currently located at 28° 52' south, 51° 12' east about 250 miles southeast of the ship.

At eleven o'clock, the barometer sat at 29.69 inches. The stars were gone now, and the wind had increased to thirty-two knots with gusts of forty. The waves were topped with white crests, twenty to twenty-five feet high.

The *Bengal* had begun to yaw as she came up out of the deep troughs. Jack ordered the helmsman to hold constant left rudder to keep her head on course. Her roll deepened. Often, the inclinometer showed a twenty-two-degree roll to starboard with a slow return.

He could feel the ship shake violently for a few seconds each time she plunged and her prop partially cleared water. To lessen runaway, he'd rung down for Pepper to drop speed to six knots.

A half hour later, he called Pepper on the power phone. "Chief, she's getting damn sluggish in roll recovery. And I can still feel the prop clearing."

"Aye," Jeremiah hollered back. "It's them bloody timbers. There's no mass to 'em. She's settin' too high."

"How much fuel have you got in the starboard tanks?"

"Thirty percent."

"I think we'd best ballast."

Pepper hissed. "Hate to muck the buggers up with salt water. But I think it's wise."

"All right, transfer fuel and start ballasting. Let me know when it's done."

"One other thing," Pepper said. "Over the last half hour, we been showin' a gradual pressure drop. I think those new boiler seals are leaking."

"Any chance we'll lose steam?"

"Don't worry about it. We'll keep her up. But we're gonna damn sure have to post repair time when we refuel at Capetown. Get those bleedin' seals redone and roll some tube."

Jack notified the captain of the situation. O'Mallaugh merely acknowledged and clicked off. Soon after, it began to rain, heavy, pounding drops against the bridge bulkhead. Feathers of water blew through the seams of the wing doors.

Jack went out on the port wing again. The raindrops stung. There was a sudden, powerful flash of lightning. Everything for a single moment was frozen into stilled motion—the foredeck with a rush of foam like waves of snow, the stark angular thrusts of the derrick posts. Beyond the ship, the clouds were low, dense as oil smoke.

He grinned happily into the face of the storm. Everything inside himself was alive, as if he had absorbed energy out of the howling wind. All around him he could hear and feel the strain in the ship. She creaked and groaned and crashed. And now her boilers were acting up. But, by God, the old lady *was* holding solid like Pepper had said.

Just before midnight, O'Mallaugh came to relieve him. His eyes were red-rimmed, as if he had just then risen from sleep. Jack updated the ship's status, shouting over the wind.

The captain nodded. He checked the course, then stepped out onto the wing. A moment later he was back, the skin of his face red from the impact of the rain. His beard glistened with droplets.

Jack said, "Sir, I request permission to keep the watch."

O'Mallaugh wiped his face and stared at him. He had a golden fleck in his left eye. He grunted. "Fancy the wind, do you?"

"Yes. I'd like to ride her out."

O'Mallaugh nodded brusquely. "Keep an eye on that steam." He went back through the door.

Down in the rolling, heat-drenched engine room, Pepper was everywhere, skittering up and down ladders, checking bearings, glaring at pressure gauges and pump indicators as the fuel was transferred out of the starboard tanks so they could be flooded with seawater ballast.

All the time, he listened, his small, bush-hatted head tilted like a bird detecting ground noise. He listened to the ponderous, throbbing revolutions of the engine and shafts, to the heavy sucks and whomps and hissing blows of the machine room.

He had actually detected the leakage in the boilers long before the gauges showed any pressure drop. He perceived it as a strange hissing hidden in the normal whooshing of the boiler boxes. At last, even his First Assistant, Vogel, picked it up.

The German, built like a long-distance runner with an incongruous bass voice, said, "Someting's wrong in the boilers, Chief."

From the location of the hissing, Jeremiah was fairly certain that the leaks were in the tube seatings rather than in the tubes themselves. But leakage like that was eating feed water. Sooner or later, they'd run low enough to put seawater into the lines. That could foul up the boiler tubes with salt soot.

The gauges were now reading 197 pounds per square inch. As Jeremiah stood squinting at the dirty boiler gauges, there was a sudden drop in pressure. He cut loose with a chain of obscenities.

A few seconds later, a high shrieking resounded throughout the cavernous engine space. It was the warning valve on the high-pressure cylinder. Then the valves on the medium-and low-pressure cylinders went off.

"Vogel," he bellowed. "Stand by the main circulatin' pump. She's droppin' too fast. We'll have to feed off the condenser line."

Vogel had been manning the throttle valve that guarded against engine runaway whenever the prop cleared water. He turned and went up the ladder to the second level and disappeared around the engine column to the main condenser.

Pepper bolted back through the boiler space to the panel board beside the throttle desk. The ship had just begun a roll to starboard, the foundation beams creaking like sundering timbers. He began flipping switch guards open.

"Feed in," he yelled over the scream of the saftey valves. "Now! An' check the hot-well tank. See how much lubricant seepage we're gettin'."

Vogel obeyed, turning the wheel of the valve that linked the boiler feed lines into the main circulating pump of the condenser. This main line fed a constant flow of seawater through the main condenser. Jeremiah instantly began shutting off the regular reciprocating feed pumps.

The ship hung for a few, agonizing moments in a roll, then began a slow, elephantine recovery. A few seconds passed as the boiler lines filled with seawater. Then there were several muffled explosions inside the boilers. They made the Malaysian watertenders jump back.

Shouting to Vogel to get back to the throttle, Pepper scurried to the boiler face. As the salt water began to feed into the boiler system, salt particles were being instantly heated and expanded until some blew apart. The explosions could dampen the fire line enough to cause a flare-out.

As he reached the face, the forward boiler went dead with a wild hissing. Instantly, Jeremiah spun the fuel wheel and lit off. The hissing stopped. There was a whomping whoosh. The hissing started again. Once more, Pepper lit off. This time, the boiler took and held.

He snapped around, staring at the pressure gauges.

Slowly the pressure began to come up. It read 190 . . . 200
. . . 215 . . . 220. Normal operating pressure.

The power phone clanged. He hurried back to the throttle
desk and snapped the receiver to his ear. "Aye?"

"I felt a lag there, Jeremiah," Ashdown's voice said
tinnily. "What's boiler status?"

"We're runnin' salt through now."

"Can we make Capetown before she starts clogging?"

"She'll hold."

"Latest weather indicates we'll be passing through the
storm peak at about oh-three-hundred hours."

Jeremiah snorted and reached into his beer box for a
fresh Foster's. "Too bad," he said. "It was jes' gettin'
interesting."


At three o'clock, the barometer hit 29.64 inches but went
no lower. A half hour later, it started up again and the wind
shifted direction, coming in forward of the port beam. With
her tanks now ballasted, the *Bengal* took the shift in stride.

At four, O'Mallaugh came up, still red-eyed, with the
smell of whiskey powerful on his breath. The barometer
had risen to 29.85, and both the wind and the seas had
dropped considerably. Jack turned over the watch but lingered on the bridge wing for awhile.

The sky southward gradually cleared enough to show a
widening band of stars, and as the light grew, he saw the
massive dark backside of the storm moving to the east and
north. The dense bank of black cloud seemed to lie motionless on the sea. Now and then, flashes of lightning
showed deep within the mass, etching the edges of the
clouds and the sea with light like that from siege guns.

Jack felt tired. He'd been awake now for nearly twenty-
two straight hours. But the residue of the storm's power
still lingered in him. Restlessly, he went down to the main
deck and moved forward along the port safety line.

The wind was now blowing at fifteen knots. It felt oddly
warm as it swept across the deck. The waves had dropped
to fifteen-footers, and only occasionally did the ship dig her

nose deep enough to hurl a wave of water up and back, the wind feathering it and turning it to a showering cascade.

He went all the way to the bow. Drenched and shivering, he braced himself against the apron plate where the lookout normally stood. The jackstaff stays trembled in the wind. Below him, he heard the sloughing, rushing hiss of the bow cleaving water.

Still more light came. The brightest of the stars faded into a pearly, glowing seascape stretching in from the southern horizon. The sea itself was as gray as pewter but no longer confused into peaks and foamy crests.

Behind him, he could hear the jabber of Tun and the morning watchmen working forward across the main deck. They were dismantling the safety lines and checking the deck machinery and hold hatches for damage.

Jack saw the pod of dolphin coming from the south, slicing through the gray waves, their shiny backs humped and looking like black plastic for an instant in air before they dipped out of sight again.

They were running a school of flying fish brought to the surface by the storm churn. The school scattered ahead in a flurry of whipped water. Then single fish began to arrow through the surface and glide above it for a hundred yards. Their silver sides flashed, and their pectoral fins looked like diaphanous wings.

Suddenly, Jack's heart froze.

One of the dolphins was pure white.

A few seconds later, he heard the crewmen shouting. They rushed to the starboard bulwark, stood on chocks and bitts to see over. They pointed and chattered, their faces rigid.

To a seaman, the sighting of a white dolphin was one of the most evil of omens.

DAMASCUS, SYRIA
SEPTEMBER 12

FOR FIVE DAYS, DUFF HAD GONE TO GROUND IN DAMAS-
cus. He knew Hibril's kin would be looking for him, watching the airport and bus and train terminals. As a point of
honor, Isfahan would have informed them of the duel, to
prove that Hibril had died without shame.

There was also the matter of the Syrian *mukhabarat*, the
secret police. They'd be watching people and running ID
checks everywhere, using the death of a known terrorist as
an excuse to roust the Muslim Brotherhood and other op-
ponents of the regime. He could easily be caught in the
turmoil.

He lived in a single room above a spice and medicinal
shop in the Souqal al Hamadiyyeh, the covered market of
Old Damascus. The room was filthy, contained a cot and a
tiny table, and smelled of garlic and cinnamon and lemons.
In the shop below, the proprietor was scrawny as a camp
refugee. He had shelves of herbs and talismans and bottles
of goat penises and bird embryos to stimulate a man's sexual strength.

Duff remained in the room during the day, sitting at the
single window to watch the pigeon racers exercising their

birds on the roofs. In the street, young men in leather jackets sold contraband American cigarettes on corners while ragamuffin children watched the television cartoon show called *Captain Majed* in tiny shops and stalls.

Only after hearing the cassette tapes of the *muezzin* calling the faithful to evening prayer and seeing the minarets of the Omayyad Mosque glow a misty green in the night did he venture out to wander aimlessly. Sometimes he returned with cartons of *mulukhieh* and *labneh*, a mixture of spinach and strained yogurt. It was all he could keep down. It made his stool, when he managed a bowel movement, green and brackish smelling.

Eventually, he had to risk going to Jerusalem. He chose to take an overland service taxi. Since it was illegal to go directly to Israel from Syria, he decided to go first to Amman, Jordan, and then cross the open border into Jerusalem.

The taxi was a battered, yellow Ford Galaxy with little bells and plastic grapes hanging from the front header. The driver, a Bedouin with a Jordanian accent, was named Salim. He wore a dirty towel around his neck, smoked incessantly and drove very fast, using four different horns to chase people out of the way.

It took them three hours to get to Der'a on the Jordanian border, desert all the way with a boiling wind coming through the window and Salim singing along to a tape of the Lebanese pop singer Fayruz.

Duff sat quietly in the passenger seat, staring out at the shimmering, khaki-colored boulder fields, his wound aching when he moved. But it was the deeper sickness in him that never went away. It hung there like a silent ghost in the shadows, riffling pain through his lower abdomen.

At the border, he had to turn in his yellow Syrian visa card, but the Swiss diplomat passport still held, although the border guards gave him studied looks.

It took them another hour and a half to reach Amman. They first passed through Jeresh, once a beautiful Roman city. Then they went into the frenetic traffic of Amman so

Salim could refuel. Afterward, they turned west toward Israel.

It was early afternoon when the driver pulled to a stop at the Al-Malek plaza beside the Allenby/Hussein Bridge, which separated Jordan from Israel. Hired taxis were not allowed to enter Israel. Carrying his gear, Duff walked across. Below, the River Jordan was a mere stream of dirty brown water.

It took him nearly an hour to get a visa at the Israeli border office and then hire a taxi. They passed through the deserted refugee camp at Maale Adumim. Along the highway, there were Israeli soldiers, hitchhiking. Thirty minutes later, they passed through the Damascus Gate and entered Old Jerusalem.

The apartment was small but well furnished. It was in the Jewish Quarter of Old Jerusalem, a block from the HaKotel HaMa'aravi, the Wailing Wall.

Too fatigued to hunt up living quarters, he had boldly gone to the Jewish Foreign Placement Division in Rose Park and requested assistance in finding something for a month's stay. He told the clerk he had been on a fact-finding jaunt into the Negev for the Swiss government. He was assigned the apartment.

The clerk mentioned that it had previously been occupied by a young married couple, both lieutenants in the Israeli Defense Force. A month before, the man had been killed in a riot in the Gaza Strip.

Walking through the rooms, Duff detected the couple's presence—the lingering smell of aftershave lotion, a whisper of perfume in corners; a few forgotten mementos and, in a drawer, a framed snapshot of two beautiful, vibrant strangers in green fatigues at a *kibbutz.* Duff placed it atop the bureau.

He sat on the bed. He was exhausted, the fatigue like a glove of lead. He lay down and was quickly asleep, into deep caverns of semidarkness where sounds were muffled and voices spoke to him without comprehension from crevices issuing a cool breeze.

After a long time, he awoke and found that the breeze was from the window, mountain-cold with the smell of pine and cedar in it. It was now night.

He lay listening to his body. It was as if he could hear it, tiny silkworms feeding on his innards. *Death.* He stared at the ceiling. A pattern of faded leaves crossed through the stucco. He thought of dying.

It was too ironic. In his life, he had always seen death come swiftly—a blow of powder, the wet whisper of a knife's cut. Instantaneous. He had assumed his own would be likewise. The whole thing was unacceptable.

In the bathroom, he vomited violently, retched until his protruding stomach ached. He lifted his head and stared at his face in the mirror above the toilet. It was haggard, pallid with a grayness that was the mark of human functions shutting down.

He smiled at himself, saw himself smile back. A death mask. It struck him that he resembled Richard Burton in those last, gaunt days of his life.

He managed to shave and then stood under steaming water in the plastic shower stall with its Mickey Mouse curtain. He re-dressed his wound and put on clean but crumpled clothes. Then he combed his hair and stepped out into the front room.

She was standing there.

Her name was Talia Rosenfeld.

She gasped at sight of him, her lovely face going open with shock. Then she came swiftly to him and embraced him, and he could smell the aching familiar scent of her hair, the feel of her body in his arms.

She wept silently, her eyes misting with tears. She sat on the edge of the bed and looked at him. "You're dying," she said with horrified surprise.

He looked at her without comment.

Talia was a senior agent with Mossad, a thoughtful

woman of forty-two with beautiful brown eyes and a certain appealing serenity that occasionally sundered into fury or desire. For four years before his banishment, she and Duff had been lovers.

He sat in a chair. "You found me quickly," he said. "I'm impressed."

"There were sightings of you in Cairo. When Klein was killed, we suspected you were back."

"Rose Park?"

"Yes." She watched him. "What is it? Cancer?"

"Yes."

"Have you found the others?"

"One. In Damascus."

"Who else?"

"A Syrian named Toufiq Nidali. I was told your people may have killed him already. True?"

She nodded. "Yes. In the desert."

Duff inhaled deeply, let the air slip from him slowly. It was over.

Talia brushed fingers through her hair. It was full and rich and vibrantly thick. "We suspect something else," she said. "We know MI-6 contacted you in England. Leigh-Simmons?"

"You *are* thorough."

"Would you have expected less?"

"No."

"What do they want?"

"Haven't you already assumed that?"

She rose and quartered the room, paused a moment to pick up the photo of the two lieutenants. She studied it distractedly and then gently replaced it. "How did they know of the theft? Our codes?"

He shrugged, shook his head.

"Obviously, they don't know precisely *what* was taken." She turned. "Do they?"

"No."

Her eyes went soft, deeply pained for a moment. Very

softly, she said, "Please don't get too close, Duff. We can't allow the world to know about this."

He smiled. "What will you do? Silence me?"

"What would you do?"

"Silence me." Now he chuckled. "A rather redundant exercise, wouldn't you say?"

"God, I can't bear the thought of this."

"It's a Red Bomb, isn't it?"

Her head lifted sharply. She stared at him.

"So it is," he said. He grunted. "This is bad."

Silence filled the room. Through it came the sound of a siren, the wailing drift of it like a prophetic comment on what had just been spoken.

At last, Duff said, "Do you know who did it?"

"We have strong suspicions. A new Iraqi terrorist group calling itself the KIE—*Kanun ittani Elhamar*. They've already tucked a murder and a bombing in Eilat under their belt."

She paused. Then, wistfully, she said, "Remember Eilat? That weekend we spent in the small chalet on the beach." She stared at the floor, remembering. "We drank that horrid strawberry wine and got very drunk and then made love all—"

"Stop it," he said sharply.

Her eyes were moist again. She turned away from him, went to the window and looked out. Across the Old City shone the great Dome of the Rock. It was golden in the night, like a giant parachute underlit with a brilliant lutescent glow as if it had just wafted gently to the earth.

"Has this KIE group made precise threats?" he asked.

She nodded, came back. "Several. One in particular seems very ominous. It contained excerpts from an ancient Persian poem that tells of the destruction of the city of Lagash by King Hammurabi." She paused, frowning.

"And?"

"One line says that, quote, all the land was visited with death and darkness in the twinkling of an eye."

"The twinkling of an eye," Duff repeated. He nodded. "That's ominous, indeed."

Talia sat on the bed again. "We've gone over the entire poem a hundred times, looking for a clue. There is one thing. The original poem always referred to Hammurabi as 'the Lion of the Desert.' The KIE version is slightly different. It calls him 'the *Tiger* of the Desert.' We don't know why the change."

"A mistranslation?"

"Perhaps. But it uses the same reference three specific times."

"What do your people think?"

She shrugged. "Only that it's very peculiar and completely out of character. The ancient Persians *never* used the specific term for tiger. They didn't even speak it. It was cursed."

"Then the switch had to be deliberate."

"We think so."

Duff frowned thoughtfully. "There's a clue there, Talia. These people are taunting you. They're like warriors telling you before battle precisely what they're going to do and then challenging you to stop them."

"Yes, I agree. But how do we do it?"

"I don't know. But don't give up on it. The clue's there."

They talked into the night. The soft undertone of the city faded into silence. The night air grew colder. At last, she said she must go. They embraced without words, and then she was gone and the room seemed suddenly, unbearably empty.

Duff lay on the bed. Without volition, the memories swept through him. He couldn't stop them. His heart mourned. The rage and the hunt that had sustained him were now over. He found the sense of revenge, its catharsis, as empty as the room.

Near dawn, the sickness exploded in him with savagery. He lay in sweat and agony.

---

## CAPETOWN, SOUTH AFRICA
## SEPTEMBER 14

"BOLT AND LOCK THE LOT OF THEM UP," O'MALLAUGH said. "In the afterhouse. As soon as we tie up to drydock."

Ashdown looked at him, shocked. They were standing on the starboard wing looking down at the deck watch as the men prepared for docking.

"What?" he said.

"The lot of 'em, in the afterhouse," O'Mallaugh growled. "Are you bloody deaf?"

"We can't do that. It's against international law."

"Fock the law. You want thim jumpin' ship? That bloody white dolphin's spooked the buggers bad. They'll be bailin' out like rats if we don't stop thim."

"Again, sir, that's an outright breach of—"

The captain swung around. "I'll not argue with you, Ashd'n," he snarled. "Either lay thim aft or I'll bloody well put you in *with* the bastards."

Jack stared at him for a long moment, then turned away. He went below to the main deck to set the fore and aft docking parties.

By order of the harbormaster, the *Bengal* was hove to three miles off Capetown's Table Bay for cargo inspection.

All ships arriving at Capetown had to be inspected for contraband munitions before they could enter the harbor area.

Two inspectors came out on the Customs House launch. They wore spotless white uniforms and spoke Afrikaans-accented English. They went methodically through the holds, engine room and living quarters.

Eventually satisfied, they cleared the ship to proceed to the huge offshore drydock complex located a mile inside the curve of Table Bay for her boiler repairs and refueling.

O'Mallaugh took the ship past the harbor's container depot and then Duncan Dock. Forty minutes later, he eased her smoothly into slip number three at the drydock.

The structure was gargantuan, like a floating city with soot-grimy derricks and workshops and fueling gantries. Two moderate-sized tankers were already moored, with work gangs and gear all over their decks.

It was mid-morning. A hot breeze blew from the south, capping Table Mountain with a coverlet of clouds. Closer in, the green slopes of Devil's Peak and Signal Hill and the city itself lay in brilliant sunshine.

Jack gathered the entire deck force on the afterdeck, beside the number-five hold. The men were grim-faced, giving him steady Oriental eyes. Tun took him aside.

"Sor," he barked, his blood-red gums showing. "Captain want my boys inside?"

"Yes."

"Lock up? Like jailhouse?"

"Yes."

Tun snorted. "Dis no right, sor. God damn, I tink maybe my boys no obey."

Jack looked off toward Capetown. The traffic along Table Bay Boulevard was heavy, light sparking off mirrors and chrome like the bursts from rifles. He turned back.

"Don't let them disobey the order, Tun," he said slowly. "The captain'd have police here in five minutes. He'd charge them with mutiny."

The bosun shook his head angrily. "I been sea long time. Dis shit no right. Captain say I gotta go inside, too?"

"I say you don't."

Tun spoke to his men, shouting at them in Malaysian. They stood around, glaring at the floor and at Jack. But finally all of them filed slowly through the single door of the afterhouse.

It was a sweltering hot steel box that contained backup machinery for steering and hatches down to the main shaft tunnel for inspection and repair. During the war, the house had contained bunks for the navy gun crews.

Pepper had been watching from the boat-deck railing. As Jack came up, he chortled mirthlessly, "Them boys is mad as cut snakes."

"They got good reason to be," Ashdown commented. "I don't like this bullshit, Jeremiah. O'Mallaugh's way out of line."

"Aye, that's true enough. But, you know, he's right. Them Malays'd ditch this ship as soon as night come on. They're frightened about the dolphin. To them, this ship an' everthing on her's cursed."

"How about your black gang? The captain order them in, too?"

"No. But I'll keep the buggers too busy rollin' tubes to think about curses."

Jack snorted. "I still don't like it."

By noon, Jeremiah was good as his word. He had the black gang, along with two burly Afrikaaner ship fitters, busy installing fresh seals on the boiler tubes.

Next, they rolled new tubes, a tiring process of installing steel and then firing up to check the tubing and blow soot. Great puffs of black smoke periodically belched from the stack, sending a coating of gummy soot over the midhouse and deck.

At the stern, the afterhouse sat baking in the sun.

With no deck force, Jack decided to spend the time inspecting the ship. He and Tun went about with clipboards, poking into compartments and alleyways and checking the emergency gear in the lifeboats.

In the crew's quarters, Jack smelled the strong odor of marijuana. He found three stashes and a rusty twenty-two-caliber handgun, which he confiscated. The entire time, Tun remained sullen and said very little.

Once, Jack spotted Jadid peering out a boat-deck companionway. He looked pallid, wan, with stains on his shirt. As for Collins, his explosive seasickness had subsided with remarkable rapidity.

Jack found him in his radio room listening to South African stations and eating Blue Tiger candy. He offered him a cup of coffee.

"Check this out," Keyshawn said. "I been dialin' in Xhosa stations? The strongest one is WKSI out in Goodwood." He laughed. "Damn Xhosa language sound like the announcer got marbles in his mouth. And, man, they play some *funky* music. Sound like that old belly-rubbin' drag-and-mooch shit."

"Maybe you got Xhosa blood running in you, Keyshawn."

"Shit," Collins said disgustedly. "I'm Swahili, man. Fuck this South African tribal jive. My daddy told me once, he say, 'You Swahili, boy. Don't never forget it.' So I ain't."

He chewed, the candy sounding like peanut brittle. He studied Jack a moment. "When's the old man gonna let them Malay boys out?"

"When we leave."

"Don't seem right, do it? That fuckin' tin box back there must be hittin' a hundred fifty degrees by now. He's gonna roast them poor motherfuckers."

Jack silently sipped at his coffee.

"What's the big deal, anyway? They see a goddamn albino fish and get shitface scared. What for? I learned a long time ago, man, don't be scared of *nothin'* white."

"Sailors are superstitious. They believe in portents and omens." He looked mischievously at Collins. "Hell, you're aboard a cursed ship now."

Keyshawn sucked a piece of candy around in his mouth. "You ain't tellin' me something I don't already know."

Two hours later, Ashdown was in the engine room watching the black gang finish the boiler tube replacement. The two hulking Afrikaaners, stripped to the waist and both muscular as weight lifters, sang dirty barroom songs while they worked in the thick, oil-and-carbon-smelling air. Pepper was down there, too, looking like a gnome beside the twin Tarzans.

After awhile, Collins came below. He crept down the ladder to the throttle station and stood looking around with distaste. "Man, how these dudes stand livin' in this hellhole?"

"To an engineman, this is heaven."

Keyshawn turned to him. Looked at him from under his brows. "Captain sent me down. We got some trouble."

"What?"

"Them Malays in the afterhouse? They raisin' a ruckus. Sounds like they bustin' up the place. The old man said for you to go stop 'em."

"Where's Tun?"

"He's back there yellin' at the dudes through the door."

Jack, with Collins right behind him, headed up the ladder. They emerged onto the after boat deck. Now he could hear the sounds from the afterhouse—men shouting, the heavy impacts of metal against metal, and Tun, yelling at the door. He hurried down to the main deck and went aft.

"When did they start?" he asked Tun.

"Ten, maybe fifteen minute." He watched Jack search through the ring of keys at his belt. "What you do?"

"Go in to talk to them."

Tun looked shocked. "No, sor. Dis boys very dangerous now."

"It'll be okay."

"Then take gun."

"No."

"Jesus Christ, man," Collins cried. "You fuckin' crazy to go in there unarmed."

He ignored them. He found the key, leaned down and unclipped the lock. He swung the dogwheel and pulled the door open, the hinges squeaking. A wave of foul air smelling of human body and urine and the under-stench of hot metal and oil swept out in a rush.

He stepped in.

It was dimly lit, the heat so strong it was a palpable substance. The deck was inch-deep in thin oil. On both sides of the small passageway were the bunk rooms for the wartime gun crews. They had recently been packed with wooden crates and small barrels of storm oil, strapped to the metal piping. All the crates were now broken open, their contents scattered. The barrels were bungless and turned upside down on the deck.

On the opposite end of the cross passageway were two crewmen. They wore only loincloths. One had a short pipe; the other, a strip of crate wood with a pointed tip. They watched Jack like two cornered animals.

A wide hatchway with a ladder was between him and the men. It led down into the emergency steering compartment. A wire netting was around it on railings. Just visible on the lower deck were some standing machinery and a network of valved piping. Now and then, the whole house would resound with loud hammering and Malay curses.

Tun started yelling at the two men in the passageway. They just looked at him. The bosun started around Jack but stopped as the men lifted their makeshift weapons.

"Stay behind me," Jack said quietly. He felt his heart beating heavily. In the thick, boiling air, it was as if his breath didn't come quite completely, as if most of it hung up there in his upper chest under pressure.

He moved to the hatchway and glanced down. Several Malays, all completely naked, turned and looked up at him. Then they shouted excitedly. A moment later, several more came out from the steering machinery area. One was Datuk, the AB that Ashdown had prevented Boyle from beating.

Jack put his hands on the railing net. First one, then the other. The men milled below, their faces moon-round and dusky and shiny with sweat, all looking up like a herd of suddenly motionless wildebeests caught in that fragile, unpredictable moment before flight or fight.

"You men, listen up," he said as evenly as he could force his voice to be. "As first officer of this ship, I'm ordering you to stop this."

For a tiny moment, no one moved. Then several Malays bent and picked up objects—a piece of pipe, a broken valve housing, a bulkhead bracket.

"I don't like this situation any more than you do," Jack went on. "But you've been locked in here by direct order of the captain. To disobey that order is mutiny."

He gave his voice a sudden rise in volume. "Mutiny! You understand what I'm telling you? He's already called the shore police. In five minutes, they'll be aboard. They'll put you in chains and throw you in a South African jail. And you'll rot there. Is that what you want?"

Again there was that still, ominous moment of motionlessness. Then one of the men slipped his hand out of sight. It came back, moving swiftly. Something liquid came up through the dim air. It splattered across the hatchway netting, plopped softly against a railing post. Human excrement.

It was like a trigger. There was instant agitated movement among the men. Everyone started yelling. It sounded animal-like, overpowering in the confined space. Two Malays with pipes started up the ladder.

Jack's heart went solid. Instinctively, he took a step back, bracing himself, his eyes suddenly focused on the head of the ladder and his arms coming up, fisted, his body's weight shifting to strike at the first head that appeared. He heard Tun say something, felt the bosun's body press against his.

Then a single voice rose above the clamor. There was the sound of grunts, the sharp smack of skin. The yelling of the men subsided slightly. Several moved back into the machinery area.

When Jack looked down again, Datuk was standing beside the ladder. He had pulled the two on the ladder off. He bellowed at the men, his body naked, the muscles long and lean and scarred along the forearms, his voice dominating and then going on alone as the men fell into total silence.

At last his own voice dropped away. He turned and looked up at Jack. For a drawn-out moment, the two men stared into each other's eyes.

Then Datuk said, "You go away now, First Officer. I make these obey."

Jack nodded, turned and followed Tun to the doorway, where Collins stood just inside. The three men exited, and Jack relocked the door. He was covered with sweat. It streamed down his face, dripped from his chin. Across on the drydock, workers had gathered on a high beam to watch.

Collins shook his head. "God *damn,* man," he said. "I thought for sure them boys was gonna take you out."

Jack felt his body going slack and the tension creaming off. He grinned at the radioman, wide and fierce.

Up on the after boat deck, Captain O'Mallaugh shoved away from the railing and disappeared into the midhouse.

At ten minutes to midnight, the *Bengal*, sporting new tubes and blown-clean boilers, steamed away from the Capetown drydock and made for open ocean. O'Mallaugh was on the conn. He set her course for the northwest, a diagonal crossing of the South Atlantic.

Datuk had kept his word. He even got the men to clean up the afterhouse. After they were released, Vogel and one of the black gang checked the damage to the emergency steering machinery. It was superficial. They quickly jury-rigged repairs, leaving the more extensive work to be done at sea.

The Malays, most still naked, spread out on the deck as

if they wanted their bodies to suck up as much of the evening breeze as possible. They were silent and obedient.

It wasn't until morning watch muster that anyone realized one man had actually left the ship. Jack figured it must have happened as the *Bengal* moved slowly away from the drydock. Had the man made it past the ship's props? he wondered.

Now the night sky was clear, star-studded. The ship picked up speed as she drew beyond the peripheral glow of Capetown. Gradually, the beacons from Lion's Head and Signal Hill faded astern until they were gone completely and the ship was once again alone with the sea.

Off the coast of western Africa, five thousand miles north-northwest of Capetown, lie the Cape Verde Islands. All summer, these islands and the surrounding waters that lie along the Tropic of Cancer are warmed by the sun and a steady trade wind from the northeast.

As the summer progresses, great volumes of evaporation from the warm seas, heavy with stored heat in vapor form, lift off the ocean surface and rise into the atmosphere to form gigantic cumulus cloud fields.

As the uplift passes twenty thousand feet, the clouds are bombarded by erratic winds. Sometimes these winds are powerful enough to deflect the normal pattern of the trades. A kind of dent in them is created. This forms a trough that moves northeast, against the normal flow.

Within this easterly wave, breaks develop in the boundary between moist surface air and cold, dry high-altitude air. The lower moist air then slips through, turning into violent thunderheads.

Twisted by the Coriolis effect of the turning earth, these moving wave fronts sometimes deepen into vortices, forming tropical depressions. Some will go on to develop into full-blown Caribbean hurricanes.

Precisely thirty-one minutes after the *Bengal* left Capetown, the National Oceanic and Atmospheric Administration satellite GOES-3, at its geostationary position east of the Cape Verdes, picked up a cloud pattern that indicated the possible presence of an easterly wave.

The National Hurricane Center in Miami immediately tagged it as a tropical wave depression and began to track its movement and intensity. Within six hours, however, the wave dissipated, and the center's TWD watch was canceled.

But the Caribbean hurricane season was still comparatively young. There would be other waves.

---

## OFF THE CAROLINA COAST
## SEPTEMBER 17

For two weeks, the U.S. carrier *America* and her small task force composed of the cruiser *Gettysburg,* four destroyers and three frigates, had been conducting antisubmarine exercises west of Burmuda.

Using its S-3 aircraft and SH-60 Seahawk (Lamps III) helicopters in conjunction with satellite reconnaissance and the undersea sound detection system called CAESAR, the carrier force had run locate-and-interdict operations against decoy submarines maneuvering in the shallow waters off the continental shelf.

Phase One of the exercise was complete, and the flag commander ordered the task force to turn southeast to initiate the second phase of the exercise mission, a FlexOp off the Puerto Rican coast. The *America* group would be in support of elements of the First Marine Strike Force carrying out tactical helicopter assault exercises in the Virgin Islands. Coordinating with the *America* would be the helicopter carrier *Enterprise* and her support vessels based at Bradenton, Florida.

\*   \*   \*

The two American F-14 Tomcats came up off the ocean like rockets, afterburners going full-out. They left two thin brownish streaks of smoke in the air as they hurtled for altitude.

So quickly had they come that Lieutenant Castile's radar hadn't picked them up amid the surface clutter before they were streaking past, bracketing the Cuban helicopter. Ensign Perez gave a surprised shout and then cranked his head sharply upward to watch them disappear.

Oddly enough, Ana had sensed something seconds before they were there. Perhaps it had been the heavy military radio traffic from the approaching U.S. ships and aircraft, which had been sparking the air for hours. An expectation suddenly become real.

She felt the helicopter shake for a second or two as the wash of the Tomcats rolled into them. Then she snapped it onto its side in order to look upward through her window.

The sun flashed on her Plexiglas and then she saw the fighters, two dots in the immense expanse of pastel blue, still going up but losing climb energy now. At last they reached apogee and arched, almost motionless for a fleeting instant; then they separated and both went into a dive.

Ana blinked, and they were gone.

For a moment, she relished the picture of pure beauty and power of the American aircraft. She loved jets. They possessed a ferocity of speed, a majesty of freedom that was the ultimate goal of all flight.

During her training at San Julian Air Base, she had flown Czech-made Slin-326s and MiG-17s. She had wished desperately for assignment to a fighter squadron. But in Cuba, women were never sent to tactical attack units.

Perez was already relaying word of the presence of the American jets to Eastern Flotilla Headquarters at Camaguey, and also down to a Zhuk-class fast attack patrol boat that had been running surveillance patterns northwest of them.

Excited cross talk snapped into Ana's helmet earphones, radio sites cutting across transmissions. There was always a deep and instantaneous paranoia within the Cuban military psyche whenever the U.S showed its face. Now jittery staff officers were anxiously trying to interpret and respond to the intrusion, the first actually over Cuban territorial waters.

Havana Command had long known about the American carrier group headed their way. Forty-eight hours earlier, one of their Tactical Air Command Il-14s had spotted it approaching the outer reaches of Cuba's surveillance space.

Within minutes, the Ministry of the Revolutionary Armed Forces (MINFAR) had declared a high-priority alert. In the immediate deployment of units, part of Ana's squadron had been reassigned to the fighter base at Moa in eastern Cuba.

Since then, she and her crew had been flying recon-and-track flights almost constantly, over the waters of the Windward Passage near the Haitian coast and up through the cays of the Turks and Caicos Islands off the southern Bahamas.

As she re-leveled the helicopter, Ana caught sight of the Zhuk patrol boat coming in fast, leaving a trail of white on the ocean like a streamer. She saw that the patrol boat's guns were now uncanvased.

Three hours later, Ana closed her eyes and leaned back in the plastic chair. It had been made in Korea and was spindly legged and wobbly. In the darkness behind her lids, she felt the exhaustion come up into her body like a menstrual cramp.

Ensign Perez said, "Wouldn't you know it? The damn rice is half-cooked again."

They were sitting in the Moa base officers' commissary, drinking Canadian soda pop and eating beans and rice. Perez was irritable. There were dark circles under his eyes. He always developed such circles when he was exhausted. They made him look like Valentino in a desert movie.

He and Ana had just completed their flight debriefing. It was conducted by the squadron adjutant, Lieutenant Commander Sosa, a very fat officer with dark skin who constantly sucked on his teeth.

Another man was present, obviously a MINFAR agent. He was visibly nervous and took hurried notes. The entire debriefing had been handled like an interrogation. Had Lieutenant Castile provoked the Americans in any way? Had her instruments indicated that the F-14s had actually *locked* onto the helicopter? The agent pressed hard on that one, his black eyes staring almost accusingly into hers.

Now she opened them, reached for the can of pop and took a drink. It tasted like kerosened strawberries. "You'd better go get some sleep, Jesse," she said, "while you can." They were scheduled to return to their patrol area in six hours.

"I'm too tired to sleep. I always get insomnia when I'm too tired."

"Try." She slid off the Korean plastic chair and stood up.

"You, too," Perez said. The roar of a jet bomber taking off rumbled into the building for a moment. The sound gradually faded off into a whisper of engines.

Ana nodded. "I will."

Perez studied her. She knew he had heard about her father's disappearance. News always traveled with mysterious but incredible speed in Cuba.

He leaned forward. "He'll be all right," he said softly, then quickly put his head down and began to eat again.

Ana headed across the commissary. At 3:30 in the afternoon, it was nearly empty. The base personnel would not be coming off duty for another hour.

The building was old, made of wood, and sat near one of the maintenance hangars. The flooring was worn along the food lines and between the tables, and darkened by years of harsh cleaning fluids. Two messmen in sweaty T-shirts idly mopped near the front door.

She went into the women's rest room. It was painted a drab green, and the walls had tiny fungus pockets in the corners. It smelled of disinfectant.

She washed her hands, looking at her face in the mirror. She ran a finger along her chin line, up over one eye, pressing the skin. She wore no makeup save for a little lip coloring. Cosmetics, like everything else, were very difficult to obtain on the island.

Studying herself, she felt a sudden, womanly anger and disgust well up at all of it. At the restrictions and ration books and long lines and constant frustrations. At the always watching and being watched. At the ubiquitous slogans and Fidelista pictures that proclaimed a wonderment of revolutionary existence—which had, in reality, long since disappeared. At the shabbiness that had descended upon her Cuba, the frayed seediness of place, of life, of soul.

She shook her head, forcing the feelings away. She washed her face again and dried it on the soiled towel. She understood that this emotional response was actually a surface reaction to a much deeper anxiety: fear for her father.

Dear God, she thought, where was he? Did the GRU have him in some tiny cell somewhere, torturing him? Was he already dead? The thought brought chilling goose bumps to her arms.

There was worry over Pilar, too. When Ana was reassigned, she had intended to leave Pilar with a neighbor until she returned to Mariel. But her squadron commander had specifically ordered that Pilar be temporarily quartered at the Maximo Gomez Training Facility.

The school was a division of the UJC, the Union of Young Communists, a secluded indoctrination center that presented a curriculum of advanced studies in Marxism-Leninism along with intensive athletic work. It was located on the Isla de la Juventura, the island once called the Isle of Pines, in the Gulf of Batabano south of Havana.

She suspected the obvious. Since her father's disappearance, the government was fearful that Enrique had somehow "contaminated" his granddaughter, so she would now be taken under its wing, protected. But when would Ana see Pilar again? The question constricted her bowels.

She turned and went into one of the stalls, pulled the door shut. Quickly shedding her flight suit, she sat and urinated, her water foaming noisily. Over it, she heard the outer door open and close quietly.

A moment later, she sensed someone standing in front of her stall. She dipped her head to see under the door. She saw work fatigues, black shoes.

A woman's voice that she didn't recognize said, "Ana?"

"Who's that?"

A folded piece of paper came over the top of the stall door. It landed on her thigh. There was the sound of footsteps. Then the outer door quickly opened and closed.

She unfolded the piece of paper. There was writing on it, printed without capitals. It said: *your father alive. mountains. one of us now.*

Quickly drying herself, Ana dressed and left the women's toilet. She paused at the door to the commissary, scanning. Perez was still at their table, drinking his pop and watching the messmen. Two senior officers drank coffee near one of the windows.

She hurried over to Jesse and sat down, leaning close to him. "Did a woman just come through here?"

"No," he said. "Why?"

Ana looked away. *One of us now.* My God, she thought.

They came at sunset, two Moskvich sedans with four GRU men in each. Behind them came two jeeps full of paratroopers in field green. The vehicles came barreling along the sugarcane road and swung down into the workers village.

The village was called a *batey*, a collection of thatch-roofed houses with a small store and dogs and chickens in the dirt streets. There were small banana patches between the village and the cane fields, and pens for the oxen that pulled the cane wagons. It was dinnertime, and the village women were cooking over outdoor ovens. Smoke hung still in the air.

The vehicles skidded to a stop in a whirl of dust. People

began coming out as the soldiers and security agents dismounted. But they were hurriedly shoved back by the troopers, who carried Kalashnikov assault rifles. The men began a methodical search of the houses.

A few minutes earlier, Enrique had gone down into the banana groves to collect fruit with a six-year-old boy named Manuelito. The boy's father was Gustavo del Pino's brother, Rafael. Enrique had been staying with him for the past two days.

Since leaving Havana, he had been hiding in Las Tunas Province in eastern Cuba. At night, he traveled with Tavo to meet members of a counterrevolutionary organization called *El Tiempo:* The Time.

Many had been political prisoners called *plantados,* housed at the infamous Boniato prison. One was a writer; another, a major in the army. They showed him their torture scars and told of night arrests and brutality and political murders. Slowly, Enrique's blood had grown hot.

Now he lay with his heart pounding as he watched the soldiers and GRU men. Beside him, Manuelito murmured. Enrique touched his arm and whispered for him to be silent. The boy obeyed but kept lifting his head to look over the lip of the banana grove.

Rafael's house was the third on the right. The paratroopers reached it. Rafael's wife met them at the door, looking anxiously up the road. The soldiers roughly pushed past her.

A moment later came a shot from inside. Another, and then the quick, throaty bursts of twin automatic weapons. Bullets blew through a wall of Rafael's house, tearing out pieces of mud-brick.

Out on the street, people instantly dove for cover. The GRU men ran toward the house, their guns drawn. Suddenly there was a small explosion inside. The thatch roof seemed to lift slightly with the concussion.

Then came a more powerful second explosion. It literally blew the house apart. Mud-bricks and thatch whirled out, and dust fumed up in a violent, sucking cloud. Several oxen bolted, tore down their small corral and broke into a humping lope off toward the cane fields across the upper road.

Enrique shoved his face into the black loam and felt his body tighten with horror. Manuelito began to scream. He held the boy down.

People in the village were screaming, too. Then a soldier came out of the ruins of Rafael's house and stumbled and fell. His clothes smoked and his right leg was gone. Blood streamed from the stump.

A woman, terror-stricken, rose from the road where her husband had flung her and began fleeing toward the groves. Instantly she was cut down by a wild-eyed GRU man, firing with both hands.

Manuelito broke away from Enrique. Still screaming, he came to his feet and ran off, Enrique coming up and going after him, yelling. The GRU man who had shot the woman turned, looked his way.

"There he is!" he shouted. He instantly pulled off three shots.

Enrique heard a round hit. Manuelito was lifted into the air, his small head snapping back, blood appearing suddenly on his face. His little body somersaulted in the air and came back over and hit the ground. He lay crumpled.

Rage and terror hit Enrique like a bolt of lightning. He rose, bellowing a growl. Then he turned and ran down into the grove, running high, the banana leaves whipping across his face. Bullets zipped through the leaves, impacted into the trunks.

He reached the road, dashed across and plunged into the ten-foot wall of cane, sweeping the branches and leaves away from his face, the leaves cutting like paper edges. The ground was littered with dry fall.

It was dim in the cane. His chest began to burn. He could faintly hear men shouting, then the rapid staccatto of Kalashnikovs, and bullets slashed through the cane to his right.

He stumbled and fell, lay for a moment, his breath gasping.

More bullets, and the sound of jeep engines whining up,

crashing through the cane. He forced himself to his feet and went on.

He ran until his legs refused him even a single additional step. He collapsed, unable to rise. The firing had stopped, but the sounds of shouting and engines were confusing. He couldn't tell from which direction they came. He tried to listen above his gasps. He couldn't.

He noticed a small yellow snake slither out from under the cane brush, cross near his leg and disappear. Then he saw that, above the cane stalks, the sky had turned a deep yellow. It shimmered.

Then he heard something that stopped his gasping. A crackling, hissing sound and, following it, smoke began seeping lightly through the stalks. They were burning the cane!

He forced himself up, stumbled on. The smoke grew thicker. He turned, went in another direction. Again the smoke thickened. He heard the fire turning into a roaring now. It seemed to come from everywhere. High above him, sparks and dark smoke blotted out the yellow sky.

The air around him grew, furnacelike, the smoke thick as cotton, smelling of burnt sugar and oil and ash. It burned his eyes until he could no longer hold them open.

He fell down again. Air wouldn't pass through his mouth or nose. His throat muscles spasmed. A heavy black cloud of smoke rolled over him. With all his might, he tried to scream. It was only a whisper.

**00:13**

---

# THE CANCER RAVAGED HIM.

For hours, Duff lay in his bed, foul-smelling sweat oozing from the pores of his deteriorating body. His upper abdomen flamed with excruciating pain. The yellow hue of his skin deepened; his fingernails grew brittle.

At last, he forced himself to move. He went down into the Moslem Quarter and scored a small brick of Lebanese hashish from a fat Palestinian woman in black in a filthy stone alley.

Back in his room, he rolled a pinch of hashish into a tiny marble, a fine red clay. It smelled oddly like the Christmas cookie dough he remembered from long ago when he was a boy in the orphanage at St. Clemens in Southampton. He swallowed it. Bitter.

It took twenty minutes for the drug to take complete hold. The pain receded. He walked about the room, pausing here and there to listen to the tremor of his blood, to the rapture of the drug absorbing the heat of the cancerous violence in him.

After awhile, he went out again, into the night. The hashish made him pensive. Shapes seemed absurd and profound:

# CONTENTS

## 00:13

RUSALEM
PTEMBER 19

HE CANCER RAVAGED HIM.

For hours, Duff lay in his bed, foul-smelling sweat ooz-
g from the pores of his deteriorating body. His upper
domen flamed with excruciating pain. The yellow hue of
s skin deepened; his fingernails grew brittle.

At last, he forced himself to move. He went down into
e Moslem Quarter and scored a small brick of Lebanese
ashish from a fat Palestinian woman in black in a filthy
ne alley.

Back in his room, he rolled a pinch of hashish into a
y marble, a fine red clay. It smelled oddly like the Christ-
s cookie dough he remembered from long ago when he
s a boy in the orphanage at St. Clemens in Southampton.
swallowed it. Bitter.

It took twenty minutes for the drug to take complete
d. The pain receded. He walked about the room, pausing
re and there to listen to the tremor of his blood, to the
ture of the drug absorbing the heat of the cancerous
lence in him.

After awhile, he went out again, into the night. The hash-
made him pensive. Shapes seemed absurd and profound:

114

began coming out as the soldiers and security agents dismounted. But they were hurriedly shoved back by the
troopers, who carried Kalashnikov assault rifles. The men
began a methodical search of the houses.

A few minutes earlier, Enrique had gone down into the
banana groves to collect fruit with a six-year-old boy
named Manuelito. The boy's father was Gustavo del Pino's
brother, Rafael. Enrique had been staying with him for the
past two days.

Since leaving Havana, he had been hiding in Las Tunas
Province in eastern Cuba. At night, he traveled with Tavo
to meet members of a counterrevolutionary organization
called *El Tiempo:* The Time.

Many had been political prisoners called *plantados*,
housed at the infamous Boniato prison. One was a writer;
another, a major in the army. They showed him their torture
scars and told of night arrests and brutality and political
murders. Slowly, Enrique's blood had grown hot.

Now he lay with his heart pounding as he watched the
soldiers and GRU men. Beside him, Manuelito murmured.
Enrique touched his arm and whispered for him to be silent.
The boy obeyed but kept lifting his head to look over the
lip of the banana grove.

Rafael's house was the third on the right. The paratroopers reached it. Rafael's wife met them at the door, looking
anxiously up the road. The soldiers roughly pushed past
her.

A moment later came a shot from inside. Another, and
then the quick, throaty bursts of twin automatic weapons.
Bullets blew through a wall of Rafael's house, tearing out
pieces of mud-brick.

Out on the street, people instantly dove for cover. The
GRU men ran toward the house, their guns drawn. Suddenly there was a small explosion inside. The thatch roof
seemed to lift slightly with the concussion.

Then came a more powerful second explosion. It literally
blew the house apart. Mud-bricks and thatch whirled out,
and dust fumed up in a violent, sucking cloud. Several oxen

bolted, tore down their small corral and broke into a humping lope off toward the cane fields across the upper road.

Enrique shoved his face into the black loam and felt his body tighten with horror. Manuelito began to scream. He held the boy down.

People in the village were screaming, too. Then a soldier came out of the ruins of Rafael's house and stumbled and fell. His clothes smoked and his right leg was gone. Blood streamed from the stump.

A woman, terror-stricken, rose from the road where her husband had flung her and began fleeing toward the groves. Instantly she was cut down by a wild-eyed GRU man, firing with both hands.

Manuelito broke away from Enrique. Still screaming, he came to his feet and ran off, Enrique coming up and going after him, yelling. The GRU man who had shot the woman turned, looked his way.

"There he is!" he shouted. He instantly pulled off three shots.

Enrique heard a round hit. Manuelito was lifted into the air, his small head snapping back, blood appearing suddenly on his face. His little body somersaulted in the air and came back over and hit the ground. He lay crumpled.

Rage and terror hit Enrique like a bolt of lightning. He rose, bellowing a growl. Then he turned and ran down into the grove, running high, the banana leaves whipping across his face. Bullets zipped through the leaves, impacted into the trunks.

He reached the road, dashed across and plunged into the ten-foot wall of cane, sweeping the branches and leaves away from his face, the leaves cutting like paper edges. The ground was littered with dry fall.

It was dim in the cane. His chest began to burn. He could faintly hear men shouting, then the rapid staccatto of Kalashnikovs, and bullets slashed through the cane to his right.

He stumbled and fell, lay for a moment, his breath gasping.

More bullets, and the sound of jeep engines whining up,

crashing through the cane. He forced himself went on.

He ran until his legs refused him even a sin step. He collapsed, unable to rise. The firing but the sounds of shouting and engines were c couldn't tell from which direction they came. listen above his gasps. He couldn't.

He noticed a small yellow snake slither out the cane brush, cross near his leg and disappe saw that, above the cane stalks, the sky had tur yellow. It shimmered.

Then he heard something that stopped his g crackling, hissing sound and, following it, smc seeping lightly through the stalks. They were bu cane!

He forced himself up, stumbled on. The smc thicker. He turned, went in another direction. A smoke thickened. He heard the fire turning into a now. It seemed to come from everywhere. High ab sparks and dark smoke blotted out the yellow sky

The air around him grew, furnacelike, the sm as cotton, smelling of burnt sugar and oil and ash. his eyes until he could no longer hold them oper

He fell down again. Air wouldn't pass through or nose. His throat muscles spasmed. A heavy b of smoke rolled over him. With all his might, scream. It was only a whisper.

people, lights and sounds, amplified and strange and oddly soothing.

He reached the Sha'ar HaAshpot, the Dung Gate, and went up the ancient steps to the wall's ramparts. He strolled along, watching the lights of the traffic down on the Ma'ale Ha-Shalom Highway. They seemed suddenly like souls lining up in the darkness, passing like good citizens into an unknown region. He laughed at the thought.

The night was cold, but he didn't feel the mountain breeze. Mesmerized, he gazed down at the Old City, a jewel of light with distinct lakes of brilliance that were the Church of the Holy Sepulchre and the Dome of the Rock and Wilson's Arch and the El Aqsa Mosque. A beautiful city, an ancient city, forever unwilling to die.

*To die.*

The words rustled stealthily into his mind. With them came again the irony of his own passing. A mockery, the pathetic rotting into eternity.

He smiled, recalling a moment from the past. St. Clemens. Once, a priest had tried to explain the concept of eternity. Assume, he said, that the earth were a solid steel ball, and every thousand years a tiny dove came and brushed its wing against the surface. Just once. Eternity would be longer than it would take that dove to wear down the whole earth.

Now Duff wondered, as he had then, how that dove could have lived so long. And if it had, then it would have been older than eternity. . . .

*All the land was visited with death and darkness in the twinkling of an eye. . . .*

His mind swung to the phrase from the poem of Hammurabi, fuzzily at first, then fully blown as he set his concentration to it. He probed it with his mental fingers, held each word, turning it over and over like a child with a wooden block.

Meaning lay there somewhere. But where? What?

*Tiger of the Desert . . .*

Something solidified—a thought, a link. But it passed so swiftly that he was unable to grasp it.

His name was Mordecai Haimon. He was a professor at the Ismael-Stone Yeshiva for Studies of Traditional Scripture on Rabbi Meir Street in the Geulah Quarter of Jerusalem. A surprisingly young man, he had a thick blond beard and broad shoulders.

He ushered Duff into his study. It was small and high-ceilinged with stacks of books on shelves and chairs and the floor. The odor of old leather, ancient paper and cooked fish pervaded the room.

"Sit, sit," Haimon said. He was dressed in a white shirt with the sleeves rolled up to expose huge biceps. Near the door was a single window. Outside, it was noon, bright sunshine with the sound of black-garbed children from the yeshiva playing among the olive trees in the yard.

The professor settled into his chair behind a cluttered desk. He studied Green narrowly. "You're not well, my friend," he said. His English carried an American accent.

"That's unimportant. I need some information."

"Ah? On what subject?"

"Tigers?"

"I don't understand."

"They told me at the Israel Museum that you were an expert on Old Persian poetry. Is that correct?"

"Yes."

"Then you'd be familiar with a poem telling of Hammurabi's destruction of the city of Lagash."

Haimon nodded. "There are three, actually." He leaned forward. "Would you care for some tea?"

"Yes, that would be nice. No cream."

The professor rose and went into another room. When he opened the door, the rich scent of baking bread wafted out. Duff heard a woman's voice. Haimon returned with two thick mugs.

"Now, about these poems," he said, returning to his chair. "I can't imagine what they'd have to do with tigers."

Duff took a sip of tea. It was very hot and bitter. "Was Hammurabi ever referred to as 'the Tiger of the Desert'?"

"No, never," Haimon answered instantly.

"Could a translator have made a mistake? Used 'tiger' instead of 'lion'?"

The professor shook his head. "Not possible. You see, in the ancient Elamite and Akkadian languages, the word for tiger, *sharrum,* was forbidden. The animal was considered a very evil entity. To write or even speak its name was to invoke immediate malediction."

"Then how *did* they refer to it?"

"Obliquely. In euphemistic terms."

"Such as?"

"Well, unlike the lion, which always attacks boldly in broad daylight, the tiger is a night creature. So they called it things like the Night Spirit or That Which Comes in Darkness."

Darkness, Duff thought. Night. Was there something there? He looked up to find Haimon staring at him.

"You need a doctor," Haimon said gently. "Please, allow me to call one."

Duff waved that off. "What other references were used?"

The professor drew his eyes away reluctantly. He sighed, stared at the ceiling and absently stroked his beard. "Oh, the Dark Demon. The Silent One." He lowered his head. "I recall an episode in Tablet Five of the great Epic of Gilgamesh in which he's called the Evil Deliverer. For bringing lightning to the monster Humbaba, in his great cedar forest."

Duff sat forward. "Deliverer," he repeated. *"Deliverer!"*

"Yes."

*Of course.*

Green shoved to his feet. "Thank you, sir."

Haimon looked puzzled. "Have I enlightened you?"

"Indeed." He made for the door, wrenched it open.

"I don't quite—" But Duff was already through, onto

the outer landing. "*Shalom*, my friend," the professor called out. "*Tee'hi'yeh baree shuv*. May you be well again."

Sitting in a filthy coffee shop across from Talia's hotel on Derokh Shekhem Avenue, he waited all through the heated afternoon for her to come home.

The hotel, all modern white limestone, sat on the edge of a *shtetl*, a tenement where artisans and intellectuals and Socialistic students lived in old wooden buildings with tar-paper roofs and courtyards where tiny chicken coops and sparse shrubbery were crisscrossed with laundry lines. To the south lay the Damascus Gate to the Old City; to the north, high-rise hotels and business buildings.

When evening came, the traffic thickened on Derokh Shekhem. Lights came on in the tenements and Talia's hotel. It was six stories high with an outside glass elevator. He watched it go up and down, reflections from the pool in the courtyard giving the glass a shimmering tint of blue.

Talia had lived there for twelve years, ever since her divorce from a captain in the Defense Force, in which she had also been a captain. Afterward, she was picked to train for Mossad. Her apartment was on the third-floor corner, which overlooked the tenement.

At two minutes after nine, he spotted her, swinging into the underground parking area in a blue Ford convertible. He paid his bill, crossed the avenue and went up into the hotel lobby.

It was nearly empty. Two women were talking to the desk clerk, and an electrician worked on a power panel. He took the elevator. Below, the pool was shaped like the ace of clubs. A man was doing laps from point to base.

At his soft knock, Talia said, "Yes? Who is it?"

"Duff."

She opened the door dressed in a yellow bathrobe. She stared at him, then silently stepped aside to let him in. She closed the door very gently, never taking her eyes from him. They were the color of melted chocolate. Deep in them was melancholy.

"Why?" she asked softly. "I told myself I would never see you again."

"I have something for you."

She stared a moment longer, then shook her head. "It can wait. Come, sit down."

He chose a beige chair made of Danish curves. The room was airy and light-colored, with a clean yet feminine spareness. She sat on a divan.

She studied his eyes. "The pain is very bad now, isn't it?"

"At times."

"Hashish? I smell it on your breath."

"It helps."

"Are you able to hold anything down?"

"Later, perhaps."

He reached into his pocket, took out the hash brick. Talia immediately rose and went into her kitchen. She returned with a jar of honey. He made a marble, dipped it into the honey and swallowed it.

Talia lit a cigarette and smoked quietly, looking out the window. "Is there no hope at all?" she asked softly.

"None."

She continued to smoke slowly, methodically. Finally, she sighed. "So, what is this thing you've brought to me?"

"A possible answer for your Hammurabi tiger."

She swung around. "What?"

"I think it refers to the Red Bomb's delivery system."

She frowned.

"More precisely, a delivery system designated 'Tiger.' "

Talia continued to look at him. Then she squashed out her cigarette and stood up, began pacing about with her head down, arms across her breasts.

"Yes," she said, "that *does* make sense. A Tiger missile, for example, or a Tiger aircraft." She stopped. "But that designation could apply to any of a thousand things."

"Indeed. So let's make a few assumptions and narrow the parameters a bit."

Duff felt the first tendrils of the drug beginning to move through him. The pain eased. But it left a sharp, icy clarity in his mind.

"First off, it wouldn't be a military vehicle," he said. "Whatever nation's backing the KIE would expose itself once it allowed its own military equipment and facilities to be used."

Talia nodded.

"A long-range missile or aircraft? Not likely. That would mean highly sophisticated gear and crews to make it all operational. And even then, no such missile or enemy aircraft could possibly penetrate your air security nets."

Talia made another loop of the room. "What about a ground vehicle? The standard parked car? A suicide run."

Duff shook his head. "They wouldn't risk it that way. They've only got the one bomb; it's far too precious to waste. Also, MI-6 believed that the Russians used a smaller nuclear charge to detonate it. If so, nothing that complicated could be set up in a car or a van."

Talia grunted, staring at him.

"Your people had only the bomb itself, correct? No detonator assemblies?"

"No, just the bomb."

"Were they able to back-construct enough to pinpoint the precise detonation system?"

She nodded. "Yes. It *is* a small nuclear charge that acts as a trigger. It creates a pressure vacuum, which then initiates the main detonation sequence."

Far away, a covey of horns sounded suddenly like disturbed geese in the night. Talia sighed again and sat down, ran her hands through her hair. "So what are we left with?"

"A ship," Duff said.

Talia's computer equipment was in her bedroom, which was precisely as Duff remembered it. The scent of jasmine and warm feminine flesh . . . copper-and-yellow-motif silk sheets . . . Talia's sensual appreciation of silk.

He stood a moment, stunned into memory. Talia's skirt and blouse lay on the bed. Beside it was her hip holster with its small nine-millimeter Glock. He looked and looked, time dissipating for a terrible moment. The vestige of an old lust trembled in his groin.

He turned to find her watching. With an effort, he drove the memories away.

Talia's computer was a UNIX-8 linked through encryption codes to the main data banks of the Mossad and the heavier mainframes of the Israeli Defense Force's Milnet. She logged into the system. Her password was *g'veret*, lady.

"As a starting point," Duff said, "we'll accept our ship theory as true. So, what kind of a ship will it be, then? Private or commercial?"

"My God, there must be hundreds of private yachts and motor launches all along the coast."

"But I assume your coastal patrols are already stopping everything of that size coming in?"

"Yes. At least at Haifa and Tel Aviv."

"They should work the whole Israeli coastline." He thought a moment. "But, frankly, I don't think KIE will try it with a small boat. It would be just as risky as a car. No, for the moment, I'd say we focus on commercial shipping."

"That's a big order. Where do we start?"

Duff walked back and forth, energized. "With shipping companies that run scheduled stops at any of your ports. We'll begin with the cruise lines. I would imagine there's a central clearinghouse somewhere that monitors that traffic. See if you can pull it up."

While Talia searched, Duff hunted through her encyclopedia for the entry: TIGER. *Panthera tigris.* There were six accepted racial names: Bali, Caspian, Javan, Sumatran, Siberian and Bengal.

Talia found the Association for Cruise and Short-Sea Operations, based in Frankfurt. She quickly accessed its

World Wide Web site and requested a listing of all cruise lines with Israeli stopovers. Then, using the key "Tiger" and its six type names as an isolation base, she checked the names of each ship and owner company.

Nothing came up.

Duff grunted. "So, we scratch the cruise lines. Now let's search the commercial lists. I'm afraid that's going to be a bit more difficult."

"Wouldn't there be a similiar clearinghouse for commercial vessels?"

"Yes, but I have no idea where. Perhaps Lloyd's Registry of Shipping in London."

Talia ran a company search, quickly obtained Lloyd's Web site and logged into it. She typed in a request for listings of all current world shipping contained in the company's insurance files. Lloyd's computer refused entry.

"Dammit," she snapped. "Their files are protected."

"Break into them."

She glanced up. "I could compromise our whole OPT net."

"Theory or no, I think the risk is acceptable."

She nodded and turned back to the computer. For the next twelve minutes, using a remote base site to cover her footprints, she attacked the Lloyd's system with hacker techniques—a trapdoor entry. A Gateway Tab.

At last, she broke through using the Trojan Horse attack, collected key passwords, doubled back and reentered the main system by logging on with a user password.

Instantly she was welcomed into the Lloyd's Data Processing Unit. Requesting the protected shipping files, she watched as the data began reassembling itself on her screen, line, by line.

"Bloody hell!" Duff cried suddenly. "We've forgotten something. Foreign words."

"Oh, God, that's right. A ship could have one of our key words in a foreign language."

"Pull up your Mossad language base. Get translations for all seven terms."

"In which languages?"

The hashish was winging through Duff now, yet it still left that cold snap-and-crackle of thought in his mind. "Wait a minute, I just thought of something else. Lloyd's will list only ships *they've* insured. That means their file list would be incomplete."

Talia shook her head. "Damn, this is getting too complicated."

"Not really. What we need is a database that keeps records of every deepwater ship ever built." He leaned down beside her. "Check Lloyd's for cooperative links with shipbuilder's organizations."

She found two sites: the Comité de Maritime Constructeurs International, Paris, and the Baltic and International Maritime Shipbuilder's Federation, Copenhagen. She logged off the Lloyd's system and reentered the main Mossad data bank.

Suddenly, her screen went blank. A second later, a verification demand came on. "Oh, oh," she said. "Somebody's been monitoring. They want my ODP clearance status."

Hurriedly she typed in her mission number sequence. There was a pause, then a tag-date on her logged time and a master-user clearance.

She chuckled softly. "I'll have some explaining to do tomorrow."

But Duff wasn't listening. He moved from point to point, his brow furrowed with thought. He came back. "Get those translations logged. Then we'll enter the Paris and Copenhagen sites."

Again using the Trojan Horse, Talia entered first the CMCI file bank in Paris, then the BIMSC's in Copenhagen. Their records went back to 1873. Arbitrarily choosing 1940 as a baseline, she downloaded the files. Forty minutes later, she backed out of the BIMSC data bank and covered her tracks.

Her list contained 21,000 entries, each with a short data bio and update status report.

Using a search engine, she picked out only those ships in current service. The list dropped to 6,322. Next, she searched for ships with any of the 105 key words for tiger and its racial groups in their names.

The final list contained thirty-eight ships.

Nine were immediately eliminated since they were scheduled carriers operating only in the Pacific. Another fourteen exclusively transited the North Atlantic. That left fifteen. Two of these regularly serviced ports in the Mediterranean, the rest were free-roving tramps.

They started down the list, methodically reading each bio for clues. The *Siberian Woodsman.* The *Leeds Tiger.* The *Sumatora no Yanagi.* The *Caspian Handelschafft.*

The ninth entry was the *Bengal:*

```
Name: SS Bengal
Keel Laid: May 6, 1943
Launched: June 19, 1943
Chief Builder: Bethlehem-Fairfield Inc., Baltimore,
    Maryland, USA
Class: EC2-S-C1 (Designated Liberty)
Type: Steam screw
MCE Hull No.: 812
Yard Hull No.: 241
```

The entry went on to list technical specifications of the hull, decking, tonnage and propulsion horsepower. The last part of the entry was a short summary of the *Bengal*'s service:

```
1943–1947: Operated under auspices of the US Mari-
    time Commission for war cargo transit in North At-
    lantic.
1948: Decommissioned and staged at Benicia, Califor-
    nia, USA
1962–1973: Recommissioned and operated by US
    Navy for cargo transport to Southeast Asian TO
1976–1980: Operated under Argentinian flag in accor-
```

dance with US Lend-Lease agreement (Note: see En:
37836)
1980: Purchased by IJK Corporation of Indonesia for
general cargo handling in South Pacific
1991: following IJK bankruptcy proceedings, ship
held in lien by Bishop/Townsend Corp., Singapore
Addenda:
1997: Purchased by TTT Group (Res. Lisc.: Yaoundé,
Cameroon) for general cargo handling. Current
Master of Record: Sean P. O'Mallaugh, lisc.
M82501 (?) see log ref.: Interpol

Duff slowly leaned back, making a soft hissing sound
through his teeth. "Oh, yes," he said softly. "There it is."
Talia glanced at him. "What?"
"Sean Padrick O'Mallaugh," he said. "The bastard's
IRA."

It was called the Tomb Garden, a tiny sanctuary of olive
and cedar trees in East Jerusalem near the Damascus Gate.
Some believed that it was Golgotha, where Jesus had been
buried and then rose from the dead.

Now it lay in empty, night-chilled silence at three in the
morning. Its pathways were made of ancient limestone.
There were tiny blue lights along the edges like chips of
sapphire scattered in the shrubbery. The faint traffic sounds
from the streets and the occasional diesel moan of a bus
from the central bus station were only vague whispers in
the air.

Duff and Talia walked along under the trees. Neither
spoke. After their discovery of the *Bengal,* Duff had become restless. Add the hashish keening through him like
an adrenaline rush, and he felt an overpowering desire to
be uncovered, to look at the sky, to smell the earth.

Talia could not bear to leave him, not yet. Instead, she
transmitted a short summary of their findings to Mossad
headquarters, and then they left the hotel, walked along
Derokh Shekhem and turned down Nablus Road.

They reached the tomb entrance. It was unlit. The rock face resembled a skull with eye sockets and a dark doorway. In front of it were a small courtyard and the remnants of an ancient cistern and a wine press. Everything smelled of roses and stone, like a monument maker's workshop.

Duff paused before the entrance. A sudden hunger filled him. To pray. To speak words he had not spoken since St. Clemens. He felt darknesses moving through him. There was a moment of excruciating fear. He felt Talia's fingers lightly touch his shoulder. He dropped to his knees.

The assassin's weapon carried a silencer, and its five explosions were no louder than the sound of five pebbles being flung violently into a still pond.

In that precise instant, Duff saw their flashes on the tomb face, felt the rounds sunder the air over his head, rounds meant for him. He heard the vicious impacts as they went instead into Talia's body.

Instincts exploded. On the other side of that instant, he was turning, drawing his own weapon, his right leg under him, coming up.

A shadow loomed over him, one with the trees. Its weight landed and slammed him back against the stones. He heard a knife blade slurry across rock. The muzzle of his pistol found the assassin's chest. He pulled the trigger three times, the sound muffled.

The man went limp and grew profoundly heavy. Growling, Duff shoved the corpse away with all the strength he could muster. He scurried to Talia. There was a great deal of blood. It looked black against the white limestone. He felt her carotid. She was dead.

He did not move for a long, bewildering moment. Then he took off his jacket and covered her face. He walked to the cistern wall and sat down and looked at her. Whispers of traffic. A jaybird, roused by the sounds, chittered sleepily in a tree.

He wept.

## 00:14

MID-SOUTH ATLANTIC
SEPTEMBER 21

THE *BENGAL* WAS SEVEN DAYS FROM CAPETOWN AND three hundred miles west southwest of the island of Ascension. The weather had remained good since they'd left the African coast, the sea smooth and glassy blue. They had logged nearly four hundred miles a day.

It was a few minutes after midnight. Ashdown, bone-tired, had just finished an eight-hour watch. He and O'Mallaugh, as the only deck officers, were pulling double watches.

The whole thing was grueling, with short, tossing bouts of sleep in between. Unfortunately, Jack had been forced to leave much of the handling of the deck duties to Tun. That worried him.

The crew's sullenness had deepened since Capetown, and it was obvious that the stocky little bosun was having difficulty controlling his men. Ever since the incident in the afterhouse, they seemed to turn to Datuk for leadership.

Jack stopped at the radio room on his way to his cabin. Collins was idly listening to a weather report, an automatic-repeat tape running from the weather station on Ascension. The weatherman had a deep, rich British voice.

Earlier that evening, Jack had asked Keyshawn to request a position fix from the Ascension station's radar facility, just to check the accuracy of his own chart positioning.

Collins now grinned at him and snapped his log shut. "Yo, Jack. How's it hangin'?"

"Limp."

"I hear you, man. These double shifts get dirty quick, don't they? Go get some sack time."

"I will as soon as I check the deck."

Keyshawn dropped his voice. "How's the old man holdin' up?"

"All right."

"Yeah? Well, I gotta tell you, man, that dude look like shit. You understand what I'm sayin'? He got them dark circles under his eyes make him look like a fuckin' raccoon."

Jack didn't comment. But Collins was right. He, too, had been watching O'Mallaugh, noting the stress coming onto the man. It was true that all captains lived with tension, but lately O'Mallaugh appeared to be a man with something beyond that. As if he were hiding a dark secret that created a furtive terror in his eyes.

"He sure does like his booze, don't he?" Keyshawn said.

Ashdown grunted noncommittally.

"Smells like a goddamn distillery all the time. But he don't never seem to get drunk. Must have a wooden leg. Look here, tell me something. You been around. Do all captains soak it up like him?"

"Not all."

Collins snorted. "Well, that's good. Else we'd all be runnin' into each other out here."

"Sometimes ships do."

Collins reached up to turn down his radio. "Where the hell are we headed anyway?"

"South America."

"Shit, I figured that much out. But where, exactly?"

Jack shrugged. "I don't really know. All O'Mallaugh gives me are the daily watch course positions."

Collins scratched his jaw. "You know when I ran your radar fix? The old man said he wanted me to get a six-day weather forecast from Ascension, too. But check this out. He wanted to know the weather for the Fernando de Noronha area. What you think of that?"

Jack frowned.

"Where the hell is Fernando de Noronha?" Keyshawn asked.

"It's an island off the north coast of Brazil."

"He also said that as soon as I get clear signal, he wants constant monitoring of weather stations *and* shipping traffic from French Guiana."

Keyshawn suddenly glanced up at the door and instantly fell silent. Jack turned in time to see the owner's rep, Jadid, move by down the passageway. He turned back.

Collins gave him an under-the-brow look. "That dude? He's one jinky motherfucker. I mean he's cold, man. He always sneakin' around all the time, lookin' at shit."

"I've noticed." Then Jack chuckled. "Old Jeremiah got on his case, though. Threw his ass out of the engine room yesterday."

"Oh, yeah? All right for the Aussie. You know, couple times that Jadid stopped here. Looked through the door like he's trying to catch me doin' something I shouldn't. I say hello but he don't answer, not a fuckin' word. Just looked at me with that cobra stare of his."

Jack nodded. "He's a strange one, all right." He sighed. "Well, I'm outta here."

"Hold it a minute." Collins lifted his leg and shoved the door shut. "Am I trippin' or are them Malay boys startin' to act funky again?"

Jack studied the radioman. Keyshawn didn't miss much. "Yeah, they *are* getting restless."

"I knew it," Collins said. He smacked his hand lightly on his desk. "I been watchin' the fuckers. I got bad feel-

ings, man. Something's about to happen. An' soon, I think.
My asshole's beginning to pucker.''

The ship was nearly still in the water.

That awareness came through Ashdown's sleep con-
sciousness like a violent sound. His eyes opened. And then
he was rising, as the last tendrils of momentum faded from
the *Bengal.*

Faint dawn light came through his porthole. He quickly
slipped from the bunk and began to dress. He washed his
face, put on his shoes and left the cabin. He could hear the
whoosh of the boilers and felt the ship easing over and back
in a gentle, stationary roll.

Before he reached the bridge, he heard someone above
him yell. His heart kicked up. He dashed onto the bridge.
It was empty; even the helmsman was gone. He glanced
out the port wing, then dodged onto the starboard wing.

It was gray-black overhead with the stars still visible.
Back toward the east, the sky merged with the sea, separated only by a thin yellow line along the horizon.

In the dimness, he saw several crewmen sitting on the
number-three hatch cover. Pacing around the hatch was
Tun, violently railing at them in Malaysian.

Suddenly, O'Mallaugh's voice boomed from above.
''Thirty seconds! Tell them they've got thirty bleedin' seconds to obey my command.''

Jack hurried up the outside wing ladder to the flying
bridge. The captain's body was rigid, defiantly pressed
against the forward railing beside the binnacle as he glared
down at the sitting crewmen.

Jack slipped up onto the bridge platform. ''What the
hell's happening, Captain?'' he asked. ''Our helm is abandoned.''

O'Mallaugh cursed under his breath. Then he turned and
rushed past him. ''Take the conn, Ashd'n,'' he growled.
''I'm breakin' out the arms chest.''

He disappeared down the ladder.

Jack paused for a moment to look down on the men.

Several more had joined them by now. All were simply sitting, their legs crossed.

He whistled at Tun. Everybody's head lifted. He motioned for the bosun to come up. Then he descended the ladder and returned to the lower bridge.

He rang Jeremiah. "We've got a problem up here, Chief," he said.

"I already know about it, mate. The crew's pullin' a sit-down. Bloody bastards even snagged two of my black gang. What's O'Mallaugh doing?"

"Breaking out the arms chest."

Pepper moaned softly. "This could get spikey, Jack. I'm coming up."

Tun reached the bridge before Pepper. He scooted through the port wing door, his face covered with the sweat of anger. Jack glanced at him. "Take the helm."

Tun instantly obeyed.

Ashdown started to ask him something but was interrupted by O'Mallaugh lunging in. He carried a shotgun and two gun belts with pistols, old British Walthers with leather thongs on their hasp loops. He also had something under his jacket.

He tossed one of the gun belts to Jack. "Get Pepper up here," he said grimly. At the helm, Tun stared wide-eyed at the weapons.

"He's on his way."

"Arm yoursefs and then both of you two come fo'ard." O'Mallaugh hung the second pistol belt over the back of the conn chair and started for the port wing.

"Do I issue a general-assistance Mayday?" Jack asked.

O'Mallaugh twisted around. "No fockin' Mayday," he snapped. "This is my ship. I'll take care of the bloody yellow swine meself."

"What are you going to do?"

"Show the scum just who the fock is captain." He rushed out the port door.

Dawn was beginning to filter in more powerfully. Gray

light fused thicker through the forward windows. It settled across the wing railings, picking up detail.

Jack swung toward Tun. "God dammit, what started this?"

"It that Datuk," Tun answered. "The bastad, he talk to my boys. Make dem angry. He say the captain deliberately run over Mah Swee, chop him up with the prop." Mah Swee was the man who had jumped ship in Capetown.

"That's bullshit."

"But Datuk, he make dem believe."

"What do they think this'll get them?"

"He tell if the ship no go, den another ship come and he take ever'body and go back home."

*"Shit!"*

Collins walked onto the bridge. He looked sleepy, his eyes puffy. "What the fuck is goin' on, man?" he said. "Some cat's hollerin' woke me up."

"The crew's defying the captain," Jack said.

Keyshawn caught sight of the weapon in Jack's hand. He said, very slowly, "Oh, yeah."

Jack handed him the gun belt. "Secure the bridge."

Collins slid off the tiny leather loop that held the Walther. He handled the weapon with expertise, giving it a half cock and spinning the cylinder to check the load.

He looked up, eyes narrowed. "We gonna have to bust cap on these people?"

"I don't know. But this goddamned thing could blow into a full mutiny."

Jack darted out into the corridor and went below to his cabin. He withdrew the Mannlicher shotgun from under his bunk, slammed two rounds into the breech and snapped it shut. He put the four extra rounds into his pocket and went out.

He met Jeremiah coming up. The Aussie was scowling. "Where's the Mick?"

"On the forward deck with the men."

"Whot's he intendin'? To start shootin' people?"

Jack simply shook his head.

They crossed through the bridge. Jack gave Pepper the other pistol. The Chief slung the belt over his bony shoulder.

At the port door, Ashdown looked back at Collins. "If anybody tries to take the bridge, shoot to kill."

Wordlessly, O'Mallaugh prowled around the hatch, glowering at the Malays. The shotgun was tucked under his arm. There were ten men on the hatch now, including the two mess boys, everybody looking frightened.

Except Datuk, who sat slightly off by himself. He watched the captain make his rounds, looking directly into his face, turning as he rounded the hold. The others stared at their feet.

It was silent save for the soft slapping of wavelets against the hull and the steel creak and moan of the vessel as she rolled gently.

Jack and Pepper took up positions on each side of the hold. They waited, watching. After a moment, Ashdown noticed Jadid come quietly up along the port rail.

A minute passed. Another.

Suddenly, the captain stopped. He lunged over the batten bar and grabbed the nearest crewman by the throat. Roughly, he dragged him from the hatch cover to the deck. The man's knee banged into one of the cleats. He yelped. His leg began to bleed.

Jack stiffened. He quickly scanned the faces of the other men for their reaction. Everybody had gone absolutely motionless, their features stark.

Pepper hissed, "Get ready, mate."

O'Mallaugh manhandled the crewman, forced him to kneel. He was a small, spindly man with a broad face. He hung his head, allowing himself to be pressed against the lip of the hatch. O'Mallaugh shoved the man's arms under the batten strapping and bound them to the metal with cord.

Jeremiah uttered an oath.

Jack stared at O'Mallaugh's face. It was stonelike, the eyes burning. He instantly realized what the captain was about to do: use this man to cow the others. If he could frighten him enough to give up, the others would follow. It was obvious that O'Mallaugh had taken time to choose the weakest-looking of the men.

But how would he do it? Jack wondered. Jesus, would O'Mallaugh actually shoot this man? His hands tightened on the shotgun.

The captain straightened up. Once more, he let his smoldering gaze sweep over the others. Then he reached under his jacket and brought out the cat-o'-nine-tails, the one Jack had seen hanging on his cabin wall. He jerked it to untangle the thongs, and they snapped in the air.

But before he could bring it down on the cowering crewman's back, Datuk made a quick, sinuous movement, an unfolding, and then he was standing, glaring down at the captain.

O'Mallaugh looked at him.

Silently, Datuk walked across the hatch and lightly dropped to the deck. He turned his back on O'Mallaugh, knelt and untied the crewman's arms. The captain did not interfere. Freed, the terrified crewman, holding his leg, retreated hastily back to the safety of the hatch cover.

Datuk quietly knelt in his place. He put his arms under the battens and hung his head, waiting.

Pepper said, "Bloody Jesus!"

Jack couldn't believe it. A surge of admiration welled up in him. Datuk was going to take the whipping, test his own strength against the captain's.

This has gone far enough, he thought.

He moved, went around the hatch and placed himself between the Malay and the captain. "You can't do this, O'Mallaugh," he said. "I won't stand by and allow this."

The captain's raging eyes swung slowly to him.

"This is against all civilized laws of the sea," Jack said.

"Get out of the way."

"For God sake, Captain, this is barbaric."

"Stand aside, I say."

Ashdown didn't move.

O'Mallaugh watched him from under his thick brows, like a bull about to hook. Then a devilish smile touched his mouth. He straightened. Flipping the whip around, he held the handle out to Jack.

"I won't do it," he said. "*You* will."

Jack was shocked.

With his other hand, O'Mallaugh lifted his shotgun. "That's a direct order, Ashd'n. Carry it out or I'll blow your fockin' head off for the bastard mutineer you are."

Pepper came scurrying forward, eyes wide. "O'Mallaugh, ya crazy son of a bitch, put it up!"

The captain shoved him back. "Do it," he repeated to Jack.

Ashdown didn't move. He looked at the shotgun muzzle. It caught a glint from the bridge lights. He felt the air, suddenly minutely aware of its substance: cool, salt-laden. There was a buzzing in his head.

At that moment, Jadid stepped forward. "I will do it, Captain," he said quietly.

O'Mallaugh swung around.

"I said, I will do it," Jadid repeated.

For a moment, O'Mallaugh stared at him. Then a look of confusion came over his face. He glanced at Jack, then back to Jadid. He hesitated.

"Give me the whip," Jadid snapped harshly.

O'Mallaugh obeyed.

Jadid looked at Ashdown. "Stand aside," he said.

Jack turned to O'Mallaugh. "This man has no authority here."

"He acts in my stead," O'Mallaugh answered. "Do as he says." His finger on the shotgun trigger went slightly white.

"Back off, Jack," Pepper yelled. "Fer Chris' sake, back off. The crazy bastard'll kill ya."

Several slow, heavy seconds passed.

At last, Ashdown stepped away.

\* \* \*

The whipping was savage. Jadid went at it with all the strength in his body, his face contorted with fury. The leather thongs sliced Datuk's back. Each time they struck, Datuk's back heaved up and then settled again. The blood ran down onto the deck. But he made no sound.

Jack could hardly watch. O'Mallaugh stood with his shotgun on him. Pepper hissed curses, his tiny Aussie eyes filled with a kind of outraged sorrow.

Dozens of times the whip struck.

Finally, Jack could bear it no longer. He stepped forward, feeling Pepper's hand come instantly to restrain him. He shrugged it off, continued toward the captain. He saw O'Mallaugh's eyes widen. Ashdown shoved the muzzle of the shotgun aside and bent forward to grab Jadid around the waist. He flung him away.

He turned to kneel. From the corner of his eye, he saw Jadid rise up, coming at him, the whip raised. He thrust himself upright. Jadid's arm came down, the whip's thongs spread, drawn back by the downward stroke.

He blocked Jadid's arm at the elbow, wrapped his own arm around it, opening the man's stance. He stepped in, swinging his elbow. It slammed against Jadid's face, and the man went down.

Jack quickly turned and knelt beside Datuk. The smell of his blood was raw, mixed with a sharper, muskier odor. The Malay had urinated in his shorts.

He lifted Datuk's head. It was limp. He felt for his carotid artery, his own hands trembling. Nothing. He pressed harder. Datuk was gone.

He came up slowly, turning. He stared at O'Mallaugh. "You murdering bastard," he hissed. "You brutal, butchering son of a bitch."

Instantly, all the crewmen silently scurried off the hatch. With terror-filled eyes, they paused only long enough to stare at Datuk's corpse. Then, wordlessly, they fled toward the bow.

Jack trembled with rage. He looked and looked at the

captain's face, wanting to strike it, to give it another substance.

"You'll pay for this," he yelled into that face. "You and that fucking scum there. I swear to Christ, I'll see you hang."

Only then did O'Mallaugh lower his weapon. It came down to his side quickly, as if his arm had grown suddenly tired from holding it. He frowned. Again that strange something passed over his features, an expression of—deep melancholy. For a moment, it actually seemed as if he might weep.

But he simply turned and plunged away.

"I TELL YOU, *PRIMA*, IT'S NO PROBLEM," SAID PEPE MAR-
tin. He grinned at his cousin, Ana Castile, and bobbed his
head. He was small and puny with ringlets of jet-black hair.
"It's simple. You agree on the arrangements and pay him
the money. No problem."

Ana was unconvinced. She sat at the table near the window of the dark bar and felt her insides flutter with apprehension. She was in the seaside town of Nicaro, forty miles
from the air base at Moa.

The bar, called the Malecon, was on the first floor of a
shabby three-story hotel located in a neighborhood of crum-
bling old houses with unkept lawns. The hotel was a *po-
sada*, a government-sanctioned location where lovers could
obtain a room for only five pesos for three hours. Most of
the women in the bar, however, were *jineteras*, free-roving
prostitutes.

Across the street was a sea wall. Shirtless boys drank
beer along the top and hissed at the sexy teenaged girls
who passed in twos and threes dressed in jeans and T-shirts.
Beyond the wall, the waves made hushed whispers in the
night.

Ana turned and watched the dancers in the center of the bar. It was so dark, they looked like shadows crossing the purple neon ripples that ringed the room, everyone gliding to Maria Christina tapes. The air smelled thickly of sweat and an accumulated, smoky lust.

She and Ensign Perez, given their first twenty-four-hour pass, had driven over from Moa in a borrowed car, along the coast road past cashew and date groves, and crumbled sugar mills back in the hills. She had asked Perez along for appearances.

Earlier, she had arranged to meet Pepe at the Malecon. It took several days for her to make contact with her cousin. He lived in Holguín and was a musician with a salsa band. But she knew he was also a hustler who often worked the black market. He knew a lot of people, including *contra-bandistas*, smugglers.

When she finally got him on the phone, she spoke in a kind of family patois they had used as children. She asked him to arrange a meeting with a smuggler in Nicaro in order to get Pilar off the island and to America.

It had been an agonizing decision for her, one in which her loyalties had been tested. Since the clandestine note in the commissary, she had not received any further word about or from her father.

She was in turmoil. There was the real possibility that the note had not been genuine, but a deliberate plant by the GRU, to entrap her in some way, draw her into the same dark conspiracy they believed her father was involved in.

Either way, it signified extreme danger—for her, for Enrique and mostly for young Pilar. If her father were actually part of a counterrevolutionary plot and he got caught, she as his daughter would immediately be suspect, undoubtedly also arrested.

What then? Pilar would be in serious trouble—tainted, in disgrace. As such, she would become the automatic ward of the state, which would deal with her in any way it saw fit. She might even be imprisoned!

Perez and his dance partner emerged out of the gloom

and sat down, laughing. Jesse was half tight, grinning at everything with his beautiful smile.

The girl's name was Cari. She had asked him to dance soon after they arrived. She was dark-pretty, with eyes that danced and a cigarette-thickened voice that was very sensual. She wore a frilly silk *blusita* with tiny sweat stains under her arms.

Ana studied her a moment, then glanced questioningly at Pepe. He shook his head. No problem.

"Let's have another drink," Jesse said.

"Oh, yes," Cari cooed.

"Go easy with that," Ana said. "We fly again in another fifteen hours."

"That's tomorrow," Perez said expansively. "Now is time for some fun."

The ripples of neon light blinked. Twice.

Jesse said disgustedly, "*Hijo de puta,* not another power-out."

The lights came on steadily again.

Pepe leaned close to Ana. "Go now," he whispered. "Room two-ten."

Ana rose immediately and melted off among the dancers.

She went up the stairs to the second floor. The stairs were covered with carpet embroidered with jungle leaves and blossoms. It was scuffed and worn, showing the weaving. The railing was made of tarnished brass.

The upper floor was shaped like the letter *I,* the stair carpeting continuing along the corridors. The doors were all painted brown, and each bore a picture poster or a slogan—Che or Fidel, *Socialismo o Muerte.* Now and then, she heard a soft male moan, a female chirp of ecstasy.

At number 210, she listened and knocked lightly. A man coughed, then said, "Come."

She eased the door open. The room was in semidarkness. There was a bed and, on a small table, a lamp that glowed a soft yellow. She closed and locked the door behind her.

A man was sitting on the side of the bed wearing only

undershorts. The bed was crumpled, and there were stains on the sheets. The room smelled of crotch and pudenda.

The man looked at Ana. He was about thirty with a scraggly El Jefe beard and a fine muscular definition to his shoulders and back. He was tanned the color of old mahogany.

He looked her up, down. "From Pepe?"

"Yes."

"What is his blood?"

"He's my cousin."

"What is his middle name?"

"Tomas."

The man nodded to himself. Finally he asked, "How many?"

"What?"

"How many will cross?"

"One. A young girl." She thought a moment. If it were possible for her to find Enrique, she would send him away, too. A big if. "Perhaps there might be two."

"No perhaps. I must know precisely."

"One, then."

"How much money you got?"

"How much does it cost?"

The man looked up angrily. "I say how much you got?"

"Three thousand."

"American?"

"Yes."

The man thought a moment. He rubbed his eyes tiredly. At last, he looked up. "Okay. One."

"When?"

"Now is closed the Strait. The American navy is everywhere."

"I know."

"Afterward I take her."

"When exactly?"

"I will choose."

"How will I know?"

"I tell Pepe." He reached for a cigarette, lit it by scratching a match with his fingernail.

Ana shifted her weight. "Where will you leave her?"

"Maybe one place, maybe another."

"I have to know exactly."

"Impossible. It depends on where the American patrols are. And on the weather."

"But there has to be someone there to meet her."

"That is not my problem."

Bullshit, Ana thought with sudden heat. How could she leave her daughter's fate in the hands of one such as this? *Maybe here, maybe there.* But what choice did she have? Chances were, another *contrabandista* would be the same. A terrifying gamble.

"Let's see your money," the man said. He moved, hiked his leg onto the bed. There was a long scar on his calf. It looked waxy against the tan.

"Not until I get reassurances," Ana answered evenly.

The man stared at her. His eyes went flat. He waved his hand in dismissal. "Then get out."

"Wait, I just want—"

"Get out," he hissed. "I don't want your fucking job."

Frantic, Ana braced herself for a moment, regaining composure. At last, she said, "Look, all I want is to know where—"

There was a hard knock on the door.

Then things began to happen rapidly. . . .


"Ana," Jesse Perez called through the door, his voice tense. "Are you in there?"

The man on the bed lunged to his feet. In the same movement, his hand swept beneath the pillow and came up holding a silver-plated Colt automatic.

In one step, he was beside Castile. He grabbed her by the hair and shoved the pistol under her chin. It felt cold and metal-hard.

"You make trap for me, *puta?*" he growled hotly into her ear, "Then I kill you first."

"It's no trap. He's my *compañero,* a fellow officer."

"Ana," Perez said again. "For God sake, open the door. The police are searching the rooms."

Again the man cursed. With the hand holding the gun, he unlocked the door and pulled it open a few inches.

"Where's my lieutenant?" Perez demanded through the crack.

The smuggler viciously shoved Ana away, swung the door open and threw himself out, knocking Jesse aside. He ran off down the corridor and disappeared around the far corner.

Perez stepped into the room. "Ana, are you all right?"

"Yes."

"What the hell's going on here? Pepe told me to get you out."

"Where is he?"

"He ran off."

"That little bastard. Come on, let's go."

They stepped into the corridor. From both ends of the building, they heard heavy footsteps coming up the stairs. Several men called to each other; there was the static sound of a dispatch radio.

Quickly, they went back into the room and closed the door, leaving it open a crack. Jesse peered out. "Here they come," he said. "Police and GRU agents." He closed the door completely, dumbfounded.

Ana listened to the men in the corridor. They began to pound on doors, calling out their identifications. Shit, she thought, we're going to be arrested. Right now.

The agents were at the next room. There was a splintering of wood, a woman's yelp. Ana looked at Jesse. He had his head down, listening, staring at the floor.

A thought struck her. She began tearing at the zipper of her uniform.

"Jesse," she whispered harshly. "Take your clothes off."

He looked up.

"Hurry, goddammit."

Within seconds, they were both naked, and Peres totally
understood her intention. They scurried to the bed and got
in. The sheets felt cold-wet on Ana's back.

"Get on top of me," she said.

Jesse swung over and mounted her. She flung her legs
around his lower back.

"Enter me."

"I'm not hard yet."

The police were at the door opposite theirs. A man was
pleading, whimpering. Another man cursed.

Ana quickly massaged Perez's penis, felt it harden, lying
flat against her belly. She guided it into herself, dry, skin
pulling, and then he was in. She felt his back muscles
tighten. "Yes, all right," she said.

There was a pounding on the door. "Open up. Police."

"Start fucking me," she whispered. "Make it real."

Perez began pumping up and down, the shaft of his
member moistening and then moving swifter.

The door was broken open. Around Jesse's shoulder,
Ana saw three men rush into the room, weapons drawn,
muzzles pointed at the ceiling. Two wore the gray uniforms
of Holguín Province policemen; the third man was a GRU
officer.

Perez turned and looked at them. *"Tremenda cagada!*
What the hell is this?"

The two policemen hurriedly searched the room; Ana
and Jesse, untangled now, watched. The GRU man looked
hard at them a moment, then bent and picked up Ana's
uniform. He looked at the insignia, glanced down at
Perez's. He flipped the uniform away.

"Let's go," he snapped to the policemen.

Wordlessly, the two officers went out the door. The
agent did not look at them again and closed the door when
he left.

Ana lowered herself gently. She stared at the ceiling, felt
herself tremble. The sound of other doors being struck came
for a few minutes, and then there was silence, the kind of
vacuumed silence following an explosion.

In it she heard soft, frightened murmurs and then the distant sound of the music from the bar starting again, Maria Christina singing *El Pitillo*.

Jesse chuckled. "Want to finish?"

She hit him with the pillow.

Ana drove very fast. Still, her thoughts ranged out there ahead of the car, on the winding two-lane road with palm trees snapping in a strong onshore breeze and the occasional *guajiro,* peasant, walking along in the darkness.

What if the *contrabandista* had been caught? And he talked, told them that the lieutenant related to Pepe Martin had tried to hire him to smuggle someone out? Distractedly, she brushed windblown hair from her face, felt her other hand tense on the wheel.

She glanced at Perez. He was scrunched down in the passenger seat, his hat low. She felt a wave of affection sweep over her. He had deliberately endangered himself for her, even though he had not known why.

"Asleep?" she asked.

"No."

"Do you want to know why I was there?"

"If you want to tell me."

She thought about that. Perhaps it would be better if he didn't know. He could honestly deny knowledge if questioned. She smiled at his shadowed face.

"Thank you for what you did," she said. "You're a good man, Jesse Perez."

He chuckled. "You didn't give me the chance to show you *how* good."

She continued to smile, letting the comment pass. Then, slowly, the smile faded and she was back in dark waters. Even if the smuggler had not been caught, what could she do now? Where would she find another man willing to take Pilar out? Pepe was beyond trust. And she herself could very well have been compromised now among the other *contrabandistas.*

Oh, Lord, she thought. . . .

TEL AVIV, ISRAEL
SEPTEMBER 21

DUFF WAITED FIFTEEN MINUTES, SITTING ON A CEMENT
bench in a small park a block from the massive Dizengoff
Center mall. It was a brilliant noon, the air drenched with
the scent of the Mediterranean, thick as salty smoke.

The park was filled with fig trees, and the fallen fruit
smelled sour, a decayed essence fit for the old men who
sat among the trees speaking disgruntled, vaguely obscene
Yiddish.

Duff was nauseated and shaky. He clasped his hands as
if to hold himself together. He had not slept in nearly thirty-
six hours. After Talia's death, he had wandered Jerusalem
in an uncontolled rage, deliberately exposing himself, wanting desperately to draw attack. None came.

At last, the rage had banked itself. He knew he had to
seek out Leigh-Simmons, to tell him of their discovery.
Using a computer in a small department store, he sent an
X-message tagged Canaan to the MI-6 station in Tel Aviv,
then took a taxi there. He followed the standard procedure
for a meet, setting up three separate locations. The park
was the last.

Leigh-Simmons finally approached. He wore a blue suit,

his skin pale and thin in the sunlight. He had a newspaper under his arm. He paused a moment, then sat down beside Duff, ignoring him. He unfolded his paper and appeared to be reading. A scruffy vendor in shorts and a tattered sweater passed selling fruitcakes and music cassettes.

"You look ghastly, old man," Leigh-Simmons said quietly.

"Talia Rosenfeld's dead."

"Yes, we picked up a Mossad dispatch on it. I'm terribly sorry." Leigh-Simmons watched two girls skim past on skateboards. "You've been quite active, haven't you?"

"The situation is very bad."

Nigel turned a page of the newspaper and casually scanned the articles, waiting.

"The KIE has a Red Bomb," Duff said. "I'm certain they intend to use it against Israel. Probably a detonation in an Israeli harbor."

Leigh-Simmons's face showed nothing. For a long moment, he continued to look at the newspaper, then folded it neatly and stared out at the sea beyond the Esplanade.

"It's aboard a ship called the *Bengal*," Green continued, "an old Liberty freighter that was in a dray yard in Singapore. An organization called the TTT Group bought it, refitted her and licensed her under the Cameroon flag." He paused. "Her captain's Sean O'Mallaugh."

Leigh-Simmons sighed heavily. "Bloody hell. The IRA's part of it, then. Why?"

"Who can be certain? Most likely an arms exchange."

"Where's this *Bengal* now?"

"I don't know."

Nigel was silent for a moment. "Well, that certainly explains the sudden Israeli naval and air activity along the coast."

"Obviously Mossad's giving high priority to Talia's computer data."

Leigh-Simmons nodded. "You have to come in, Duff. We need you now."

"Now you know as much as I do."

"You can't stay out, man. You're too vulnerable."

Duff smiled coldly. "Indeed."

Leigh-Simmons turned and looked directly at him. "The final revenge, is it? Bloody Hamlet to the end?"

"Yes."

Nigel turned away, gazed at the sea again. A sailboat curved back into the wind, heeling. An Israeli patrol cruiser lingered out beyond the roadstead.

Three tourists went chattering by, two men and a woman. They wore bright Hawaiian shirts and shorts, and their legs were very white.

Duff watched them go on up the sidewalk. "Look at that tall chap," he said bemusedly. "Rather reminds you of Sillitoe, doesn't he?"

"Sillitoe? Oh, yes, old One-Knob."

They both chuckled. Sillitoe was once an MI-6 agent, until he was caught in bed by an enraged husband and got his right testicle shot off.

The memory passed. Leigh-Simmons said, "You won't reconsider?"

"No."

"Is there anything you want me to do?"

"No."

They were silent. Sparrows clustered for a moment nearby, then flared away. Nigel exhaled slowly and tucked his paper under his arm.

"Good-bye, old man," he said softly. "Good hunting."

He rose and walked away.

John Cairncross, MI-6's director general in London, listened without comment while Leigh-Simmons told him of the *Bengal* and the lethal plot involving the Red Bomb, yet an aura of rising consternation came clearly through the faint modulation of the LMI scramble phone.

When Nigel finished, the DG exhaled audibly. Then he said, "A Red Bomb. Good God, it stuns the mind to think what that bloody thing could do in a populated area."

"It does indeed."

"And your people had absolutely no hint that the Israelis actually possessed one of these damnable things?"

"Unfortunately not. It's always been a sort of penny gaff among intelligence circles. No one ever really established that it actually existed."

The DG's voice cut nastily. "Apparently we intelligence circles were decidedly wrong, weren't we?"

"Yes."

There was a moment of thoughtful silence. Then: "Look here, before we all hurl ourselves into hysteria, who on your team made contact with this Mossad agent? Is he absolutely reliable?"

"Very." Nigel blinked and braced himself. "It was Duff Green."

"Green?"

"Yes."

"What in God's name was *he* doing down there?"

Nigel briefly explained how he had brought Duff in. He finished and waited for the explosion.

There wasn't any. "Well," Cairncross said quietly, "that was a rather neat twist, I must say. Admittedly, a dangerous and potentially compromising one, of course. But Green was always a crack field agent who knew his ground." He grunted. "And I would say he obviously had incentives of his own."

"Yes."

"I take it he was involved in the Klein wipe?"

"I suspect so."

"Well, at least bravo for that. Where's he now?"

"I don't know."

"What's that? You mean he's not under station protection?"

"He refused to come in."

"Refused?"

"The man's dying."

"Of course he's dying. He's a walking target, for God sake. It's a damned wonder he's lasted this long."

"You don't understand, sir. He's *literally* dying. Of cancer, I believe. Apparently, it's in a very advanced stage.''

The DG grunted. "Well, be that as it may, you can't leave him out there. My God, man, if word of this Red Bomb affair leaked out through him, it would be disastrous. Just a ruddy rumor of it would be enough to set the entire region ablaze.''

"That's true enough. But I can assure you, sir, Duff would never divulge it.''

"Dammit, man, that isn't good enough. I want him in.''

"I'll try.''

"Don't try, do it.''

"Of course.'' Nigel inhaled and thoughtfully pinched the skin of his forehead before continuing. "There is one hopeful possibility here, sir. The plot is still totally theoretical. Until someone actually locates this *Bengal* and thoroughly searches her, we can't be certain Duff is correct.''

"Yes, there is that.'' Cairncross sighed. "But, God save me, I have a terrible gut feeling that this is more ominous than a mere theory. With the IRA involved, the thing reeks of potential bloodbath.''

"I agree.''

"Look, I'm going to set up a meeting with the JIC and the Prime Minister immediately. But, as you point out, our first priority now is to find this freighter. I'll initiate a full C3 track from here. But you get your team cracking on it, too.''

"Right. One last thing. Should we liaison with Mossad? Tell them what we know and offer assistance?''

"Damn,'' the DG said. "That's a dicey bit. We'd have some heavy explaining to do, wouldn't we? No, I think for now we'll leave that decision to the JIC.''

"How about U.S. intelligence?''

"There, too.'' Cairncross snorted contemptuously. "Christ, that's all we'd need now, the bloody Americans flying off into another frenzy.''

"Yes.''

"All right, I want all your field people out in force. Have

them pick up anything and everything. And I want constant updates. Understood?''

The British embassy building was on Mazor Avenue in Tel Aviv, an anachronism built in 1887. It stood among glass and steel skyscrapers, as out of place as a Victorian dowager in Soho.

The MI-6 offices were located in the basement, a small warren of cubicles and staff rooms dominated by the communications center, which contained sophisticated radio banks, surveillance and signal analysis modules, and high-speed encryption units.

After the Cairncross conversation, Leigh-Simmons ordered his radio team onto the track of the *Bengal,* then met with his chief field agents and the vice ambassador to apprise them of the situation. The ambassador, Sir Donald Avery, was at that moment at a high-level conference in Vienna. Predictably, everybody sat around stunned.

Since there was no MI-6 station in Singapore, the ship trace had to begin through the Malaysian station in Kuala Lumpur. Fortunately, it had contacts in the Singaporean government.

Within forty-one minutes, full particulars on the *Bengal* came back, including its list of officers that showed her captain to indeed be Sean O'Mallaugh.

London was also picking up identical data along with other leads. It quickly established that the TTT Group was a phony corporation that had set up a false *lex mercatorium* status in Cameroon. That was enough to cause the senior levels of the British government to start taking the whole affair with extreme seriousness.

It ordered the Admiralty to divert a small destroyer force, currently exercising off Greece, to the waters near the Suez Canal. The carrier HMS *Gallant*, with her support ships, was sent into picket duty off the Straits of Gibraltar on the chance that this mysterious *Bengal* might approach the Mediterranean from off the West African coast.

Meanwhile, Israeli activity had continued to increase in

intensity. Patrols were rousting known terrorist enclaves, and all coastal positions were being reinforced. Everything coming into or leaving Israel was being thoroughly searched.

All of this was not missed by other foreign intelligence groups. Sensing something big in the wind, they were making frantic probes to find out what the hell was going on. Particularly active were the French and the Americans.

Unfortunately, it didn't take long for the *Bengal* search to run into a blank wall. Her last sighting had been made at Sri Lanka—a short stay offshore to take on a passenger. Then she had simply disappeared into the Indian Ocean.

Like many tramp freighters, with their ports of call dependent on at-sea cargo consignments, the *Bengal* had not filed a voyage summary with any international trip-monitoring service. As a result, no one knew precisely where she was or where she was bound.

Desperate for clues, Leigh-Simmons haunted his comm center, now fully linked with the London C3 track effort. They both began exploring every conceivable source of information that might relocate the ship—shipping reports, port inquiries, captain's logs, trans–Indian Ocean and trans–Arabian Sea airline summaries, even weather satellite scans.

So far, no trace of the *Bengal* had turned up.

Nigel studied his wall maps. The Indian Ocean and Arabian Sea formed a great expanse of soft blue. He stared at it. My God, he thought, there was one hell of a lot of water out there.

Night rolled over Jerusalem, clear and slightly cold with stars far up beyond the glow of the city. Duff moved through it constantly, seemingly beyond rest, across the Old City, one leg in front of the other, the pain held in check by the hashish and some deep mental discipline from a long-forgotten part of his soul.

The Jewish Quarter. The Christian. The Moslem and Armenian. Crisscrossing streets and alleys and busy thoroughfares. Passing through the ever-swirling babble of life and the silent, ancient stone edifices that had withstood the passing of time.

His own time ebbed sluggishly. There were moments when it even seemed to stop completely. He would stare at an object, a face, a window, a lighted doorway, and the image would be pinioned in a kind of internal eternity.

But always was the pain. It ebbed and surged. Sometimes he would pause in shadow—the deepest prohibition against embarrassment still intact—and vomit, vile-smelling bile like the stench of rotting sheep carcasses.

Around again he went. The night quieted; the streets emptied. He saw police and military patrols moving. He was not stopped. He passed the Church of the Holy Sepulchre, traveled along the Via Dolorosa. For a moment, he stood near Antonia's Fortress and thought in his inward stillness that he could detect the scent of ancient war.

At last, exhaustion drove him back to his room. He lay and listened to the rapid pulse of his body. A curious sensation. After awhile, dawn light seeped through the window. He slept.

When he awoke, it was night again. He tried to move his head; couldn't. His arm felt as if all the veins had been sucked of blood. Thankfully, the pain seemed dulled.

At last he was able to rise, the room suddenly whirling. He went to the bathroom and urinated. It burned like fire, blood-colored. He sat on the toilet seat and took two more pellets of hashish. Behind his eyelids, slivers of light burned, and then a resurgence of energy came.

On the move once more, into the Armenian Quarter. Tourists and vendors and young girls in Syriac black and a church on Habad Street lit with candles as tall as giant men. Shops with the scents of lamb's flesh and almonds. A jewelry kiosk, a crippled boy begging, two young men debating God.

At first, the motorcycle was merely a part of the moving montage of car lights. Up the block, coming swiftly, weaving in between vehicles, its whine was as yet only a faint trill amid the traffic sounds.

Duff had paused beside a light pole. He inhaled. The night seemed suddenly so alive about him. He distractedly listened to the two men debating, to the soft hustling challenge of the beggar child.

Then his instincts rose up.

He snapped his gaze this way, that, across the busy street, back at the two men. Then around. He spotted the cyclist. A half block away, coming, the lights around him gleaming for an instant on his black leathers, on his helmet as shiny as an ebony cannonball in flight.

He was thirty yards away now, skimming right beside the sidewalk. And then his arm was coming up. A new gleam appeared, the sawed-off barrel of a shotgun braced atop the handlebars, themselves shining chrome in the cast glow from the motorcycle's headlight, the fender red and the engine now rising above the other sounds as the rider gunned it.

Duff's hand had already gone to his waist, the grip of the Browning Hi-Power suddenly solid and unutterably heavy. He willed all his strength to pull it free and it came, swinging up, the sight crossing sidewalk and blurring for a moment in the motorcycle's headlight.

He didn't hear the shotgun blast. He only saw an orange-white flame leap at him. A nanosecond later, the load of buckshot struck him in the chest with a pain so horrendous, it was as if all his body's nerves had exploded at once. It hurled him against the light pole.

In a kind of red, suddenly numbed mist, he felt the Browning go off. The recoil took it from his hand. He saw the rider, twenty feet away, somersault backward off his cycle like a clown taking a pratfall.

He heard himself moan, a distant sound; then a scream, and himself sliding slowly, wetly down the side of the pole and the motorcycle, riderless, hurtling on. He closed his eyes an instant before it crashed into him.

IT WAS RAINING HARD WHEN THE *BENGAL* MADE LAND-
fall at mid-afternoon. Passing to windward of the islands
called the Îles du Salut fifty miles off the French Guiana
coast. The islands sat out there in the rain, low and dark
and misty, the last one in the chain named the Île du Diable,
Devil's Island.

Thirty minutes later, they cleared a French weather ship
stationed offshore, a stubby, high-staked vessel with its
white hull and upworks streaked with orange rust. They
were still more than twenty miles from shore, but the ocean
was now brown from the mud washed into the sea by the
Sinnamary River.

Collins raised the weather ship. She was called the *Baraka,* which meant "luck" in French. O'Mallaugh talked
to her captain, a lieutenant named Jean Masse who spoke
very good English. O'Mallaugh informed him that they
were bound for the river town of Mana, located three miles
from the coast. He requested clearance to enter the Sinnamary estuary.

"Have you traversed these waters before, *capitaine?*"
Masse asked.

"Negative."

"Be most careful. This is flood season, and shoals shift quickly. Your most appropriate approach is from the north. Once on the river, hold to the center."

"Yes."

"Two words of warning. First, do not allow your crew into the waters. The piranha and crocodiles are voracious at flood. Second, be alert for pirates. *Qui fait les poubelles.* How you say? Scavengers, freebooters from the gold mines. Very dangerous men."

"Thank you, Captain," O'Mallaugh said and signed off.

He took them into the estuary very slowly, using the ocean current and his engine to maintain control. Tun was at the wheel with Ashdown standing the bow, using the walkie-talkie to relay shoal sightings. All the off-duty crewmen lined the railing to watch.

The rain stopped for a few minutes and then came again. The deluge pounded on the deck and churned the channel water into a dark, opaque mass that made it nearly impossible for Jack to read shoal sign.

The river mouth was about a mile wide. Three hundred yards to starboard, just off the shoreline, the water was a lighter brown. Beyond were thick mangrove forests, flooded now save for small grass and debris islands that had washed against the higher trees. Lying on them were clusters of black caiman crocodiles, some at least fifteen feet long.

The ship reached the main river current and immediately fell off to port. O'Mallaugh turned hard to starboard, working the engine in and out of reverse until the current swung the stern. The bow finally turned sluggishly, directly into the river current.

O'Mallaugh called for more power. The ship responded quickly, her prop pulling in the deepest part of the river now. The bow wave *V*'ed off her hull like rolling humps of milked coffee, riffling off and away into the mangroves where it sent the crocodile packs exploding in lightning-quick lunges back into the river.

The river curved to the left with true jungle now on both sides. The trees, thick as black-green fungus, came right down to the water, which was filled with flood debris.

Rain squalls constantly roared over the ship as it made its way upriver. In between the rain, there was a deep, humid, stifling silence broken only by the thud of the *Bengal*'s engine and the wash of her prop.

They reached Mana late in the afternoon and anchored in midstream. The town was a dilapidated collection of tin-roofed shacks that came down to the river. Farther upslope were a few civic buildings of dirty white bricks, and there was a church steeple and a high radio tower with a flashing red light on top.

A narrow pier ran off the bank with two small freight barges tied to it. Ranged on either side of the pier were a dozen houseboats moored to tall poles driven into the mud. The boats were made of wood and were round and flat-bodied, resembling cheese boxes. They belonged to prospectors who worked the gold and emerald fields farther up the Sinnamary and Orapoque Rivers.

Forty minutes later, a small, dirty-blue motor launch came out, and a French Foreign Legion captain in grimy uniform boarded the ship. He was tall with a raw, bony face and typhus scars, and he smelled of brandy. In total silence, he perfunctorily went over the ship's papers, accepted a case of Irish whiskey and then went back to shore.

The rain started again. Soaked, Ashdown went about securing the ship for the night. To repel boarders, he ordered the water mains charged and their hoses run out. Then he turned on all the deck lights and posted fore, aft and midship lookouts. Each man was given a whistle and would stand a two-hour watch.

At twilight, a canoe with a small outboard engine came out. There was a single man in it. He was dressed in a pink shirt and wore a large gold medallion on his chest.

O'Mallaugh and Jadid, carrying a satchel, came out on

deck. They spoke for a moment; then the captain ordered
the Jacob's ladder lowered, and Jadid climbed down to the
canoe, the boatman holding the little craft steady against
the current with his outboard idling. A moment later, with
Jadid sitting in the bow, he spun the craft in a sharp turn
and they sped away.

The boatman's name was Dade Caine, an ex–U.S. Navy
chief petty officer who now owned a small café in Mana
called Le Sauvage, the Wildcat. He was fat, with big shoulders stretching his pink shirt tightly over thick arms that
bore fading tattoos. His face was swollen from too much
drink, and when he grinned he looked like Babe Ruth.

He yelled over the whining buzz of the motor, "Hey,
*patron,* you speak English?"

Jadid nodded.

Caine studied him narrowly. "What the hell are you?
Italian? You look like a fucking wop."

"It does not matter."

Caine grunted. He spat over the side and dodged a floating log that tumbled past in the current.

After serving two hitches in the navy, Caine had gone
to Venezuela to wildcat for oil. He soon discovered, however, that it was much more lucrative to transship drugs and
weapons to the fanatical bushfire revolutionists in Venezuela and Suriname and the Tupamaros in northern Uru-
guay. French Guiana was a refuge for him, where he
maintained jungle staging areas near the borders.

Jadid said, "Has the object arrived yet?"

Caine laughed. "Yeah, it's here," he said.

Le Sauvage sat on a corner near the town's church graveyard. The graves were above ground and covered with
boxes of concrete. Some were decorated with roof tiles and
broken statuary.

The café was two-storied, the bottom half painted with
red lead. It had two entrances, both hung with steel shutters.
The upper story had a balcony running the length of the

front with wrought iron trailing on the bottom like something from New Orleans. Caine and his French wife lived up there, where he also ran three whores in the back rooms.

The interior of the café was lit with kerosene lamps, the air damp and smoky and foul with the stench of dung and lamp fumes. The bar was made from a single log cut in half, with the top ground and polished. Two large jars sat on it, each containing a small brown snake curled in a hollow mound of rock.

Caine's wife was a sparrow of a woman named Lillian. She was down at the end of the bar watching three men in filthy T-shirts playing a pebble game called *cascajo* for tiny gold nuggets.

On the other side of the room were two legionnaires with two of the upstairs whores. One girl was doing a tiny dance with her feet, pouty and loose-hipped. The other sat on the lap of one of the soldiers. Her blouse was pulled down below one breast. The legionnaire poured a little beer on her nipple and licked it, and the girl laughed.

Caine led Jadid into a back room.

"Okay, *patron*," Caine said, "let's see the *chnouffe*."

Jadid put his satchel onto a table beside a Coleman lantern. The lantern hissed softly. He opened the satchel and took out a small packet wrapped in black plastic. There were six altogether in the bag. Each weighed a kilo.

Caine's eyes were bright, watching. He quickly made a tiny hole in the first packet with an ivory-handled penknife and delicately lifted out a little of the white powder inside. It was crystals of heroin, which glistened in the lantern light.

He wet a forefinger and dabbed it into the heroin, put it to his nostril and inhaled powerfully. He lifted his head as if listening. After a moment, a smile touched his heavy lips.

"Oh, yeah," he said. "Pure as God."

They replaced the packet into Jadid's satchel. Taking it, they left the room and stepped onto a walkway at the rear. It was raining heavily again, the drops ricocheting off the tin overhang like bullets.

Caine led Jadid over a bridge that crossed a small stream now in flood. The water roared along the bank. On the other side of the stream were several small wooden cribs, all connected by a tin overhang.

He knocked twice on the door of the second crib, paused, knocked again. The door opened and a man peered out, holding the door with the muzzle of a French assault rifle. When he recognized Caine, he stepped aside and let them in.

The crib consisted of a single room with a bed and a lamp stand that held a white-gas lantern. There were two nearly empty bottles of whiskey on the stand with a small porcelain cup, several syringes and a butane lighter. Against the other wall was a tin washstand and an open toilet. Clothes and military jungle gear were scattered on the floor.

A naked Creole girl lay on the bed. She had smooth, creamily tanned skin and streaks of blond in her hair. She was half conscious and occasionally murmured to herself.

The man rested the rifle against the wall. He was also naked, tall and lean with a shaved head and a rather youthful, handsome face. He had tattoos of snakes and daggers and naked women on his shoulders, and a tiger on one pectoral. His forearms bore fresh needle marks. He had half-lidded, angry black eyes.

"Where is it?" he growled to Caine in French.

"Right here, sergeant."

"Give."

"Not yet."

The legionnaire's name was Amoise. Two weeks earlier, he had deserted from the huge French Space and Research Center located in the jungle at Kourou, a hundred miles to the south. It was from Kourou that the French, as a prime member of the European Space Agency, sent up satellites. They also conducted secret nuclear research there.

Cursing, the sergeant rummaged through his camouflaged jungle pack and came up with a small wooden box about the size of a loaf of bread. Across it was stenciled:

MATERIEL    DANGEREUX—CENTRE    POUR    RECHERCHE
D'ESPACE.

Jadid immediately took it from him. The top of the box
had been opened. He pried back the cover. Inside, fitted
snuggly into Styrofoam, was a metal shaft about eight
inches long and four inches wide. It was highly polished.

He lifted it out. It was very heavy, weighing perhaps
thirty or forty pounds. One end was shaped into a cone
with varying rings of screw threads. The other end was
domed and contained two tiny holes drilled into the metal.
Below the holes was a small digital indicator window.
Taped to the shaft was a needle-thin punch.

Jadid nodded to Caine. The American grinned. He took
out the packets of heroin and laid them on the lamp stand.
"There you go, friend," he said to the legionnaire.

The sergeant scooped up one of the packets and pulled
the plastic open. His hands shook. He spilled some of the
powder. "How pure?" he asked Caine in French.

"Forty percent."

"*Vache!* You said it would be total pure."

"You can still cut it many times."

Amoise swore vehemently, his eyes blazing. But finally
he slashed his hand through the air. "Get out, you fucking
thieves!"

Caine smiled benignly. "Nice doing business with you,"
he said.

He and Jadid stepped through the door onto the walkway. Caine pulled the door shut softly, holding the knob.
He held up his other hand for Jadid to wait. The rain had
lessened somewhat. Tiny white bats flitted around them,
going for the insects driven under the overhang by the rain.

At last, Caine eased open the door softly and peered in.
The legionnaire sergeant was seated on the bed, preparing
a shot in the tiny porcelain cup. He mixed it with whiskey
and heated it over the lighter, mesmerized.

He hurriedly tied a bandanna around his left bicep and
flexed his muscles until a vein bulged in his forearm. He
put the shot right into the vein. A burst of bright color came

up into the syringe. It left delicate patterns on the glass as
the full shot went in. On the bed, the girl murmured.

For a few moments, the sergeant stared straight ahead.
Then his eyelids closed and opened lazily. Suddenly, he
leapt to his feet. He twisted his head sharply. He began to
gag, hunched over.

His entire body began to convulse. Foam formed at his
mouth. Still gagging, he cursed. Again. Then he began
retching. Suddenly, he slumped to the floor. The muscles
throughout his body twitched and jerked, looking like insects beneath the skin.

Caine shoved the door wide open and moved swiftly to
the lamp stand. He made up another heavy shot, and as he
did, he explained to the corpse, "My mistake. This shit
must be pure." Using his handkerchief, he then leaned over
the girl and pulled open her vagina. He put the needle deep
into the smooth, pink flesh inside the lips. The girl trembled
once, twice and lay still. Her face turned blue.

Jadid watched silently.

Five minutes later, in the café's back room, Caine transferred the heroin into a leather bag. They packed the box
from the space center into Jadid's satchel.

For a moment, Caine stared steadily at Jadid. "You
know, *patron,*" he said finally. "I don't know what you
intend to use this thing for. And I don't the fuck *want* to
know. But I'll tell you this. I hope that when it goes, it
takes *you* out, too."

Jadid simply looked at him, said nothing.

They left Le Sauvage and walked back to the river. The
rain had stopped completely now, but the night was filled
with the rush and drip of water and the occasional distant
roar of a caiman.

Twenty-one minutes later, Jadid was again aboard the
*Bengal.*

The whistle came suddenly out of the night like the cry
of a strange jungle bird that had landed on the stern of the
ship.

Jack, about to take the watch, was in the galley drinking a cup of coffee. He paused for a second to locate the whistle's position, then dove through the galley door and headed aft.

He emerged onto the boat deck, heard men shouting. The afterdeck was lit from the after midhouse lights and the spot on the stern gun pit. He immediately saw grappling hooks and lines over the port bulwark. Two bearded men in shorts were using machetes to cut security lines on several small barrels of storm oil. They paused long enough to heave two over the side.

"Open the mains!" Jack bellowed and started down the companionway. As he hit the main deck, there was a sudden burst of water from the port side, and then a narrow stream of white water shot out against the number-four hold, spraying upward. For a crazy moment, the stream cut wildly all over the deck.

Three more grappling hooks came sailing over the starboard bulwark, clanking and then locking onto the scupper's lip. Within a few seconds, three more men scrambled aboard. One man had a rifle strapped to his back. He instantly knelt, swung the rifle around and opened up, spraying indiscriminately. Bullets whanged and sang off metal.

By now the crewmen on the port main had gotten the hose spray steadied and were moving astern, blowing water at the two men on that side. The water knocked them off their feet. On the opposite side of the stern house, the rifleman started firing again as his companions heaved overboard anything they could find unlashed.

Ashdown picked up a four-foot piece of steel. Dodging and darting between the number-five hatch and stern winch, he crossed to the starboard side. A man with a machete suddenly appeared in front of him. The man wore narrow dark glasses. He twisted, swinging his weapon, yelling something that sounded German.

The machete whistled past Jack's shoulder and struck a winch spool. As the man began a backswing, a solid stream of water, barrel-thick, struck them. It came from the starboard hose. Jack and the man went down, skidding entangled together across the deck. They slammed up against the scuppers.

On his knees, Ashdown slammed his fist at the man, struck him in the throat. The man clawed at him frantically for a moment. Then he grabbed for the grappling line, pulled himself over the bulwark and disappeared from the light.

Water continued to spray powerfully against the stern house bulkhead, making rainbows against the spotlight. Vaguely, Jack saw the rifleman through the mist. One-handed, the man fired once, and again. Then there was a powerful explosion close behind Jack. He saw the rifleman bodily lifted and flung over the bulwark. A few seconds later, he heard a wild thrashing in the river and the man screaming.

Collins ran over. He had Jack's shotgun and was wearing only his skivvies. "You hit, man?" he yelled at Jack.

Ashdown shook his head.

Slipping and falling on the flooded deck, they started around the stern of the afterhouse. Water was blowing against the outside port bulkhead, flooding loudly through the scuppers. By now, the crewmen, with O'Mallaugh anchoring a second hose, had driven the first two men over the side.

Twin outboard engines started in the darkness below the slant of the deck lights. They revved suddenly and sped off downriver.

"Eat this, motherfuckers," Collins yelled after them and let loose the other barrel of the shotgun into the darkness.

For the next half hour, they watched tiny lights moving downriver as the pirates went slowly about picking up whatever they had managed to heave overboard that was still afloat.

By first light, Pepper already had steam up. There was a light fog on the river; it deepened over the jungle, making the treetops look as if they were shrouded in dirty gray cotton. Overhead, the sky sagged with dark clouds.

The anchors were hoisted. Using engine power, O'Mallaugh let the current swing the bow back downriver, the prop gouging coils of brown water and the low, steady pound of the engine coming up out of the depths of the hull like the heartbeat of the river.

There were a few dim lights in Mana as they eased away. The antenna beacon of the town seemed like a tethered red star in the mist. A few fishermen in single-log pirogues worked the river's edge, the men carrying long spears.

When they reached the river's entrance, they swung northward, directly into the ocean current, angling slightly until they were free of the pull of the shore. O'Mallaugh ordered a course to the northwest.

Collins raised the French station ship for the latest weather. He was informed that a long system of rain squalls lay all the way to the Lesser Antilles. To the east was a high-pressure pattern with southwesterly winds at eight knots.

The final item stated that a tropical wave depression had formed off the North African coast. . . .

---

**MIAMI, FLORIDA**
**SEPTEMBER 28**

THE LUNCHROOM LOUDSPEAKER OF THE NATIONAL HURricane Center's headquarters building blared: "Would the DD please come to TAFO."

Warren Anholt, deputy director for the NHC's new facility located on the campus of Florida International University, had just finished his lunch, a Jack-in-the-Box steak sandwich. He quickly finished his milk and hurried out into the main entrance hall.

Anholt was a youngish-looking man of forty-nine with close-cropped brown hair and a trim, tanned body that came from his main obsession, scuba diving.

The NHC structure was a huge block of gray concrete that housed a vast array of state-of-the-art weather tracking and forecasting equipment. Its walls, ten feet thick, could withstand a Category 4 hurricane.

Operating as an arm of the National Oceanic and Atmospheric Administration (NOAA), it was staffed by crack meteorologists and weather forecasting specialists. Their responsibility was to keep constant watch over a vast area of ocean comprising the tropical and subtropical North Atlantic, the Caribbean Sea and the Gulf of Mexico.

Anholt entered the Tropical Analysis and Forecast Operations room. It was filled with mainframe computers and workstations showing computerized mappings, statistical grids and real-time satellite pictures of various ocean areas.

Harry Tanaka, chief of the TAFO section, sat at one of the workstations. He waved Warren over. "Look at this," he said. He had a faint Texas accent and jet-black hair cut in the style Brian Bosworth had tried to make popular ten years before. "I've been monitoring the latest dial-ups on TWD-46."

Using coded messages from the geostationary satellite GOES-3, which transmitted every six minutes, Tanaka had created a filtered, enhanced and colorized visual animation of the tropical wave depression, tagged TWD-46, that had recently formed off the African coast.

Anholt studied the screen. It showed an undulated wave pattern that ran from the northeast to the southwest, three hundred miles off the Cape Verde Islands. The display was colored in shades of blue, red and white.

The blue indicated rain densities; the red, temperature readings; and the white, pressure gradients. A series of arrows and barbed symbols showed the complex flow of windfields behind and in front of the wave. Along the edges of the screen were relative error and time marks.

Warren grunted. "She's strengthening, isn't she? Have you input the latest EWFN ATOLLs?" ATOLL stood for Tropical Oceanic Lower Level. It consisted of data pertaining to near-ocean conditions that could often be missed by the satellite scans.

The data came from ground and buoy stations and low-altitude balloon ascents off southern Europe and North Africa. The system was co-operated by the NOAA and the European Weather Forecasting Network.

Tanaka nodded. "They're showing developing shower and thunderstorm coalescence, too. Overall windspeeds're still holding under forty, but I don't like their sync tendency."

"Shit," Anholt growled. "And the forward motion's

slow enough to keep her alive. A dollar to a doughnut, we start seeing verticals in the next three to four hours, Harry.''

Tanaka nodded.

When a wave depression's winds at all levels began to synchronize and blow essentially from the same direction at the same speed, they created rapid concentrations of vertical uplifts of surface heat. This rising warm air would eventually begin spiraling inward toward the center of the system, which would then begin to feed off its own evaporation energy.

Anholt picked up the workstation phone and punched the button marked TAFS. It stood for Tropical Analysis and Forecast Support.

A woman answered: ''Jacoby.''

''Laura, Warren.'' Laura Jacoby, thirty-one years old and a graduate of MIT, was head of the unit. ''Check your latest GOES dial-ups.''

''I just did. Looks like we might have a seedling about to bloom, doesn't it?''

''Yeah. Okay, let's run off an NHC embryo model, see if we can figure what she'll do.''

To track a hurricane in an attempt to understand and forecast its dynamics and energetics, the most useful tools were computer simulated models. Several systems were used simultaneously, each with at least eight to ten option packages.

The models were fed large doses of observation data collected from satellites, field stations, ships at sea and flights into the storm itself. Unfortunately, the models were more advanced than the data input. This made analyses and prediction parameters very tricky for any time span over twenty-four to thirty hours.

''Will do,'' Jacoby said.

''I'll be in Operations.''

''Right.'' She hung off.

Anholt turned his attention back to Tanaka's screen. Harry was typing in the newest six-minute GOES-3 readings. Warren sighed. The center's director, Allen New-house, was currently in the hospital. He'd suffered a serious heart attack two days before and was still in intensive care. Now the center was Warren's bailiwick.

He picked up the phone again. He needed to call his wife. Apparently, he was going to be around for awhile.

## MOA AIR BASE, CUBA

The chief officer of the base, Commander Alberto Torralba, stood at the window when Ana entered his office. She snapped to attention. Two other men were present, GRU agents in their ubiquitous white *guayabera* shirts, Rolex watches and Ray·Ban glasses.

"Be at ease, Lieutenant," Torralba said without turning. "Sit."

Ana did as she was told.

The taller of the agents eased one buttock onto Torralba's desk. He had a long, narrow nose, a mustache and large hands. The other man quietly took out a small tape recorder from his shirt pocket and put it on the desk. He flicked it on.

Ana's heart tripped.

The first agent stared at her for a moment. "When did you last see your father?"

She glanced at her commander's back. He seemed absorbed in watching a flock of seagulls near a distant runway. She returned to the agent and answered his question.

"Why did he flee Havana?" the agent snapped.

"He didn't flee. Why should he? I believe he's merely visiting relatives."

"What relatives?"

Ana shrugged. "We have many. All over the island."

"Do you know his friends?"

"Some."

The agent lifted his face and stared at the ceiling. "Do you know what Alpha 66 is?" he asked suddenly.

"Yes. Cuban dissidents who live in America."

"They are more than dissidents," the agent said sharply. "They're counterrevolutionaries. Garbage. Traitors."

Ana remained silent.

"Was your father one of them?"

"What?"

"*Was* he?"

"Never," she answered angrily. "My father fought at El Comandante's side from the beginning. He was a patriot then and he's a patriot today."

The two agents exchanged Ray·Ban glances.

The interrogating agent lifted his hand and smoothed his mustache. "Have you ever had any contact with *contrabandistas?*"

Again Ana's heart tripped. But she stared directly into the man's dark glasses, seeing her own twin faces. "No."

"Why were you at the Malecon in Nicaro?"

There was the slightest hesitation. "To be with my lover."

"Ensign Perez, I believe."

"Yes."

"You are aware that it is a breach of military discipline to fuck an inferior officer?" He emphasised the word *fuck,* made it sound very ugly.

"I love him. I am prepared for any reprimands."

The agent chuckled quietly and stood up. He left the tape running. Commander Torralba turned and looked at him. The agent nodded.

Torralba walked to his desk and opened a drawer. He took out an oversize cedarwood box. The single word COHIBA, the name of a famous brand of Cuban cigar, was carved into the top. He shoved it across the table. All three men stared hard at Ana.

"These are the remains of your father," Torralba said quietly. "He was killed while trying to escape the police."

For one tiny moment, her body remained still. Then, like a fever chill, she felt her insides begin to shake. Her throat felt suddenly constricted.

She stared at the box. Dear sweet God! My father?

There, in a cigar box? A sense of overwhelming sorrow struck at her heart like a knife blade. With it came a sickening outrage at the indecency of it.

*A stinking cigar box.*

She stood, looked directly into Torralba's eyes; forced her hands not to shake as she picked up the box, not to let the bastards see. The box was heavy. For a fleeting moment, the commander's eyes flicked down, then up again.

"You have a twelve-hour furlough to bury him at his birthplace," he said.

She willed herself to come to attention, standing there rigid, holding her father's remains in both hands. Then she made a perfect about-face and walked out.

Enrique had been born in a small village called Valle Blanco in the western highlands of the Sierra Maestra Mountains—coffee country, where the nights were always dry and cool, lying in the lee of the mountains.

Ana drove there in a rented Toyota, along the coast to Mayari and then inland at Cuento. The main highway became a dusty country road that ran through fields of sugarcane. She passed no cars, only the occasional donkey cart. In the distance were the smoke puffs of cane trains.

At last she was into the highlands, where the slopes were groved in coffee trees. She passed the remains of an old coffee baron's mansion, overgrown with jungle. Now and then, in the dust thrown up by her tires, she caught sight of the two GRU men following in a Lada.

Ana drove numbly, aware of the cedar box on the passenger seat. Now and then she'd reach out, touch it, run her fingers along the edge. It drew up images of her father, the sound of his voice, the passion of his eyes, which could crinkle with quick laughter.

She sobbed.

It was evening when she reached Valle Blanco. Before leaving Moa, she had telephoned Enrique's only living relative there, his older sister, Placida. The town was nestled in a small valley. There was an old coffee-processing plant at the apex of the valley; below it, the town had cobblestone streets lined with yellow and green and blue houses.

Placida lived in a stonecutter's cottage near a small Catholic church that sat on a hillock among mountain apple trees. She was sitting on her porch when Ana drove up. She stood, a straight-backed woman with white hair and a narrow, lined face the color of tanned hide. Like her brother, she had once fought alongside Castro in the mountains.

When Ana came up the steps with the cedar box, Placida stared at it. Her face went stony. "So this is his casket," she said bitterly. Then she hugged Ana fiercely, the box pressed between them, her body stiff with repressed rage.

Down the slope, the Lada stopped beside the church. The agents remained inside.

The two women went into the cottage. The walls were made of blocks of mountain stone chinked with cement that had yellowed. It was cool and smelled of tobacco and kerosene smoke and the faintly sour odor of an old woman's body.

Placida told Ana about her father's death, the police, the burning cane field. Ana listened, looking out the window as the day deepened into twilight.

When her aunt finished, she said, "Was he a counter-revolutionary?"

Placida shook her head. "He had not yet decided."

"Are you?"

"Yes." She smiled. "I am not too old to pull a trigger." She watched her narrowly. "What are *you, carina?*"

"A soldier."

"But a blind one?"

Ana stood and walked to the window. "I've believed in the revolution my whole life."

"We all did. But it was a dream, one that has become a nightmare." Placida went on to tell of the atrocities that had become commonplace in Cuba—the sudden disappearances, the *jinete de la noche,* the night riders, who came with automatic weapons and dogs.

Then she paused a long moment before speaking again. "Your husband was also murdered by the regime," she said softly.

Ana swung around, stunned.

"It is true." Her aunt went on to explain, finishing with, "You must get out of Cuba now, Ana. Go to America. There you can be valuable to the Cause." She glared at the cigar box. "You can repay them for *this*."

Ana walked back slowly and sat down. My sweet Antonio, too? she thought, stricken.

"If you won't go," Placido said, "then at least send little Pilar. If she remains here, they'll poison her mind until she's like one of those." She jerked her head, indicating the agents parked down the slope.

"But how? I've tried."

"There are ways. I know men who can do it."

"She's on the Isla de Juventura. It wouldn't be possible until she's back with me in Havana."

Placida shook her head sadly. "No, Ana, they will never give Pilar back to you."


Using flashlights, they buried Enrique's cedar box in a small patch at the edge of the church's graveyard. The GRU agents watched silently. The priest came out, an old man with a shriveled, bald head. He was nervous and told them that since their loved one had been cremated, his remains could not be placed in hallowed ground. He gave them a shovel.

Ana dug a shallow hole in the tall grass. The earth smelled raw, and tiny black beetles scurried in the flashlight beams. She placed the box in the hole, then took off her aviator's silver wings, put them on the box and replaced the dirt.

The women stood for a moment, each whispering a prayer. Ana's was only a fragment of the Hail Mary, vaguely remembered from a night six months earlier when she had overheard her father, who had rejected his Catholicism after the revolution, saying the Rosary in the darkness.

They walked back to the cottage. A warm wind started, sweeping down off the higher foothills. It shook the palms, made them clack and snap.

The women embraced. Placida ran her finger along Ana's cheek. "Think long on it, *mi carina.*"

"I already have," Ana said. "Arrange to take Pilar out."

She got into the Toyota and drove away.

LEIGH-SIMMONS HELD UP HIS ID CARD FOR THE GUARD at the embassy gate, then eased the black Land Rover utility van on around the curving driveway toward the entrance. Before reaching it, however, he swung off onto a narrow cement side road that went around to the delivery entrance of the building. He backed down to the small loading ramp.

He switched off the engine and sat, swiveling his neck tiredly. After a moment, he glanced back at the plain wooden coffin in the rear of the van. He had covered it with a small British flag that had nearly slipped off from the movement of the automobile. He reached over the seat and straightened it.

Nigel was exhausted, hadn't slept since the previous night. Earlier that day, in the afternoon, he'd driven over to Jerusalem to claim Duff Green's body. According to Mossad intercepts, it was in the Mishkenot Military Hospital.

As expected, he'd run into a roadblock. He had to wait two hours before finally being allowed to speak with someone. A curt Israeli Defense Force captain told him the circumstances of Duff's killing and of that of his assassin.

The killings were under intense investigation, and, therefore, the body of Green could not be released. . . .

He climbed out and rang the delivery bell. Two men in work coveralls came out. Together, they got the coffin onto a dolly and wheeled it through a storage area to a small refrigerated room where the corpses of British subjects who had died in Israel were held for shipment back to England. It was now empty and smelled sharply of disinfectant and iodine.

Leigh-Simmons went back out to the loading dock and up the main basement corridor toward the MI-6 suite. . . .

He had finally gotten Duff's body released through the intercession of his Mossad counterpart, Darron Hareven, and even that had taken until nearly two in the morning.

Hareven, a robust man in shirtsleeves, was well informed about Green. He knew of his affair with Rosenfeld, of his return to the Middle East, of his suspected activities there. Nigel assured him that Duff had been conducting his travels completely without MI-6 sanctions.

Hareven nodded. "A sort of Rambo mission, you might say?"

"An apt appraisal."

The two men discussed the sudden increase in Israeli security and the new movements of British fleet elements in the Mediterranean. No hint was given of the Red Bomb. Both were like pugilists shadowboxing with each other, probing and feinting, giving nothing yet closely reading each other's eyes.

Now Hareven fell silent for a long moment, thoughtfully tapping his thick fingers on his desk. At last, he rose. "All right, I'll see what I can do about releasing the body."

"Thank you," Nigel said. "I'm indebted."

Now in his embassy office, he nodded to his secretary and snapped, "Coffee, if you would."

"Yes, sir."

His desk bore a small stack of telexes and radio reports that had come in over the past eighteen hours. He began going through them. His secretary brought in a tray with a carafe of coffee, a cup and a plate of biscuits and Swiss cakes.

"The ambassador returned while you were gone, sir," she said. "He wishes to see you as soon as possible."

Nigel nodded. "Who's on radio watch?"

"Stuffert, I believe, sir." The secretary withdrew.

Nigel lifted his phone and punched the radio section button. He poured a cup of coffee as it buzzed.

A man answered: "R and A section, Stuffert."

"Nigel here. Update me."

Stuffert quickly explained that the C3 track had developed an in-depth dossier on the *Bengal,* right from the moment of her launch. As for the TTT Group, several hints were surfacing that indicated a Libyan connection.

"And the ship's location?"

"We've traced her first to Madagascar, where she picked up a load of lumber. Then she went on to Capetown, stopped there for minor repairs on her boilers. We checked the pulled seal manufacturing stamps back to her builder in the U.S. A—" Stuffert shuffled his notes. "A Bethlehem-Fairfield shipyard in Baltimore, Maryland. The numbers checked out."

"Did anyone in Capetown pick up a hint of where she was headed?"

"I'm afraid not. But we're checking everything transiting the entire African coast. So far, not a blip."

"When was your last report to Cairncross?"

"Two hours ago."

"All right." He hung up.

Ambassador Sir Donald Avery was writing a poem when Nigel knocked lightly on his office door. "Come," he called. He laid down the pen and leaned back in his deep leather chair.

Avery was six feet, six inches tall and narrow as an aspen, with curly ginger hair. In times of stress, he always had an overpowering urge to put his thoughts down in poetic rhymes. At Cambridge, he had been famous for his obscene limericks.

"Ah, Leigh-Simmons," he said as Nigel walked in. He nodded for him to be seated.

Nigel sat, the milk-soft leather of his chair whispering gently with his weight. Before him loomed the ambassador's desk, huge as a dining table and made of rare Indian red mahogany.

Sir Donald eyed him quietly. "Seems we have a sticky situation on our hands, doesn't it?"

"Damned sticky, sir."

"All right, I have the basics. You fill in the chinks."

Leigh-Simmons quickly summarized the entire situation, including the Capetown sighting of the *Bengal* and the report of a possible Libyan connection to the TTT-Group.

As Nigel talked, Avery lit a cigarette. It was a cork-tipped Shekeer, a cinnimon-spiced brand imported from Turkey. He was addicted to them, yet never allowed himself to smoke in public. His office, however, always held the faint scent of apple dumplings.

When Leigh-Simmons finished, the ambassador exhaled and leaned forward. "I've already spoken to the PM. Needless to say, everyone is deeply concerned. As you know, our entire Eastern Command's in a bloody facer trying to find this damned *Bengal*. Seems rather odd someone hasn't sighted it yet, doesn't it?"

"It's a very big ocean, sir."

"Of course." He took another pull on the Shekeer. "Well, I'm scheduled to lunch with the Israeli deputy prime minister today. Any items in particular you suggest I explore?"

"Depends. Has London decided on coordinating with Mossad yet?"

"No, the JIC's still debating the advisability of that. Frankly, I've recommended we do. What do you think?"

"Ordinarily, I would say no, in order to keep our intercept capability secret. But the potential gravity of this situation makes it very tricky."

Sir Donald grunted and squashed out his cigarette. "Oh, one other thing. This Green affair. As I understand it, this chap was booted from the organization before I got here, correct?"

"Yes."

"Something about a killing that caused quite a cat among the pigeons?"

"Yes."

"Then what the hell was he doing out here?"

Nigel hesitated. Had Cairncross kept silent on his involvement in bringing Duff in? Or was the ambassador simply out of the loop?

"His wife was murdered by terrorists," he finally answered. "We assume he was seeking out her killers."

"And they finally got to him."

"Apparently so."

The ambassador nodded slowly. "You know, I might ask if he had any assistance from our offices. But let's just say I prefer to assume he didn't and leave it at that."

"Of course, sir."

"Well, keep me apprised." His face went solemn. "And let's hope we're not all turned into bloody cinders in the meantime."

"Yes, sir."

Back in his own office, Nigel called Cairncross. The MI-6 chief was agitated. He explained that further information about the Libyan connection was coming to light from deep plants in Gadhafi's headquarters. However, the outlines were still very hazy.

"But there certainly seems to be a link with O'Mallaugh," he went on. "We've been tracing his movements over the last eighteen months. There's strong evidence he was in Tripoli and possibly Bengazi last year. Four months later, he turned up in Singapore."

Well, Nigel thought, the pieces are beginning to come together.

They went on to discuss the KIE. Nigel said that one of

his field agent's informers had mentioned an Iranian link to the terrorist organization—just a whisper, something to do with the Kurds.

"The Kurds?" Cairncross said. "Interesting."

"Yes. Still, it could be a false lead."

Cairncross grunted. "Everybody seems to be running into those. We're also being bombarded with Western intelligence probes. I talked with the CIA station chief yesterday. Cheeky bastard, that one. But I think the Americans are beginning to sniff things out. He mentioned Egyptian sources."

Egyptian? Odd. "What about the French?"

Cairncross snorted. "The bleeding frogs couldn't find their own asses in a steambath."

They talked a few moments longer and then rang off.

Fifteen minutes later, Stuffert buzzed him. He was excited. "Nigel, I've found something."

"Be right there."

Stuffert was studying a workstation monitor when Leigh-Simmons entered the radio section. He paused beside Stuffert's desk. The monitor screen contained entries from what appeared to be ship and land site radio logs.

Stuffert glanced up. "Wait till you see *this*," he said, his eyes sparkling. "Sort of puts the deuce in our mix." He began to scroll back. "On a hunch, I started monitoring shipping and weather station logs deeper in the South Atlantic. This is what I found."

He had reached three entries that were highlighted. The first two were standard station tape repeats of weather in the South Atlantic.

But the next entry read:

AI station: VPA-BBC
9/21/97: 2214:16 SAT
OSX: BENGAL
2670 mH
Req rad fix (15.32W/07.15S)

dt WX des N quad: ZVA-ZVZ
Via Fernando de Noronha
Trans end: 2216:07

Nigel's gaze instantly picked out the word *Bengal*. He leaned in while Stuffert explained.

"This is a log notation from the weather station on Ascension Island. They received a transmission from *Bengal* at twenty-two hundred hours their time on twenty-one September. The ship wanted a standard radar position check."

Stuffert pointed to the sixth line of the entry. "But it also wanted a WX. That's a weather forecast. For the northern coastal quadrant of the ZVA-ZVZ area. That's the international call allocation for Brazil."

Leigh-Simmons's head snapped around. "What? You mean they wanted to know the weather off the northern Brazilian coast?"

"Precisely. And another thing—the position coordinates show that the ship was southwest of Ascension Island, had already passed it. That means it was headed *west*."

Nigel put his head down, walked a few feet away, came back. "Brazil? What the hell're they doing going to South America? That's a bloody long way round to the Mediterranean."

He looked at Stuffert. The obvious was in his eyes. *Maybe the* Bengal *wasn't going to the Mediterranean.*

He snapped up a phone and began to punch in Cairncross's scramble codes.


## NATIONAL HURRICANE CENTER

Anholt entered the TAFS room, poured himself a cup of coffee and leaned against Jacoby's workstation. He'd just finished a short weather update for Miami TV channel 4 pertaining to TWD-46. The depression, as the embryonic model predicted it would do, had by now become a tropical storm and was assigned the name Emma.

"We're getting another ST downlink," Jacoby said. She was a tall, athletically slender woman with short blond hair and a quiet smile.

The ST she referred to stood for Storm Trackers, the name given the 815th Weather Recon Squadron stationed at Miami International. Operated under the auspices of the NOAA, it maintained a small liaison unit in the Center and at a field base at San Juan, Puerto Rico.

Using Lockheed WP-3D Orions, the Trackers flew directly into storms, including hurricanes. Loaded with electronic sensors and analysis gear, they gathered dense data on the storm. It was then satellite-downlinked to the NHC in three-to six-second bursts.

Actually, Anholt's earlier prediction that TWD-46 would produce verticals had been an hour off. As expected, their NHC embryo package had come up vague. Too few data parameters. It hadn't been until evening that the trade wind inversion, the boundary that normally divides the moist lower air from the dry upper air, finally broke down completely.

Immediately, great funnels of heavily saturated air were driven into the troposphere, creating violent thunderheads. Yet it was still another nine hours before a vortex, the next stage in the birthing of a hurricane, appeared.

As the verticals speared upward, they threw the entire atmospheric environment above the storm into turbulence. Cyclones and anticyclones, great eddies of air, formed and were hurled away from the funnel tops.

This caused pressure drops within the upward flow of moist air. In turn, more heated air off the ocean was sucked into the bottom of the storm. Wind speeds increased. Coupled with the spin of the earth, a spiraling of the winds began until a completely closed vortex was formed.

At 4:00 A.M., the upgrade to tropical storm status was established, and TS watches were issued to the Virgin Islands and Puerto Rico. Just after dawn, one of the San Juan Orions was dispatched to study Emma. She now lay 1,400 miles east of the Virgin Islands, moving westward along a path near the eighteenth parallel.

Anholt and Jacoby silently watched the data as line after line rapidly ran across the monitor. It included meteorological readings, such as temperature, pressure, wind speed and humidity. It also showed nuclei formation and cloud physics along with radiation, $CO_2$ parameters and C-and X-Band radar scans.

Suddenly Jacoby grunted and glanced around at Warren, her eyebrows raised. He knew what she had spotted: wind velocities and core temperature.

There are always several clues in a tropical storm profile that indicate a high probability of its turning into a full-blown hurricane. One is the increase of internal wind velocities. Emma's had now climbed to sixty-eight miles per hour.

But the second data clue was even more ominous. In a tropical storm, the vortex core temperature is always slightly cooler than its surroundings. In a hurricane, however, it is higher. The more vicious the storm, the hotter the core.

Emma's vortex core temperature had already increased six degrees Fahrenheit since the last aircraft downlink.

"She's starting to ripen, Warren," Jacoby said.

Anholt cursed, downed his coffee and slammed the cup onto the desk. "Start preparing for progression models. I'm going on conference."

Whenever a storm reached this level of growth, protocol designated that the Hurricane Center director utilize a conference loop with the NOAA office in Washington, the National Weather Service headquarters in Biloxi, and the U.S. Navy meteorologists at Jacksonville and Norfolk.

He paused a few seconds longer to scan the monitor once more, then darted from the room.

## 00:20

"Yo, CHECK THIS OUT," COLLINS SAID SOBERLY, STEP-ping onto the bridge. Ashdown was on the forenoon watch. Keyshawn handed him the latest weather report.

Jack glanced at it. The National Hurricane Center in Mi-ami had now categorized Tropical Storm Emma a full hur-ricane. With winds at eighty-nine miles per hour, she was now eight hundred miles east of San Juan, Puerto Rico, heading almost due west.

Hurricane warnings had already been posted for Puerto Rico and the Dominican Republic, with watches on Cuba and southern Florida. Present forecasts indicated that the storm should reach San Juan within the next forty hours.

"Sweet Lord Jesus," Collins said. "I hope that slag bitch doesn't come huntin' us."

The *Bengal* was now in the Caribbean Sea. She had passed through the Lesser Antilles between Tobago and Grenada the day before. Once out of the line of rain squalls along the South American coast, the weather had turned beautiful—warm, crystal-clear days.

Jack handed back the pad. "It's too early to worry. Be-sides, forecast says she'll hold to the north, cross over the

He leaned in. "We come from Singapore, right? Well, take it from me, jack, south Malaysia's one of the biggest transfer points there is for heroin. There's probably kilos of the shit stuffed all over this boat."

Jack tended to agree with the idea of contraband aboard. So did Jeremiah. They had discussed that possibility in the past.

As the Aussie put it, "I'll lay you a dingo's arse it's weapons. Hidden down in those timber loads. An' I'll tell you something else. That drongo Jadid ain't along for the ride. He's 'ere to see that everything goes the Bob."

There was something else that reinforced their theory. The moment they passed into the Caribbean Sea, O'Mallaugh had ordered Collins to maintain total radio silence. No transmissions, no requests for radar fixes. In effect, they were now running invisible. To be sure Keyshawn obeyed, the captain had put a lock on the ship's transmitter. . . .

Now Collins studied Ashdown narrowly. "You the First John on this ship now, man. And maybe I should watch my mouth. But I tell you, if that hurricane starts bearin' down on us, I'm gonna bypass the old man's transmitter lock. Orders or no orders. I'll lay out a SOS so loud the fuckin' brothers back in Dee-troit gonna hear me."

The heavy hammering shot through Jeremiah's dream like the firing sequence of a cannon. The dream—something about a long-ago bar in Dirranbondi—disintegrated if hit by a shell. He was on his feet before his eyes were en, moving.

Over the past week, he'd taken to sleeping in the engine m, in the alleyway near the high-voltage panel. He 't trust leaving the area. Too many things had been wrong.

w, as he came around the HV panel, he immediately at the cylinder heads were swaying slightly. His first t was that the holding-down bolts had loosened or roken.

Leewards and then turn up into the Bahamas and
Florida. That's four hundred miles from us.''

"But what if that goddamned forecast is wrong, m
What if that sucker changes direction?''

Jack shrugged. "It's always possible.'' He knew that b
ing *anywhere* near a hurricane was always an unpredictabl
and very dangerous business. "In fact,'' he said, "I remember a *baguio* in the South China Sea back in the eight-
ies. That's what they call hurricanes in the Philippines. This
one made a ninety-degree turn against all forecasts. Finally
went ashore near Manila and tore the hell out of the place.''

"Oh, shit,'' Keyshawn groaned. "Why you tell me crap
like that, fool? A ninety-degree turn? If this one does that,
she be comin' straight *at* us.''

Jack chuckled. "Think positive.''

"Fuck positive. I'm gettin' premonitions again, baby.
My goddamned bones're talkin' to me.''

Ashdown shook his head. "Even if she did turn, the
captain would lee port us right away.''

For all his brutality, Jack knew O'Mallaugh was too wise
a master to allow his ship to be caught at sea by a hurricane
Jack had noted that O'Mallaugh had been watching th
storm's progress very closely. Had, in fact, ordered Coll
to bring him its latest position and status reports every h

"Why don't he do it now, then?'' Keyshawn cried.
stead of us digging fuckin' ocean doughnuts out
Screw them drug runners. We can off-load to the
the goddamned storm.''

Twelve hours earlier, O'Mallaugh had in
slowed the *Bengal*, holding her to five knots an
ing a constant two-degree turn to starboard, tr
circle like an aircraft in a holding pattern. He v
checking off time.

Collins was positive he was doing it beca
to rendezvous with high-speed drug boa
you,'' he'd commented, "we're carryin' p
You understand what I'm tellin' you?
white horse.''

He headed for the pressure station, bellowing for Vogel. The safety valves atop the low and intermediate cylinders blew open, hissing wildly. He reached the station, saw immediately that the low-pressure cylinder was up to thirty pounds and the intermediate was double what it should be.

He scurried back to the throttle desk and shoved the throttle down to mid-speed range. Instantly, he felt the deck shift slightly as the prop slowed. The hammering in the engine faded. A few moments later, the safeties shut off.

Vogel came sliding down from the upper walkway. Pepper glared at him. "Whot the hell you think you doin', you bloody Kraut?"

"The captain rang down and wanted eighty revolutions."

"Eighty? Jesus H Christ!"

Vogel shrugged, puzzled. "First we go around and around slow, then all of a sudden we go fast."

The power phone buzzed. Jeremiah snapped it up. "You're a bloody fool, O'Mallaugh," he bellowed.

"Why the fock have you cut speed?" the captain came right back.

"To keep my engine from tearin' itself out of its foundation plates, goddammit."

"I want maximum revs."

"Do you? Well, all you'll get is sixty-eight. An' maybe not even that. We push her past it, we'll have babbitt runnin' in the bleedin' bilges."

The captain cursed and rang off.

Jeremiah slammed down the phone. He paced around for a while, then began easing throttle up again, constantly listening to the engine. He finally settled on sixty-five revolutions.

For the next two hours, he, Vogel and one of the black gang had to reset the links and balance up the engine. It was a bitch job, all of them pouring sweat and constantly backing off to run pressure checks.

Under normal conditions, a Liberty's engine operated at a top speed of seventy-six revolutions. For a short time, it could even be pushed to eighty-three. But ever since leaving Capetown, the *Bengal* had begun to show her age.

Things were breaking down. Hydraulic systems blew. Shaft bearings overheated and had to be shimmed up. Evaporators were switched back and forth so salt scum could be chipped off the coils. Pressure packing blew and had to be jury-rigged with ballast cement.

Once they'd even been forced to go cold iron at sea for a major repair. The low-pressure crosshead had started screeching and throwing smoke. They were down for three hours, pulling the crosshead and re-machining the oil box.

Fortunately, the anchorage on the Sinnamary River had allowed Pepper a little time to work on a potentially very serious problem. For days he'd been listening to the main crankshaft, catching an increasing metal-on-metal chuff. It was obvious that the thrust collars were worn, allowing no clearance for the crank webs.

They worked all night on it. Using a jack between the IP web and the main journal, they sledged the shaft ahead enough to get to the adjusting screws and reset the collar clearances.

But these were all temporary fixes. Sooner or later, Jeremiah knew that something major would go. Already his pressure log was showing a gradual but steady drop in steam pressure. That meant all three cylinders had to be re-ringed, a task that would require shutdown and at least two days of intensive work.

Now, with the crazy Mick wandering the hell all over the ocean, there was the weather to consider, too. If they hit heavy seas again, with the lightness of the timber cargo and the resets down as tight as possible, there was a good chance that the main shaft could warp when the ship pitched too deeply. Bearings would burn out and cause enough vibration to shear the crankpins and webs and tear the whole forward section of the engine off its welded foundation frame.

They finally completed the link resets and balancing. Jeremiah, Vogel and the Malaysian black ganger gathered at the control desk. He handed out beers, cracked his open and stood, head down, listening. His sensitive ear picked out discordant thuds and metallic clinks amid the slow, heavy throb of the engine.

He spat disgustedly into his wastebox. "Dumb fuckin' Paddy," he snarled and gulped down his Foster's in one steady pull.

The increasing terror, coupled now with a deepening sense of remorse, seemed locked inside O'Mallaugh's body. Like a scream he couldn't release, all the exits closed. Only in those rare moments when he slept, too exhausted to keep conscious, did the scream come, a silent wailing that did nothing.

Ashdown had relieved him on the bridge at midnight. It was now 1:35 A.M. O'Mallaugh walked slowly back and forth in his cabin, bottle in hand. The room was silent save for the normal low drumroll of the engine, the metallic creaks and groans of a ship at sea. He drank. The liquor bit into his stomach, sent pain thrusts like needles.

He moaned audibly.

It was almost here, O'Mallaugh thought wildly. The final moment. Drawing ever closer in a whirling wind. Dear God, so many people. So much agony.

For a horrible moment, he felt as if he might collapse onto the floor of his cabin, his body driven down by the weight of all those souls. Sweet Mother Mary, how would he climb to Heaven against such weight?

He tore his mind away from the thought, moved to the door and slipped into the corridor. He quickly unlocked the chart room and went in. He sucked in the familiar smell of old paper, the clean, oily scent of navigating instruments.

He had recently taken to locking Ashdown out of the chart room. Ever since the mid Atlantic, he'd kept their destinations secret from his First, giving him only necessary watch courses. But now he was overtaken by black paranoia. He didn't want Ashdown to look at the charts at all.

He bent over the map set spread on the slanted table.

Just before being relieved by Ashdown, he had taken a sextant shot at the star Polaris, fixed the ship's position off the Bowditch tables and logged it.

That position was marked on the course line with a running fix symbol, the line extending beyond it toward the west. O'Mallaugh swung the double parallels and drew a second course line. It was eighty-five degrees to the right of the present one. At the point where the two course lines intersected, he drew a circle.

The tip of his pencil began to shake, and the circle came out lopsided. Again the terror struck full bore. O'Mallaugh stared horrified at the new course line, the thin black streak of lead. It exuded a terrible menace.

A violent urge gripped him. He must turn his ship in the opposite direction, run to the south, flee, away from what lay ahead.

Then a sudden rage enveloped him, absorbing the fear. He lifted his right arm and smashed his fist down onto the chart table. Instruments jumped; the bottle fell to the deck. The impact sent a stinging pain up through his wrist.

Focusing on the pain, he jammed his mind into furious concentration. He glanced up at the chronometer. It was 1:41.

Mentally, he estimated how far the ship had traveled since his Polaris shot, and he marked the chart point. He then measured the distance from it to the intersection of the two course lines. Next, using the ship's speed and drift, he calculated the time to convergence.

Twenty-seven minutes.

At two o'clock, Jack unsheathed the sextant and stepped onto the starboard wing. It was a windless night with a quarter moon lying just above the western horizon. It sent a shimmering silvery pathway across the sea.

Fixing on Polaris, he took a quick sighting and returned to the bridge. He consulted the Bowditch, logged the time and position coordinates, then returned the logbook to its slot in the binnacle.

Tun was at the wheel. Ashdown leaned back slightly to check the compass. Heading 279 degrees. The little Malaysian had the lubber's line dead on.

One minute later, O'Mallaugh came onto the bridge. Without a word, he crossed to stand before one of the small forward windows, hands clasped behind his back. Out there on the deck, the lowering moon threw long blue-white shadows.

Seconds passed. A minute.

At last, the captain turned and looked at the clock on the starboard bulkhead. "Prepare for starboard turn," he barked. "Bring her to heading zero-zero-four degrees."

Instantly Jack repeated the heading. To Tun, he said, "Stand by to change course."

"Aye, sor."

He stepped around the wheel and pulled the annunciator handle down to HALF SPEED. Bells sounded. A few seconds passed, and then he caught the slight change in engine sound and felt the gentle pull of inertia as the *Bengal* slowed.

"Right to zero-zero-four degrees."

Tun repeated and eased the wheel over.

There was a momentary lag and then the ship, sluggishly at first, then smoother, began to swing to starboard. The compass moved under the lubber's line.

Jack glanced over at the captain. In O'Mallaugh's gaunt, pallid face, his eyes blazed. The fierceness of the stare startled Ashdown for a second, distracted him.

What the hell?

But he quickly came back to the compass. "Coming to three-two-zero," he called out. "Begin easing off."

"Easing off," Tun answered. His hands were white-knuckled on the wheel.

Gradually, the *Bengal*'s turn slackened. Jack could now hear the whoosh of the ship's prop wash. Under the lubber's line, the compass drifted lazily, trembling.

330 . . .

345 . . .

"Counter the helm," he snapped.

"Counter helm."

"Call it."

A few seconds passed, the *Bengal* straightening.

Tun said, "I have zero-zero-four degrees, sor."

"Maintain."

Jack waited a full minute while the ship settled to her new heading, then returned the annunciator handle back to FULL AHEAD. The bells rang. As their sound died, O'Mallaugh lunged through the door.

Ashdown logged the course change, then walked to the forward window and gazed out thoughtfully. Something was up. Where in hell were they going now? Had all their suspicions about contraband been wrong? Or had the supposed pickup boats simply failed to show?

Maybe O'Mallaugh had chosen to shelter, at Cabo Rojo or Mayagüez in Puerto Rico, perhaps Romana in the Dominican Republic. But that didn't make sense. Why would he scurry to a lee port so soon? The hurricane was still moving in the Atlantic and showing no indication of crossing south into the Caribbean Sea.

He turned and walked to the small chart slot below the flag rack, slipped out the top map. Locked out of the chart room, he had been keeping his own course track on this smaller chart.

He unrolled it onto the wheel's hydraulic box. His track symbols marked off the progress of the *Bengal* since she had passed through the Lessers—all except his last sextant sighting. He marked these coordinates. His eyes lifted, tracing out the new heading.

004 degrees.

"Sweet Jesus," he murmured, and an icy chill crept across his shoulders. They weren't bound for the coasts of either Puerto Rico or the Republic. Instead, the new heading would send them dead-center through the Mona Passage.

*O'Mallaugh was taking the* Bengal *back into the Atlantic, into the storm.*

THE SOFT BUZZ OF ANHOLT'S TRAVEL CLOCK WENT OFF. Instantly, he sat up, tiredly rubbing the two-day stubble on his face. He was on the couch in his office. He'd managed to get three hours of sleep, and it was now 6:01 A.M.

The NHC was operating full-up now. Both day-and night-shift employees were remaining on station around the clock and grabbing sleep whenever they could in the small Ready Room dorm.

He stood and went into the tiny office bathroom, brushed his teeth and washed his face. He felt thick-headed, heavy in the body tissues. Popping a Certs into his mouth, he headed out the door.

As he passed the director's office, Newhouse's secretary, June, poked her head out the door. ''Morning, Warren.''

''Hi, Junie. What's the word on Allen?''

''Still in intensive. But I wanted to remind you that you've got a TV interview at six-ten. They're setting up now.''

The channel 4 people had requested that the interview be held up on the NHC building roof—a dramatic effect,

**193**

with the plethora of antennae and radar dishes in the background.

"Right."

In the TAFS section room, he held a short update conference with Jacoby, Tanaka and Phil Deyer of Operations. Captain Lorrin Breedlove, the center's air force liaison officer, sat in. Around the room, workstation monitors showed model grids and scrolling data sets along with three-dimensional satellite pictures of Emma.

Tanaka started the round-robin. "She's now about 350 miles from Puerto Rico," he said. "The frontal edge should reach San Juan in about nineteen hours. But she's still holding to Category 2—sustained winds at ninety-eight, gusts to one-ten."

"Well, that's hopeful," Warren said.

"Pressure readings in the outer rain bands are at 993.6 millibars," Tanaka continued. "Internals range from 988 to 968. The eye's showing 948.3, nearly a ten-percent drop from the wall wind field. And she's moving pretty fast, between seventeen and nineteen knots."

Anholt scratched at his stubble. "At least we might get lucky and she won't cross heat."

A Category-2 hurricane, though dangerous, usually created only moderate damage once it made landfall. If, however, it passed over warmer surface water, it would immediately feed off it. Wind velocities would increase and internal pressures drop rapidly, intensifying its power.

Anholt glanced at Jacoby. "Laura?"

"So far, all our results are giving nearly identical track forecasts: a northward curve starting in the Bahamas and then tightening to parallel the south Florida coast. She should come ashore around Jacksonville and probably turn back to sea between Wilmington and Morehead City, North Carolina."

Jacoby's section was now running all model systems: the HURRAN analog model, which used data from hurricanes as far back as 1886 to glean potential track lines, and the CLIPER, NHC-83 and SANBAR models, which were statistical regression systems that created track and intensity predictions by analyzing climatology and range of persistence equations, deep layer potentials, and wind field and cloud patterns.

Anholt grunted. "That's a good chunk of coastline. What's the PE?"

"A bit dicey. Could be as high as twenty percent."

The PE was the prediction error inherent in all forecasts. It was the difference between the projected track and the actual track of the storm. As the forecast time increased from twenty-four to seventy-two hours, the PE percentages also increased.

"What's landfall estimate?"

"Seventy-two to seventy-five hours."

Anholt sighed and turned back to Tanaka. "All right, Harry, you better crank up SLOSH."

"Right."

The SLOSH model was used to show the vulnerability to flooding from the storm surge at specific coastal locations along the hurricane's path. By using bathymetry data and topographical mapping, the grid results would pinpoint danger zones for possible evacuation.

Warren glanced at his watch—6:58. He'd have just time enough to shave, toss on a clean shirt and get to the roof for the interview. He glanced at Deyer. "Phil, I want you to handle the NWS update. You know the drill."

"Will do."

"Okay, people, keep cracking," Anholt said and headed for the door.

## TEL AVIV

All through the day, Leigh-Simmons had the distinct feeling he was falling out of the loop. Ever since he'd told Cairncross about the Ascension Island radio logs, which indicated that the *Bengal* might be headed west, his conversations with the MI-6 director had trailed off.

Then, at noon, Cairncross informed him that they had

uncovered positive proof that the *Bengal* was in South American waters. A French weather ship called the *Baraka*, anchored off the French Guiana coast, offered them an actual sighting.

The two captains had spoken, and O'Mallaugh had openly identified himself. He'd requested permission and instructions to enter the Sinnamary River. He claimed he was headed for a small river town called Mana. Apparently, the *Bengal* had stayed upriver overnight, then exited the Sinnamary the following morning and headed north.

After that call, the conversations with Cairncross ceased completely. Instead, Leigh-Simmons' calls were taken by one of the director's staff assistants, someone he didn't know, named Oakley. The man seemed reticent to exchange data. Even a bloody bit cool.

Frustrated, around five in the afternoon, Nigel finally sought out an old friend, Hal Grantham from MI-6's Cypher and Radio Security section.

"Hal, Leigh-Simmons here," he said the moment Grantham came on.

"Nigel, what a pleasant surprise." The scramble synthesizer gave a slight warble to Grantham's voice. "It's been a bit."

"Yes. Look, what the hell's afoot over there on this *Bengal* affair? Cairncross has shunted me off to some damned tea boy named Oakley. Won't tell me a bloody thing."

Grantham chuckled. "That'd be Reggie. Always a bit stiff, that one. In any case, Cairncross has been in briefings with Denham and the foreign secretary all day." Stephen Denham was chairman of the Joint Intelligence Committee.

"And?"

"So far, general consensus is that the ship is definitely headed for an American port. Since the Grenada sighting, it most likely will be one along the Gulf coast."

"What Grenada sighting?"

Hal explained. Two hours earlier, a Royal Naval Intelligence agent had located a pilot who flew for a small Trinidad charter air service, A one-time RAF captain whose father had sailed on Liberty ships during World War II.

"The bloke says he spotted a Liberty off the coast of Grenada island," Hal went on, "on the twenty-ninth. Said the ship was heading west into the Caribbean Sea."

Nigel tried to form a mental picture of the string of islands that made up the Caribbean. He couldn't, exactly. But, at least timewise, this sighting complemented the one off French Guiana.

"He was certain it was a Liberty?"

"Absolutely."

"Well, that about locks it, doesn't it? A Gulf port it's to be, then."

"Unless the bugger's after Cuba or Mexico. But that's about as likely as a fiddler attending services."

Nigel thought a moment. "D'you know, there's still a mystery here."

"You mean, why the *Bengal* went up a jungle river in French Guiana? We think O'Mallaugh intended to retrieve something, probably smuggled out of the Ariane missile facility at Kourou. As you know, the Frenchies conduct secret nuclear research there along with their missile launches."

"A pence for a pound it was a trigger," Leigh-Simmons said quickly. "That damned Irishman needs a nuclear trigger for his bomb."

"Everyone pretty well agrees with that."

"Have the Americans been told of the situation?"

"Not quite yet. There's been discussion about precisely what line of communication to use. Naturally, it should be directly to the U.S. president. But he's at an economic conference in Mexico City at the moment. JIC feels it would appear too ominous if he were to receive a call from our PM and then suddenly head for Washington."

"So what's been decided? The foreign-minister level?"

"No. Those bleeding diplomat types move too slowly.

We'll probably go through the intelligence network instead. Denham to his CIA counterpart, Hershhaur.''

"What about the Israelis? Do they intend for me to inform the Mossad of this new development?"

"I doubt it. JIC thinks it would be wiser to let them remain on high watch, along with keeping our naval units in the Med. There's a chance O'Mallaugh could still go after Israel, you know. A hurricane's out in the Atlantic right now, but he could always shelter and then cross over afterward.''

"The bastard would have to be damned tricky to evade being seen for that long.''

"I suspect he hasn't the least idea we know he's in the Caribbean." Hal snorted contempuously. "The arrogant bugger probably thinks he's still invisible out there. Intends to keep us all looking the Charlie.''

"So far he has.''

"Indeed. Hold a sec, would you?" Grantham spoke to someone, then came back. "Sorry, Nigel, have to rush off. Look, I'll try to keep you in the link.''

"Thanks, Hal.'' He rang off.

For a long moment, Leigh-Simmons sat at his desk staring at the phone. Finally he took a sip of his tea. It was cold. He felt suddenly very useless.


### CENTRAL INTELLIGENCE AGENCY
### LANGLEY, VIRGINIA

At precisely 1:03 P.M. Eastern Standard Time, a coded telex was received from the CRS section of MI-6 headquarters in London. It stated that the chairman of the Joint Intelligence Committee was requesting immediate contact with CIA director, Andrew Hershhaur. The request was taglined ULTRA URGENT.

Hershhaur was in a meeting with two members of his accounts department. It was always a crappy task, pruning appropriations requests that would be sent up to the Office of Management and Budget.

The red light on his phone blinked. He picked up. "What is it?" he snapped.

It was his assistant director of communications, Alex Frankoni. "Sorry to interrupt, Andrew. But we've just received a Double-U telex from the Brits. The JIC chair, Denham, wants a one-on-one with you immediately."

A Double-U? he thought. What the hell now?

"Get the security line set up. I'll be right down." To the accountants he said, "Sorry, guys, gotta go."

The men left.

For a moment, Hershhaur sat frowning, bringing up the image of Stephen Denham. He'd met him several times in the past. A rather stuffy bird, as he remembered, but not one prone to panic. Something goddamned big must be up.

He finally rose, headed out the door and strode off down the corridor. He was a tall man in his early sixties with a long, horsey face and a receding hairline of gray. A one-time captain in Naval Intelligence, he'd been a member of Bush's National Security Council. Usually even-tempered, he could get nasty when the situation warranted it.

He entered the communications room. It was full of electronic and signal equipment. Frankoni and an operator were seated before a security encryption panel. Three red telephones were lined up in front of it. The operator immediately rose and stood aside for the director to take his chair.

"Denham'll be on line two in a few seconds," Frankoni said.

They waited. There was a buzz, and an internal light went on inside the second telephone. It lit up the whole unit.

Hershhaur picked up the receiver. "Hello, Stephen," he said. He could hear a slight feedback from his own voice.

"Hershhaur," Denham said in a cool British voice. "Damned nice of you to speak with me so quickly."

"What's up?"

"I'm afraid I have some shocking information for you."

Hershhaur's eyes narrowed. He waited.

"We have extremely telling evidence," Denham said,

"that a ship, at present somewhere in the Caribbean Sea, is headed for one of your gulf ports. We believe she's carrying a Red Bomb aboard."

"Good Lord, is this for real?" Hershhaur cried, knowing as he asked it that it was. He quickly scribbled on a notepad: *get tony*. Frankoni shoved himself out of his chair, moved to a nearby workstation and scooped up its phone.

"Unfortunately, *too* real," Denham answered. "Ironically enough, the ship is an old American Liberty called the *Bengal.* Her captain's a known IRA officer named Sean O'Mallaugh."

O'Mallaugh? Hershhaur vaguely remembered seeing that name somewhere, on some distant report. "Where is she now?"

"No one knows for certain," Denham said. "We have two solid sightings, however. One off the French Guiana coast, the other in the Caribbean Sea."

He explained the general situation, starting with the loss of the bomb by the Israelis and then moving on to the first word of the ship and its lethal cargo from the MI-6 station in Tel Aviv.

As Denham talked, Tony Persigian came in. He was in charge of the CIA's Crisis Assessment division. Hershhaur looked at him from under his eyebrows, then shook his head balefully.

The JIC chairman finished. After a moment, he added, "Of course, we'll give full cooperation in this, Hershhaur. Is there anything you'd like me to do on this side?"

"Yes. Would you allow us access to your files on this? Combined with our own area data, maybe something might pop up that you've missed."

Denham was silent for a long moment, obviously a bit perturbed by the reference that his people had missed *anything*. At last, he said, "Yes, I suppose something can be worked out. A certain *limited* access. Instruct your people to enter through our A Branch port."

A Branch, nicknamed the Watchers, was MI-6's Counterintelligence department. Denham gave Hershhaur the day's entry code.

"All right, I have it," he said. "Thank you, Stephen."

"Yes, well, let's hope we can check this ungodly thing in time. Good luck."

The line buzzed.

As Hershhaur put down the receiver, Persigian said, "What the hell's happened?"

The director told him. Persigian's face showed no emotion, but his eyes grew narrower and narrower. When Hershhaur finished, he simply said, "Christ Almighty."

Hershhaur stared off into space, thinking. His Middle East agents had been diligently investigating the sudden upclick of security in Israel, along with the British repositioning of naval units in the Med. Sources, particularly out of Cairo, had been slowly illuminating a trail. It was obvious that somebody was going to hit the Israelis. But like Mossad, the CIA focus had been on Iraq and the KIE.

He disgustedly blew air through his lips. His people had screwed up, never even had a clue that the Israelis actually *possessed* a Red Bomb. Well, dealing with that was for another time. Now the goddamned thing was headed for *their* yard.

He turned back to Persigian. "Set up a Red Op meet, stat. At the Pentagon." He glanced at his watch: 1:31. Traffic on the George Washington Parkway would not yet be after-work heavy. He'd get there easily enough. "Make it in an hour."

"Right," Persigian said and scurried away.

The Red Op meeting started at 2:51 in the staff room on the fifth floor of the Pentagon. The room was dark-paneled with a large window that overlooked the five-acre central court.

Seated around the oblong mahogany table with Hershhaur were Allen Washburn, vice president; Admiral James Rebeck, chairman of the Joint Chiefs of Staff; Manuel Santia, head of the National Security Council; and Herbert For-sell, director of the FBI.

Normally, the secretary of defense, George Gilliland, would have been included in such a meeting, but he was now in Canada.

The men waited for the CIA chief to begin, their arms crossed—all except Admiral Rebeck, who sat forward, el-bows on the table. At fifty-two, he looked thirty-two. A one-time Top Gun in Nam, he wore his blond hair close-cropped, and his light blue eyes were penetrating.

Hershhaur got right to it: "Gentlemen, we have a poten-tially catastrophic situation on our hands. We've just re-ceived word from British Intelligence that a ship is heading for our Gulf coast with a Red Bomb aboard."

No one said anything, but the faces of both Rebeck and Forsell registered shocked comprehension.

"The captain's an Irish Republican Army officer," Hershhaur continued. "According to the Brits, there ap-pears to be some link to Libya."

He quickly went over the data that MI-6's A Branch had allowed his people to download. The others listened si-lently. Some occasionally shifted uncomfortably in their seats or scribbled a note on the yellow pad each had been given. Only Rebeck didn't move a muscle, his eyes boring into Hershhaur's.

When the CIA chief finished, Rebeck immediately snapped, "Where's this ship now?"

"Somewhere in the Caribbean Sea. That's all anyone knows."

"Then we slam every goddamned ship and aircraft we have into the Gulf," the admiral said. "Barricade the damned thing. When we find it, we take it out."

"How much surface and air can we immediately put into that area?" Santia asked.

"There're several major fleet and air bases all along the Gulf coast. And there's Guantánamo Bay." Rebeck thought a moment. "We've also got two carrier task groups that were running a FlexOp off the Virgin Islands. They've been ordered out of the area because of this incoming hurricane, but there's enough time to send them safely into the Gulf.''

The vice president leaned forward. ''This Red Bomb, what is it precisely? I've never been briefed on the thing.'' Washburn was a handsome man with an easy, rather bland smile, like a slightly apologetic salesman. He wasn't smiling now.

''It's a small Russian nuclear device that uses red mercury for its fusion reaction,'' Hershhaur explained. ''Actually, it's a tactical field weapon, small but able to create an extremely dirty radiation throwout.

''The Russians were known to be working on it during the Afghan War. But there was never any hard evidence that they had actually built one. Then, in 1989, rumors circulated that a Soviet aircraft carrying two of these devices had crashed in a lake on the Iran-Afghan frontier.'' He shrugged. ''Apparently, not only were the rumors true, but somehow the Israelis actually got their hands on one.''

There was a long moment of silence. Then Santia said, ''Well, the president has to be told as soon as possible. All national emergency activation procedures must start with him.''

Everyone agreed.

Forsell said, ''Unfortunately, this is going to create a major problem. When he leaves that ECA conference so abruptly, it'll scream catastrophe. The media'll jump all over it.''

''We don't have any choice about that,'' Santia said. An intimate friend of the president, Santia was a sharp-speaking man with a weight lifter's shoulders. His father had come from Mexico; his mother, from a black township in Georgia. A grad of Stanford law school, he'd once played linebacker for the Washington Redskins. ''We'll just have to handle the flak.''

''How much do we tell them?''

''That'll be up to the president.''

''Well, he'd better be well aware of the consequences,''

Forsell said. "If he releases too much, there'll be panic in the streets down there."

Washburn had been frowning. Now he said, "Let's consider something before we go off half-cocked. Is this whole scenario really *true?* It seems to me, the original British sources were a little shaky. A single Mossad agent and a fired MI-6 operative? With just a theory as a starting point?"

Hershhaur shook his head. "It's far beyond that now. Way too much is checking out."

He went on to quiz the others for their opinions on the matter. starting with Forsell. "What do you think, Herb?"

Forsell nodded slowly. He looked like a young Walter Cronkite. "The whole thing's very likely true. Particularly since it looks like Gadhafi's in it."

"Admiral?"

"Sounds real enough to me."

"Manuel?"

"I agree that it's very likely true. In any case, we can't afford to assume it isn't."

The vice president inhaled. "All right," he said. "I'll call the president."

Rebeck instantly rose and moved to a side table where several phones were located. He snapped up a receiver and barked orders, then brought the phone over to Washburn and placed it on the table.

"The president's on-site security comm won't be complete," Hershhaur said. "I suggest that we wait for a conference line as soon as Air Force One is airborne."

"Right," Rebeck said. He turned to Washburn. "Sir, I suggest that you be very discreet when you speak with him."

The vice president nodded.

For the next sixteen minutes, there was a grim discussion, everyone inputting suggestions and exploring contingency plans and operational implementations. Eyes kept glancing at the phone.

It rang.

Washburn picked it up.

It was now 4:08 P.M.

Ashdown, once more on the conn, had just logged the end of the afternoon watch and was now entering his double up, the first dog watch. O'Mallaugh had turned the bridge over to him at noon, having taken the watch himself at four that morning. . . .

The captain had taken them through the Mona Passage, skimming close to Mona Island and then into the passage itself. To starboard lay Puerto Rico; to port, the Dominican Republic.

As the morning sun climbed higher, it turned pale, without rays, and a misty halo formed around it. The peculiar thin light made the high green headlands of the islands look misty. The ripe, earthy smell of vegetation drifted in the air, and flocks of seagulls and shearwaters came out. They raucously swooped and glided above the ship's wake, searching for garbage.

The *Bengal* cleared into the Atlantic at 10:30. It immediately encountered a long cross swell from the east. It was still windless, but now the air felt humid. The ocean had a slick, oily cast to it, the swells running low and far apart like ripples in a disturbed pond.

A half hour later, O'Mallaugh turned the ship to the northwest, holding to a course of 315 degrees. Now the swells passed under the ship from off the starboard quarter, giving the ship a slow, even roll. . . .

When Jack took the conn at noon, he'd openly confronted the captain, stood right in front of him so the man would have to step around to get by.

"I want to know what your intentions are," he demanded.

O'Mallaugh glared at him. "It's not for you to ask, Ash'dn."

"The hell it isn't."

"You just mind the course you're given." The captain tried to push past.

Anger flared up through Jack's throat, into his head. He again stepped in front of O'Mallaugh. "Listen," he said throatily, "you're putting this ship in the path of a goddamned hurricane. And you're also heading it for shoal waters. If that storm hits us in shallows, the swells'll break our back."

O'Mallaugh's jaw muscles went to stone. "You'll do as I say, goddammit," he hissed. "Or I'll see your focking arse in irons."

He continued glowering at Ashdown, then bulled his way past, shoving Jack against the binnacle. For a moment, Ashdown had a wild desire to reach out, turn O'Mallaugh about and beat him to the deck.

Instead, he inhaled deeply and slowly released the air, drawing back control. He glanced at the wheelman, a tiny Malay named Sungei who stared back at him, shocked.

He crossed to the power phone desk and snatched up the walkie-talkie. He clicked it several times.

A moment later, Tun's voice came on: "Aye, bridge?"

"Set up your working parties and secure for heavy weather," he said. "Lifelines on all weather decks. And everybody in life jackets."

There was a long silence before Tun said, "Yes, sor."

Jack walked to the forward window and looked out. He watched the bosun making up the deck parties near hold number three. And he wondered, with the safety of land disappearing below the horizon, how the men would react to the order to secure. To *any* order, now.

Earlier, as they transited the passage, the Malays had been excited at the closeness of land. Word quickly spread among them that the captain was taking the ship to shelter. They all lined the bulwarks, pointing at the islands.

Although never being privy to Collins's weather reports, most of them were wise enough to read the signs of an approaching hurricane. Now they knew they were heading into what could be very serious trouble. Would their fear of O'Mallaugh continue to keep them obedient?

He felt a swell cross under the *Bengal,* the ship rolling to port and yawing slightly, then rolling back. With anger still in him, Jack swung around to yell at the wheelman. Sungei's eyes were frightened.

Jack caught himself. Poor bastard, he thought. Instead, he said quietly, ''Bring her head back.''

''Aye, Meester Ashden,'' Sungei said.

Collins, too, had been joyous during the run through the Mona Passage. He'd actually left his radio room long enough to have a look at the islands himself. Jack found him leaning on the port railing of the boat deck, staring out at the Dominican Republic.

Keyshawn turned and grinned broadly at him. ''I guess the old man ain't so stupid after all, huh? He's gonna jook that Emma bitch an' tuck us neatly away in some port.''

Jack said nothing.

Collins shook his head. ''Man, she was makin' me bad in the head, you know? Gettin' too damn close. Radio traffic has turned heavy as hell, from all over. Hurricane warnings, aircraft reports, ships tellin' how they're gettin' out the way. All that shit.''

Jack remained silent.

Collins looked over. A frown slowly formed between his eyes. ''What?'' he said.

''We're not headed for shelter.''

''Say what?''

''We're going into the Atlantic.''

Collins stared. The pale sunlight sheened his dark glasses, reflected the yellow sky. ''Bullshit,'' he said.

Jack shook his head.

''Oh, man,'' Keyshawn groaned with angry despair. ''Into the fuckin' Atlantic? *Where* in the Atlantic?''

''I don't know.''

''What the fuck the old man doin' this shit for?''

''I don't know that either.''

Collins' face grew tight. For a moment, his lips pulled back against his teeth as if he were about to let go a jet of spittle. Instead, he blurted, ''You know what? That mother-fucker's *crazy!*''

At 5:00 P.M., Jack checked the barometer: 29.81 inches of mercury. He logged it. For a moment, he scanned back over his other hourly entries:

> 1300: Barometer 29.89. Temp 81F. Wind 2 from 063.
> Sea smooth with long low swell from 092, spacing
> 3.4 minutes.
> 1400: Barometer 29.88. Temp 81F. Wind 3 from 059.
> Sea agitated with low swell from 097, spacing 3.0
> minutes. Mackerel clouds from 090, sky ⅓ cov-
> ered.
> 1500: Barometer 29.85. Temp 83F. Wind 3 from 048.
> Sea slight chop. Low swell from 101 degrees, spac-
> ing 2.8 minutes. Mackerel cloud cover complete.
> 1600: Barometer 29.85. Temp 84F. Wind 4 from 051.
> Sea chop with breaking peaks. Swell steepening,
> spacing 2.8 minutes. Overcast thickening.

And his latest entry:

> 1700: Barometer 29.83. Temp 84F. Wind 4 from 054
> Sea chop peaks, occas. white horses. Swell holding,
> spacing 2.7 minutes. Overcast heavy, nimbostratus
> clouds visible at 098 degrees.

He made some quick mental calculations. The barometer had dropped six-hundreths of an inch in four hours, and the wind had increased two clicks on the Beaufort scale, from four to sixteen knots. The swells had steepened at least ten percent with a forty-two-second spacing decrease. As a storm approached, he knew, its outcast of swells always grew steeper and closer together.

The *Bengal* was rolling heavier now. He glanced at the clinometer on the starboard bulkhead and watched it as the ship rolled, peaked and then recovered. Twelve degrees.

The hurricane was getting ever closer. Using dead reckoning, Jack figured they should now be about eighty miles northeast of the San Francisco Macoris peninsula of the Dominican Republic. According to Collins's latest storm position report, that would put the hurricane approximately four hundred miles east-southeast of them.

Jeremiah poked his head through the door, glared at Ashdown, then disappeared. A moment later, Jack heard him pounding on the captain's door.

"Open up, O'Mallaugh," Pepper shouted. "I wanta talk to you."

"Go away."

"Come out 'ere, God damn you to hell."

"Get out!" the Captain roared.

Jeremiah came back onto the bridge, his eyes narrowed to fiery slits. He was drenched in sweat. Droplets rolled down his wrinkled jaws, glistened in his mustache.

He paused to stare at Jack. His lips drew back against his teeth. "That fuckin' Mick's gone total *shonky*," he shouted. He glanced at the little Malay at the wheel, then jerked his head at Jack. "Let's you'n me step onto the wing, mate."

They went out. The warm wind came up the face of the deckhouse and made little whipping swirls under the overhang. Under the thick overcast, the color of the ocean, etched with spindrift, had deepened to a blue-black.

"So?" Pepper said, his grizzled face thrust forward pugnaciously. ''Whot the bloody hell you intend to do about this?''

''Nothing.''

''For God sake, man, O'Mallaugh's lost it. Enterin' shallows in the track of a bleedin' willy-willy? Runnin' silent? He's crazy as a flippin' meat axe. You know it 'an I know it. The whole fuckin' crew knows it.''

''What do you expect me to do?''

''You're First. Either you convince him to shelter, or *you* do it.''

Jack watched him. ''You're talking mutiny, Jeremiah.''

Although he had not spoken of it, the identical thought had already entered Ashdown's mind, back at the very moment O'Mallaugh ordered the turn toward Mona Passage. Yet his deepest instincts, prohibitions honed by years at sea, had rebelled against it.

But it kept pushing itself back in, wouldn't let him alone. With time flying away from them like spindrift, he knew that, sooner or later, he might *have* to act.

But by then, would it be too late?

Pepper turned, looked forward for a moment, came back. ''Under Articles, when the safety of a ship an' its crew is at risk because of the mental state of its master, it's the duty of the first officer to intercede.'' His cheek quivered with anger. ''I assume you learned that in your fuckin' maritime academy.''

''It looks neat and clean in writing,'' Jack shot back. ''But we're not in a goddamned classroom on the finer points of maritime law here. There are consequences.''

Pepper studied him icily. ''Aye, we're *not* in a bleedin' classroom. And there *will* be consequences. This ship's packin' death, mate. When that dirty weather hits us, there's a damned good chance she'll break.''

He stepped around Jack and slammed through the bridge door.

In the engine room, the temperature had climbed to 125 degrees. Whenever a ship was secured for foul weather, all deck ventilators were spun to face the stern. As a result, the induction effect was lessened. Along with the increasing humidity, the below decks spaces had now become hellish.

Pepper came back looking grim. Vogel was guarding the throttle. He silently watched Jeremiah crack himself a Foster's. Finally, he asked, "What did the captain say?"

"Not a fuckin' thing," Pepper snapped.

Jeremiah went off to circle the engine, cocking his head to listen for a moment. There was a slight pounding in the low-pressure cylinder. He moved on, interpreting the vibrations coming up from the floor plates, gauging the roll of the ship.

In preparation for dampening the *Bengal*'s increasing roll, he had earlier transferred fuel oil from the number-six deep tank to the number two. Then, without command from the bridge, he pumped seawater ballast into the numbers one and five tanks, both port and starboard.

Afterward, he sent Vogel to test the water service piping in the shaft tunnel. It was used for emergency cooling of the steady and stern tube bearings. Meanwhile, he had checked the entire power panel, doubling insulation at vulnerable connections.

Despite the stark certainty that the *Bengal* was headed for fatal trouble, Jeremiah continued working from a powerful, natural stubbornness in himself. But the knowledge of impending death enraged him. As a sailor, he'd always known that one day he'd die at sea. He considered it the only fitting way to go. This was sheer idiocy though. Senseless.

After leaving the bridge, he'd even momentarily considered wresting command from the captain *and* Ashdown. Put both the bloody cockers in chains. But he quickly dismissed that. He was an engineer. There would be no way to get this ship to safety without at least one experienced bridge officer.

He came back around to the throttle desk, aware that the Malay boilermen and wipers were eyeing him with apprehensive, ferret eyes.

"That pound in the low-pressure cylinder," Vogel said. "What do you think?"

"There's oil caked on them ring springs," Jeremiah answered. "But they'll hold fit enough."

Vogel stared at him with his quiet, mournful eyes. "This isn't good, is it, Chief? I think maybe we're going to die here."

Pepper returned the stare and felt a sudden, odd rush of affection for the younger man. He smiled at him. "The game ain't over yet, Claud." Then, embarassed by his own emotion, he cut off the smile. "Well, bugger off with ya now. Go check them bleedin' feed pumps again."

Silently, Vogel turned away.

Jadid looked at his watch. In the darkness of the cabin, the tiny luminous hands showed that it was forty-one minutes after eight.

He stood, holding the edge of his bunk. The ship was rolling heavily now, pitching as the swells crossed under her. His stomach had become somewhat accustomed to being at sea, but he found it a tricky business moving around a shifting deck.

He switched on the cabin light, knelt and withdrew his satchel and suitcase from under the bunk. In the suitcase was an Uzi. He checked the clip and put the gun into the satchel, beside the wooden box from Kourou. Then he ran his belt through the satchel's handle and rebuckled it.

He eased open the door. From up the passageway, he heard Collins's radio: static-filled cross talk. He stepped out, closed the door and went down the stairs to the boat deck level.

He emerged from the midhouse on the port side next to one of the lifeboats. There was a stiff wind now, a thin warm rain in it. It made the lifeboat's falls snap against their davit posts.

The sky and sea were black, but close-in Jadid saw trails of white foam on the surface skittering in the wind. Feeling his way, he went forward, down to the main deck. At the leading edge of the midhouse, he paused to survey the darkness ahead.

The ship lifted slightly, rolling, and then came back, her bow pitching down into the passing swell's trough. A feathering of spray flew up over her bulwarks.

Slipping on the wet deck and banging solidly into standing machinery, he took several minutes to reach the anchor windlass at the bow. He found the forepeak hatch and quickly undogged it. He stepped onto the ladder and pulled the hatch shut just as a gust of wind caught it, slamming it down noisily. He locked it.

Heart pounding, he switched on his flashlight. The slimy red-leaded shaft disappeared down into dank darkness. He began his descent.

The ladder swayed like a sailboat's mast, and he heard the rush of the ocean across the hull plates and the creaking and moaning of stressed metal throughout the ship. Now and then it shuddered, the rush of the water's hiss rising, and then a boom as the *Bengal*'s bow plunged deep.

He reached the bottom. He squatted there, holding tightly to the ladder. He was panting with excitement and the exertion of climbing down. He played his light onto the bow junction, on familiar piping and wheel valves, and then the tank with the canister tied beneath it.

Gripping one of the pipes, he went to it. He braced the flashlight against the bottom angle iron, then undid the strip of cloth that held the canister. His hands shook. He pulled the unit free and, holding it tightly against his groin, sat down on the floor plate. It was oily, sticky-wet.

He reached under the satchel's handle, zipped it open and lifted the metal cylinder from its wooden box. As he did, his legs opened slightly and the canister slid away from him. Jolted, he watched it roll with the tilt of the deck and slam into a channel flange.

For several seconds, Jadid remained paralyzed. Slowly, the canister began to roll foward. With a gasp, he leapt to grab it and pull it back. Once more he sat.

His mind whirled—joys, terrors, memories, the thoughts

all flashing past, leaving strangely dissolving images like dissipating smoke.

He locked the canister between his knees, the beveled side up. Using both hands, he slowly lowered the tapered end of the cylinder's shaft into the canister's dish-shaped bevel. There was a moment of resistance.

Then the seal broke and the shaft went in, struck metal. He twisted it. Wrong way. The other way, and the shaft went deeper until it was solidly locked into the canister.

He skiddered his buttocks to the tank. He tried to fit the canister back under the cross brace, where it had been tied. But it would no longer fit with the shaft connected.

He finally worked it around until he was able to tie it to the tank stanchion. He took off his belt and wound it over the strip of cloth to secure the full weight. The domed end of the shaft with its twin drill holes and indicator window were now facing him.

He untaped the needle punch from the cylinder and tried to insert it into the left hole. His hands shook so violently that he kept missing it. At last he got it in and pushed the tip down until he felt a tiny click. Instantly, the indicator window lit up with a preset—a glowing red field with white numbers: 28.92.

He paused, overcome with emotion. The moment was here. One final act, and his mission would be completed. He closed his eyes and slowed his thoughts until his mind drew up the scene, the one that had transfixed his heart, had haunted and driven him for nine years. . . .

*They came on an April dawn when the sun was still below the peaks of the Zagros. The Kurdish village, his village, was tiered up the rocky slope in gray shadow, with wispy cooking smoke drifting in the cool air and mingling with the scent of apple blossoms.*

*There were three aircraft—Russian MiG-17Cs, creamy white and marked with the green crescent of the Iraqi air force on their tails and small pods under the rocket tubes.*

*He was on an opposite ridge, gathering his father's goats. He didn't hear the aircraft coming. They were just suddenly there, engines screaming as they flashed past, holding close to the ground.*

*He watched them climb sharply and then turn almost lazily against the ceramic gray-blue of the sky, each pivoting in sequence and then coming down again, one behind the other. Villagers ran from their houses to look up at them.*

*Then the pods were falling, tumbling like gray watermelons with vicious momentum. They struck the earth, exploding in the apple orchards and in the village itself. Boiling cloudbursts of thin yellow smoke swept through the trees and over the houses like a rushing liquid.*

*In the yellow fog, villagers and their animals began to fall to the ground. They lay writhing. The three MiGs disappeared beyond the southern mountains, sucking their thunder after them. In the sudden silence that followed, he heard the choked screams drift faintly in the still air like the bleating of goats from a far ridge. . . .*

In the darkness behind Jadid's lids, the scene dissolved. In its place was the face of a man, large as the sky, evil as Dajjal, the one-eyed angel of hell.

*Saddam Hussein.*

Jadid's soul brought up the hatred as it had done so often before. Now it was so profound, so magnificent that it made him sob. He began saying the *shada*, rapidly, the words tumbling over each other.

He leaned forward. His hand was steady now. He plunged the tiny punch into the second drill hole. In increments of five, the numbers in the indicator window began to change rapidly: 28.77 . . . 28.72 . . .

Click . . . click . . .

28.67 . . . 28.62 . . . 28.57 . . .

Then the last one:

*28.52*

He sat back. It was done.

At PRECISELY 12:47 A.M., THE PRESIDENT STRODE briskly into the Cabinet Room. Accompanying him was the NSC director, Santia.

Everyone seated around the huge conference table rose. Those from the earlier meeting—all except the FBI director, Forsell—had been joined by Secretary of Defense Gilliland and a Colonel Abigail Trautloff from the army's War College at Carlisle, Pennsylvania. Trautloff was an expert in small tactical nuclear ordnance.

The president took his chair at the head of the table. A tall, vigorously handsome man with well-formed shoulders and wavy gray-black hair, he now looked tired, and there was a slight puffiness under his blue eyes. During the flight back to Washington, he had been briefed and constantly updated by Hershhaur and Rebeck.

Six hours earlier, the Joint Chiefs had sent all military ships and aircraft from bases ringing the Gulf out to search for the *Bengal*. Commercial and fishing fleets in the area were also notified to watch for her. In addition, the two carrier forces that had been on exercises in the Atlantic were ordered to turn back and cross the Straits of Florida to enter the Gulf.

Also, SUBCOMLANT, command headquarters for submarine operations in the Atlantic, diverted two Los Angeles attack subs into the Caribbean, one from its patrol sector east of the Lesser Antilles, the other from south of Bermuda. The Atlantic Control of SOSUS was alerted to listen specifically for a ship bearing a Liberty-class prop signature that might cross near their sensors. SOSUS stood for the navy's sonar surveillance system: arrays of highly sensitive sonar receptors deployed on the ocean bottom of numerous areas around the world.

The president sat back, his elbows resting on the sides of his chair, his fingers tented. The tips of his forefingers touched the slight cleft in his chin.

"First off," he said, "I want to know precisely what this Red Bomb is and how much damage it can do." He glanced at Trautloff. "Colonel, I believe you're the guru on the subject here."

"Yes, Mr. President," Trautloff said. She leaned forward. "There's very little hard data on this particular unit. But from what we *do* know, it appears to be a small fusion device designed specifically for tactical field use.

"We believe the fusion material is an isotope of Mercury, Hg 204. We've never been able to isolate it ourselves. But we think the Russians successfully created a so-called type HgR2 organometallic compound of the isotope, probably using sulfur. The compound would be a red dust, thus the name Red Mercury. It would have a comparatively low excitation energy yield but an extremely high ionization avalanche potential."

"Which means?" the president said.

The colonel adjusted her glasses. She had narrow features and short brown hair that made her look like a librarian. "The destructive force would range between twelve to fifteen kilotons," she said, "similiar to the Hiroshima bomb. But radiation concentrations would be extremely intense, somewhere on the scale of five thousand rads per gram of air.''

Eyes around the table narrowed. The president asked, ''Would the damage be similiar to Hiroshima's?''

''Yes,'' the colonel said. ''Within the hot zone, destruction would be almost total—from impact and disintegrative forces as well as radiation burn. Farther out, the contamination would create varying levels of blood, lymphoid, brain, bone and muscle tissue damage.

''But even at a distance of two to three miles from the hot zone, the radioactive concentrations from this particular bomb would cause at least ninety percent victim mortality, primarily from brain damage and bacterial blooms within the intestines. Most would die within several hours to several days.''

Everyone just sat there, faces somber, absorbing the implications of what had just been said. Finally Gilliland snapped, ''If this thing is so contaminating, how could it be used in a contained combat area?''

''Theoretically, Hg 204 has a half-life of approximately sixty-eight hours,'' Trautloff answered. ''After that, the hot zone would be stable enough for ground troops to enter it safely.''

The president turned to Admiral Rebeck. ''What's the latest on the search?''

''Nothing yet, sir. With this incoming hurricane, there's a helluva lot of sea traffic entering the eastern Gulf.''

''What are satellite scans showing?''

''We're downlinking everything from the GOES-3 weather sat. But it has very limited multispectral scanning capability—nowhere near the resolution necessary to pinpoint a single ship.''

''What about our NavSats and KH-13s?''

NavSat satellites were part of the Global Positioning System used to pinpoint ships at sea. The series of KH or Keyhole satellites were secret space vehicles that scanned certain specific areas of the globe. The 13s, latest in the series, contained highly sophisticated surveillance gear including microwave and infrared scanners and three-dimensional radar imagers that provided resolutions down to one square foot, even at night.

"The NavSats are inquiry-pulse activated," Rebeck said. "The *Bengal* would have to request a position fix for the satellite to log a position." He turned to Hershhaur. "As to the KHs, CIA can better brief you on that."

Hershhaur nodded. "As you already know, Mr. President, we've got two KHs in the area, one that crosses over Central America, the other over Cuba. But their outer-scan cross sections don't overlap. That leaves a pretty fair chunk of the Gulf and Carribbean Sea in the dark."

"We've already moved to correct that," Rebeck put in. "Four of our 3A AWACS from VAQ 33 Squadron out of Key West are running TACAMO patterns over the dark zone. I've also dispatched a U-2 from Beale Air Force Base in California. That *should* cover it."

He frowned. "Unfortunately, this hurricane's shoving heavy overcast and squall lines across most of the area. That'll cut our imaging precision quite a bit. Even the radar scans will be somewhat smeared."

The president grunted, shifted slightly in his chair. "Tell me, do we have any hard evidence as to just who the hell's responsible for this?"

Everyone turned to Hershhaur. He said, "We think Gadhafi's involved, but there's nothing that absolutely points the finger at him. British intelligence did track links between Libya and this ship, but it's not that simple. There also appears to be an Iraqi connection."

"Oh, shit," the president said wearily.

"When this whole thing started," the CIA director continued, "the assumption was that Israel was to be the prime target—final, decisive strike by this new terrorist organization, the KIE. From the little we've been able to pick up about messages from the KIE to Mossad, it seems obvious to assume that Iraq is backing the group.

"But now there's a third possibility. Our deep plants in Turkey and Syria found some clues indicating that Kurds might be involved. Even the Brits got a whisper of it. In fact, two specific Kurdish men were mentioned in our Area Station reports. We're tracing the specifics on them now.''

"Kurds?" the president said, frowning. "Why in hell would they come after us?"

"That's an interesting point," Secretary Gilliland said. "I got to thinking about motive here, too. So, several hours ago I ordered Clark at JAD to run some mock-up scenarios using everything we have, including this Kurd business."

Scott Clark was operations director of the Joint Analysis Directorate, a strategic think tank connected to the Pentagon's National Command Center.

Using top-level military officers, politicians and experts in various fields, JAD ran war games, "what-if" scenarios in which the experts were confronted with situations and then continually challenged by computers. Their conclusions, called hot wash-ups, were then analyzed and used in option formulation for strategic decision protocols.

"Out of six mock-ups," Gilliland continued, "two pointed to Libya, two to Iraq, and one to a coalition of the two. But the sixth hot wash, after the Kurd data was input, came up with a whole different scenario. It said that the motive was revenge and the prime target was Iraq."

"Iraq?" the president snapped. "Then why hit us? That makes no sense."

"The mock-up lays out a theory," Gilliland said. "As you recall, Hussein slaughtered thousands of Kurdish people in northern Iraq in '88—used mustard and other neurological gas on them. Naturally, the Kurds wanted revenge, but they were helpless. There was only one option: a surrogate to do their fighting for them. A nation powerful enough to take out Iraq totally."

"That would, of course, be us."

"Yes. But they still had a big problem. How to get us to unilaterally act? And do it with enough force to destroy Hussein. The mock-up indicated a solution: a terrorist attack against the United States—one so horrendous that it'd enrage the entire nation, just as Pearl Harbor did. We Americans would demand revenge, immediate and massive.''

The president thought about that. ''But how would we be certain it *was* Hussein?''

''Through the false trail laid out by this KIE. Remember, two mock-ups have already shown Iraq to be responsible. This sort of thing is what we *expect* that crazy bastard to do. Once a terrorist attack of that magnitude occurred, there'd be no waiting around to find the smoking gun. No, every American in this country would cry out to wipe that son of a bitch and his regime off the face of the earth.''

The president's eyes narrowed. ''Sounds a bit convoluted to me.'' He scanned the faces around the table. ''Opinions?''

There was a moment of silence. Then Hershhaur said, ''It does sound out of left field, sir. But the idea connects up some otherwise disparate angles here. It could just possibly be true.''

''Jesus Christ,'' Santia said. ''Kurds? But where do the Libyans come in?''

The president took a shot at that one. ''Maybe they're the ones who are really backing these terrorists. After all, once Iraq was eliminated, Gadhafi would get a lion's share of the restructuring of power in the whole region.''

Gilliland nodded. ''That's precisely what the sixth mock-up says.''

The president exhaled tiredly, rubbing his eyes with thumb and forefinger. ''All right, let's put culpability and reaction aside for the moment and get back to this damned ship.''

Vice President Washburn spoke for the first time. ''What exactly do we do once we locate it, Mr. President? Do we bomb it? Board it? I mean, as soon as the crew realizes they've been spotted, they could blow that bomb immediately. And what about verification? We can't just destroy a ship on the high seas because we *think* it's carrying a nuclear weapon.''

''Good question.'' The president turned to Rebeck. ''Admiral?''

"Well, my first reaction was to take it out right away," Rebeck answered. "But that could be dicey—not only because of verification, but more importantly because we might cause detonation ourselves." He glanced at Colonel Trautloff. "*Is* that a realistic possibility?"

"Depending on the particular trigger mechanism they're using, yes," she said.

Rebeck turned back to the president. "In that case, Chief of Naval Operations thinks it would be advisable to put a SEAL extraction team aboard her, armed with radiation detection gear to locate and disarm the bomb."

Colonel Trautloff put her hand up. "Mr. President, I must point out that this matter of disarming the unit is extremely crucial and dangerous."

"Why, precisely?"

"All nuclear fusion reactions are initiated by a smaller nuclear explosion. They create an intense thermal energy environment, which then sets off the main reaction. The critical question here is, what exact trigger system is being used for the initiating charge? We have to know that before we can disarm."

"We know the ship stopped in French Guiana," Hershhaur responded. "Obviously to pick up something. It must have been a trigger mechanism somehow smuggled out of the French nuclear research facilities at Kourou. So the French are the only ones who can tell us what kind of trigger."

"Have we made *any* contacts with the French government?" the president asked.

"Not yet, sir. We were waiting for your decision on how to handle the approach. The Brits tried through the foreign ministry, without tipping their hand to the real show. But they were shut out completely."

"I think it'll have to be a one-on-one," Santia said. "You and Lariviere. If we've got to know about that trigger, we've got to know."

Everyone at the table nodded.

"Yes, I agree," the president said. He pushed back his

chair and stood up. Silently, he went to the door, opened it and headed down the corridor toward the Oval Office.

Even through the encryption resonance, the voice of the French president, Andre Lariviere, was low, throaty. It had a Charles Boyer timbre. After the formal greetings, the U.S. president briefly explained the situation. When he paused, Lariviere cried, *"Quell horreur!"*

"The reason for my call, Mr. President, is to ask for your assistance," the American chief executive went on quickly. "This *Bengal* ship is known to have entered the Sinnamary River in your Department of Guiana. We believe it was for the purpose of obtaining a trigger mechanism stolen from your research facilities at Kourou."

"Ah?"

"We must know precisely what kind of trigger it is in order to be able to disarm it."

"I see."

"Will you give me that data?"

There was a pause while Lariviere weighed the security implications of such a disclosure.

The president gently spun his chair around, looked out across the veranda at the giant magnolia trees on the White House lawn. It had rained earlier, and now the leaves glistened in the mansion's lights as if they were made of finely pounded metal.

He waited.

At last, Lariviere said simply, "I will seek out that information for you."

"Thank you, sir," the president said.

At thirty minutes past two, the president ordered the meeting to move to the Situation Room located in the basement of the White House. It was a spacious area filled with communication, coding and computer equipment manned by NSC and navy personnel.

It was busy. Every thirty minutes, analyses of the downlinks from the GOES-3 and the twin KH-13s were transmitted from Satellite and Analysis Command at Fort Belvoir, Virginia.

There was also a continuous stream of reports from the office of the chief of naval operations, Admiral William Becker. His staff was monitoring deployment status through CINCLANT and CINCSCOM, headquarters for the Atlantic and Southern Commands.

A total of over seventy naval ships, along with a virtual fleet of military and commercial aircraft, was now searching the Gulf. The *Enterprise* task force had already cleared the Straits of Florida. The *America* and her escorts were scheduled to begin the passage within three hours.

Elements from the Mexican and Colombian navies were also involved, although they had no idea why the U.S. government wanted to find this particular ship. Even Cuba had been contacted for assistance in the search, by ambassador to the UN Wendell Simon, who personally knew Castro.

El Comandante refused to speak with him. Simon informed the president and pointed out that he had gotten the distinct impression that Cuba's MINFAR was in a state of alert.

"They're plenty nervous over there," Simon said. "Their patrols have obviously spotted the sudden increase of military shipping in the Gulf. There's a distinct chance these people might actually think we're setting up for an invasion."

"Oh, Christ, that's absurd," the president said.

"With these people, you never know, sir."

Now the president led the way to a smaller, enclosed conference area within the Situation Room. Everyone took a seat around a large oval table. On the right wall of the room was a huge electronic plotting board showing the world. Coffee was served. It took a few minutes for the pace of the discussion to get back up to speed.

Washburn probed a delicate question. "Mr. President," he began, "I think we ought to consider worst-case contingency options here. What if, God forbid, that ship actually gets through our blockade? Actually detonates that ghastly thing in one of our harbors. Should we inform the public now? Get evacuations started immediately?''

The president looked at his vice president for a long moment, his eyes still in thought. Finally he said, ''I want some opinions on that.''

He began questioning each person at the table. All except Washburn quickly rejected the idea, at least for the time being. Total chaos would result if the millions of people living on the gulf coast were suddenly told that they might be struck by a nuclear bomb at any moment, with nobody knowing exactly where or when.

The vice president pressed: ''But what if it *does* happen? Hundreds of thousands of innocent citizens would be killed.''

The president's eyes flashed. ''Goddammit, Allen,'' he snapped angrily. ''We can't afford that negative 'what if' crap at this juncture. This ship *will* be found. *And* disarmed. I believe that. I must believe that.''

Washburn's eyes looked at him from under his brows. ''God help us if we're wrong,'' he said softly.

''We all better damned well pray I'm not,'' the president said.

He turned to Santia. ''All right, no public announcement doesn't mean we sit on our asses. I want every federal emergency coordinating organization contacted, starting with the Federal Emergency Management Agency. Speak only to senior directors. I want specific contingency plans and timetables for evacuations from every major port in the Gulf. They've got four hours to get those plans here. You handle it.''

Santia instantly came to his feet and hurried from the room.

The president looked at Gilliland. ''Where do we go for radiation experts?''

The secretary thought a moment. ''Well, we could start with the people at the Institute for Chemical and Radiation Studies at Price, Utah.''

Colonel Trautloff said, ''There's USAMRIID, the

army's medical research facility for infectious diseases, at Fort Detrick, Maryland, Mr. President. It has leading experts on radiation burn medicine there.''

''Okay, George, you take that. Same parameters. Be discreet, but drive home the reality of this thing.''

Gilliland left.

At precisely 3:41, Lariviere's call came through. The president took it at the conference table.

''Thank you for your haste, Mr. President,'' he said. He listened silently for a full minute—gazed at his hands, nodded slightly now and then.

Finally, he said, ''I appreciate this, Mr. President. The American people appreciate it. . . . Yes, I will, indeed. . . . Thank you.'' He hung up.

Everyone leaned forward, waited.

''A trigger mechanism *is* missing from the Kourou inventory,'' he said slowly. ''A pressure device coded PCU dash XO dash 14.'' His eyes flicked to Trautloff. ''Are you familiar with this unit, Colonel?''

''Not with this particular one, sir. But I am with our own prototypes of similiar units. They're all designed for low-altitude detonations of nuclear missile warheads. The reaction mechanism initiates as soon as a preset pressure level is achieved. Under normal conditions, the drop in atmospheric pressure near the earth is one inch per thousand feet. So, once a missile reaches an altitude with an ambient pressure level equal to the preset, the trigger will immediately detonate. Its focused thermal field, usually in the range of one-five-thousandths of a kiloton, then starts the primary bomb reaction.''

''Lariviere said this one had a preset range of three. What does that mean?''

All eyes turned back to Trautloff.

She nodded slowly. There was a tiny frown between her eyes now. ''They're using an aneroid barometer, sir,'' she answered, ''so the trigger setting window will show the pressure in inches of mercury rather than in millibars. The three indicates that they can preset the triggering pressure down as much as three inches below the normal sea-level pressure of 29.92.

"In order to prevent accidental detonation on the ground, a base level is always used—usually the pressure that would exist at a thousand-foot altitude, or 28.92 inches."

She stopped. Her frown deepened. For a moment, she stared straight ahead.

The president noted it. "Problem?" he asked.

The colonel drew her attention back. "It's just that I find this very unusual, sir. There's no way a bomb on a ship at sea level could be detonated by this type of—"

She stopped abruptly. For a second, her gaze lifted, something working deep in her eyes. Then they shot open. The blood drained out of her face, and her lips parted. "Oh, my God!" she gasped.

The president leaned forward tensely. "Colonel? What is it?"

"That ship," Trautloff cried, her voice thick with shock. "It isn't in the Gulf at all. It's heading for the hurricane!"

After roaring by the British Virgin Islands, the eye of Emma lay ninety miles north of San Juan, Puerto Rico, by 4 A.M.

Fortunately, the Virgins were on the periphery of the storm, and damage was moderate—except on the islands of Sombrero, Anegada and Tortola, where torrential rains and a twelve-foot storm surge had created serious coastal flooding.

The hurricane was still a Category 2 but seemed to be increasing in force. Fly-through data showed that eye-wall wind fields contained sustained winds of 108 miles per hour with gusts reaching 140. The storm's forward speed had increased slightly, and its track was now showing a twenty-degree veer to the north.

The fisherman was a short Portuguese with a knife scar on his cheek and a wrinkled bald head. Pimpled with drop-lets of rain, it looked like a cantaloupe. He was wrapped in a red blanket that the winchman, Escalera, had given him. Still, he shivered, squatting beside Ana Castile's command seat.

The Helix jerked and slewed in the strong wind gusts that were now registering nearly forty knots. Now and then it spooled up in a rush, the engines overspeeding for a moment to compensate for the sudden rotor loading. Then the governors caught up, and it would drop sharply before finally recovering.

Ana expertly maintained control, anticipating the gusting patterns. Her face was tense, her lips unconsciously working between her teeth as she focused.

The fisherman leaned forward now and tried to kiss her hand on the stick. His eyes watered with gratitude. His fishing boat had gone down sometime during the night, about a hundred miles north of Cabo Isabela off the Dominican Republic.

They had picked him up from a small rubber raft six minutes before, homing to his emergency radio. It was a very touchy rescue, the harness line blowing out in the wind with the ocean, fifty feet below, a churning cauldron of wind-slashed water the color of gunmetal, with swells running twenty-five feet.

The fisherman shifted his legs. He pulled at Ana's sleeve, slapped his hands together twice and then chopped his arm in the air toward the right, as if indicating something in that direction. She glanced down at him.

He jabbered excitedly in Portuguese, his eyes suddenly flashing with anger. *"Eh vi o barco de cargo,"* he shouted over the roar of the engines and wind. *"Mas O Capetao Deixoume!"*

Is there someone else out there? Ana thought.

She indicated for Perez to take the controls and slipped off her flight helmet so she could hear the fisherman. *"Que dice?"* she asked.

He started again, still speaking Portuguese.

*"No,"* she yelled back. *"Hable en español."*

The fisherman shook his head. *"No español. Inglês?"*

Ana nodded.

The fisherman grinned. He had a silver tooth. "First I must telling chu," he cried. "Chu are my sav-ee-or, *senhora.*"

"What were you pointing at?"

"A freighter, *senhora.* Before chu come, she go dat

way.'' He angrily moved his palms back and forth, an inch apart. ''Like dis close she come to me. I call my radio, I call an' call, but she no answer.''

''They probably couldn't find you.''

''Oh, no!'' the fisherman yelled agitatedly. ''I so close I see da crewmens. Dey look down on me, dey point. But she no stop, joos' go on. I can even see name on the stern.''

Ana frowned. A ship deliberately leaving a man helpless in the sea?

''When was this?'' she asked.

''Joos after daylight come.''

''What was the ship's name?''

''*Bengal,*'' the fisherman said. He lowered his head and spat again between his legs. ''Fuckin' shit *comandante.*''

Ana took back the controls. *Bengal?* It sounded familiar somehow, from some radio message.

But what was a freighter doing in these waters in the first place? With a hurricane only 250 miles away, all commercial shipping had already either vacated the area or gone to a safe port.

The jolting stick drew her attention back. They were at five thousand feet now. She swung to a heading of 278 degrees. Instantly the wind, striking them directly from the right, sharply slewed the helicopter to the left. Ana eased the Helix back, crabbing into the wind to maintain a correct ground course.

She fixed all her senses on operating the bucking, jigging craft—and was thankful for it. The concentration held off the terrible worries over Pilar, encapsulated the dark mourning for her father and the stunning knowledge of her husband's murder.

She had heard nothing from Pilar or anyone since leaving Valle Blanco. On the ground, her anxieties ate at her like worms in the belly. She became jumpy and quick to anger, even with Perez. Patiently, he had kept his silence.

Her earphones crackled. ''HCC one-four-four, Green Base, over.'' Green Base was Moa comm control.

Ana turned to the fisherman, pointed to the rear. He nodded and crawled away. She keyed, acknowledging the call.

Green Base came right back. "One-four-four, switch to Arrow frequency, over."

"One-four-four, switching." She frowned as she swung the radio selector. Arrow frequency was an encoded transmission system used by MGR, the Revolutionary navy headquarters at Punta Santa Ana, only during a national emergency.

She keyed her mike three times to indicate that she had achieved frequency. Instantly, a tiny light on a small encryption box near the Heads-Up panel began blinking. Long, wavering impulses sounded in her earphones.

Finally, the sounds ceased. There was a pause and then the encryption box display window glowed, showing the decode. She read the decode in spurts. It said: mode palmira in effect . . . return immediate alternate baracoa for refuel and ordnance . . . maintain vector two-six-eight at five and guard arrow to approach control . . .

Ana felt a tiny shiver of cold creep up the back of her neck. Mode Palmira was a full-up combat condition. And they were to be loaded with live ammunition. This was no exercise.

She and Perez exchanged a silent glance before she eased the Helix onto the new heading, still holding the seven-degree crab into the wind.

Both pilots had sensed that something was up at their preflight briefing. The squadron captain had been nervous. He repeatedly stressed that they diligently watch for American aircraft and surface vessels in their patrol area.

Then, after takeoff, the air had been alive with radio traffic, quick transmissions with an aura of urgency about them. They came mostly from air and sea craft out in the Gulf. Much of it was coded stuff transmitted on the frequencies used by the U.S. navy and air force.

Ana knew that the two American carrier forces that had been exercising off the Leewards had already moved out of the way of the incoming hurricane. Yet the strength of the coded signals they were picking up was very strong, indicating that the force vessels were still close by, perhaps had even turned back into the area.

Her heart went cold. Was it possible that the Americans were going to attack Cuba? She quickly dismissed the thought.

## WHITE HOUSE

The atmosphere in the Situation Room had changed. It was as if an icy chill had crept into the room, lodged in spaces, gathered at the ceiling. People moved with greater urgency, speaking in quick, sharp phrases. Faces that had been grim were now stark. . . .

After Colonel Trautloff's stunning statement, those remaining at the table had gone totally silent in jolted astonishment. Then Washburn whispered, "Sweet Mother."

The words seemed to rouse the president. He leaned forward and punched a button on a panel beside his two telephones. A moment later, the operations officer of the Situation Room, a commander named Hand, appeared at the door.

"Mr. President," he said, smartly snapping to attention.

The president nodded at the plotting board. "Can you bring up satellite visuals of Hurricane Emma on that thing?"

"Yes, sir," Hand said. "It'll take a few minutes to download from Fort Belvoir." Out in the main room, Santia and Gilliland were still talking on telephones.

"I want National Hurricane Center pictures, too. When you raise the NHC director, put him on conference."

"Yes, sir." Hand scurried off.

Admiral Rebeck said, "Sir, I'll need to confer with my people."

"Go."

The admiral rose, hurried into the main room and sat beside Gilliland. The president studied Colonel Trautloff. "What happens if this Red Bomb actually explodes inside a hurricane?"

"I'm not qualified to give you a definitive answer to that, sir," she said helplessly. "I'm unfamiliar with the dynamics of hurricanes."

"Who can?"

She shook her head. "This is such a unique situation, Mr. President. All I can think of is to put meteorologists and radiation experts together and run a computer model."

He turned to Washburn. "Notify Fort Meade that we'll need their big Crays for a model setup. Prepare them for data downlinks from the National Hurricane Center and from whatever radiation expert base Gilliland finds."

Washburn started away.

The president stopped him. "As of now, Allen, this is a Condition-One."

The Vice President nodded, left.

The conference speaker buzzed. Commander Hand said, "I have the NHC on line, Mr. President."

"Hold it." He turned and signaled Santia in.

"Is this hurricane business really true?" Santia blurted, hurrying through the door.

"Yes," the president said. He closed his eyes as he spoke to the speaker system. "Who am I speaking with?"

"Good morning, Mr. President," a man said. "This is Deputy Director Warren Anholt."

"What I'm about to tell you, Anholt, is classified ultra top secret. You share it only with senior personnel of your choosing. If anything leaks beyond the confines of your facility, you'll be held responsible. Is that understood?"

"Yes, sir."

The president explained, speaking rapidly but concisely.

When he finished, Anholt made a small choking sound.

The president had been watching the plotting board as it clicked through several highlighting steps. Now it was tight-focused on the eastern coast of the U.S. and the northern islands of the Carribbean. Superimposed over the map was the great cloud spiral that was Emma.

"Give me your latest update on this hurricane," the president instructed. "Start with the landfall forecast."

Anholt was trying to control his shock. "Well—ah—I—I'm sorry, Mr. President." He cleared his throat. "Our models show that it should reach land in forty-nine to fifty-one hours, sir."

Trautloff and Santia took notes. The president, like Hershhaur, listened with his eyes riveted on the plotting board. The grids were shifting, and data sets were being flashed along the perimeter. "How solid is that?" the president asked.

"Fairly solid, sir. A hurricane is very unpredictable. It could speed up, slow down, even stop completely. But at this point, it seems to be increasing steering speed very slightly."

"Where will it come ashore?"

"Our models say Jacksonville, Florida. After first touch, it'll move north along the coast of Georgia, then cross over South and North Carolina. It should move back over ocean somewhere near Morehead and the southern tip of Cape Hatteras."

"How solid is *that?*"

Now several satellite pictures of Emma appeared on the plotting board. Since the satellites sent transmitted visuals at the rate of one every three minutes, the pictures of the storm had a slight jerky motion.

"Our prediction error," Anholt said, "is now down to eight percent for a forty-eight-hour forecast. Unless there's a drastic and completely unexpected change in the storm's dynamics, landfall estimates will be very close."

"Excuse me, sir," Hershhaur said. To the speaker: "How far inland will the winds go?"

"Emma's approximately 238 miles in diameter," Anholt answered. "So, from Jacksonville to Savannah, the outer storm winds would penetrate about seventy miles inland. Beyond Savannah to the cities past Wilmington, penetration would be about 120 miles with the deepest at Columbia, South Carolina."

The president looked to the side a moment, then came

back. "In this specific scenario, if this bomb hurls radiation into the hurricane's winds, will it remain there? Or will it spread out into the entire atmosphere?"

Anholt was silent for a long moment. Then: "A very difficult question for me to answer, sir. I know nothing about nuclear radiation. All I can say is that essentially a hurricane is a closed weather system. Its winds remain within the system, continually spiraling around the center."

"Does it throw out any wind into the atmosphere at all?"

"Yes, there's *some* loss of the storm's winds along its periphery. But this volume loss is replaced by downdrafts in the eye, which are immediately sucked into the eye wall by centrifugal force. So in effect, the body of the storm itself remains almost totally intact."

The president blinked slowly. "All right, Anholt, I want updates on this storm every thirty minutes. If any conditions change in between, I want to know that immediately."

"Yes, sir."

"Also, your computers are to be linked with those at Fort Meade. I want everything you people know about hurricanes in general and this one in particular to be fed into their Crays."

"Yes, Mr. President," Anholt said.

The president closed his eyes, absently rubbing his forefinger back and forth just above his nose. "What's your estimate of the population within this storm's path?"

Again there was a pause before Anholt said, very softly, "Between twenty-five and thirty million people, sir."

From that point on, there was confusion within the inner sanctum of the Situation Room—angry words, differing opinions. The smooth crisis decisions portrayed in movies did not exist. Instead, there was a constant movement to act and react, harangues over technicalities, instant decisions born of momentary character flaws or strengths.

The SR's communication systems now operated at an

intense level—in and out messages, command center reports, data telexes. Also, it was packed with newly arrived people, experts and directors and deputies of this or that. Their faces were masks of individual coping. *Thirty million people!* Minds rebelled.

At the center was the president. His own emotions slid through indecisivenesses, terrors, angers, fortitudes. To relieve the tension, he paced around like a football coach in the last three minutes of a tight game.

Yet he did act. At 7:07 A.M., he activated the Defense Master Mobilization Plan, the nation's contingency program for actual war. Immediately, numerous subagencies became operational.

Evacuation logistics and mobilization would be handled through the JDA, the Joint Deployment Agency, working in coordination with the Industrial College of the Armed Forces headquartered at Fort McNair in DC.

At 7:31, in conjunction with the DMMP, he signed a presidential order activating national guard units in Florida, Georgia, and South and North Carolina. Federal troops were also put on ConOne alert.

Now he listened to Admiral Rebeck summarize JCS actions and recommendations. "We've turned the larger ships out of the gulf and into the straits," Rebeck explained. "But only cruisers and Kidd-class destroyers. They'll be able to handle the storm seas. All remaining vessels will hold station in the Gulf. It's possible that the *Bengal* could still be there. We're also shifting as much air surveillance as possible over and around the storm."

"Are you putting the carriers in?" the president asked.

"No, sir. In this scenario, they'd be useless. Once they got anywhere near the outer storm wall, they'd never be able to launch or recover. Besides, it'd be too dangerous, putting fighters into hurricane conditions."

"Dangerous?" Santia cried. "For Chris' sake, look at what we're staring at here! We need eyes in there, man."

Rebeck glared at the NSC director. "It isn't only dangerous, God dammit, it's also stupid. Carrier aircraft don't have powerful enough radars to handle that hurricane. And if we put them on the deck, their scan and visual capability in those squall lines would be zilch."

"But they'd be *there*," Santia insisted sharply. "We don't go in, we can't see anything, right?"

The president cut off the debate. "What about the AWACS?"

"Even their microwave radar capability will be downgraded," Rebeck said. "There's too much ionization in those storm walls. It absorbs pulse energy, distorts bounce."

"So what's our best bet?"

"Subs and SOSUS," Rebeck said. "SUBCOMLANT's already pulled two SSNs from their patrol sectors and ordered them into the area inside and ahead of the hurricane. They've also deployed the three subs from the *America* FlexOp. Unfortunately, the closest boat's two hundred miles out. That's a three-hour AOS."

He went on: "We might have a fair chance with SOSUS. Atlantic Control has good receptor lines north of Cuba and west of the Bahamas. If the *Bengal* comes within range of one of these, we'll have her."

"Is our Cuban KH-13 showing anything?" Washburn asked.

Rebeck glanced at Hershhaur, passing the question to him. The CIA man said, "We're getting good peripheral tracking, but like the admiral says, the microwave and radar scans are smeared. Belvoir's recalibrating to wash out as much as they can."

The president paused in his ranging of the room and stood there, hands on his hips, staring at the floor. "Son of a *bitch*," he said abruptly, then starting walking again.

Fresh pastries were brought in. Hardly anyone ate, but the coffee went rapidly.

A navy lieutenant on Commander Hand's staff entered and notified Hershhaur that he had a call from the CIA's Office of Strategic Research. Hershhaur took the call at the conference table. He listened for a few moments, then hung up.

"We've just hard-fixed the Kurdish link," he said to the president. "One of the men mentioned in the earlier report, a Mashhad Jadid, is definitely aboard the *Bengal*."

Heads swung around.

"He was picked up by the ship at Colombo, Sri Lanka. MI-6 tracked down the taxi-boat driver who took him out. The man knew Jadid's cousin. The cousin and his family are now being interrogated by Sri Lankan intelligence."

"Well, that's terrific," the president said sarcastically. "But it doesn't do us a helluva lot of good at this point, now, does it?"

Santia got up and went out into the outer room. He talked for a few moments at a panel phone. The president stopped in front of the plotting board and stared up at it, hands behind his back. His shoulders seemed somehow smaller now.

Santia returned. "I just talked to the director of the National Disaster Medical System," he said. The NDMS, like FEMA, had automatically been activated by the president's mobilization order. "He and Stussy at FEMA are coordinating every source they can find which deals with nuclear radiation medicine. They've already set up guidelines for the takeover of medical facilities on the entire Eastern seaboard." He lifted his eyebrows. "But we've got a legal glitch."

The president turned, scowled. "What?"

"Under federal law," Santia went on, "they can't commandeer any facilities or medical personnel without written permission from the governor *and* legislature of each state involved."

The president looked shocked. "Not even under the Disaster Mobilization Protocol?"

"No."

"Oh, for God sake," the president groaned. He inhaled deeply. "All right, I'm overriding procedure."

Both Hershhaur and Santia looked shocked. "But that

would interfere with constitutionally mandated state protections.''

''Yes, but it'll also bypass a pissant technicality in the DMMP statute. We can deal with legalities later.''

''Well, even your bypass order will have to be in writing.''

''Screw writing. I'll give it verbally. What's this NDMS guy's name?''

''Hoskins.''

''Get him on conference and log it.''

Santia turned, caught the eye of a panel operator and twirled his finger. A moment later, through the speaker, a man said, ''Hello?''

''Hoskins, this is the president of the United States. I'm verbally ordering you to disregard the requirement for state governmental permission to take over all local medical facilities and personnel. As of now, they're under direct presidential control. Is that clear?''

''Yes, Mr. President.''

''Then move it.''

Hoskins clicked off.

Washburn waited a moment, then asked, ''What about the press? Undoubtedly they're already in the loop. How much do we tell them?''

During emergencies, television and radio companies always offered their facilities for the broadcasting of essential information. Since the practice was not mandated except under martial law, the press, in return, expected constant and accurate updates from the White House on the particular situation.

The president thought a moment. ''For now, we keep this a simple hurricane emergency.''

''That won't hold them long,'' Washburn said.

The president paused, staring hard at his Vice President. ''It's either that or instant panic in the streets. Which do you choose?''

''But sooner or later we may have to come clean anyway. If we hold off too long, it could badly damage our credibility.''

"Well, you know what, Allen?" the president said sharply. "At this moment, I really don't give a flying fuck about credibility."

Washburn dropped his eyes to the table.

One minute later, the results from the Fort Meade computer model came in. It was called a QEE for quantitative evolution estimate. A Major Thomas Updike summarized the findings.

He started off with a highly complex explanation of what would occur within the hurricane at the moment of detonation. It contained phrases such as spurring of radicals, nanosecond track reactions, knock-on lattice displacements and ionization of gas phasing.

The president listened for a full minute, then cut Updike off. "Dispense with the esoterics, Major. Give it to me in plain English."

"Sorry, Mr. President," Updike said. "Essentially, the moment the bomb explodes in the eye, or ground zero, it will create a tremendous electron stress field. Immediate radiation waves will be hurled throughout the entire hurricane spiral. A huge column of superheated ocean will also be sucked up within the eye itself.

"This will feed the storm's internal thermal state. Wind speeds will increase within thirty to forty seconds to approximately three hundred plus miles per hour. Due to what is known as molecular swelling, the storm's rain bands will increase in size by forty to fifty percent."

He paused a moment, gathering further notes. Then: "The electromagnetic pulse from the detonation will create fields of eddy currents that will disable all electronic-based equipment and processes within a radius of at least two hundred miles. Also, through magnetic resonance effect, the explosion will be heard at least two thousand miles away."

Major Updike stopped again. The people around the table and those who had gathered at the door of the conference room were stark still, listening.

Updike picked it up again. He spoke flatly, unemotionally. "Because of ionization collision and decay within the rain bands, half-life contamination will be decreased from seventy to sixty hours. But the radiation fields will be intense. Mortality rates within twenty miles of the hot zone will be ninety-eight percent. Collateral contamination will extend to three-hundred plus miles. Estimates of contamination deaths are between sixty and seventy millions of people, with mortality occurring in three seconds to twenty years."

There was a general intake of breath. It sounded like the soft whispering of a breeze through a pine tree. People suddenly found it impossible to remain still. Now they shifted, turned their heads, fumbled unconsciously with pencils and pads.

"The QEE recommends," Updike continued, "immediate evacuation of track and adjacent states under conditions of martial law—the implementation of theater-sized operations for dispersal of immediate population. The—"

The president's agonized voice cut him off again. "Evacuate those people out of there," he shouted. *"Now!"*

There was a general scramble for the door. In a moment, the president sat alone, the soft slur of the speaker drifting in the air. Very slowly, he leaned forward, put the heels of his palms to his eye sockets.

He looked like a man who had just glimpsed a vision of hell.

Ashdown's anger was inexorably heating up, like coals blown into flame by the wind.

He and Tun were in the number-two hold, checking the timber lashings. It was pitch-black. The men used flashlights, their beams like shafts of gold. The cavernous space resounded with stress creakings from the cables and the soft groans of hull plating. The air was stifling and muggy and smelled of camphor from the timbers and sour dampness and rusted steel.

Now and then, as they crossed between center skids, a misty shower of water came down out of the darkness. The *Bengal* was now taking occasional water over her bow, and the wash back was finding tiny cracks and openings in the hatch covers. Water dripped off the tween-deck cross beams.

Jack swore. He had been timing the ship's rolls, which gave an indication of the wave spacing. It was now down to a minute and thirty seconds. He estimated that the rolls themselves were about twenty degrees.

Once the swells steepened enough to send the ship into deep bow plunges, the cascade of water would increase.

The timbers directly under the hatches would become saturated and start to swell, putting a heavy strain on the tiedown cables.

*Nothing sank a ship quicker than shifting cargo . . .*

Earlier, at midnight, O'Mallaugh had relieved him on the bridge, the man's face the gray color of soggy newsprint. As Jack brusquely went through the litany of conn transfer, the captain's eyes darted about in a confused fashion.

Then, suddenly, they narrowed, eerily, as if he had just caught sight of something distressful in the air before his face. Afterward, he stood at the forward window and appeared to be murmuring to himself.

Around five in the morning, Collins sought out Jack in his bunk. "I'm pickin' up an emergency call," he said. "The signal sounds like it's from one of them hand-cranked manpack transmitters. I think it's real close, man. The dude's talkin' Spanish, but he actually used the word *Bengal*."

Jack immediately went to the bridge and told O'Mallaugh. He suggested that they turn and begin a search pattern. Since the caller had mentioned the ship's name, that meant he was somewhere astern of them.

The captain said nothing.

"Well?" Jack insisted. "Do you give the command, or do I?"

"Get off the bridge," O'Mallaugh said quietly, staring at the bulkhead.

Ashdown was shocked, speechless. He stood there and waited. The captain said nothing more. Finally, cursing, Jack left and headed for the stern.

By the time he reached the afterdeck, he saw three crewmen up on the gun pit. They were excitedly looking toward the south. At that moment, the ship was passing through a rain squall. Thunder rumbled faintly in the distance, sounding like furniture being moved in an upstairs apartment.

Jack went up to the pit. The men pointed out a small yellow raft that lay out about three hundred yards. The raft would slide up the steep face of a swell, disappear for a moment and then reappear, bobbing. A single man was in it, waving frantically.

"Who first spotted him?" he snapped.

One of the Malays said, "Bow lookout."

"Did he call the bridge?"

"Yes, but the cap'n no answer."

They watched helplessly as the tiny raft drew farther and farther away until it was lost in the rain.

It was that act that finally decided something for Ashdown. Deliberately leaving a man helpless in the sea clearly told him that O'Mallaugh had passed beyond rationality, into some dark place where his instincts had become warped and disconsonant.

But even then, Jack's own reasonings, though profoundly repelled by what he had seen, couldn't rise above the same moral code that condemned it. To take the command from O'Mallaugh would be mutiny, and that was as heinous an act as the other.

With him thus entrapped, his rage grew. . . .

Now he paused for a moment, gripping a turnbuckle to maintain his balance as the ship rolled to starboard. It was getting more difficult to move about. He heard a peal of thunder come cleanly through the hull, jarring the stagnant air in the hold. A closer sound, booming.

Instantly, the sound drew a memory out of the darkness: that day in the rain at the small cemetery where he had buried his wife and child with the Texas thunder rolling across the prairie bluebonnets like an invisible giant walking the earth.

The old shame and guilt rose in him and brought on an ache to his soul. *If only* . . .

When Jack stepped through the main doorway of the engine room, a wave of watersoaked heat smothered him for a moment. It instantly pulled sweat from his pores.

He and Tun had completed their inspection of the forward holds. He'd then sent the little bosun with two crewmen to check holds four and five, while he headed for the engine room.

He moved to the edge of the fiddley grating and looked down at the floor of the machinery space. The air was misty and smelled of fuel oil and burning stones. The railing dripped condensation and was hot to the touch.

The grating shook with the slow, ponderous revolutions of the engine's pistons. He could just see the edges of the thick connecting shafts as they moved up and down in the crank pit. Beside them, the thinner eccentric valve rods went faster, like smaller copies hurrying to keep up. Everywhere was sound, heavy and pounding and clattering and shrill, all of it coming together into that deep, singular resonance of heavy machinery at work.

He started down. Vogel was guarding the throttle, leaning against the standing desk as the ship rolled. Sweat drained down his long, solemn face. He nodded at Jack.

"Where's Jeremiah?" Ashdown yelled. One of the main overhead blowers washed slightly cooler air over them.

Vogel pointed forward. "In the settling tank compartment. We had a coil leak."

Bunker C fuel is as thick as partially hardened Jell-O. To keep it moving through the lines, it must be heated at several points by steam coils—in the main tanks and also in settling tanks located fore and aft of the engine space.

Occasionally a leak develops in a coil, which allows water into the fuel. Once in the boiler, the water droplets cause tiny expansion explosions that can sometimes extinguish the burners.

Jack glanced at the control panel. The RPM counter showed forty-five revolutions. He started around the desk. The *Bengal* began a heavy roll to port as another wave front came into her from off the starboard quarter.

He braced himself against a bulkhead and glanced back at the clinometer on the control panel. As the ship finally peaked the roll, it showed a thirty-degree angle.

It started back, the deck slanting forward slightly as the stern lifted off the back slope of the wave. Vogel instantly slowed the throttle. Gradually the ship came back fully, settled a moment and then began a quick, snapping roll to starboard.

"You better shift ballast water into three and six," Jack shouted to Vogel. "Keep that damned stern low."

"Already done," Vogel said.

Counter-leaning as if in a wind, Jack went forward into the firing alley beside the boilers. Beyond it was the secondary electrical panel and the hatchway to the forward settling tank.

The hatch was open. Jack leaned in. It was half lit inside by a small hanging light hooked to a cross beam. Jeremiah and a Malay fireman were working between the bulkhead and tank frame. Silhouetted by the light, their crouched figures looked like hunters around a campfire.

After several minutes, Pepper came out, his legs appearing first as he pulled himself through the doorway like a submariner. He glared at Jack. His face and hands were smeared with fuel oil. Behind him came the fireman with the light and spacer wrenches.

Wordlessly, Jeremiah moved to the second boiler. He squinted through the viewing window, then picked up a lighting torch that hung from a small can of fuel oil at the base of the feeder valve.

The torch was a steel rod with asbestos wound around one end. He doused the asbestos with oil, lit it with a cowboy match and thrust it through the opening to the firebox. At the same time, he turned on the oil valve and then the air register. There was a soft woosh. He closed the firebox, gave one last look through the viewer and turned aft.

"Where the bloody hell are we now?" he snapped at Ashdown.

"I'm not sure. I think somewhere southwest of the Turks."

The two men moved along, tilted like drunken sailors, Jeremiah checking the main pressure gauges as he passed, tapping his fingernail lightly against one of the steam drum gauge tubes.

At that moment, O'Mallaugh's voice came through the speaking tube at the control desk. "Engine, stand by."

"Engine, aye," Vogel yelled back into the tube's mouth.

Jack and Jeremiah exchanged frowning glances. Pepper said, "Whot the bloody hell's the Mick got to now?"

They reached the control desk. Pepper took the throttle from Vogel. Jack picked up the power phone. "Bridge, Ashdown," he said. "What is your intention, Captain?"

No answer.

"Dammit, what is your *intention?*"

Still no answer.

"Son of a *bitch,*" Jack hissed and slammed the phone back into its cradle.

The *Bengal* began another roll to port. It deepened, the three men holding onto objects. At last it peaked out and started back, coming up slowly, the deck tilting down.

A few seconds passed, and then Jeremiah eased off the throttle. The great connecting rods slowed their heavy reciprocate pulse, and the main shaft shook for a moment as the prop cleared water and then re-caught.

The ship came back to level, began her snap to starboard. At that moment, the annunciator bell rang, a loud chirp in the engine noise. AHEAD FULL.

Cutting loose with a chain of Aussie cuss words, Pepper set the annunciator order and moved the throttle up. A few seconds later, they felt the heel of the ship steepen as her bow began to swing to the right.

"The bastard's turnin' back into them wave chains," Jeremiah cried.

Holding to a stanchion, Jack drew up a picture of the *Bengal* coming about, racing the next wave front. Mentally he clicked off the degrees of the turn, the ship straining as she heaved her weight and wave-driven momentum into an arc of constantly changing direction.

A minute and a half into the turn, a wave took them aft the starboard beam. The ship rolled hard over to port, everyone watching the clinometer, the dial swinging, jigging.

Thirty degrees . . . thirty-five . . . forty . . .

They heard the distant whooshing rumble of water as ocean passed along the lee weather deck. The *Bengal* stopped her roll and began a sluggish return.

At last the ship leveled out, the turn complete. Instantly, the annunciator rang again. AHEAD SLOW. Pepper answered and eased off the throttle. The RPM indicator dropped through revolutions, steadied on thirty-five.

The deck slanted sharply then as a wave front came into the starboard bow. Up the head went. There was a slight pause as the ship topped and then plunged down into the trough, the wave passing under the waist. Jeremiah eased off more throttle until the wave cleared the ship's counter and then pulled the RPMs back to ten.

Jack watched all this through slitted eyes. He calculated that O'Mallaugh had taken them through a full ninety-degree turn. To the east! He pictured a chart, the ship a tiny dot; off to the north somewhere, the Turks. Eastward were the deadly shallows of the Mouchoir Bank.

Why was O'Mallaugh doing this, he thought furiously. For God sake, why?

He looked up to see both Pepper and Vogel watching him closely. Their eyes were dark, their gazes constricted.

Silently, he turned and headed up the ladder.

## NATIONAL HURRICANE CENTER

Over the past six hours, Anholt had been frantically shuttling from section to section in the NHC, checking and rechecking data flows, running constant updates on his prediction models and generally coordinating the whole network of statistics coming off his own machines and those from the Weather Processing/Analysis Department at the University of Wisconsin.

In essence, the center had become the main clearinghouse for all data on Emma, and Anholt was the lead expert source to the White House Situation Room. He carried a cell phone linked directly to the president, to whom he gave his thirty-minute status updates.

Inwardly, he was terrified. A nuclear nightmare in the making! Sweet God in Holy Heaven. Yet he hid his fears. He saw the same terror in the others, in their eyes, a glazed numbness. He realized that word had leaked out from the senior staff people.

He tried desperately to assuage it, pushing the technicians hard so they'd keep their minds occupied. He did allow each to call his family, but he ordered them to say absolutely nothing about the real situation.

It wasn't until 7:30 that he got a chance to call his own wife. Her name was Jo-Ann, her voice sparkly and morning-fresh on the line.

He said, "Honey, listen very carefully. Take the kids and go over to your mother's place." Jo-Ann's parents lived in Naples, on the gulf coast.

"What?"

"Do as I say. Do it now."

"What is it? My God, is something wrong with Mom?"

"No." He felt a silent agony. "There's just a chance this hurricane might come into Miami."

"Really? The TV's been saying it should hit around Jacksonville."

"That's true. But I want to be sure you people are all right. Just in case."

"Oh, we'll be fine. Remember, we've been through this sort of thing before."

"Dammit, Jo-Ann, do what I tell you."

A slight, puzzled pause, then: "All right, okay."

"I love you and the kids."

"Me, too."

He hung up.

Now Elaine Martin called to him in the corridor. "Ah, Mr. Anholt, sir." She came closer, a pretty blonde who always had a dazzling smile. Martin was one of the staff assistants to whom he'd given the permanent job of handling updates to the media. He hoped her coquettish charm would distract.

She wasn't smiling now. "These newspeople are getting

antsy as hell,'' she said. ''Word's seeping out about the
extent of those evacuations up north, even rumors of martial
law. What the hell do I tell them?''

''Nothing. Just give out the normal stats.''

''But they're throwing hard questions at me.''

''Downplay them.''

''I'll try.''

''Do the best you can.''

In the TAFS room, Jacoby said, ''There's no doubt now,
Warren. Steering speed's increased dramatically. Thirty-
two knots. And she's leveled the curve. Headed straight for
the western Bahamas.''

*Shit.*

''What's the projected landfall now?''

''Cape Canaveral. Sometime over the next twenty-two
to twenty-four hours.''

''Will she fall farther out of the curve?''

''CLIPER and the NHC-83 say no.''

Thank God, he thought. At least all of southern Florida
would be spared fallout if—

''What are the pressure gradients?''

Jacoby tore a sheet from her printer and handed it over.
It bore a series of number sequences, ID words and in-
house code phrases. His eyes went straight to the storm's
pressure bands, focused on the inches-of-mercury readings:

Barometric field patterns
DS pack/aerial recon
2-10-97/GMT 0132

Outer ring (ref ts 5–6): 990.2 mb/ 29.64 in
Internals (ref ts 2–5): 985.4 to 970.1 mb/ 29.50 to
    29.04 in
Center (ref ts 1–1.9): 945.6 mb/ 28.31 in

He turned and walked to a window. Outside, the sky was
gray with overcast. He watched it a moment, seeing the
slow churn of high cloud.

At last, he pulled out his cell phone and punched in the code-number sequence he'd been given. There was a click, then another. Then a man said, "CVSD clear for voice sample."

He repeated the word "absolute" three times. There was a series of high-pitched squeals. Then the president's voice said, "Go."

Collins was strapped into his chair, hunched over an old Omega Marine Radio System manual range map when Jack reached the radio room. Days earlier, O'Mallaugh had taken all of Keyshawn's frequency charts.

"What's the position of Emma's front?" Jack asked, coming clumsily forward on the moving deck, grabbing for handholds. The radio crackled loudly with static, throwing hot needles of sound into the air.

The *Bengal* was now taking wave fronts off her starboard bow, pitching and plunging strongly with seas blowing back across the fo'c'sle and forward decks. Coming up, Jack had paused on the boat deck to check the wind. He estimated it to be about a nine, or forty-five knots.

Keyshawn swung around and looked up at him. Sometime before, he had caught spray. It had left tiny salt dots on his dark hands and face. He looked ill, jaw muscles taut. But his eyes held a hard bead, like shiny black agates.

Silently, he turned back, pointing to the coordinates he had scribbled on the manual map: 10:31 AM/ 18.8 N: 68.9 W. "There's where the motherfuckin' *eye* is at," he said.

Jack checked the bulkhead clock. It was 10:41.

He turned back to the small map. There were no latitude or longitude lines, and the land masses were only outlines. He tried to draw up the position. He estimated it to be somewhere north-northwest of the Mona Passage.

Since earlier reports had given the entire hurricane's size as over two hundred miles across, that would put the western front about fifty miles from them.

Keyshawn watched him. "This is bad, man," he said finally. "You hear what I'm sayin'? We gonna die in this motherfuckin' steel coffin.'' His eyes blazed with a flash of fire. "Fuck this shit, man."

The radio crackled with a burst of cross talk. It was faint and deep in the static. Jack caught only the words *tandem* and *checkdown.*

"Listen to that," Collins said, jerking his head at his receiver. "Signal ain't worth shit with this thing. The air's too full of refraction interference."

For a moment, their eyes met. Jack momentarily wondered why Keyshawn had not bypassed the captain's lock as he had said he would—tell the world he wasn't going to die. But he knew the answer. Collins was a soldier, trained to obey orders.

Just like him.

He went back to the map. Keyshawn had logged earlier position reports of the hurricane on the page, along with reception times. He chose the first and mentally figured the distance the storm had traveled to the last position; saw immediately that it was moving very fast, probably in the range of twenty-five or thirty knots.

*Damn!*

He slapped Collins on the shoulder. "Hang tight," he said and headed for the door.

The voices had started four days before, coming out of the cabin walls and the overhead and from behind objects.

O'Mallaugh, fear-sweating, his face tight as a thin sheet of gray leather over bone, crept about, searching for their hiding places. He peered under the wall chronometer; turned on the faucet of his wash basin, his head tilted to catch words in the stream; explored corners and heater pipings; shook curtains.

Nothing.

Yet still they came, sometimes whispering, sometimes screaming. They spoke obscenities to him, lewd distortions of sexual fantasies enlarged into monstrous incest. They spoke of ancestry and kin and memories deep. They murmured fragments of prayers and songs and poetry:

*You, too, have come where the dim tides are hurled*
*Upon the wharves of sorrow, and heard ring*
*The bell that calls us on; the sweet far thing.*

But mostly they spoke of death.

An inferno of death. Innumerable bodies writhing in eternal agony. Some moments, in the utter darkness of the room, he actually caught glimpses of these horrors, floating in the air. And he held his breath, lest he suck them into his own body, lend his own blood to their tortures.

Now he stared through the tiny forward bridge window and heard a voice. Had it raced past in the wind? His heart began to pound; his hands shook. He leaned into the bulkhead and gripped the railing, listening fiercely.

There, again.

Dear God, what was it saying?

*Black Hell!*

He frantically studied the steel bulkhead, glanced up at the cable wheels, the flying bridge light panel. Then he snapped around and glared at the helmsman, eyes blazing. The Malay looked back at him with stark fear.

"Was it you?" O'Mallaugh bellowed. He lunged at the helmsman, his body bending over the binnacle and wheel power box. He gripped the man around the neck with his right hand. "Was it *yow,* ye bloody fockin' savage?"

The Malay choked and gasped, pleading, holding wildly onto the wheel. O'Mallaugh screamed curses into his face. Then the *Bengal* lifted suddenly on another wavefront, shoving the captain hard against the brass-ringed searchlight in its slot on the power box.

*Black hell!*

Sweet Virgin, it was coming from the air. O'Mallaugh released the Malay and searched the bridge, his terror like a beast in him. The ship hung for a moment, and then the deck dropped sharply as she plunged.

He heard the cascading water tumbling and roiling across the forward decks, heard the shotlike drumming of the rain against the bridge house and wings.

*Black hell!*

Now it screamed at him, over and over again. He hung desperately onto the binnacle, his eyes shut. He smelled the acrid stench of his own fear, heard the voice still screaming, mingling with the howling of the wind beyond the wing doors.

And he realized, with a horrified, heart-gripping shock, that it was his own voice.


The door to the chart room gave easily under Ashdown's full weight. The wood was old and splintered around its Kendrick lock. He shoved the door open and stepped in.

A chart was half spread on the slanted table, a straight-edge and spanners laid across the half-fold. The ship began a climb up the face of a wave. Instruments tinkled in their slots, and those on the chart slid down to the stopper board. When the ship plunged, they slid back.

Gripping a map slot to keep his balance, Jack looked down at the chart. O'Mallaugh had marked the turn point with a tiny triangle, then drawn a line toward the northeast, trailing it off at the second line of longitude.

It ran squarely through the Mouchoir Bank.

He stared at it. The line had been made with a dark grease pencil. Even along the straightedge, it bore a slight wavy imperfection, like a flutter in the flow. A trembling hand?

His gaze went the other way. Due west lay the shrimp shape of Great Inagua island. He counted the grid spaces. Eighty miles across deep, open water. He fixed the heading.

*And in that instant, he crossed it: the point of no return.*

Quickly, he scribbled the turn coordinates on a Night Order form: 20.8 N: 71.8 W. Then he swung around and dashed back into the passageway.

In his cabin, he pulled the old Mannlicher shotgun out from under his mattress. He cracked the breech to check the load, then snapped it back. It felt heavy in his hand, the oil coat gummy where the stock met the steel.

A moment later, Collins's head snapped around when

Jack touched his shoulder. He saw the look in Ashdown's eyes. His own dropped for a moment to the shotgun, then returned to Jack's face. A tiny smile touched his lips.

Jack laid the Night Order slip on the desk. "Bypass the radio lock," he said. "Notify the Coast Guard and all ships within range of our position. We're approximately eight minutes northeast of those coordinates but will be turning to a new heading of two-seven-two."

"You gonna do it, ain't you?"

"Yes."

"All *right!*" Keyshawn said.

And then Jack was gone.

THE HELIX LIFTED OFF ITS PAD, THE WIND ROCKING IT slightly. Ana immediately put it into a climbing turn to the right. They swept over the outskirts of the town and the commercial airfield near the beach, and then they were paralleling the steep Sierra Maestra cliffs of the Canete coastline.

Despite the increasing hysteria coming from the MIN-FAR general staff and what had been said in their preflight briefing, Lt. Castile now flew with an enigmatic smile on her lips. At least one great load had just been lifted from her shoulders.

They had landed at Baracoa at 9:15. The Portuguese fisherman was taken to the base infirmary, and the two pilots went to Operations to file a prelim report on the rescue incident.

Meanwhile, their aircraft was refueled and loaded with ordnance: two modified 406-millimeter torpedoes and a half dozen magnetic-detonated depth charges in the weapons bay, and two small AS-4 antiship missiles externally mounted beside the front wheels.

At 10:05, Ana and Perez, along with several other helicopter officers, were briefed by a two-star captain on the staff of the DGI, the Directorate General of Intelligence. A steely-eyed man with very dark skin and stubby boxer's fists. He gave them a grim pep talk. There appeared to be, he said, an approaching invasion by the imperialistic United States. Under the transparent guise of searching for a certain ship, American war vessels were massing out in the Gulf. Also, two carrier groups were at that very moment crossing through the Straits of Florida. Some of the ships were suspected of carrying crack assault units.

He grew extremely heated, cursed all Americans for their monstrous deceit and greed. He shouted ringing El Comandante slogans and bravuras on the eternal sanctity of Communist Cuba. Then he extolled them to go forth and fight, to die if necessary, for their beloved motherland.

Afterward, the base commander assigned them their patrol areas. He paused before solemnly informing them that *Operación Espada de Sangre,* Operation Sword of Blood, was now in effect.

Everyone stiffened. *Mierda!* This was for real.

*Operación Espada de Sangre* represented the final, glorious stand of the Cuban people—battles on the beaches, house-to-house combat to the last man and woman. The crown of the scenario would be a full-out air and submarine attack against nuclear power facilities all along the southern coast of the U.S. In essence, it would be the ultimate sword thrust that would carry Cuba's fiery death into history.

The base commander then issued the patrol sectors and went on to remind them of the now-operational rules of engagement. If any American vessel crossed into Cuban territorial waters, they were to be given two warnings before being fired upon.

To facilitate this, he issued a listing of frequencies known to be used by the U.S. Navy, along with decryption cards. Although undoubtedly outdated, these would allow some access to the American naval ships.

Ana and Perez silently walked back to their aircraft. The air was clammy, and a hot wind came across the airfield.

There seemed to be an air of desperate, almost fatalistic haste among the ground crews. At the Helix, they separated to run preflight checks, Jesse in the armament bay and Ana going over the ship itself.

As she completed her inspection, Ana turned to her crew chief. He was a warrant officer named Olivas. He handed over the maintenance clipboard for her to sign off. A small slip of paper was clipped to the top of the OM form.

Her heart jumped. The note said: *Pilar safe. In American consulate, Grand Caymans.*

She glanced at Olivas. He said nothing. Helplessly, her gratitude rose in her, shone silently through her eyes. Still he said nothing. Yet she saw, deep in his own eyes, a profound sadness—the embodiment of all the tragedies and lost hopes that had become modern Cuba.

She signed the form and gave it back. For just a tiny instant, her fingers caressed his.

At two thousand feet, below a close ceiling, they passed Maisi on the tip of Cuba and headed out over open ocean. The helicopter rocked and bucked in the wind. Below, the ocean was a mosaic of gray and white. To the north and east were the dark, slanted lines of rapidly moving rain squalls.

Perez had been watching her closely. Now, on the intercom, he said, "What is it?"

"What?"

"The smile."

She shrugged.

"Pilar's out, right?" he said.

Ana looked over at him. He gave her back a grin. She nodded.

"So, what do you think about all this?" she asked.

"Insanity," Perez answered heatedly. "It makes no sense for America to attack us now. And to use such a flimsy excuse as looking for a ship? Shit, if they wanted to do it, they'd do it." He shook his head disgustedly.

Ana closed her eyes a moment, a thousand things racing

through her mind. She opened them again. "Are you prepared to die, Jesse?" she asked.

The ensign snorted contemptuously. "Isn't that what El Comandante expects us to do?"

They flew along for a couple of minutes, each caught in the web of his own thoughts. Their assigned patrol area was S Sector, a hundred-mile triangle with turning points off Haiti's Cap Haitien and Great Inagua.

At last, Ana keyed her intercom. "Check out those U.S. Navy frequencies. Maybe we might pick up something."

Perez first radioed their position to Baracoa, then took out the encryption sheet and punched in the first frequency. Ana went off intercom. Through her earphone, the air was filled with surging static. They both listened for a few seconds. Nothing.

Jesse punched in a second frequency. Still nothing but the growl and waver of dead air. On the third frequency, there was a clear signal, a series of sound pulses interspersed with whistles and sequenced hums. U.S. Navy code.

It began to rain, pounding against the aircraft. Some of the heavy droplets slanted in under the chopper's blades and were driven hard against the windshield. The wipers sliced off thick films of water with each sweep.

They tried the decryption cards. Each one brought up the same response on their code unit: non-key signature.

Jesse went back to the frequencies. On the sixth, he got voice. They listened to a slurry of intercepting transmissions, then a clear, one-sided conversation:

Click: "That's an affirm, *Clifton.* Op Diogenese target carries Liberty ship configuration, designate *Bengal.* Over."

In the silence that followed, Ana threw a questioning frown at Perez. *Bengal?*

Click: "We have ident confirmation on target assigned Kilo-3. A Panamanian Foxtrot-class merchantman. Say again your range."

Silence.

Click: "Repeating, permission to shift to Delta Quad op area and institute Sugar Pattern. Stand by."

Silence.

Click: "Affirmative on request to shift to Delta Quad op area for Sierra Papa, sector one-zero-three. Continue guarding Charlie two-two-three-point-niner. Out."

Ana went back on intercom. "That's it," she said. "There really is a ship out here. Pull our log and get the exact position where we picked up that fisherman."

Perez did so. He read her the coordinates, then quickly requested a position fix from the NavSat satellite. He entered the target coordinates into the helo's navigational computer.

Ana eased the Helix into a left bank, watching the magnetic compass swing slightly and finally settle on 099 degrees. She glanced at the computer screen. The target point had been fixed, and the aircraft's ground speed and time-to-convergence were automatically calculated.

TTS: 24 min 15 sec

*WHITE HOUSE*
*11:01 A.M.*

It was now nearly three hours since the evacuations had begun.

After a heated discussion, the president had decided not to invoke martial law. Immediate hysteria would have swept the country, causing horrendous internal reactions. One of them would have been a mind-boggling logistical logjam within the affected states.

Instead, the evacuations were to be carried out within prescribed national emergency guidelines. As a result, the communication boards in the Situation Room now worked at breakneck speed, ingesting and logging millions of bytes of data and updating source material.

There were over a hundred ships in the sea search for the *Bengal* now. Their positions formed ragged arcs from the shores of the Carolinas to the Gulf, all converging toward the hurricane like hounds to a lioness at bay.

Under the direction of the army's Electronic and Research Command, stockpiling of nuclear protection equipment was begun: TCPSs, inflatable decontamination field tents; nuclear surveillance meters; STEPO or self-contained toxic environment protective outfits; and XM-19 decontamination kits called NAEDS. Once assembled, the equipment was immediately flown into designated military airfields within the states at risk.

Meanwhile, riding the power of the president's verbal authorization, NDMS and FEMA were quietly whisking scientists and medical personnel who specialized in radiation medicine from their posts at universities and research facilities throughout the country.

In addition, field teams already in the affected states had completed their takeover of medical facilities and were now searching out and commandeering large, heavy concrete structures that could be used as protective shelters.

So far, the evacuations were running within acceptable efficiency parameters. Most of the people being moved had always lived under the threat of hurricanes and were reasonably responsive to the guard and police units that came to their doors to order them out.

Many, however, simply refused to obey. These had to be physically removed. Field reporters and their video crews shot the processes.

All over the eastern seaboard, journalists were everywhere, probing, trying to get next to officials to dig out the reasons for such extraordinary and massive displacements. They smelled an obvious catastrophe. But what the hell was it?

Since the expanding operation now involved literally thousands of people, dozens of governmental organizations and military units, it was only a matter of time before someone in the know talked.

To help hold off that inevitable moment, the president had left the Situation Room just before nine o'clock to take up his usual activities for appearance's sake. First, however, he met with key members of Congress to tell them of the situation. Naturally, everyone was stunned. The senator from South Carolina was speechless with rage.

Afterward, the president, his famous smile warm and natural, kept three low-key appointments and even ushered a Girl Scout troop through the Blue Room. Then he returned to the Situation Room, instructing his press secretary, Ron Phillips, to notify the press corps that he had possibly contracted the flu and would be several hours with his personal physician.

When Anholt told him of the updated landfall prediction, he momentarily lost it, stomped around the inner room cursing terrorists, hurricanes, the tendencies of humankind to destroy itself, and the general shittiness of being president. People looked down, embarrassed, shifting uncomfortably in their chairs.

He finally stopped before the plotting board. Dominated by the great swirl of Emma, it was dotted with tiny white lights that indicated the positions of search ships.

"Look at that," he snapped. "Ships and aircraft all over the goddamned place, and *still* we can't find that ship. I just don't believe this. It's absurd!"

There was a soft knock on the door. Commander Hand. The president waved him in.

"SOSUS's Atlantic Control just picked up a probable target, sir," Hand said. "It crossed their QA-4 array two minutes ago."

"QA-4? Where the hell is that?"

Hand moved quickly to the plotting board. Using an aluminum pointer, he indicated the position just as a tiny red light came on the board. "There it is," the commander said. "The QA-4 runs through the southern Bahamas. As you can see, the target's approximately fifty miles southwest of the Turks Islands."

"Is it a Liberty?"

"They're not certain yet, sir. Apparently, whale pods have been moving through those shallows over the last twelve hours and creating sound distortions. But the target prop is giving off a specific cavitation signal, very slow, with a profile of either cast steel or manganese bronze. It also has airfoil sectioning, indicating that the ship is at least fifty years old.''

"Will they be able to make a positive ID?''

"They're checking shipyard records. As I understand it, each ship has specific prop characteristics, so they're looking to compare those of the *Bengal*'s original sea trials with this one.''

The president studied the plotting board. "Is the SEAL team ready to take off?''

"Yes, sir. They've already been transferred to Nassau in the Bahamas.''

The president continued squinting thoughtfully up at the red target light. Then his gaze shifted toward the northeast and Nassau. "How long will it take them to get to the target?''

"Approximately two hours by chopper.''

He went back to the target light, a scarlet dot like a minuscule, phosphorescent ruby. In the huge expanse of the plotting board, it lay mere inches from the western edge of the hurricane.

Dear God, he thought desperately, let it be the *Bengal*.

Eleven minutes earlier, Jack Ashdown had paused before the bridge door, braced himself against the bulkhead and waited for the ship to take another header off a wave front. She heeled slightly to port and went down, snapping to starboard. He felt the pounding rush of sea sweep off and over the bow.

As the ship pulled herself free, leveling, he opened the door and stepped into the gray gloom of the bridge, holding the shotgun along the side of his right leg.

He scanned quickly. The helmsman's head had swung around the moment he stepped through the doorway. The man's eyes went wide when he saw the weapon.

O'Mallaugh stood before the forward windows, his huge

hands gripping the rail. He seemed to be staring not through the window but at the bulkhead itself.

Jack moved to the binnacle, wedging himself against it and the searchlight. He glanced over his shoulder at the Malay. "Note and remember the precise time. Understood?"

The Malay nodded jerkily. "Yes."

Jack turned back to O'Mallaugh. "Captain O'Mallaugh," he said, shouting clearly above the whirring howl of the wind, "I am hereby taking command of this ship pursuant to the appropriate articles of international maritime law."

At that moment, the port wing door took a powerful blast of wind. Tongues of air blew through the seams and made the storm chart, posted on the bulkhead, flutter.

Jack waited for the captain's reaction. O'Mallaugh neither moved nor spoke.

"Do you understand what I have just said, sir?" Jack asked. Still nothing.

Frowning, he waited through another plunge. Behind him, the Malay fought the wheel as the ship once more came up, things rattling metallically.

Now Ashdown stepped forward and touched O'Mallaugh's shoulder. He instantly felt tension there under the canvas raincoat. A knotted, steely power. His hand tightened on the shotgun.

Slowly, O'Mallaugh turned his head. His face was contorted, cheeks streaked with tears. He seemed to be sobbing in utter silence, his eyes quivering with an agonized despair.

"I am now in command, sir," Jack said. "I suggest that you retire to your cabin."

O'Mallaugh stared at him out of his anguished face. Then, just as silently, he turned and looked at the bulkhead again.

Jack moved to the power phone and rang the engine room. Pepper answered, the thick thrum of machinery behind him.

"Approximately one minute ten seconds ago, I took command, Jeremiah," Jack said. "Log the time."

"Bloody good-oh, mate," Pepper shouted. "Where's the Mick now?"

"Still on the bridge. He's lost it. Just stares at the bulkhead."

"Whot? Iron the mad bugger, fer Chris' sake."

"No. I won't humiliate him."

"Then ya best be bloody careful, man."

"Right. Stand by for left turn on the mark."

"Left turn she is." Jeremiah rang off.

Ashdown moved around the port stanchion and took up a position beside the annunciator. The handle was on AHEAD SLOW. The Malay stared at him. Sweat filmed his forehead, had soaked down into his oily T-shirt.

"Stand by for left turn," Jack ordered.

"Left turn, aye."

The *Bengal* shook and began another climb. Port heel, pause, hard starboard plunge. As she came free, Jack rammed the annunciator to AHEAD FULL, then backed to AHEAD HALF, the bell sounding twice.

"Hard left," he shouted.

"Hod left, aye," the helmsman repeated. The Malay swung the wheel four spokes to the left and held it. The helm power box chattered loudly.

Jack watched the binnacle card as the ship sluggishly began to swing her head to port. He could hear the direction of the rain shifting as it struck the forward part of the house, ceased for a moment and then came in against the starboard wing.

A few seconds before it struck, he felt the approach of the next wave. "Rudder amidships," he shouted.

"Amidsheeps." The wheel spokes snapped through the helmsman's hands, popping against his palms. Then the ship took a heavy roll to port, tipping hard and steady, the deck slanting dangerously.

Jack gripped the annunciator shaft, felt his feet sliding. He glanced at O'Mallaugh. His big body rolled with the deck like a metronome, hands looking bloodless on the rail.

The ship went all the way over to forty degrees before she peaked the roll and, fighting her own massive weight, began to come back. The rumble of ocean crossing along her port deck sounded like a train in a tunnel. Jets of water blew through the cracks around the wing door.

As she leveled, shuddering, Ashdown ordered thirty degrees left on the wheel. "Thurddy degree, aye," called the Malay and pulled the spokes down, his thin arms coiling with wiry muscle.

Gradually, the ship fulfilled the turn. The next wave took her off the starboard quarter, the sharp roll to port and then the snapback. But this time the heel was gentler.

"Hard right."

"Hod right."

Back the wheel came, spokes slamming the helmsman's palms again. Once more the power box chattered, louder this time, a metallic grinding like someone trying to put a car into gear without depressing the clutch. It slowly faded off.

He leaned over and read the compass chart under the glass face of the binnacle. "Ease off helm. Steady on two-seven-one degrees."

"Eesing helm. Two-seben-wan degree."

The card shimmied on its pivot and then crept slowly until it at last held beneath the red lubber's line.

"Rudder amidships."

"Amidsheeps."

Jack reached up and pulled down the horn of the voice tube. "Engine, give me thirty-five revs," he shouted into it. This would allow the *Bengal* adequate forward steerageway without the risk of driving her bow too deeply as the wave chains swept into her stern.

A moment later, Jeremiah's tinny voice came back: "Bridge, you have thirddy-five."

Each time a wave struck, the ship's stern quickly lifted up the incline of the waveface before clearing. At that moment, a momentary mushiness would come into the wheel as the *Bengal* yawed sharply to the left.

"Hard left," Jack shouted now.

The helmsman repeated and spun the wheel. Since the moving ocean was now crossing over the rudder from astern, all the wheel changes had to be reversed.

Slowly the bow yawed back.

"Counter the wheel."

"Count'ring."

The compass slid past the designated course heading. Then, as the wheel spun over and back to amidships, it settled once more under the lubber's line at two-seven-one degrees.

A burst of lightning suddenly hurled an acetylene blue-white flash through the forward windows. It etched metal surfaces with an electric brilliance, created a nanosecond of moonlike shadows in the half darkness of the bridge.

Jack jumped, his eyes blinking, the flash lingering on his retinas. Almost instantly afterward came the peal, a cracking, splintering percussion that shook the bridge. The sharp acrylic odor of ozone filled the air.

He looked across at O'Mallaugh. The captain had not moved from his position on the forward rail. Only a muscle in his neck twitched, like the last flicker of flame in a burned-out city.

For the past twenty-four hours, Jadid had not moved from his room. Mostly he lay in his bunk in the darkness and tried to keep from falling out. After awhile, he searched the cabin, found a roll of electrical wire and tied himself to the bunk sides.

Occasionally, he vomited. The balance mechanisms of his body were no longer able to withstand the violent irregularity of the ship's movements. His stomach spasmed and he threw up a frothy, creamy-yellow vomit onto himself, the blanket, the floor.

The cabin stank viciously of vomit, of feces from his toilet. It had stopped operating, the pressure valve refusing

to inject water or open the bottom slip door. His gummy
stool still clung to the inside of the metal bowl.

In this foul, clammy heat, fear assailed him and his re-
solve waned. Frantically, he forced himself to draw up images again, all the long panoply of his hatred. He pleaded
with Allah for strength and memory.

But still he worried. What if the ship sank before it
reached detonation pressure? Failure! All his solemn dedi-
cations and sacrifices for nothing. Instead, he'd sink into
the black depths cocooned within this steel room. Sharks
would come sweeping up the corridors, chew through the
wooden door and sunder him. His warrior's place in Paradise would be gone.

When O'Mallaugh turned the *Bengal* directly into the
storm waves, Jadid had felt and understood the movement.
This drew joy from his mind. Soon it would all be over.

Long, plunging minutes passed. Then, suddenly, he felt
the ship turning once more. *What?* He sat up, the wire
cutting into his belly. He listened, heard the howl of the
wind, the crash of thunder.

Quickly, he undid the wire and got out of the bunk. The
deck dropped heavily and threw him hard against the door.
He clung to the knob, legs splayed. Slowly, the *Bengal*
came up again.

Like a drunken man using both hands, he opened the
door and peered out into the passageway. It and the stair-
well were in storm twilight. Beneath the distant roar of the
gale, he heard a man's voice from the radio room, which
lay around the curve of the stack bulkhead.

A sudden lull in the wind came. For a moment, it left
only the sound of the deep creaks and heavy tremulous
moanings of the ship's plates and framings. Within them,
he heard Collins's voice.

The radioman was transmitting!

Jadid bent and slipped a knife from his boot. It had a
gray sheep's horn handle and a seven-inch blade, the edge
scored with tiny honing marks. Pitching and lunging, he
headed for the radio room.

\*   \*   \*

It had taken Keyshawn eight minutes to bypass the captain's lock. He had to pull off the faceplate of the transceiver to get to the lock switch. The radio was an old Henschel TMX-400 Marine, so he found dusty tubes, condensers and relays instead of intergrated circuit boards. With the lock switch nullified, he replaced the faceplate. Then he quickly checked the frequency manual for the international distress band, swung the dial to 2183.4 kilohertz and began transmitting.

"Mayday, Mayday, Mayday," he called. "This is *Bengal*, this is *Bengal*. Need immediate assistance. Approximate position two-zero-point-eight north, seven-one-point-eight west. Listening on two-one-eight-three-point-four. Over."

He unkeyed and listened, head bowed, murmuring encourgement to the radio. Washes of blowing static came. Deep in it were voices, far away, indecipherable. He waited. Another voice swept through too quickly to catch.

"God *dammit*," Collins shouted. He repeated the distress call, listened again. Still the riot of storm interference. He glanced up at the overhead, imagined the antennas and insulators high above him. Motherfuckers were probably caked with salt by now. Shit!

Once more he tried. Same result.

Frantically he sought out a solution. Maybe if he switched to the CW band, Morse code. He could hook up the key and tap out an SOS. Sure. He might possibly reach a ham operator who could relay. At the very least, the CW signal would carry better in storm conditions.

He scanned the manual again, attempting to remember the precise Morse code letters from RD school. He found the international CW distress frequency: 500 kilohertz.

Suddenly, a voice boomed clear as a bell through the speaker: "*Bengal*, this is Houston Approach Control. We understand you are declaring a Mayday. State nature of situation, heading and altitude. Will attempt to vector you. Guard two-one-eight-three-point-four. Over."

"Say what?" Keyshawn jerked back, surprised. Then he quickly understood what was happening. Through a freak of pulse bounce called trapping, his signal was actually reaching all the way to Texas.

He adjusted his dial and keyed. "Houston Approach Control, *Bengal*. I ain't no aircraft. This is a ship. Liberty merchantman. Need assistance immediately." He repeated the position coordinates twice, then clicked off.

"*Bengal*, we have your position. State situation and stand—" And then the voice was gone as quickly as it had come.

"Fuck!" Something banged heavily against the radio room closet. He turned.

Jadid lunged at him. Collins bellowed an obscenity and tried to come up out of his chair. The seat belt held him down. Jadid grabbed a handful of his hair, jerked his head back. Collins's elbow struck him viciously in the stomach. They struggled for a few seconds.

Then Jadid rammed the knife blade into Collins's neck between the jawbone and left ear. He cut back and across, slicing Collins's throat wide open. Blood spewed forth onto the desk, the radio, Jadid's arm and shirtfront, and dripped to the deck, raw-smelling and hot. Collins's eyes were wide open. He made a low, gurgling moan.

The ship lurched suddenly. Jadid lost his hold on Keyshawn's hair. Collins slumped forward as the Kurd tried to catch himself. Slipping on the bloody floor, he went down squarely onto his chest.

A few inches from his face, Collins's right arm hung beside the chair. His hand spasmed, fingers jerking toward his palm like a traffic cop hurrying a reluctant motorist through an intersection. Then it stopped.

Jadid crawled to the door and hauled himself to his feet. He made his way back to his cabin. He retrieved his satchel from under the bunk and took out the Uzi submachine pistol. He rammed in a thirty-two-bullet clip, ratcheted a round into the chamber.

As he again reached the radio room, he paused long

enough to fire several rounds into the radio. The sound of the burst was lost in the rage of the wind. The bullets made precise holes in the faceplate, and from behind it came several sizzling flashes of light.

Jadid turned and headed for the bridge.

*USS WINSTON-SALEM*
*1121 HOURS*

THE LOS ANGELES–CLASS ATTACK SUBMARINE ACHIEVED four hundred feet and leveled out. Forty-one seconds earlier, it had been running at periscope depth, its UHF antenna extended for an updated FLASH message from the Commander, Submarine Forces Atlantic.

Two minutes later, a radioman came to the control center with the decoded script for the boat's captain, Commander James Vantrease.

It read:

```
Z16215TOCT
TOP SECRET: CODOP DIOGENESE
FR: COMSUBLANT
TO: USS WINSTON-SALEM
INFO: CINCLANTFLT


1. SOSUS ACQUISITION ANOMALOUS CONTACT 1616Z 2OCT.
   ESTIMATED POSITION LAT 20° 44' / LONG 71° 30'. CAV-
   ITATION AND PROPELLOR CHARACTERISTICS INDICATE
   POSSIBLE LIBERTY.
```

2. ATTEMPT ACQUISITION FOR FURTHER CHARACTERIS-
   TICS IDENT AND POSITION ESTABLISHMENT.
3. INITIATE TMA FOR POSSIBLE MISSILE LAUNCH. PERMIS-
   SION GRANTED FOR UNRESTRICTED SECTOR CHANGES.

Vantrease stepped from the officer-of-the-deck station and moved to one of the nearby plotting tables. He was a short but stocky man with curly blond hair and a ruddy face. "Navigation, range and bearing on position coordinates two-zero-point-four-four north, seven-one-point-three-zero west," he ordered.

The navigation watch officer repeated the coordinates. A few seconds later, a three-dimensional fix of the SOSUS contact came onto the automatic plotting screen. A tiny box marked the contact, a cross indicated the sub's relative position. The watch officer audibly read off the range and bearing as they flashed in the left-hand corner of the screen.

It showed that the *Winston-Salem* was 240 nautical miles from the contact.

Vantrease studied the plotting screen. That contact was a long way out there, he realized. Under earlier sonar systems, it would have been far beyond the sub's range. Fortunately, this boat's BQQ-5D sonar system had been upgraded with the new TB-23 passive "thin line" towed array, capable of detecting low-frequency noise at very long ranges.

Vantrease turned to his exec, Lieutenant Commander Jerry Delannis. "I'm going to Sonar," he said. "Start the TMA manual plot."

"Aye, sir."

Two hours earlier, the submarine had received an emergency message on its Extremely Low Frequency radio system. In the ELF's slow, three-letter code, Vantrease was ordered to break out of the sub's patrol sector, Domino, and head at flank speed toward the general area within and ahead of Hurricane Emma. At the time, the *Winston-Salem* was three hundred miles north-northeast of San Juan, Puerto Rico.

Further, pursuant to an operation assigned the code name Diogenese, he was to immediately begin an intensive sonar search for a Liberty ship known to be operating somewhere within that quadrant. The ship, designated *Bengal*, was believed to contain a nuclear device with a low-pressure detonation trigger unit.

Vantrease was jolted. He'd had to read the last line twice. He then handed the decode to Delannis. The XO scanned it and glanced up, his eyebrows lifted. "Holy shit," he said. . . .

Vantrease entered the sonar room located on the port side, forward of the control center. It was a compact area with four sonar consoles and a large acoustic spectrum analyzer. The sonar watch officer was a lanky lieutenant named Boerner.

He and Boerner discussed the SOSUS contact. Then Vantrease leaned forward to study the number-four console display. Its sitting technician was Sonarman Second Class Edward Tenbow, a very sharp interpreter of acoustical signals.

The display showed a cascade of closely packed, black-and-white lines called a waterfall. The white lines indicated sound sources and were of varying widths.

"You picking up anything that sounds like a Liberty's prop?" the captain asked.

Tenbow shook his head. "Not yet, sir. There's a lot of random noise out there, ships all over hell with everybody's screws running high-speed. Plenty of cetacean activity and surface rebound, too."

Vantrease turned to Boerner. "Run our library; see if we've got any hull and prop data on those old MCE class-one freighters. And switch the WLR-9 to read off the 23."

"Yes, sir."

He patted Tenbow on the shoulder. "Tighten up your beam channel as narrow as it'll go on that contact bearing. This one's a biggie."

"Yes, sir. Could you give me a few zigzags?"

"Will do."

He left.

For eight minutes, the *Winston-Salem* ran at quarter speed and performed a zigzag pattern to give the TB-23 sensor array a better ranging spread.

Suddenly the CC intercom blared: "Conn, Sonar."

"Conn, aye."

"We have faint but positive ident on target contact designated Sierra Two. Bearing two-two-four degrees, range two-three-four nautical miles. Hull resonance, prop cavitation and bubble pattern all match that of MCE class-one merchantman design-catalogued Liberty."

"Bingo," Vantrease said. "Officer of the Deck, bring us to periscope depth. Stand by to deploy antennas." The order was instantly repeated by the OOD and divemaster.

"Fire Control, Conn. Initiate automatic TMA for firing solution."

Again his orders were repeated and executed.

Vantrease stood waiting for the voices to cease, his gaze cold-eyed. When they did, he said, "Radio, Conn. Shoot off a FLASH to COMSUBLANT. Tell 'em we've got her."

Three minutes earlier, Jadid had burst through the door into the rain-dimmed gloom of the bridge. The *Bengal* had just taken a wave astern, and her bow was now being driven downward, the deck tilting sharply.

Jadid's momentum carried him all the way across the bridge to the rail. He slammed his shoulder into it a foot from O'Mallaugh. He grabbed for the handrail, then twisted around and brought up the muzzle of the machine pistol, swinging it menacingly back and forth between the Malay helmsman and Ashdown. His eyes were wild, hot.

"Turn the ship," he shouted over the wind. "Back into the storm."

Jack was on the opposite side of the bridge near the power phone. He'd been trying to raise Collins. The Malay, eyes bulging with fright, kept swiveling his head, desperate for a command. O'Mallaugh just looked blankly at the bulkhead as if unaware that the Kurd was even there, armed and threatening.

As the wave passed beneath the ship, the bow lifted heavily and then resettled, the deck leveling for a moment. A powerful gust of rain crossed the windows, sounding like lead shot against the glass.

Jadid took a step toward the helm. "I tell you to turn around. Or I kill you both."

Ashdown stared at the Kurd, at his bloody hands and shirt. And knew. *The fucking bastard killed Collins!* A bore of scalding anger washed up under his breastbone.

He flicked his eyes away for an instant, to the flag rack behind the wheel station. He'd placed his shotgun back there, into one of the flag slots. His gaze swung back. Slowly, delicately, he lowered the power phone into its cradle.

Jadid thrust his arm straight out, sighting along the line of the Uzi's barrel. "Do this thing," he screamed. "Do it *now!*"

From the corner of his eye, Jack caught a movement in O'Mallaugh, the man's head swiveling around toward Jadid, slowly, robotlike. His dark, sunken eyes fixed on the Kurd's back. His shaggy brows lowered, and he glared out from under them with a seething, black rage.

The Malay was pleading hysterically with Jadid, "No shoot, meester. Please. I turn, I turn." He put his weight against the wheel and spun it hard over to the right, going hand over hand until the wheel hub hit the emergency stop bar. The helm power box crackled with angry hydraulic chatter.

Shocked, Jack shouted a curse and leapt away from the phone desk. Instantly, Jadid's pistol swung to him. Another wave swept into the stern, lifting it, the deck tilting forward again. Jack felt the engine slow as Pepper pulled off steam.

With a deep, bellowing "NO!" O'Mallaugh suddenly hurled himself at the Kurd. He grabbed Jadid's shirt and lifted him completely off the deck. Swinging him like a sack of flour, he viciously threw Jadid against the starboard bulkhead. The Uzi clattered to the floor.

Blood surged through Jack's body. Twisting, he dove for

the flag rack, at the same time yelling shrilly at the Malay, "Bring her back, you son of a bitch. Bring her *back*."

He finally got the weapon free and hauled it out, thumbing the safety off. He swung the barrel around in an arc, the helmsman cowering now, his hands off the wheel. It began swinging wildly back.

O'Mallaugh had again pounced on Jadid, savaging him with his fists, growling, animal-like. With a ponderous, sliding jolt, the *Bengal* responded to the wheel. The stern yawed violently to the right as the wave, moving faster than the ship, passed full force across the backside of the rudder.

Jack was knocked off his feet, back against the gear closet. He felt a deep shudder riffle through the ship. The bow continued swinging to port, the whole ship heeling in the opposite direction. Then, as the wave cleared beneath her waist and moved on past the afterdeck, she settled slightly, rocking.

Across the bridge, Jadid's hand slapped and clawed for his weapon as O'Mallaugh's fists kept flailing away with powerful roundhouses, sometimes missing totally and striking the deck. The Kurd's face was bloody. Drops flew off as he tried to dodge the incoming blows. One eye protruded grotesquely as if it had been pumped with unusual pressure.

He finally reached the gun, gripped it and shoved the muzzle deep into O'Mallaugh's side. He fired. The blast was muffled, absorbed into the whine of the wind. The expended shell casings went flying out, bright, hot silver onto the deck.

The captain reared back against the solid impact of the bullets. For a tiny moment, he glowered down at the ravaged Kurd with a kind of profound, quzzical look. Almost curiously, he probed his wounded side.

Jadid shot him in the chest, four rounds coming so close together that they made a single cracking explosion, which now tore a seam in the wind noise. O'Mallaugh fell back and away, his mouth opening and closing like that of a fish scooped from water.

Jack, back on his feet, had watched the fight over the

top of the power box. He'd actually seen two of the rounds exit O'Mallaugh's body, cutting ragged holes through the back of his canvas jacket, spewing little bursts of blood and fluttering the material.

The ship was now wallowing in the trough, heeling from side to side. The wheel swung crazily back and forth. But the powerful turn had now brought her broadside to the wave chains.

Suddenly, up came Jadid, bloody, the one eye wide like a man made insane by black speed. He opened fire again, blindly, sweeping the Uzi in an arc. Bullets whanged and slammed into bulkheads, up into the electrical conduits.

Jack felt one sizzle past his shoulder and heard another thud into the helmsman. The Malay instantly fell down, screaming. Ashdown jerked up the shotgun and held it at arm's length, pointed at the Kurd.

Around came the muzzle of the Uzi pistol. The hole looked deep and black and seeped a tiny wisp of smoke. Jack heard himself yell, an incoherent outburst of breath. The shotgun felt heavy, cold. He pulled both triggers. The twin blasts were like cannon rounds.

In recoil, the barrels jerked upward, the breech slamming hard against his thumb. Two bloody holes the size of saucers instantly appeared in Jadid's stomach and chest. Their impacts flung him up and back into the starboard bulkhead.

Braced against the power box, Jack lowered the shotgun. He was panting hard, adrenaline flashing like electrical charges through his blood and muscle. He stared at the two dead men, faintly heard the Malay whimpering. A rush of wind and water sprayed through the door cracks.

He felt the wave coming. At first, there was a faint lift of the deck as the *Bengal* responded to its foreslope, then a sudden hushing of the wind as it was momentarily deflected by the face of the incoming swell.

He dropped the shotgun and grabbed for the wheel with both hands. He gripped a spoke, felt it torn from his hand. He reached for another and got it. Then everything sped up, one side of the bridge dropping with breathtaking suddenness, the other side leaping upward as the ship went into a quick, savage roll to starboard.

His legs slid out from under him as the deck dropped away. He reached up, took hold of a conduit pipe and hung there, dangling. Below him, the Malay tried to fling an arm around the annunciator pedestal, missed and went tumbling over and over into the bulkhead.

Things began falling out of slots and brace shelves, pulled loose of clip locks. There were metallic clinks and chimes. But beneath them all was a heavy, deep-pitched rumble as the ship's cross beams and frames, hull and deck plating began to torque with mounting strain.

Jack's gaze frantically sought the clinometer bolted to the starboard bulkhead. The indicator needle trembled for a moment on sixty degrees, then moved past it. His blood went to ice.

Oh, Jesus, Jesus, he thought wildly. She's going over!

"We've got something," Ensign Perez called through the intercom.

Ana allowed herself a quick glance at the Helix's radar screen, which sat just above the twin throttles. Unlike the round American unit, the Russian SS-11A screen was square with a beam that moved from left to right.

She was having a difficult time maintaining the stability of the chopper. It rocked violently from side to side, forcing her to constantly play the throttles, letting off power as gusts lifted the aircraft sharply upward, then throttling back quickly as lift dissipated.

They were at present passing through a heavy squall. The rain came at them in almost horizontal lines. Visibility was nil. Two thousand feet below lay the ocean, unseen.

The radar scope was full of scatter mist. An older generation of pulse Doppler, the SS-11A Puff Ball radar unit possessed slow phase shifters and a gross signal-to-noise ratio. It often gave false images.

But now, as its beam crossed their position, the aircraft showed clearly as a white dot within a box. A few seconds later, an amorphous blob of light appeared under the beam. Slowly the blob faded, and then a sudden flurry of light dotlets showed, like a swarm of fireflies, as the pulse struck compacted rain and wave-bounce off the edge of the storm.

"It's a big ship," Jesse said. "Almost stationary in the water. But very close to that front."

"They're hove to."

Perez shook his head, his handsome face profiled against the gray wash of rain on his window. "Maybe. But I'll tell you one thing, that goddamned captain's crazy."

"Give me a heading."

Jesse punched a set of buttons beneath the scope. Instantly, the azimuth line and range to the target contact flashed at the bottom of the screen: 8 nm/ 021 degrees.

Ana eased the helo into a shallow left turn, watching her heading indicator swing slowly until it was on zero-two-one. A powerful gust lifted them abruptly. They climbed a hundred feet before she could counter with the throttle.

Settling, she threw her mind out beyond the windshield, at that ship out there. What was so important about it? And why had its captain deliberately brought it into this dangerous, potentially fatal situation?

"Tell Baracoa we've made a contact," she said. "We think it's a freighter named *Bengal*."

Jesse went off intercom. He took a quick GPS fix, then began calling up Baracoa Flight Control.

Why was the American navy so interested in this *Bengal?* Ana wondered. Were they really looking for it? Or, as Havana believed, *was* it a hoax, a ploy, the presage to invasion? But then why the hell would it be out *here?*

She flicked her radio, caught the tail end of Perez's tranmission: "... on present target heading of zero-two-one, range zero-eight nautical miles. Advise. Over."

Baracoa came right back. "Hotel one-four-four, Baracoa Flight. Why are you beyond designated patrol sector? Has contact requested assistance?"

"Negative," Jesse said. "But it's stationary in the water. Over."

"Urgent you return immediately to your designated patrol sector. Maintain vector one-six-eight degrees. Call when you reach outer boundary."

"Baracoa Flight, Hotel one-four-four, roger that and out." Jesse gave Ana a lifted brow look.

Ana didn't alter course. They were now heading almost directly into the wind, and the Helix's ground speed had dropped to approximately seventy-fives miles per hour. She mentally figured the time to convergence. About eight minutes.

Perez studied her.

She knew this ship out there was the key to something big—was certain of it, felt it inside. Surely MINFAR headquarters must also know of it, have heard its name in monitored transmissions. Then why hadn't Baracoa reacted to its location? She must find out why—Cuba's very existence could depend on it.

She glanced at Jesse, clicked back to intercom. "Something's very wrong here. And that ship's the answer to all of it."

Perez said nothing; simply waited.

Ana felt a jolting sense of despair. The moment had come, the single instant in time that she had dreaded for so long. She would have to deliberately disobey Baracoa's command. That would make her a traitor, commit her to that which would forever be irreversible. With all that her country had done to her, to her family, though, it was no longer a country she recognized, despite her love for it.

She inhaled deeply, let the air seep through her lips, then keyed. "Bring up that U.S. Navy voice frequency," she ordered.

For a moment, Jesse did not comply.

"This is my command decision, Ensign," Ana snapped. "Do it."

He stared a moment longer, then began swinging the frequency dial.

*HOUSTON INTERNATIONAL TOWER*
*11:26 A.M.*
Air Traffic Control watch supervisor Virgil Gisler impatiently waited on the line, tapping his blue pencil lightly against the top of his bald head. Three minutes earlier, he'd called the Coast Guard station at Port Bolivar to report the *Bengal* Mayday. He got a Seaman First named Stender, explained the situation and was put on hold.

The distress call had been logged at precisely 11:20, taken by controller number three. Under operational procedure, all Mayday calls were instantly linked to the supervisor's master screen while they were being processed.

This one was a bit odd. A ship in trouble? Still, radios did strange things, and Gisler had been in on other peculiar receptions in the past.

The phone clicked and a man's brusque voice said, "Lieutenant McKenna. Who's this?"

Gisler identified himself. "Look, Lieutenant," he said, "our approach control received a Mayday declaration at eleven-twenty this morning. The apparent source of origin was a ship named *Bengal*. The op—"

McKenna cut him off: "What was that name?"

*"Bengal."*

"You're absolutely certain?"

"Yes."

"Did you get its position?"

"Yes. I've got our log tape if you want to hear it."

"Yes. Hang on a minute."

There was a click, but Virgil could still hear McKenna yelling excitedly, "Chief, run a separate tape on this. Move it! And get Eighth District on the horn. Jesus, I think we've found the ship with that fucking hot nuke aboard."

Virgil's scalp prickled suddenly, as if a cold wind had

just passed over his head. A live nuclear bomb out there?
*Holy fuck!*

McKenna came back. "Gisler?"

"Ah—yeah."

"Run the tape."

He did, twice. It contained the original call, the AP response, the second call and the AP partial.

When it finished the second time, McKenna said, "That's the whole of it?"

"Yes. Listen—I—ah—"

"Thank you, sir," McKenna said. "We'll be in touch." He was gone.

Gisler sat frowning into space, dumbfounded. Had he actually heard what he thought he heard? He felt an overwhelming need to call somebody, tell them, find out if such a wild thing could actually be true. But who?

He remembered Ken Stark. Stark was a news anchor on channel 4. He was also a member of Gisler's Moose Lodge. They both played on the lodge's bowling team. If anybody could sniff this out, Ken could.

Virgil leaned forward and flipped through his Rolodex until he found Stark's business phone. He dialed it, then sat tensely waiting for someone to pick up.

*WHITE HOUSE*
*11:27 A.M.*
Although still racing at a headlong pace, the mood in the Situation Room had changed subtly again.

The initial shock of the situation had somewhat settled into fatigued minds. The unthinkable was accepted. Now the continuing unfolding of its parameters and the reactions to it gave to the room's activity a kind of dulled, inevitable, unstoppable momentum, like an abandoned locomotive traveling a slight, steady downgrade.

The growing weariness was also showing in other ways. There had simply been too much tension for too long. Tempers flared viciously. Radio operators snapped sarcastically at their counterparts, made transcription errors. In the conference area, military and White House officials took messages, squabbled over incidentals and constantly squinted up at the plotting board.

As for the president, he hadn't slept for over thirty-five hours now. People advised him to get some rest. He refused. Instead, he prowled around the Situation Room or went out to wander the halls, head down, hands clasped behind his back. Alone, despite his Secret Service men trailing behind.

Now one of the agents approached him, holding a phone. "Mr. President, it's Admiral Rebeck."

The president took it. "Yes?"

"We just got a definite ID and fix on the *Bengal*, sir," Rebeck said quickly, "from one of our Domino subs, the *Winston-Salem*. That SOSUS contact was right."

"I'm there." He tossed the phone back to the Secret Service agent and hurried off.

Forty-one seconds later, he stood in front of the plotting board, gazing narrow-eyed up at the little red dot that was now positively IDed as the *Bengal*. It now lay very close to the western edge of the hurricane, the storm up there in three dimensions like a huge sugar-frosted doughnut. Contour lines ran through it, showing Anholt's latest pressure gradient readings.

The number of people in the Situation Room had thinned. Vice President Washburn was in Alexandria, at a meeting with more congressmen to go over the situation. Before he left, the president had cautioned him to avoid the journalists who had become increasingly more frustrated and aggressive.

Hershhaur and FBI chief Forsell were both at Langley, shooting probes worldwide to broaden their profile of Mashhad Jadid and the Kurd connection.

Besides Rebeck and two logging secretaries, present were Secretary Gilliland, Santia and Colonel Trautloff, now supplemented by two scientists from the Blue Mountain

Nuclear Research Facility at Los Alamos. Their names were Leitch and Minkner.

Rebeck explained the *Winston-Salem*'s method of identification. He finished with, "They're heading for the target contact now at flank speed, and running constant target motion analysis and firing solutions for possible missile launch."

*Missile launch.* The president blinked slowly at that. He said, "What's the sub carrying?"

"Harpoon and Tomahawk cruise missiles. If a launch becomes necessary, we advise the 109-B Tomahawks. They're specifically antiship units with a longer range and modified radar seekers."

"What about the SEAL team?" Gilliland asked.

"We've already committed them. They're aboard two CH-53 Super Sea Dragon choppers, the fastest we've got." Rebeck pointed at a white light just off Fowl Cay in the Bahamian Exuma Sound. "There they are."

"What's their TOT?"

"Approximately two hours and ten minutes. They're hitting strong headwinds."

The president cursed. "That ship'll long be inside the storm by then." He turned. "Will they be able to board under those conditions?"

Rebeck exhaled. "It'll be rough as hell, sir. But if it can be done, they'll do it."

The president returned to the map, studied it a moment longer, then walked to his chair at the table and sat down. He clasped his fingers together, rubbing one thumb over the other. He turned to the nuclear experts.

"Looking at those pressure readings up there," he said, "what do you think the most likely pressure setting on this bomb would be?"

Trautloff said, "I think the trigger's set to go off somewhere near the eye wall. That way, there would be as dense a radiation saturation as possible." She glanced around at the plotting board, came back. "It would probably be in the range of two-eight-point-five-zero inches. Sooner than that would create a risk of centrifugal dissipation of the contaminated clouds.''

Leitch, a narrow-faced, pale man, leaned forward to speak. ''I agree with that assessment, Mr. President,'' he said, ''but with a proviso. We must remember, this *Bengal* is an old ship. She might not make it all the way to the eye wall. In that case, these terrorists would be forced to detonate sooner.''

The president thought about that statement and its implications. That godawful thing could go off within the hour. The minute. The second.

''It's obvious that the quickest sure-kill of this would be an immediate missile strike,'' he said finally, as if to himself.

''Yes, sir,'' Leitch said.

''But, dammit, you people tell me a missile could cause detonation itself.''

''Yes, it could, Mr. President,'' Minkner said. In contrast to Leitch, he had a round, sunburned face and a rather high voice. ''Unless, of course, it could be placed precisely where the bomb is located. In essence, destroy the trigger mechanism before it could begin its sequence.''

The President snorted. ''That'd have to be one helluva'n accurate shot.''

''Or we could use a Tomahawk with a nuclear warhead,'' Rebeck said sharply. ''Vaporize the son of a bitch in a blink.''

Everybody swung to him. Trautloff and the scientists shook their heads, no. ''If you did that,'' Leitch said, ''you'd have a similar contamination profile in that hurricane. Not as bad as the Red Bomb, but sufficient to cause widespread radiation fallout.''

''Okay, no nuke hit,'' Santia said. ''What about a swarm strike? Throw all the *Winston-Salem*'s Tomahawks at the ship at once. At least one could take out that trigger.''

This time, Trautloff and Rebeck both looked skeptical. Trautloff said, ''A sequential launch of that many units would take at least a full minute. If the first one to impact didn't find the trigger, the rest wouldn't matter. The entire trigger-mainload sequence only takes milliseconds to complete.''

The president went silent, head lowered to distractedly watch his thumbs. He felt his stomach coil, a gripping of bowel. He knew that, sooner or later, he would have to make that terrible decision. To order those missiles sent in—and thus, by his own hand, perhaps begin the horror.

But when to do it? When?

Without looking up, he asked, ''How long would it take missiles to get from the *Winston-Salem* to the *Bengal?*''

''From her present position, approximately twenty-four minutes,'' Rebeck replied.

*An eternity.*

There was a knock at the door. Admiral Rebeck pulled it open. One of Hand's watch officers handed over a yellow telex sheet, then departed.

Rebeck scanned it, glanced up. ''Jesus, this is from the Coast Guard district headquarters at Bradenton, Florida. It's actually a transcription of an SOS call from the *Bengal*. The thing was received by the Houston International airport approach control.''

The president's head snapped up. ''An SOS from the ship?''

''Yes.''

Rebeck hurried around the table and handed the telex to the president. As he read it, Santia blurted, ''Hey, do you see what this means? *Somebody* aboard that ship doesn't want to go through with this thing.''

The president glanced at him. His eyes were suddenly bright with a cautious but hopeful glint, like a condemned prisoner who'd just been told there was a tiny chance he might not have to die.

Rebeck, also excited, said, ''He's right, by God. And if there's one, there could be more.''

''Hell, yes,'' Gilliland said. ''In fact, there could even be a goddamned battle for control going on aboard that ship right now.''

The president leapt to his feet, walked around with his hands on his hips. "Dammit," he cried. "If there was only some way we could know for sure."

For the next several minutes, the discussion flew. Optimistic suppositions, what-ifs. Then, abruptly, it stopped as the true reality came back. There was probably only one man aboard in opposition to the others. Through fear or some sudden rebirth of morality, he had cried for help. If that were true, what could one man do?

At that moment, Commander Hand entered, not bothering to knock. "Mr. President," he said loudly. "We just got a FLASH message from Atlantic CINCCOM. The cruiser USS *Gettysburg* reports picking up a radio transmission from a female Cuban air force chopper pilot. She claims she's got the *Bengal* on her radar. And she's very close to it."

Everybody jerked up. *What?*

The *Bengal*'s roll went to sixty-five degrees, the clinometer's arrow hitting the peg. There she stayed. Water roared over her forward decks, and solid curtains of it blew through the cracks in the wing doors.

Jack turned his head to look through the forward windows. He saw the wave, a gray wall higher than the wheelhouse, torn and jagged-faced, with the wind whipping spray like a waterfall going sideways.

He felt the panic in him, a wild animal loose in his chest. He was going to die. He knew it as surely as he knew every tiny sensual impression his body was absorbing, all of them suddenly made minutely precise.

The bridge was now awash with two feet of water, most of it banked against the right bulkhead. The corpses of O'Mallaugh and Jadid had crumpled crookedly together there. In the dim light, their blood made black swirls. Over in the door corner, the Malay sobbed with terror and bawled Buddhist prayers.

Things began crashing into the outside of the bridge and both wing coamings: cables, a cork-and-canvas life raft, a boom with its cargo blocks. There was the loud rending sound of metal breaking from somewhere on the port side.

A moment later, Jack saw the partially crushed port lifeboat, trailing a single davit, go end over end into the number-two derrick, carom off and disappear over the starboard side into the gray-black sea.

The *Bengal*'s starboard bulwarks were now completely under a snowy avalanche of foam and water. It rumbled back along the main- and boat-deck alleyways with a hollow, rushing thunder.

Then, very slowly at first, the ship began to come back.

Jack hung there, feeling it coming up, heard the ship straining and moaning with the effort. For a moment, she rolled down again, caught, then continued back up. Farther and farther.

His feet touched the deck. Still she came. The water in the bridge leveled out, Jadid's body making a slow pirouette in it. And then she was right once more, wallowing.

As Ashdown still clung to the overhead pipe, his emotions flew through a series of stages, a metamorphosing. From fear to life force to rage to determination. The blood, already hot in his body, surged anew, filled muscle and tendon and brain.

An image flashed, born out of his death vision. It was the faces of his wife and daughter, seen far away, back through the tunnel of himself. And with them, the flare of guilt like fire. His failure to act, to protect back then; his absence, an empty, insufficient excuse.

*Not this time*, he thought with a kind of wild joyousness.

He twisted and took hold of the wheel, which was swinging slowly, mushily on its hub. He stopped the spokes, glanced at the binnacle. The face was beaded with moisture, the card jiggering under the lubber's line: 183 degrees.

He quickly made a decision. Realizing that the waves had grown too large for him to continue exposing the *Bengal*'s stern to them, he knew that the only way to save the ship now was to put her head directly into the storm. Fight his way through it. If they were lucky, it'd blow them far

enough westward to avoid the shoals of the Mouchoir
Bank.

With his right hand, he reached for the annunciator handle, rammed it forward, the bell jingling, back and forward
again. AHEAD FULL. He bellowed into the speaking tube:
"Engine, give me everything you have."

There was no answering bell, only the storm roar and
the hiss of water draining out from under the wing doors.
Hand over hand, he swung the helm hard to port, all the
way to the emergency hub. The wheel felt loose. But then
the power box chattered, and the wheel tightened up.

A loud, expulsive blow came up through the stack. A
few seconds later, he felt the deck begin to vibrate with the
throb of the engine. It increased gradually, the deck tilting
aft a bit as the *Bengal*'s prop began to dig deep.

The ship's head started to the left, yawing slightly as the
quartering wind now struck the midhouse off center. Still
broadside to the waves, the ship's rudder was no longer
offset by the speed of the sea. Coupled with the heavy
backwash of her prop, she was now answering the helm
efficiently.

Jack glared down at the compass card: 170 degrees.
"Come on, old lady," he shouted through gritted teeth.
"Come around, come around!"

160 degrees . . .

"Yeah, that's it! There you go."

145 . . . 135 . . .

From the corner of his eye, he saw the Malay shove open
the bridge door and crawl out. He ignored him, staring at
the compass card as it jiggled and bounced.

120 . . .

Another huge wave struck the ship from off the port
bow, snapped her over hard. But with her engine driving,
she didn't go all the way down this time. Quickly she came
back, humping as the wave passed beneath the hull, and
then she sliced back into the trough, blowing spray, still
turning.

105 . . .

He began to ease off the helm, swinging the wheel back. The run of the compass card slowed. Easing, he finally held on 090 degrees. Due east. Toward the heart of the hurricane.

Another wave came, head-on now. The *Bengal* drove her bow into it, climbed with a sudden, ponderous lifting. The bow burst through the crest, and the wave ran under her all the way to the number-two hold before she finally broke free completely and, with a stomach-dropping, thunderous plunge, went down into the trough. A mountain of water exploded over her head, completely submerging the fo'c's'le and forward decks.

Jack instantly rang the annunciator, rammed the handle to AHEAD QUARTER. He felt the engine vibration ease off. Now, he knew, he'd have to run her slowly, just enough to keep steerage way on. To ram the *Bengal* directly into the waves at speed would break her back.

He looked out the window. The rain and spray made a blanket of white just beyond. Then it began to slacken, its clattering pound fading swiftly.

Light flooded across the forward deck. The derrick posts came black and shiny-clean into view. A momentary break in the squall. Quickly, visibility opened up ahead of the ship, the sea stretching out there, rugged-edged, mountainous gray hills lashed with white foam.

And there it was: the hurricane's front!

It was less than a mile away. Jack stared and stared, mesmerized. His legs went weak for a split second. The thing completely covered all that he could see, from ocean to sky. This great, boiling, dense black wall of clouds moving, now and then scatter-lit by bursts of lightning deep inside, like the pulses of a living beast. Above the howl of the near wind, the rush of water, he could hear it clearly. A throbbing, roaring, thunderous shrieking . . .

# 00:28

EVERYBODY WATCHED AS THE *BENGAL*'S TINY RED LIGHT on the plotting board was overrun by the storm's edge, the movement of the big sugared doughnut not jerky but digitally smooth now. The light lay just inside, like a brilliant Mars caught in the hazy web of the Milky Way.

The president felt his shoulder muscles slacken. He slumped. He'd known all along that the ship would reach the storm front before the SEAL teams could possibly get to her. But hope, always dispensing with reality, had buoyed him. Now the truth was up there on the board.

"Well, shit," Santia said gruffly. "There she goes. Those poor SEALs are in for it now."

"What's the status on the Cuban pilot link?" the president asked quietly. When told earlier of the unusual contact, he'd immediately ordered that a direct radio connection be made between her and the Situation Room.

"They're still working it," Rebeck answered. "Her radio's weak, keeps fading in and out." He caught sight of Commander Hand coming to the door and stepped over to open it. Hand gave him a code transcript. He read it.

"Well, at least there's one good thing here, sir," he said.

"*Winston-Salem* reports that the *Bengal*'s cavitation profile indicates she's heading due east. Very slowly, thirty to thirty-five revolutions on her prop. That'd give her about four or five knots. Obviously, the captain's putting her head into those wave chains with as little speed as possible to keep her from breaking apart."

The president turned. *So?* his expression said.

"According to Anholt, wave speed is well beyond five knots. That means the ship's actually being pushed in the opposite direction. So the hurricane eye will have to over-*run* her. That gives us about two solid hours before she gets into any of those really low barometer readings."

The president grunted. Hope flickered up again. He walked back to the table and sat down. Rebeck did the same. He glanced around the table. "What do you all think about this Cuban pilot thing?"

"I'd say be careful with it," Santia said. "Could be a trick."

"To what purpose?" the president asked.

"With Castro, who the hell knows? Remember what Simon said. Fidel and his military may actually think we're all out there to go after *him*."

"But surely they've picked up ship transmissions indicating that there really *is* a ship we're searching for."

Santia shrugged. "Sure, but old El Comandante needs a national threat about now. You know, solidarity against the big bad imperialists to the north. Keeps the peasants worked up and faithful."

"I disagree, sir," Rebeck said. "If this chopper pilot is as close to the *Bengal* as she claims, her aircraft's way beyond Cuba's fifty-mile territorial limit. If Castro were really trying to whip up his people into believing we're going to attack, I don't think he'd allow one of his helicopters to engage us outside his own space."

The president studied that thought a moment. "Could this woman be acting alone? A renegade officer?"

"Quite possibly."

''All right, let's assume she reaches the ship. What could she do?''

''I think the first question is, will she actually go into that storm?'' Gilliland said. ''We don't know what she's flying. Those internal winds could tear that helo apart.''

''The Cuban navy flies Russian-built Hormone Ka-26s and Helix Ka-27s,'' the admiral informed them.

''Could such aircraft take a hurricane?'' the president asked.

Rebeck nodded. ''Yes. But that pilot damned well better know what she's doing.''

The president sighed. ''So *if* she decides to go in and *if* she actually locates that ship, what the hell do we ask her to do?''

''Try and raise whoever it was that sent that Mayday,'' Rebeck answered instantly.

''Sure,'' Santia said, leaning forward. ''If she can, it's possible that he could tell her exactly where the bomb is.''

The president turned to Colonel Trautloff. ''Suppose we're able to get that information. Would a missile hit— say, on the opposite end of the ship from where the bomb is—still detonate it?''

''That would depend on how many compartments were between, sir,'' she answered. ''But, yes, the explosive vacuum could possibly be dissipated enough to keep the trigger mechanism unexposed to a pressure drop.''

The president squinted at her a moment. ''You know, we've all assumed that sinking that ship is a priority. But just what the hell happens to that bomb if we do? I mean, after she actually goes under?''

''The trigger would become totally useless. The increasing water pressure of the depth would permanently prevent the mechanism from reaching its detonation set.''

The president turned to Rebeck. ''Could the *Winston-Salem* put a missile on the *Bengal* with pinpoint accuracy?''

Rebeck shook his head. ''I'm afraid not, sir. Those Tomahawks aren't smart bombs visually guided by a spotter aircraft. They're radar-guided to the target, and then they home to the mass of the ship, which means they could strike it anywhere from stem to stern.''

"Well, what about the Cuban pilot?'' Gilliland put in. "Maybe she's armed.''

The president's eyes swung to him. "Now there's a thought, George.'' To Rebeck: "What ordnance do those Cuban patrol helos carry?''

"Usually ASW torpedoes and depth bombs. But she could also have one or two modified tactical air-to-ship missiles. Probably some revised version of an AS-4.''

"What kind of guidance?''

"Radio command, I believe.''

"So she could hit the ship exactly where she wanted?''

"Only with a missile. And so long as she had visual on the target.''

"But that's a helluva lot to expect from the pilot of an enemy nation,'' Santia snapped.

The president glared at him. "Goddammit, Manuel, as long as there's a possibility, we consider it.''

"Well, I was just saying.''

The president shook his head. "No, the question is whether or not she'd obey a request to fire on that ship.''

"If she's on her own, maybe so,'' Gilliland said.

"But if she isn't, she *would* have to take a direct order from Castro.'' He nodded. "George, you and Simon get on the horn to MINFAR headquarters. Demand, cajole, plead, if necessary. But get Fidel on a line. I want to talk to him.''

Gilliland rose and darted away.

The president glanced at Rebeck. "Admiral, find out what the hell's taking them so long to get that link to this pilot completed.''

"Yes, sir.'' Rebeck got up and followed the secretary out into the main room.

It was like being hurled into the center of an explosion while wearing welder's goggles. Everything went gray-black. The only true illumination on the bridge was from the tiny red window lights, the white light on the annunciator barrel and the soft greenish glow of the binnacle.

The sudden blast of the northeast wind, which always circles a hurricane eye in a counterclockwise direction in the Northern Hemisphere, struck the *Bengal* just forward of the port beam. It was so powerful that it actually skidded the whole ship fifty yards to the right, heeling her over about forty-five degrees.

She had just cleared a wave and was now pitching deeply into the trough. Jack, fighting against the crazy inertial forces pulling at him, managed to slam the annunciator forward to AHEAD FULL, then haul the helm over to the left.

The wheel mushed up for a moment, then took hold. He knew the power box was chattering but couldn't hear it. He couldn't hear anything save the savage scream and thunder of the storm, the explosive drumming of rain against the entire midhouse.

A flash of lightning lit up the forward deck for a fraction of a second. Everything was a blurry blue-white, caught in stopped action—the plunging ship, the walls of ocean peeling off her bow. As it all sank back into the dimness, two red balls of Saint Elmo's fire appeared on the arms of the number-two cargo derrick. They danced and tumbled to the ends, and then exploded like flares.

The ship came back slowly, heavily, remaining slightly canted to starboard. Ashdown glanced down at the binnacle glass. The brilliance of the Saint Elmo bursts lingered in his eyes, made little red and orange smears on the compass card. He saw that the *Bengal*'s heading was now at 070 degrees.

He brought the helm back to midships, reached over and rang down for AHEAD QUARTER. Now the winds came at the ship from aft her port bow, the seas from aft the starboard bow. It was the one heading, he knew, that would minimize both forces as much as possible. The compass card steadied up at 067 degrees.

There was so much vibration in the deck, he could no longer feel the steady throb of the engine. But he was certain that Jeremiah was still giving him power from the way the bow had turned so quickly into the wind. Water sloshed around his ankles. It felt sticky, like blood.

Another wave heaved into the *Bengal*. Over she went to port, the water slushing past him. Another spray of sea blew in through the starboard wing door. Something hit his right calf, half coiled around it.

It was one of the bodies. Repulsed, Jack kicked it away, felt it tumble against the bolted captain's chair, then slide back past his leg as the ship righted once more.

He lifted his face and yelled into the speaking tube: "Jeremiah, I can't leave the helm. O'Mallaugh and the owner's rep are dead. Collins, too. Helmsman gone. Get somebody the hell up here to help me."

No answer. The window and annunciator lights faded suddenly, then came back with a surge of brightness before returning to normal.

Cursing, Jack stared out through the forward windows. For a few seconds, the cascade of rain dwindled. Visibility cleared. He saw the forward part of the ship as she battled against the sea, a nearly constant flood of water crossing aft, blowing upward and then enveloping deck machinery, hold hatches, the bases of the twin cargo derricks. A moment later, the rain swept across the windows once more, and the bridge returned to its gray dusk.

Yet in that single glimpse of partial light, Ashdown had experienced a sudden renewal, an animal instinct for light. He felt the sense of strength and power lift through him, rush solidly along the pathways of his body.

"Hang in there, old lady," he howled to the ship. "You and me, we're gonna come through this."

WHITE HOUSE
12:06 P.M.
The connection was very bad. The long link stretched from Ana to the *Gettysburg* to Atlantic Fleet Communications in

Norfolk to the Situation Room. Static, filtered all the way, was still heavy and splaying.

The president, standing beside a large radio console in the outer area, said into a mike, "Hotel one-four-four, can you read me? Over."

There was a short pause as the link stations handled the handoffs. Then: "USS *Gettysburg,* one-four-four," Ana Castile said in clean English. "Affirmative that. Proceed. Over."

"This is the president of the United States speaking to you. Do you copy?"

Pause. "Say again."

He repeated. Waited.

A long pause, then: "It is an honor, sir."

"One-four—no. What is your first name?"

Pause. "Ana."

"Ana, please listen very carefully to me." He rapidly but concisely explained the situation. Twice he had to stop for the waves of static and long, willowing screels that came through the loudspeaker, and the quick bursts of voice-overs as operators adjusted up.

Ana came back. He finished the explanation, again waited.

Pause. "I understand situation. What are your intentions?"

"How close are you to the ship?"

Pause. "Target approximately two miles on radar. Bearing zero-eight-seven degrees."

"Have you made any radio contact with ship?"

Pause. "Negative."

"Are you armed?"

Pause. "Affirmative."

"Do you have missiles?"

Pause. "Twin alpha-sierra-fours."

The president glanced up at Rebeck. *You were on the button.* He said, "Do you intend to enter storm front?"

Pause. "Affirmative."

"It is urgent that you achieve radio contact with ship.

We must know precise area where bomb is located. I am advised you should use channel sixteen. Over.''

This time the pause was long. Thirty seconds. Forty. A minute. "Come on, let's go," the president said frustratedly.

An operator's voice came snapping through the loudspeaker. "Sierra sierra one, this is Fleet Comm. I'm sorry, Mr. President, we've lost signal on Hotel one-four-four.''

"Shit!" the president growled.

From the moment the *Bengal* took her sixty-five-degree roll, things started going wrong in the engine room.

As the deck dropped precipitously into the roll, everyone frantically grabbed for stanchions, grating railings, brackets. Objects went flying through the steamy air: port side fittings, heavy tools, Jeremiah's beer box. Even the engineer's standing desk was partially torn loose. Everything smashed into the starboard bulkhead.

The men frantically hung on, their bodies dangling with the tilt.

As the roll steepened, Vogel, literally standing on the throttle post, was sharp enough to react. Knowing that the prop would partially clear water, he instantly pulled off steam.

A few moments later, as the sea rushed up and over the midhouse, a deluge suddenly plunged down through the four main blower outlets. It covered everything on the starboard side. The electrical switch panels began crackling and popping blue sparks.

From his position at the second deck catwalk, Jeremiah had instantly twisted around to check the red fire lights down on the boiler face. They were still on.

*Good. So far.*

He swung back, glanced down at the fuel circulating pump. At such an angle, he knew it would soon lose vacuum. If that happened, the boiler tubes would be starved for fuel and go out. The ship would be dead in the water, at the mercy of the sea.

Heavily, her plating moaning and cracking with reports like rifle shots, the *Bengal* began to come back. Men's feet finally touched decking again. Water hissed around stanchions, rolled in little wavelets toward the left as the deck began to level.

Pepper instantly slid down the steps' handrails and headed for the throttle station, bellowing orders punctuated with raging Aussie invective.

For the next thirty-four minutes, he and his men fought to keep the ship under way, responding to Ashdown's commands—first at Full Ahead, then backing down until they could feel the ship straining, just barely making steerageway. They worked in ankle-deep water and scurried for handholds each time she heeled or yawed or plunged.

First the fuel pump was manually brought back to pressure. Next, the blown circuits in the electrical panels were replaced. Then the circulation pump, hooked into the main condenser line, developed a leak and had to be repacked to maintain feed water level.

The wet-air pump overheated suddenly, forcing lubrication oil under pressure back through the hot well and into the boiler tubes. It was bypassed, the pumping switched to manual. With the constant slowing of the prop, the main shaft bearings began heating up. They were hosed down. When Ashdown called for help, Pepper sent one of the black gang up to tell the bosun, Tun, to go to the bridge. The man never came back.

All the while, through the great cavernous space of the engine room, the sound of the storm was a constant, deep rumbling like a column of tanks rolling over a wooden bridge, the reverbrations palpable in the steam-drenched air. With all but one of the main blowers out, the temperature was now at 145 degrees, and everybody was covered with sweat and seawater and oil.

Jeremiah left Vogel at the throttle station while he himself covered the rest of the engine room, blasting out orders, darting up and down levels, his wiry little body fuming energy, his squinting eyes ablaze. Now and then, he'd soundly cuff one or another of the Malays. He knew they were on the edge of panic. His blows would jolt them back, recapture them with his authority.

Now he paused for a moment beside the throttle station, panting. A Foster's floated past the stanchion. He scooped it up, cracked the top and took a long pull.

Vogel watched. His solemn eyes held tiny, bright centers. "We're into it good now, eh, Chief?" he shouted.

"Aye. And headed straight for the monster's center."

"You think we can ride her out?"

"We've got a swaggie's chance, mate." He glanced around, took in the whole of the engine room. "As long as this old sheila keeps her steel together."

A sudden, violent, booming crash blew through the storm and engine noise. The entire ship shook, the vibrations passing along the deck and bulkheads like a wave.

Everyone's head snapped foward. Another crash came, followed by a deeper rumble, lost in the storm noise but still felt in the deck.

Jeremiah's face went as hard and dark as granite. "*Damn!* We've bought it now. Them bloody cargo timbers're tearin' loose."

A swift movement caught his eye on the second level. Two Malay wipers skirted the engine and fled up the steps to the main deck. Another followed.

"Come back here, ya cowardly bag of bastards," he screamed at them.

"Chief!" Vogel yelled sharply.

Jeremiah swung around just as the two Malay boilermen came bounding through the water, one behind the other, their eyes wild with terror. He lunged for the first one, missed and went down.

As he rose, the other Malay struck him across the back of the head with a heavy wrench. Pepper felt the shock of the steel, an explosion of blood-red pain that tore through his head. He fell down. For the tiniest moment, in a spasm of light, he saw a colony of bubbles rise in the water at the level of his eye. Then everything went away into darkness.

Vogel chased the Malay, but the man darted up the ladder too quickly, his bare feet slapping on the steps. The German gave it up and returned to the machinery floor. Pepper floated facedown, swaying with the movement of the water. The back of his head looked peculiar, boneless under the skin at the edge of his hair.

Vogel picked him up by the back of the shirt. Blood ran out of Jeremiah's ears and eyes. Vogel touched his carotid. There was no pulse. "Oh, Jesus," he moaned. "Oh, goddamn Jesus."

After a moment, he carried the chief engineer to the second grating and gently laid him down. Then he went below to the power phone.

Twelve minutes earlier, Tun had collected the last of his watch-standers in the crew's mess on the boat deck. All of the off-duty men, including the cook and messboy, were already there, sitting on the worn linoleum floor in their bulky gray cork survival vests, their feet and backs braced against the bolted tables and benches.

Without specific orders, Tun had pulled his watchmen off their weather deck stations. It was too dangerous for anyone to be exposed out there now.

He paced among them, silently studying each face. He knew they were very frightened, and the fear had plunged them into a foul, sullen, dangerous mood. It would take a mere spark to shove them into full panic.

The fear came from more than just the storm. Like himself, most of these men were veterans of southern typhoons—in the Indian Ocean and South China Sea. But there was something horribly different here. It was the ship itself. She was cursed, bloodstained, driven by an insane captain. They all remembered the white dolphin.

The engineman that Jeremiah had sent up came in to tell Tun to go to the bridge. The man said he thought the captain had been relieved by the First Mate. The men began murmuring amongst themselves.

Tun considered Pepper's command and decided to ignore it. The bosun of a ship is part of the deck force, under the supervision of the First Mate. Without a direct order from a deck officer, no crewman can legally enter the bridge. So he would wait until he got such an order. Further, his primary duty was to keep control of his men, to make certain they didn't bolt.

Then, in rapid sequence, three things happened. . . .

The first was the sudden, rending crash that rumbled through the hull of the ship. Everyone jerked up. Their eyes swung toward the forward deck, knowing instantly what it was. The cargo of lashed timbers in one of the forward holds had just broken free.

The men leapt to their feet, shouting excitedly. Their faces were jolted, suddenly pale. At that instant, the wounded helmsman appeared at the door. His duck trousers were covered with blood. Jabbering hysterically, he told them about the killings on the bridge.

That news went into the men like a surge of electricity. They started for the doors. Tun screamed at them and blocked the way. He shoved two men back against a table. The others paused. Cursing, he told them he was going to the bridge and ordered them to remain where they were until he came back.

He started for the door but was instantly knocked backward by the rush of the five enginemen who came lunging in. They screamed that the ship was sinking and that the Chief Engineer was dead.

That did it. There was a general yelling, stumbling stampede for the doors. Tun again tried to stop them. He swung a fist at a frenzied face, felt it go into the man's shoulder. He grabbed a cork vest. The rotted material ripped away in his hand.

He took hold of another man. For a flashing instant, he saw the glint of a switchblade coming at him. He felt it slice across his rib cage, the pain a firebrand. He doubled over and was knocked to the deck. The last crewman disappeared out the door.

Tun, his own panic welling up, staggered to his feet.

Holding his left arm against the wound, he started after his men.

To Jack, the crash of the loose timber was like the collision of empty boxcars. His body experienced a peculiar sensation, as if his blood had ceased flowing for a moment. For shifting cargo tore up interior bulkheads and destroyed flotation integrity.

Swearing bitterly into the air in an effort to release the rising energy of his own panic, he twisted around, started pulling pennant flags from the rack. He had to go outside, he knew, to see if the hold hatches had been breached by the moving timber. Once the holds were open to the sea, the *Bengal* would be doomed. She'd plunge and go on plunging, straight to the bottom.

He quickly strung together several pennants and lashed the wheel, holding the lubber's line at 068 degrees. The air in the bridge was permeated with a subtle change in smell now. There was a solid edge of death in it, a sweetish slaughterhouse stench fused into the sharper, cooler odor of ozone.

With the wheel secure, he made his way to the starboard wing door. A body drifted into him, then away. He tried the door. It was as solidly shut as if a huge stone had been rolled against it. He rammed it with his shoulder and got it open a bit before the wind shut it again. On the third try, he got the thing open wide enough to squeeze through.

Back on the bridge, the light on the power phone began blinking.

Screeching, the full blast of the wind and rain struck him like a blizzard of gravel. He could no longer hear the shifting timbers, but he felt their periodic impacts riffle up through the wing deck.

Hugging the edge of the wheelhouse, he cupped his hands over his face, leaving a narrow space between his fingers. Through it, he looked down at the forward deck. Now out in the storm light, he could see the entire deck, the bow and the roiling sea beyond.

Several derrick booms had been washed away. The second raft was also gone. Near the fo'c'sle deck, the two preventer stays and part of the old gun pit had been torn away. The pit slab, hanging by its enforcing rods, slammed against the starboard ladder each time a sea came off the bow.

Fortunately, the hold hatches were still secure.

Momentarily relieved, he turned back to the door. It was then that he saw them, the Malay crewmen frantically trying to launch the starboard lifeboat. Several had already leaped down into it while the others cranked the davits outboard and worked the falls.

The bow of the lifeboat dropped suddenly as the after fall tangled in its block fairlead. Inside the boat, the men tumbled against the seats. Ashdown shouted at them, but his voice was instantly lost in the howl of the wind. He released the door handle and started toward the wing ladder just as Tun came lunging unsteadily out the Liberty doorway.

At that moment, the *Bengal* rolled sharply to port. The movement slammed Jack hard against the wheelhouse. Then the ship began to lift. He snapped his head around. A mountainous wave loomed over the bow. "Oh, shit!" he yelled and grabbed for a wing stanchion, his heart leaping against his chest.

The wave seemed to fold itself around the ship's bow. Over the top of the wing coaming, he watched it. Slowly, slowly it came, engulfing the bow now, and then the full weight of it struck the forward deck in an exploding, rushing avalanche of foam and water.

Two heartbeats later, it struck the midhouse. A hissing curtain of water blew straight up the face of the wing coaming, and then the main part of the wave poured over the coaming and struck him.

He held on with all the strength he could bring to his shoulders and arms, both hugging the stanchion. His legs were instantly swept off the wing deck, carried straight out by the onrush of the water.

Seconds seemed like minutes before it passed, left him crumpled on the deck, his legs resting down the ladder. He twisted to look aft in time to see Tun's head bob once and then disappear beneath the wave.

It swept on through the alleyways. Objects torn from the deck, railing sections and stanchions flew up into the air. A second later, the roaring river of ocean engulfed the lifeboat. Falls snapped like strings from a kite; blocks shot out. He saw the curved tops of the davits drop out of sight. The force of the wave hurled the lifeboat down and out. Three men went somersaulting into the sea.

As the sternward rush of water dissipated, he caught sight of the lifeboat's red bottom lying in the sea about thirty yards from the ship. As he watched, it was rammed underwater by the confusion of wave shatter. A few seconds later, its airtight compartments popped it to the surface again, still upside down. For a fleeting moment, Jack thought he saw two heads nearby. Then they were gone.

For the past eighteen minutes, Ana had been testing the hurricane front—darting into the wall at a thousand feet, taking the full blast of the wind and then hurtling back out again.

Each time, the aircraft was viciously struck by the wind, and the sudden increased speed of the air passing over its rotors would shoot it back and up, with Ana madly pulling power off the Isotov TV3-117 turboshaft engines and adjusting the blade pitch on the lower of the two contrarotating rotors to prevent being flung upside down. Once leveled, the chopper would vibrate wildly but remain under control.

The Helix-27 was well designed for heavy buffeting winds. With its twin rotors, horizontal stabilizer fins instead of stern rotors, and sets of cyclic pitch linkages in the shaft heads, it allowed Ana to quickly counteract gyroscopic precession in the gusts, a potentially fatal oscillation that could tear the aircraft to pieces.

Meanwhile, Jesse tried frantically to regain the radio link

to the White House. All he got back were blows of ferocious static and meaningless snippets of voice messages from U.S. Navy operators.

The aircraft's radar unit was nearly useless now, its screen awash in chaotic surface bounce and electron jam from lightning flashes. Now and then, however, the solid blip of the *Bengal* would emerge for a second or two, glowing suddenly amid all that gray bounce. Two kilometers out, then four or three as the Helix entered and exited the storm wall.

As Ana strained to concentrate on the controls, to take the measure of the storm, wild, random thoughts shot through her mind. Pilar. Cuba. The stunning words of the American president. A radiation holocaust! *Madre de Dios!*

Still, from the very moment the American president had told her of the true situation, she knew she would go into the storm after the *Bengal,* risk herself, her crew, simply because it had to be done. She believed the American, despite the years of Cuban enmity. Making contact with this horror about to happen allowed her no options for refusal.

The President had asked about her ordnance. That clearly meant she might be asked to sink the ship. But why didn't the Americans do that, she wondered, hurl their own missiles out here? No, there must be a reason, some prohibition she was unaware of. Instead, this scenario would be played out with her right in the middle of it.

As they prowled once more beyond the fringe of the storm, she glanced over at Perez. His face was stiff with frustration, a touch of anxiety.

She let her hands go very gentle on the stick, felt it instantly slap back into her palm. The movement was very sudden as the wind hit the solid body of the fuselage with full force. A thought occurred.

Keying the intercom, she called to her winchman in the after bay. "Escalera, open both doors. Be sure your safety line is anchored."

"Yes, Lieutenant," Escalera came right back.

Half a minute passed. Then she felt the effect of the port

door opening, a sudden, thick hiss of air. The Helix yawed as the wind sucked at the widening hole in its side. She countered, adjusting pitch, felt pressure in her ears.

The winchman then opened the starboard door. There was an immediate settling of the chopper. In effect, she had created a breezeway through which some of the force of the wind could freely pass. Both pilots felt a pronounced vacuum made by the rushing wind behind them.

Jesse gave her a stiff grin, nodded.

Next, she considered the effect of the helo's weight. They were carrying over six thousand pounds of ordnance. If they found the ship, she knew she'd have to go down as close to it and the sea as possible. Any extra weight would increase her drop rate when the gusts hit her.

Again she keyed. "Dump all the depth bombs," she ordered Escalera and turned to Perez. "Jesse, get aft and help him."

The ensign immediately unhooked his harness and mike lead, and shoved out of the seat, grabbing for projections to keep from falling. She touched his arm and patted her chest, indicating that he remember his safety harness. He nodded and staggered off toward the after bay.

A sudden rain squall swept into them. She felt water droplets come flying into the back of her head. She looked out. The window was opaque with water, but she was able to see the tip of her left missile wobbling just forward of the front wheel strut.

She glanced back at the radar screen and felt the shift of the fuselage as the first depth bomb went out. Another. Then, suddenly, there the *Bengal* was again, the glowing, misshapen blob of light.

She punched in the computer. The readout came instantly. One and a half kilometers to her right, heading 059 degrees.

The blob faded off as the echo line passed on. Then it was back, brighter this time. For some reason, the unit was picking up a sudden clear return. Once more she set the computer. Same read.

She felt the last of the bombs go out. A minute later, Jesse came climbing back to his seat and dropped into it, harnessed up, rehooked his mike lead. His clothes were soaking wet.

"I've got the ship again," Ana said. "Zero-five-nine, one-point-five kilometers."

Jesse stared through the water-misty windshield in that direction, then turned to look at her for a long moment. He tilted his head. "Okay, let's do it."

Giving herself no time to think another thought, Ana swung the helo slightly to the right, her eyes riveted on the heading compass as it swung slowly, deliberately through degrees.

She eased the turn, steadied up: 059 degrees. She became suddenly, acutely aware of things around her. The roar of the two Isotovs deep in the wind sound. The woody scent of Jesse's shaving lotion. The feel of the stick in her hand and the jolt and tremble of the aircraft as it raced straight for the unseen storm wall.

---

BENGAL
*12:41 P.M.*

"JEREMIAH," JACK YELLED INTO THE POWER PHONE, panting from the shock of seeing the crew lost, the effort to get back to the bridge. "They're all gone. The whole crew, swept away."

He was drenching wet, stood there holding onto the port wing door handle. He felt numb and cold, all over, his body pores allowing the iciness to seep inside. He heard machinery through the phone.

"Jeremiah!" he hollered again. The phone was off its cradle, he thought. He whistled. "Goddammit, answer."

Vogel's voice came on. "The chief's dead," he said simply.

"What!" *Jeremiah*. "How?"

"One of the Malays killed him. They've all deserted."

Jack's head roared, felt compacted. A few seconds passed. He came back. "You're alone down there?"

"Yes."

Christ, now there're only two of us aboard.

The ship blew through a wave, tore the crest, plunged. Jack braced himself against the sill and listened to the sea

**310**

sweep back. He glanced at the wheel, saw the pennant lashings straining.

"Can you keep up steam?" he asked.

"Yes. I—"

The phone went dead, and the window and annunciator lights went out. Only the binnacle light remained, running off its own battery. Jack took the phone away and pressed his ear against the bulkhead.

A few seconds later, he felt the automatic diesel generators kick in, the solid hum coming up through the steel. The phone made a distant whoosing sound and the lights flared, then dropped to normal.

Jack put the phone back to his ear and started to say something. There was an explosion. He caught the sound of rending wood and ripping canvas in it. Then came a crazy, discordant thundering and slamming and two solid impacts against the midhouse, the sharp, crackling snap of cables parting.

He dropped the phone and ran uphill to the window rail; the *Bengal*, climbing another wave face, tilted to the left. He peered through the center window. He saw the snow of runoff cascading back. In it, tumbling and skidding like sticks caught in rapids, were the long, black-misty shapes of logs.

The timbers had blown through the number-two hold hatch.

The ship crested and hung there; then her bow dropped with the same stomach-sickening suddenness of a plummeting elevator. As he watched, the bow disappeared into trough water, tons of it engulfing the fo'c'sle and then the forward deck, the water suddenly sheeny and smooth as it bulged over the ship and then parted as its center went down into the open hold hatch.

This time the ship stayed under for what seemed an eternity before she at last started up, struggling massively. Finally, she cleared, stablized.

Jack was aware of a new solidity to her set. His heart leapt with hope. The huge volume of water that had just poured down into the hold was acting as ballast, holding the ship's forward hull deeper in the sea. It would make it harder for her to clear the trough plunge, but at least she'd ride easier through the wave fronts.

Then a horrible realization struck. If the hold was only partially filled, the water and remaining logs would pile up on one side when she heeled. It might be enough to pull her completely over. The hold would have to be totally filled, right up to the coamings, in order to prevent such a shift of weight.

He pulled his way back to the dangling phone. ''Vogel,'' he yelled.

''Yes.''

''Number-two hold's been breached. It's taking water.''

''I felt it.''

''Give me Ahead Half. I've got to put her head directly into those waves.''

He didn't wait for an answer. Pulling his waist knife, he lunged around the power box and sliced through the pennant lashings. As soon as the wheel was freed, it snapped hard to the left as the wind bore into the ship, yawing it to starboard.

He stopped it, the spokes stinging his hands. Shoving his weight to it, he went over to the right, felt the engine throb increase through the deck, felt the *Bengal* lift on another wave. But she was answering the helm, turning slowly.

Again the sudden drop. But she was already fully into the turn and struck the trough with no heel, going deep, the wheel getting mushy as part of the rudder cleared and then, again with the massive, straining ponderousness, she came back.

At that instant, a brilliant white light flashed across the bridge windows. It was so bright, it cast shadows inside for a few seconds before it disappeared.

But he could see its thick beam out there, like a shaft of smoky white sunlight scoured with rain. It slanted out beyond the midhouse, illuminated the port bulwarks. He followed the beam back and up. There! Red and green blinking lights, the solid yellow-lit dome of a helicopter's cockpit.

The ship loomed suddenly out of the rain and wind like a gray apparition.

"There she is," Jesse shouted through the intercom. His words were immediately echoed by the winchman.

Ana had been looking at her altimeter. She snapped her eyes up. She saw it, the ship sixty feet below, its whole forward section pulling up through tons of water. It carried no running lights.

Then the Helix's search beam crossed the midhouse and flashed for a moment on the windows. She saw what looked like logs twirling and pinwheeling in the maelstrom of ocean on her decks.

She stared down at the vessel, feeling her throat constrict. It carried chaos. Yet, as she watched it fighting against the tumultuous sea, its gray hugeness all alone down there, it seemed to possess some dark, painful majesty.

Within seconds, the wind drove the helicopter past the ship, out over open ocean again. The wave tops were just below the struts. Ana lifted slightly and swung back, the Helix skidding and rocking until she got it aligned to the headwind. Slowly they drove into it until the ship was below them once more, off their right side.

Jesse was already calling the ship, using the international distress frequency, channel 16, speaking rapidly in English: "*Bengal, Bengal*, this is Cuban Patrol one-four-four. Do you read? Over."

Again and again he repeated the call while Ana fought to hold position. Suddenly a downdraft dropped the chopper. The struts momentarily dragged through a crest. She threw on power, pitched upward. The bottom of the fuselage, catching the wind, was whipped back and away.

No answer from the ship.

Again, they struggled back to it, this time fifty feet above the crest height. As they settled into hover, the radio blared: "Cuban one-four-four, this is Watchdog. Receiving your transmission to *Bengal*. We will monitor but stand clear. Over.''

Jesse immediately acknowledged. Watchdog was the code name for the USS *Gettysburg*. He began calling to the *Bengal* again, over and over. Only static-filled emptiness returned.

Ana, her eyes in a constant scan, body reacting instantly to the forces surging against her aircraft, caught glimpses of the ship's bridge. Is anyone still in there? she wondered. Or is that ship just going on its own, a robot locked into its headlong journey to . . .

A thought. She tapped Jesse on the shoulder, flicked to intercom. ''Their radio could be out. Use our searchlight and transmit in Morse code.''

Perez nodded excitedly. He switched off all the lights in and on the Helix save for those on the instrument panel. Then, fingering the searchlight switch, he quickly blinked a *Q* signal: ''QSL'' *Are you receiving?*

He repeated it three times.

The *Bengal*'s bridge lights suddenly came on, three small squares of yellow light through the rain. They went off again. Then they blinked off and on: R . . . R *Receiving as transmitted*.

''We've got him!'' Perez yelled.

A gust blew them out of hover. Pitching and powering around into the wind, Ana brought them back. Jesse blinked another message: ''QSO RDIO'' *Can you transmit radio?*

There was a long pause before the bridge lights blinked: ''N.'' *No*.

Amid the hiss of boilers and the deep cranking throb of the engine, Vogel worked at a feverish pace, locked off in his fear and the elemental awareness that if this engine stopped, he and Ashdown would die.

The periodic downpours through the main blower vents had continued. The water on the lower deck of the engine room was now mid-calf deep, the pumps falling behind. Yet, wherever he was, Vogel consciously guarded the throttle, felt for the telltale first lift of the ship as each new wave came into her.

He'd quickly break off what he was doing and race for the throttle to pull off power until the prop cleared. Then he'd slowly bring the engine back to forty RPMs.

The ship's electricity was still coming off the twin diesel generators. The main switch panel had blown all its circuit breakers when the *Bengal* heeled hard over and water was hurled against both transformers. But Vogel knew that the generators had limited capacity and if run too long would automatically shut down to prevent overheating.

Vogel quickly jury-rigged an override of the panel transformers, ran the engine-generated electricity straight into the panel. It was a risky move. Certain circuit systems could overload, and the hookup charged the entire panel, which made it dangerous to work around.

But at least the ship's mains would hold voltage. He threw the circuit breakers back on. There was a flash of light and a few sparks. The diesel generators stopped, indicating that the mains were functioning.

Next, he began transferring ballast, shifting oil to both number-three deep tanks. He hoped this would even out the forward weight of the breached hold.

The heavy, erratic rolling of the ship was dampened somewhat now that Ashdown had the bow heading directly into the wave chains. Still, the ship's pitching movement, even with the flooded hold and shifted ballast, was deep and heavy. As the wind now struck at her slightly forward of her amidships, there was a pronounced slippage to leeward.

The earlier vibration in the main shaft had also lessened slightly. Vogel didn't know why. But trouble was beginning to develop up on the cylinders. Their crosshead troughs were oozing a thick yellow foam, which meant that water from the main blowers had gotten into the siphon boxes and was contaminating the lubricating oil.

He dashed up to the second grating—forcing himself not to look at Pepper—and began hand-lubricating the ahead guides. But he wasn't fast enough. He glanced at the temperature gauges for the guides and piston shafts. They were slowly rising.

The ship took another heavy sea. In the engine room, the sound was like big stones rolling off a roof. Then there was a hollow shuddering as water struck the stack. The jolt made the water on the deck tremble as if radio impulses were passing through it.

Vogel froze. If the stack went, the entire engine room would flood, putting out the boilers.

Slowly, the ship plowed through it.

He went back to work.

## WHITE HOUSE
### 12:46 P.M.

"We have made contact with *Bengal,*" Ana's voice said. It echoed through the loudspeaker of the suddenly silent conference room. Everybody stopped in mid movement, only their eyes lifting to the round speaker. The signal was surprisingly strong and clear.

Pause. "Ship directly below. Radio not functioning. We are communicating—"

There was a violent burst of static. Still no one moved.

Pause. "—unknown." The rumble of thunder was heard for a moment. It gave a malignant resonance to the air in the room.

"Say again," shouted the president. "Say again. Over."

Pause. "Ship's radio not functioning. We are communicating by Morse code light. Status aboard unknown."

"At least *someone* on that ship's answering her," Rebeck said.

"Request her ambient pressure," Colonel Trautloff said quietly to the president. "She can calculate it off her altimeter."

"What is your ambient pressure? Over," the president called.

Pause. "Two-nine-point-two-zero. Do you copy?"

The president turned and stared directly at Colonel Trautloff. She gave him a slight frown. He swung back.

"Yes, we read. Ana, please find out who is in control of the ship. Do you understand? Over."

Pause. "Affirmative."

The crackle of static stopped. A moment later, the Norfolk operator notified them that the Cuban pilot had ceased transmission.

The president turned to Trautloff again. "Well? What do you think about that pressure reading?"

"It's lower than the NHC model extrapolations, sir," she answered. "But I still think we have a decent amount of time before trigger level's reached."

*A decent amount of time,* the president thought distractedly, bitterly. There wasn't a goddamned thing decent about this. He started pacing again, around and around the table, people's heads turning to follow him.

Commander Hand came to the door. Rebeck spoke softly to him a moment, then swung around to the president. "Sir, about a half hour ago, a television station in Houston claimed they'd received an unconfirmed report of a disabled ship off the coast of Florida with a live nuclear device aboard."

The president looked at him. His jaw muscles tightened and he lifted his head to the ceiling. "God *dammit,*" he snarled.

"Well, it's gonna hit the fan now," Santia said. "And fast."

"Deal with it," the president snapped.

Santia sighed softly, got up and went out.

The president paused to look up at the plotting board. He found the symbol for the *Winston-Salem.* "Rebeck, what's the sub's status on launch?"

The admiral instantly picked up one of the table phones. He talked for a minute, then put it down. "They're running continuous firing solutions, sir."

"Now how long to target?"

"Nineteen minutes."

The president grunted and started off around the table again.

HOUSTON
12:47 P.M.

At precisely 12:04, Ken Stark of channel 4 had interrupted the daily noon showing of *The Andy Griffith Show* to report what his bowling teammate, Virgil Gisler, had told him about a ship out there somewhere with a live nuclear bomb on it.

After talking with Gisler, he'd immediately called the Coast Guard station at Port Bolivar for confirmation. He got nowhere. He tried the Eighth District headquarters, talked to two officers but still got zilch. But he'd sensed a clear impression of urgency in their tone. These jokers were running with tight assholes, he thought.

He decided to go with a break-in announcement, make it sound big but neatly framed in the "unconfirmed" safety net. Afterward, it didn't take long for the telephone lines to light up. But the calls were mostly from little-old-lady types asking what, dear God, was going to happen.

Stark was disappointed. He'd figured a much bigger response. He walked to the huge, tinted window of the broadcasting room and looked out at Jacksonlee Avenue. Everything seemed perfectly normal.

Then, ten minutes later, the big-bore calls started coming in, asking specifically for him: staff people from CNN, CBS, ABC, Fox, everybody wanting to know the particulars, sources, substantiations.

He played it close to the vest, enjoying the sudden importance. But he did manage subtle hints that the information had actually come from the Coast Guard. Who, specifically? he was asked. Hell, he said, you-all know I can't divulge that.

Unknown to Stark as he sat with a fresh cup of coffee and gleefully punched phone buttons, the first tentacles of panic were already beginning to reach out through the coastal communities of southern Florida.

Jack, again lashing the wheel with the pennants, watched the helicopter through the right forward window, its white shape distorted by the water runoff on the glass. It sat out there blinking its light like a flying saucer come to curiously, cautiously study the agony of this huge Earth artifact in the sea.

The lashings secure, he reached over the power box and pulled the bridge searchlight from its bracket. It was heavy, brass-encased with a gun-type grip. Steadying himself with one arm around the helm stanchion, he waited.

The chopper blinked: STATS?

Jack answered, the light's switch making a solid click close to his face: CPTN / CRW DED = 2 ABRD

The helo's light stayed off for nearly a quarter of a minute before it began blinking again: CFM TERRORISTS ABRD? *Do you confirm terrorists aboard?*

Ashdown frowned, lowered the searchlight. What?

He quickly blinked: QSM *Repeat message.*

It came right back.

He blinked: N

The *Bengal* lifted on a gigantic wave. He saw the helicopter pull away instantly. The ship crested and plunged, the hull popping and cracking off rifle rounds.

When she leveled once more, he peered anxiously out the window. Where the hell are you? There, the aircraft was back, hovering. Its light immediately began transmitting rapidly.

Jack read the dots and dashes, the message complete this time, no *Q* signals or shorthand. It sent a wash across his skin. It said: NUCLEAR BOMB ABOARD

He made the aircraft repeat.

It did, added: TRIGGER SET TO UNKNOWN BAROMETRIC PRESSURE

For a moment he was too stunned to react. Then he thought, No, this can't be true. Who the hell *are* these people?

He looked angrily out the window again, began blinking:
ID SLF/DTA SORCE

The answer: CUBN PAT . . . DTA SORCE DE U S
NVY/U S PRES

Once more the chilling shock. The U.S. Navy, the president? Jesus! Was it all a lie? But to what purpose? Then
things began to fall into place. O'Mallaugh and Jadid.
Jadid's assault weapon. Collins's death. The run for the
center of the hurricane.

MyGodmyGodmyGod. It was *true*.

The chopper was signaling again: U KNOW LOCA-
TION BOMB?

N . . . N . . . N . . . N

A sudden black shroud descended over the ship as a
heavy rain squall struck. The helicopter disappeared. Jack,
staring, was still blinking, the flash of his light illuminating
the bridge, making a misty yellow hole through the rain.

Deep in the forepeak, two inches of water had collected
in the very bottom of the space. It came from leakage
through the hatchway seals high above, the water dripping
steadily down through the rope locker and carpenter's
space, giving the rust-smelling air an overlay of soaked
hemp and wet wood.

With each heaving movement of the ship's bow, the water slipped and splashed against the storm oil tank and piping, over the angle iron brace and the bomb attached to it.

The sound in the confined area was constant and deaf-
ening. The booming impacts of the seas against the bow;
the racing, deadly hiss of the water; the endless explosive
cracks and deep groans of the struggling ship.

It was pitch-black, save for a single light, the tiny, soft
glow of the readout in the bomb's casing: 28.52

Vogel held the power phone tightly against his head,
straining to hear Ashdown's words as they came in rapid,
wild bursts: A Cuban chopper out there. Nuclear bomb
aboard. Trigger on barometric pressure set.

His heart jammed for a moment. A nuclear bomb? He cut in: "Wait, wait. Is this really true?"

"The Cubans claim it's direct from the U.S. Navy and the president," Jack said. "I believe them. O'Mallaugh actually intended to blow this bomb inside the storm, contaminate the whole goddamned thing with radiation."

Vogel was stunned into silence.

"It could be anywhere," Ashdown went on. "But, Christ, we'd never be able to find it. Just the two of us. We don't . . ." His voice trailed off.

The German's mind was roiling. "Maybe it won't go off," he blurted.

"Even if it didn't, the navy would have to sink us. That means missiles." There was a string of silence through the receiver. It coiled under the noise of the ship, the sea.

Finally Jack said, "There's only one thing we can do. Put her down ourselves."

"Yes," Vogel said numbly.

"There isn't time enough for scuttle procedure. We'll have to blow her boilers."

"Yes."

"I'm coming below."


## WHITE HOUSE
## 12:53 P.M.

Ana was back, a clean signal only occasionally splurred with static bursts. She said, "Captain and all but two of crew are dead."

"Jesus," Rebeck said softly. "They must have had one helluva fight on her."

The president hissed at him to be quiet.

Pause. "Person we are communicating with denies knowledge of terrorists. Does not know location of bomb. Advise next move. Over."

The president said to the speaker: "Please stand by."

Pause. "Acknowledge. Standing by."

The president swung to look into the faces at the table.

"All right, let's have thoughts. Hurry it up, God dammit."

Rebeck said, "At this point, I'd say we tell those men aboard to sink her."

"They'd be committing suicide."

"Not necessarily, sir. They could put off in one of the lifeboats or rafts before she sounded." He shrugged. "Besides, what other option do they have? They're going to die anyway, one way or another."

That statement visibly affected everyone. Although they had been dealing for hours with the possibility of the deaths of millions, the precise, inevitable deaths of these two specific men revolted them.

The president thought a moment, his lips drawn back against his teeth. "How would they do it?"

"Open the cargo hatches," Rebeck answered. "Heave in the bilge petcocks. Lash the helm and deliberately breach the ship till she went fully over."

"Could only two men do all that?"

"It's a long shot but possible, sir." He thought a moment. "Still, even if she went completely over, she could remain afloat like that for quite a long time."

The president murmured something.

"There's one other possibility," Rebeck said. "The *Winston-Salem*'s still picking up cavitation noise. That means the *Bengal*'s engine is still running. They could blow the boilers, tear out part of the hull."

"How long would it take to go under then?"

"No way to know, sir. If the breach was large enough, maybe minutes. If not, it could take hours."

The president glanced at Trautloff and the two scientists. "Would a boiler explosion detonate the bomb?"

"No, sir," the colonel answered. "A pressure blowout is a deflagrating explosion. That means it presents a heaving *outthrow*. Surrounding pressure would actually increase."

The president nodded and went back to the plotting board. "How much time before she reaches the eye wall?"

"I talked to Norfolk two minutes ago," Rebeck said.

"They estimate approximately an hour and forty-eight minutes. NHC concurs."

"Is Anholt on-line?"

"Yes, sir." Rebeck pointed to one of the phones.

The president picked it up. "Anholt?"

"Yes, sir."

"Can you estimate what the pressure will be near the ship in forty-five minutes?"

"A moment, sir," Anholt said. Five seconds passed. Eight. He came back. "We estimate it should be about 28.90, maybe 28.80."

*Maybe.*

"Thank you." He hung up and looked at the admiral. "What's the *Winston-Salem*'s missile time-to-target now?"

Rebeck picked up another phone, spoke a moment and put it back. "Sixteen minutes, twenty-eight seconds, sir, with some lag time for the Tomahawk's seeker unit to run its search pattern. Exact time depends on where it enters the target quadrant."

The president put his head down, rubbing his face vigorously with both hands like a man just risen from a long sleep. He paused, holding the tips of his fingers under his chin.

"How deep is the sub running at this moment?" he asked.

"Probably at four hundred feet. It's an ideal speed depth."

"How long does it normally take from there to reach launch depth?"

"With a crack crew, about three minutes to achieve a hover and launch position, sir. Another thirty seconds to actually launch."

The others exchanged glances. Was the president about to play the big gamble? He remained very still, silent, his eyes squinting at the air in front of him.

"Sir?" Rebeck said, "Do I order the *Winston-Salem* to go to launch depth?"

"Not yet." He turned slowly and faced the loudspeaker. "Ana, can you read me? Over."

Pause. "I copy, sir. Go ahead."

"Order those men aboard her to sink the *Bengal*. They have forty-five minutes to do it. Or we will. Do you understand? Over."

Pause. "I understand. Will comply. Stand by."

The president slowly sat down.

*BENGAL*
*1:00 P.M.*

JACK LEFT THE BRIDGE AND DUCKED INTO THE CHART room to check the barometer. It was bolted to the inboard bulkhead. It glowed softly from the phenomenon called barometric light. Whenever pressures dropped to low levels and the mercury inside the tube was vigorously shaken, a luminous, scarlet glow formed on the glass. It made it appear like a thin shaft of ruby.

**29.18 inches.**

A rush of explosive images assailed Ashdown's mind. That nanosecond of nuclear light, a burst as brilliant as the sun. Heat beyond comprehension. Then nothing, the self utterly, infinitesimally gone.

The images sucked into him an overwhelming sense of sadness. For Pepper and the crew and Vogel and himself. And for the *Bengal,* too.

He'd come to love her as only a seaman can love a ship. His home, his battlement against a vast and sometimes vicious sea. It was a bond that extended far beyond mere affection. And it carried a kinship to that deep, vague, unspoken need for maternal protection that all men carry forever from birth.

She'd fought long and hard for her life, for all their lives. Her exhausted body had strained to hold together; her engine, the heart of her, to beat. Now everything was reversed. Where once he'd tried to save her, he now had to kill her. With his own hands. It wrenched his heart.

He reached out and gently touched the bulkhead, felt its old, cold steel. "Good-bye, old lady," he said softly.

He returned to the bridge. The Cuban chopper was back, madly signaling. Flashes coming quick and clean. He picked up the searchlight, cut them off: BK . . . BK *Break*. QSM. *Repeat*.

The flashes came right back: PRES ORDR U SINK SHIP

C . . . C *Yes . . . Yes.*

U HVE 45 MIN// THN MISLE ATAK

Missiles. Oh, yeah, Jack thought.

**Forty-five minutes** . . .

He wondered why the navy hadn't already launched. He thought a moment. Wait, a missile could possibly detonate the bomb itself. Sure. So, they were going to wait, see if he and Vogel could sink her first.

He clicked the searchlight: WILL BLO BOILERS// OPN CRGO HATCHS

QSL . . . HW MUCH TIME?

CNT CNFRM

WILL REMN FR RSCUE ATTMPT U

TU . . . SK. *Thank you. End of transmission.*

He checked the wheel lashings, then headed into the passageway. This time Jadid's body floated through the doorway when he opened it. A distortion of a human being, boneless as an empty rubber wetsuit.


Vogel was stripped to the waist, his skin shiny with sweat and oil. He was on the second grating when Ashdown reached the engine room.

For a moment, Jack knelt beside Jeremiah's corpse. He saw that Pepper had clearly died of a skull fracture. Blood had come from his eyes, nose, ears. It still dripped off the grating. He slipped off the Aussie's bush hat and laid it over his face.

Then, wordlessly, he and Vogel went down to the machinery floor. They stood close beside the throttle desk. Jack shouted over the noise. "The Cubans say we've got forty-five minutes to put her under. Then the navy starts firing missiles."

Vogel's eyes narrowed for a moment, as if he had looked into the sun. He nodded gravely.

"How long to get the pressure up to explosive level?" Jack asked.

"Thirty, maybe forty minutes."

"All right," he said. "We'll set everything in motion here and then go into the holds. We've got to break down the cargo cables and get those timbers free of the ship. Otherwise, they'll keep her afloat."

The *Bengal* took another solid wave front. Before leaving the bridge, Jack had lashed the helm so the bow would maintain a heading of due east. As the deck tilted sharply upward, both men grabbed for handholds. With his free hand, Vogel eased off throttle.

The ship cleared the crest and plunged. Everything shook as if an earthquake were shuddering through the hull. At last, the bow broke free and the *Bengal* settled, heaving slightly to starboard. The German eased power back.

A flurry of electrical arcs crackled across the secondary power panel. The lights went out. A few seconds later, one of the emergency generators kicked in. The lights flared up, steadied. The generator began to miss, sputtered, caught again. Then it died abruptly.

The entire engine room was plunged into a flickering blackness. The only illumination came from the yellow glow of the boiler ports, which threw narrow rings of light onto the shimmering deck water, and a soft, delicate green iridescence of static electricity that rippled and played about the engine cylinder shafts and crank pits.

Both men cursed.

Although the lights were gone, the numerous engine and

boiler pumps and fans continued to operate, drawing their electrical power into the main panel directly from the engine.

Vogel fumbled for a flashlight. A moment later, he switched it on. The beam was a misty shaft in the dark. They waded to the secondary power panel.

Vogel played the light across its face. Several U-shaped circuit breakers had been badly scorched. He threw one off, then snapped it back on again. A string of small lights on the second level immediately came on for a second, then went off.

Vogel threw the breaker off again and back. His left hand touched a second switch, and there was a flash. He was instantly thrown backward into Ashdown, and they both went down into the water.

The moment Vogel touched the second switch, Jack had felt a fiery riffle bolt through the water and into his legs. A million pinpricks swept through his body. For a millisecond, his heart felt as if it would burst. Then Vogel's limp body had crashed into him.

He came up out of the water in a gasping lunge and immediately caught the stench of burnt flesh. A familiar smell: Nam, burning corpses along jungle roads. The flashlight was still clasped in Vogel's hand. It formed a foggy brown smear of light under the water.

He bent to examine the German. He was partially submerged. The entire left side of his body was black, the skin shriveled as if its juices had been instantly sucked away. His face was also charred. The skin around his mouth was gone, and his teeth showed like a skull's.

Jack moaned. Jesus, no. He closed his eyes, put his head back and drew air deeply. Behind him in the flickering darkness, the shafts and headers and cranks continued their ceaseless, throbbing churn.

*Now he was totally alone.*

Real fear hung on the edges of Ana's mind, a prowling wolf pack seeking out a hole in her concentration. She held it back, focused on the aircraft.

She and Jesse had talked little over the last few minutes. Both were white-faced. Once, the winchman came forward, soaking wet, looked silently at both pilots, then went aft again.

Ana constantly checked her instruments, tried desperately to foresee the aircraft's movements. She sensed that the storm was getting worse. She shot a look at her altimeter. It indicated that they were flying at 200 feet.

Whenever the ambient pressure drops below the mean-sea-level setting of 29.92, an altimeter will register a higher-than-true altitude. Back when the president asked her for her ambient pressure, her altimeter had actually read over a thousand-foot altitude. By adjusting the altitude indicator back to her true altitude of 50 feet, the actual ambient pressure immediately showed in the setting window.

Now she reset the indicator again, read the field pressure: 29.00. She glanced at her watch: 1:17. The pressure had dropped a full two-tenths of an inch in thirty-one minutes!

She keyed her intercom. "Jesse, what's our fuel?"

He already had figured it. "One hour, fifty-seven minutes at present rate of consumption."

Then all the lights on the *Bengal* had gone out. At the same moment, a deep gray-black rain squall swept over them. Visibility was completely lost. She lifted the Helix slightly, regained hover.

Jesse leaned forward, peering intently through the windshield, the wiper blades carrying berms of water away.

She clicked off intercom and began calling the *Gettysburg*. It took two full minutes to obtain a clear signal to the White House.

She keyed: "Ship has communicated intention to explode boilers and open cargo hatches. All lights gone now. Possible main electrical power loss."

Pause. "Did they give estimate of time to complete sinking? Over."

"Negative."

Pause. "What is your ambient pressure?"

"Two-nine-point-zero-zero. Over."

Pause. "Acknowledge. Will you be able to recover survivors? Over."

"Will attempt if possible. Have not—"

The signal was suddenly drowned in a violent crackling of static. The whole atmosphere around the Helix lit up in a blue-white lightning flash that lasted several seconds, the thunder coming with it like cannon fire all around them.

The aircraft shook violently. For a fleeting moment, cobalt-colored electrical charges spiderwebbed down through the rotor blades. Two red circuit breaker lights flashed. Jesse quickly flicked the breakers back on.

There was a sudden clearing in the squall, the downwash instantly sheening off the opaque film of rain. Less than thirty yards directly in front of them was the forward derrick post of the *Bengal*. The ship's bow lifted up under them, hurling spray up against the bottom of the aircraft's fuselage.

With her heart suddenly in her throat, Ana rammed on power and pitched to the right. The Helix caught the wind and heaved away, the bow visible for a flashing moment, clearing the wave crest as the tips of the helicopter's rotors slashed the air only a few feet above it.

They skidded downwind for a few seconds. Then Ana, her hands shaking, swung the helicopter back and struggled toward the *Bengal*.

Standing in the firing alley, Jack tried desperately to remember things. He drew up images of the engine room of the coastal freighter he'd served on. Pictures of the engineering classes at the Maritime Academy with the schematics of triple-expansion reciprocating steam engines.

To blow a ship's boilers, he knew, certain procedures had to be performed in a sequential way. And all the safety systems that were deliberately built into the machinery had to be disabled.

Gradually, flashes of memory began to solidify. Piping systems. Safety backups. Integrated pressure lines and gauge readings. Yeah, yeah! Frantically, he traced them out in his mind, aware that terror hung back there in the darker recesses.

At last, he was ready.

First he moved back to the throttle and dropped the revolutions to thirty. This would give the ship steerageway, yet still keep her prop from tearing out the main shaft when it cleared water.

Next, he located and turned up the forced draft valve. It immediately increased the pressure of the fuel going into the boilers. He checked the steam gauges. The needles began climbing.

Then, one by one, he turned off all the steam line bypass valves and manually locked their red-line seal vents. He did the same to the surface condenser return lines. Afterward, he went up to the top grating and locked off the relief valves on all the cylinders and steam chest covers.

He was still up there when the *Bengal* took a particularly huge wave front. Jack froze, felt it cross under the hull. A few seconds later, the prop wound up as it cleared water.

It sent a violent vibration up the main shaft and into the bedplate. Bearings ground with a bass-toned, bone-chilling rasp. A shim fired out of a link block and smashed into a thrust shoe with the impact of a bullet.

As the ship leveled once more, he hurried back to the machinery floor. Ducking and lunging, he closed all the bottom cylinder and steam chest drain valves. Then he returned to the throttle and locked down its pilot valve so steam couldn't back up through the poppet.

Panting from exertion, his nerves vibrating with tension, he waded to the firing alley and checked the steam and temperature gauges. There was an opaque layer of condensation on the glass faces. He wiped it away.

Pressure: 300 pounds per square inch. Temperature: 550 degrees Fahrenheit.

Using his light, he cast the beam upward and followed the steam lines. Had he forgotten a valve somewhere? He scanned the boilers and panels, then tipped his head back to look up at the network of piping that crisscrossed below the high overhead.

Two red warning lights suddenly began blinking on the boiler faces. Jack peered through a port. Both boilers were roaring now, the sound like water rushing through a flume. Inside, the fuel tubes were red-hot. He twisted around, checked the gauges.

Pressure: 420 psi. Temperature: 600 degrees.

A whistle went off on the gauge panel. He ignored it. Instead, he waded back and forth in the firing alley, grabbing the gauge panel post with each lift and plunge. His body tingled with adrenaline that forced constant movement.

Pressure: 480 Temperature: 685.

Three minutes passed. Four.

The pressure at last reached 500. Jack immediately opened the sea chest valve and began flooding the deck. He felt the swirl of its current around his legs.

He returned to the throttle desk. Vogel's body had lodged itself between a power box and the back of the ladder. He stared at it a moment, then went up the steps.

Pepper's bush hat had fallen off his face. His robin's-egg-blue eyes stared upward emptily, void of substance, like two buttons poked into the face of a scarecrow.

Jack replaced the hat and went on. Up the ladder. Faster and faster. Then his utter aloneness overwhelmed him, drew hopelessness from his soul. He stopped. This won't work, he thought. It's too late.

But something in him fought back. No! Not yet. He headed up the ladder again, taking three steps at a time.

**WHITE HOUSE**
**1:21 P.M.**

Things were coming at the president like rounds from ambush. After Ana's shocking revelation of the big drop in ambient pressure at the ship, everybody's face tightened into grimmer lines. Anholt verified that his models were also showing steeper drops in the storm's pressure bands.

"Well, at least they've begun sinking her," the president said, groping for slivers of hope. His eyes swung to Rebeck. "Dammit, you must have *some* idea of how long it takes for a ship to go down once her boilers are blown."

Rebeck shrugged helplessly. "I'm sorry, sir. As I said, she could go in minutes, especially if her cargo starts shifting. Or she could stay afloat for hours. We'll just have to depend on Ana's visuals to tell us what's happening out there."

"Then get her back."

"Yes, sir."

At that moment, Secretary of Defense Gilliland returned from his attempt to raise Castro. Like everyone else, he was in shirtsleeves now, nervous sweat rings under his armpits.

The president gave him a questioning look.

Gilliland shook his head. "No dice, sir. Either Castro *won't* talk to you or his ministers are deliberately sequestering him. Simon even tried to speak with his brother, Raul. Nothing."

"Well, screw the son of a bitch," the president said angrily. "We won't need his chopper's rockets, anyway."

"There's something else," Gilliland said. "It's not good. Langley received reports from two separate sources in Cuba that claim Castro's activated his Sword of Bloody operation."

The Sword of Blood scenario had long been known to American intelligence. Both the president and Admiral Rebeck swore.

Gilliland went on: "These sources also say Cuban Tu-16 Badger attack bombers have been seen loading ordnance in at least two bases: Campo Libertad and San Julian." The secretary shook his head. "If that bomb goes off so near his coast, that insane bastard would probably send over those Badgers."

The president's head snapped around to face Rebeck. "Is

there time to get those two carrier groups back into the Gulf?''

''Yes, sir: And I think we should put everything along the Gulf and southern Atlantic coasts on two-minute alert.''

''Do it.''

Rebeck rushed out.

The president started his walking again, back and forth, his arms crossed, suddenly aware of the icy coldness of the air-conditioning. One of the phone lights blinked.

He picked it up. ''Yes?''

It was Santia. ''We traced that television report. Some pissant local anchor from channel 4. He won't disclose his source, but we think it's somebody at Houston International's approach control.''

''What's happening down there?''

''Telephone switchboards all over southern Florida are going nuts. And state highway patrol and local police are reporting a horrific surge of northbound traffic.''

''Oh, God.'' The president inhaled deeply, let it out. ''Are we looking at real panic down there?''

''I don't think so. Not yet, anyway. I figure everybody's watching their TVs to see what the hell the networks say. Now *those* big honchos are really starting to break down the doors. Phillips is sweatin' bullets trying to hold them at bay.''

''What about the evacuations along the eastern coast?''

''So far, things are still moving efficiently. But rumors are starting to take hold.''

The president thought a moment. ''All right, tell Phillips to set up a press conference for two-thirty.''

Santia was silent a moment. ''Isn't that cutting it a bit tight?''

''Two-thirty.''

''All right.'' Santia was gone.

The president glanced at the clock, frowned. He'd forgotten the precise time he'd issued his forty-five-minute deadline. He turned to Trautloff.

"How much time to launch deadline?"

"Twenty-one minutes, sir," she said.

The trunk hatch shaft down into the number-five hold was as black as a lava conduit straight to hell.

Jack climbed down the ladder with the flashlight off, feeling along the rungs, the walls of the trunk slimy with condensation and rusty scum. It smelled of bilge water, a diesel and rotted wood stench.

The sounds from the storm and the *Bengal*'s shuddering impacts into the wave chains sounded hollow and muffled here, like heavy thunder way up in the clouds. But there was another sound, a low-pitched humming that seemed close at hand, from somewhere below him.

Near the bottom of the ladder, he hit water. It blocked the end of the trunk shaft. Apparently, ocean leaking through the main hatch covering had risen above the foot of the trunk shaft. With power off, the bilge pumps were now useless.

He continued down until he was fully into the water. It was pitch-black, the water like thin gelatin. He cleared the bottom of the shaft and surfaced inside the hold.

The water was at least ten feet deep. He turned on the flashlight. A constant rain from the hatch cover glistened as it passed through the beam. Strips of dunnage and chock wedges floated around him.

The humming was thick in the stifled, clammy air. It was like a tape of a million bees played at slow speed. Jack understood its cause. Water had swollen the logs so much that the cargo cables were now taut enough to vibrate with the strain.

He sculled his legs and realized it would be futile to attempt to loosen the handy billies and screw jacks that held the cargo cables to the hold's deck eyebolts. And way too dangerous. If one of those cables parted, it'd whip around like a strap saw flung off its hub.

He turned back toward the trunk shaft. There was a loud, cracking explosion. Jack's skin jumped. One of the cables had snapped. He instinctively ducked back against the trunk shaft. He heard the cable end slash up against the hatch boards.

Then things began to rumble. He felt the reverberations all around him. As the ship crested and plunged, more cables parted. The second tier of timbers suddenly rammed forward en masse into the bulkhead that separated this hold from number four. Jack felt the trunk shaft crumple somewhere above him.

He was trapped.

His mind went flying away from him for an instant. It came back, whirling. Wait. Wait. He remembered there was a small hatch in the cross bulkhead that led into the number-four hold.

Sucking in as much air as he could, he went under and swam beneath the bottom of the trunk ladder. A moment later, his shoulder rammed into the bulkhead. He dropped his flashlight. In the pitch darkness, he saw it twirl away and down.

Blindly, he felt along the bulkhead for the hatch dog. He reached a bilge bracket, lowered himself to the deck and started back. There! He found the dog.

He tried to turn it, but it was snugged tightly. Straining, he finally got it moving counterclockwise. Through the water came fearsome squeaks and impacts as the timbers were hurled about with the shifting motion of the ship. Fear clamped around his throat. His lungs screamed for air.

He pulled on the hatch. The seals were stuck. Oh, God, he thought wildly. Was there enough water on the other side of the bulkhead to allow him to open the hatch?

He braced his feet and heaved. It opened. Somersaulting, he kicked his legs and jetted through the hatch into the number-four hold.

Down in the engine room, the air was blisteringly hot and saturated with moisture. Each time the ship lifted, the deck water, now several feet deep, receded from the firing alley. Then, as the *Bengal* crested and dropped, the water shot forward again, slamming against the electrical panel and forward bulkhead like a wave hitting a seawall. Some of the water was flung up onto the boiler faces, where it was superheated and instantly vaporized with furious, sizzling bursts.

The roar of the boilers had reached the pitch of twin jet engines. The color of the light from the boiler viewing ports went from acid yellow to pure white.

Pressure: 665. Temperature: 710.

The inside of the boiler was like a piece of the sun, everything blinding with a fiery incandescence. The fuel discharging into the headers was reaching explosive heat level now, the long narrow tubes resembling near-liquid steel coming off a wire-casting machine. Even the back plates and firebricks of the water wall were a brilliant scarlet.

There was a sudden, whomping flash aft of the firing alley. A fire had erupted under the feed pump drum. The oil and grease extracted from the condenser water were so hot, they had spontaneously flared when they hit the air in the extractor traps. The flames threw dancing shadows across the condenser columns and upper gratings.

Another sound came, a hissing throb. The main condenser was losing suction. The level in the gauge glass that indicated the boiler water instantly dropped to half. Soon the boiler crown plates and tubes would begin to melt.

Pressure: 832. Temperature: 781.

One minute later, the boilers blew.

There was a tremendous explosion, a brilliant white-hot flash of light. Parts of the boilers smashed into bulkheads, steam pipes, into the main engine plant and condenser housings. There was the cracking sound of rending hull plate. Smaller bits of metal went zinging through the air, ricocheting off and away.

A vicious, voluminous hissing came, then the sudden, gushing, explosive roar of an erupting geyser. There was a second, more powerful explosion as water hit the ruptured, superheated boiler remnants.

This time the ship heaved to starboard as the explosion blew a huge hole in her port side.

Three minutes earlier, the president's deadline had run out.

He'd been staring up at the wall clock as the seconds ticked off. He felt a developing sense of hollowness, a peculiar sensation, as if some of his breath had been pumped out of his lungs.

Finally, Rebeck stood slowly. "Sir?" he said. The others shifted in silent expectation.

Over the preceding twenty minutes, the *Gettysburg* operators had managed to regain a radio link with Ana, twice. But each time, the signal was badly static-fouled. They could only pick out bits of phrases. From these, they were able to deduce that the *Bengal* was still fully afloat.

Now the president nodded sharply, once. "Order the sub to get ready to launch."

Rebeck left.

A minute later, Commander Hand came to the door. "Mr. President?"

He turned away from the clock.

"We just got a code from SOSUS, sir," Hand said. "Their QA-4 array picked up a surface detonation from the *Bengal*. About three minutes ago."

The president's face went slightly pale. Santia said, "Oh, Jesus, no!"

"It's non-nuclear, sir," hand quickly said. "They've analyzed it as a probable boiler explosion. Lots of exothermic harmonics. That means her hull's been breached. Now she's open to the sea."

"All *right!*" the president cried. "I'm extending the deadline fifteen minutes as of now. Notify the admiral."

"Yes, sir."

The president turned to the people at the table. There

was a hard smile in his eyes. "Maybe those boys'll just do it yet."

"I'm prayin' like hell," Santia said.

## WINSTON-SALEM

Sixty seconds after the president's deadline passed, the sub's CDC speaker had blared: "Conn, Sonar."

"Conn, what is it?"

"We have an anomalous signal on lateral, sir. Possible detonation. Bearing two-four-zero degrees, range one-three-niner miles."

Commander Vantrease shot a glance at his XO. Detonation! Then he shook his head. "Not a nuke. Otherwise our laterals would be going off the spectrum. What do you think?"

Delannis grunted. "Maybe she's going under and water's hitting her boilers."

"Sonar, are you still picking up cavitation from Sierra Two?"

"Negative, sir. Her prop has stopped."

"Can you ID a boiler explosion off the harmonic profile?"

"We're running tape analysis now, sir. It's possible that we could get a decent profile off the oscilloscope."

Thirty-seven minutes earlier, the sub had risen to four hundred feet below the surface. She had been running in good, dense water at six hundred feet. Then an EAM from COMSUBLANT ordered Vantrease to stand by for a possible launch command. Since then, the sub had continued flying through the water while her tracking party ran continuous TMA plots.

Her sonar watchmen were still receiving a barrage of random noise along with the extremely faint and often fading sound of the *Bengal*'s prop. In reality, they'd picked up the sounds created when the cargo timbers tore open the ship's two holds. But the BC-10 analysis computer had been unable to classify them precisely.

Vantrease turned and moved to the port plotting table. The bearing of the *Bengal* matched the bearing of the possible detonation. He stared down at the plotting screen. The sound *had* to have come from the ship. His gaze swept back, followed his sub's track marked in a segmented red line.

They'd come a long, fast way over the last ninety minutes, he thought.

"Conn, Sonar."

"Go ahead."

"Sorry, sir, we can't get a pure definition off the signal tape."

"All right."

Thirty seconds later, the speaker came alive again: "Conn, Radio."

"Conn, aye."

"Another EMA coming in now, sir."

"Read off the decode when it's completed."

"Aye, sir."

Vantrease tilted his head back, waiting patiently.

Finally, the speaker sounded: "Conn, message reads: Achieve launch depth. Spin up two—repeat, two—TASMs. Stand by for launch command."

Vantrease instantly swung around. "Stand by to achieve launch depth," he snapped. "Diving officer, make your depth six-zero feet, smartly."

"Six-zero feet, smartly, aye," the officer responded. "Fifteen degrees up-angle on the planes."

"Fifteen degrees up, aye," repeated the planesman, pulling slowly back on his wheel. A moment later, the deck tilted slightly.

Vantrease reached up for a loudspeaker mike. "This is the captain. We are now in Condition 1-SQ, Missile." He replaced the mike and turned to the CCS-2 console on his right. "Tracking party, give me sixty-second updates on sequential mission plan."

"Sixty-second updates, aye."

"Weapons, Conn, stand by to initiate preset spin-ups for VLS tubes three and five. Hold for final mission program and firing command."

"Conn, Weapons, standing by on VLS three and five, aye."

All through the CDC, men had become suddenly more intent than usual, leaning over their consoles and instrument controls. The watch officers paced slowly behind them.

Vantrease, still at the plotting table, again glanced down at it, visually spanning the distance between the X and the Sierra Two's marker box. His eyes were hard as stone.

Jack's surge through the access hatch into the number-four hold had taken him so deep into it that when he surfaced, he was disoriented. He felt around, banged into the edge of a log.

The seepage through the hatch cover came down in streams. Outside was the storm roar and the constant crashing of timbers into the bulkhead. Then he heard them exploding through the hatch.

Closer in, he could hear the humming from the cables, and the timbers creaked and popped as they continued soaking up water. The sound resembled that of a wind passing through a pine forest, bending the trees.

His knee struck a cable. It was hot from the tremendous tension. He followed it down to a bilge strut. Pulling himself from one margin plate to the next, he at last reached the bulkhead and then the foot of the deck hatch trunk.

Ducking under water, he came up into it. He grabbed a rung and began to climb frantically to the deck, the ladder swaying.

He was halfway up when the boilers exploded. A quick jolt. The metal casing of the trunk rang. A few seconds later came a second explosion, much more powerful. The ship yawed sharply to the right, the movement so quick and shearing, Jack lost his hold. He slipped down several rungs before he managed to catch on again.

At last, he reached the deck hatch. He heard a mass of water washing across it. He waited a few seconds, then undogged it and tried to lift the hatch. Water shot in around the seal. He managed to get it up a few inches. Another wall of water struck it and slammed it fully open, the water flooding over him and down the trunk.

He clung to the ladder as the deluge sucked at his body. Gradually it eased. He pulled himself through the hatch and crawled out onto the main deck. He shot a glance astern.

Logs, caught in the wash, were slamming against the afterhouse and gun pit. Two quick flashes of lightning came, the thunder cracks right behind them. They illuminated the nearly horizontal rain into streaks of silver, made the foaming wash of ocean glow like snow in moonlight.

He struggled to his feet and headed for the boat deck ladder. He could feel the ship already beginning to list to port. He reached the ladder and raced up, cut across to the port door. Snapping the dogs over, he hauled it open and lunged through.

There was a foot of water in the passageway. To his left, a cloud of steam and smoke poured from the engine-room door. He heard the sea rushing in. It sounded like a swift, shallow river crossing a rock bed. Now and then came a hissing explosion as water got through packing to the hot steam pipes.

He turned and headed up the main passageway. He had to get to the forward holds, he knew, open them to the sea. Seconds zipped past him like dynamite fragments.

*How much time was left?*

For a stunning moment, his mind drew up a picture of the missiles. Already on their way. Like the Viet Cong rocket barrages in Nam where he had gripped the earth and listened to that heart-stopping rush and fluttering keen of incoming ordnance just before the target impacts, the ground heaving, each explosion in a neatly spaced sequence . . .

He willed the thoughts away and ran on.

\*       \*       \*

From their position above and to the right of the ship, both Ana and Jesse had witnessed the second boiler explosion: a quick flash of orange-white light, the ship visibly trembling as a great outburst of pure white steam with pieces of metal in it shot out through a hole in the port hull. The wind caught the steam and swept it back through the weather alleyways and railings, up around the stack, where it curled in the backdraft.

On the afterdeck, they watched as long gray logs came blowing through the hatch of the last hold. They went up into the air as if driven by an explosive force, then were caught in the sea and sent tumbling across the deck.

A moment later, Perez yelled through the intercom, "There's a man."

"Where? Where?"

He pointed down and to the right. Ana finally spotted him, emerging from a deck hatch. He wore shorts and a yellow T-shirt. She stared at him. Until this moment, the only life aboard this doomed ship had been a blinking light. Now there was a real human being down there. She watched him disappear through a door into the midhouse.

Jesse attempted to raise the *Gettysburg* again. Since losing the White House, all they'd picked up was a lot of scattered, incoherent feedback—snippets of voice-overs; long, wavering sound lines and sudden blows of hard static.

Ana took over the call. Twice she repeated the same message: "Watchdog, Watchdog, Cuban one-four-four. *Bengal* boilers have blown hole in port side. Two holds also open to sea. Ship beginning to list but is still afloat."

She keyed off and listened, the Helix jumping suddenly in a blast of ricocheting wind shear coming off the ship's rising starboard hull. She got the aircraft settled.

The radio gave her nothing back.

At midship, Jack turned right toward the Liberty door. It was called that because it opened onto the deck where the accommodation ladder was set in the gangway while in port.

Inboard the door was a small head; beside it, a bosun's chest. Toilet water flooded from under the head door. When the boilers exploded, back pressure had blown all the utility valves.

He tried the door to the bosun's chest. It was locked. Cursing, he ran back along the cross corridor to the galley on the port side. The galley was strewn with pots and broken bottles. The huge cooking stove had been torn off its foundation. The room stank of butane gas.

Holding his breath, he yanked open the refrigerator door. Slabs of meat and whole, frozen fish were down on the wooden deck boards. He spotted what he wanted: a rack of large open-ended wrenches used to service the galley's compressor and condenser units.

He grabbed a heavy, two-foot-long wrench. Returning to the passageway, he sprinted back to the Liberty door.

Ana keyed the intercom. "Escalera, can you see anyone?"

"No."

"Shit."

She eased the chopper slightly to the right so she could get a better view of the upper decks of the ship. The *Bengal*'s heel was steepening. Already the starboard waterline was exposed.

She turned to see Perez watching her. "It's past the deadline, Ana," he said. "We've got to get out of here."

"Not yet. I want those men."

"But we can't even see them now."

"No."

Jesse shook his head and shot an anxious glance at the MRP indicator lights on the overhead electronic countermeasure panel. There were two, both red. When the first flashed, it would mean that the unit had detected radar search pulses from an incoming missile. The second lit up once a missile locked onto the Helix.

Ana felt her blood pounding in her head, in her fingertips. She keyed the intercom again. "Escalera, stand by to lower a harness. We can't use the ground line, so attach a weight to it. Maybe the wind won't lift it too high.''

Escalera didn't acknowledge.

"God dammit, Tony, did you get that?"

"Yes, Lieutenant."

She glanced at Jesse. He was still looking out. She suddenly realized how black and shiny his hair was. Crazy thought. She turned away, scanned the ship again.

Escalera came on. "Harness set."

"All right, lower about thirty feet of cable. Let's see how it acts in the wind."

She waited, stared out at the rise of the *Bengal*'s stack, huge and dangerous, the metal of it scoured and covered with impregnated soot.

"The harness is blowing almost horizontal," Escalera said.

"Reel in and add more weight."

A minute passed. The thought of the missiles came. She forced it out, keying, "What the hell's taking so long back there?"

"Harness set."

"Lower."

She looked back, tried to see the cable and harness. Couldn't. A moment later, Escalera said, "It's holding at about forty degrees."

"Good enough. Stand by."

Jack had to put his full weight to the Liberty door to get it open. He squeezed through and was instantly hit by the full blast of the wind. Bracing against it, he checked the afterdeck.

The ship's stern was sitting low in the water now, the seas sweeping over the port bulwarks and against the afterhouse and gun pit. All but three logs from the number-five hold were gone; the remaining three were jammed under the stern canopy.

At that moment, timbers began exploding through the number-four hold hatch. Whirling and tumbling, they smashed into the after derrick booms and bull chains and tore them away. Another log sheared off a cowl vent and sent it sailing up onto the boat deck.

Jack turned and struggled forward along the lee alley-way. At the forward boat deck ladder, he hunkered down as another sea came off the bow and slashed its way back and up against the lifted starboard bulwarks, then flooded over him. He put his head down and hugged the ladder against its vicious pull.

At last, it washed past him, left him choking, his mouth full of seawater. He became aware of the hard rapping crack of the chopper's props close by. He looked up.

The aircraft was fighting its way against the wind sixty feet above him. A cable trailed out the right door, swinging at a slant in the wind. There were a harness and two weights at the end.

He turned back to the forward deck. All the booms and stays on both forward derricks were also gone. A glut of chains and stay cables was tangled around the main winches. As the deck rolled, water poured out of the open number-two hold.

Pitched into the wind, he crab-walked to the starboard winch platform located just aft the number-three hold. He looked at the hold hatch. Part of the canvas ducking had been ripped away by the wind, exposing the cover boards.

But all eight of the metal cross battens that snugged them down were still intact, each batten a thick strip of two-inch steel joined in the center by a turnbuckle.

Jack felt the ship's head lifting abruptly on another wave, saw the thing loom over the fo'c'sle deck like a tidal front, a gray-blue monster scarred with wind peaks and scud.

From the edge of his eyes, he caught sight of the heli-copter suddenly veer up and away just as the wave crashed down onto the forward deck. For a fleeting moment, its spray completely covered the aircraft, the props creating downdraft curls of mist like those at the bottom of a steep waterfall.

Then he had to duck behind the winch as the wave wash

roared across the deck and overran him. But this time, the winch housing protected him somewhat from the main strength of the rushing water. Instead, a small back current was formed, strong enough to slam him into the winch's drum casing.

As soon as the bulk of the wash drained off, hissing through the scuppers, Jack leapt to his feet and started toward the number-three hatch. A twisting explosion of wind instantly knocked him down and slid him on a cushion of water all the way to the bulwarks.

He clawed his way to his knees, the wind roaring across his ears, the rain driving into the top of his head and shoulders and legs like birdshot.

It gradually lessened enough for him to crawl to the hatch coaming and climb up onto it. Using the narrow end of the galley wrench, he began to loosen the first batten's turnbuckle, slamming it over, withdrawing, then slamming it over again. The bolt screw began to give.

Over the screech of the wind, he heard the helicopter coming back.

## WHITE HOUSE
## 2:06 P.M.

There was utter silence in the conference area of the Situation Room when the second deadline passed, everybody waiting for the president to say it. An odd, musky odor permeated the area, seeped from bodies that had been under stress for too long.

The president was still walking slowly around, his head down, hands in his pockets. An aura of separation surrounded him. He finally paused before the plotting board, stood there silently.

The phone rang. Santia grabbed it, listened, then said, "Bring in the telex." He hung up. "Norfolk Comm managed to filter out some of the last transmission from Cuba one-four-four."

A moment later, Commander Hand came into the con-

ference room and handed the president a yellow sheet. He
read it. It said:

```
GMT060615ZSPT
CINCOMLANT OP
OPDES: DIOGENES

INFO: TRANS D CUBN-144

WATCHDOG . . . DOG   CUB . . . ONE- . . . -FOUR . . . BOILERS
BLO . . . HOLDS OPEN . . . SEA . . . NNING . . . LIST PORT . . .
UT . . . AFLOAT
```

The president stared at the last word. *The Bengal was
still out there, alive!* He handed the telex sheet to Rebeck.
The admiral scanned it and passed it to Santia, who also
read it.

Santia slumped. "Well, there goes the last card," he
said.

The president put his hands back into his pockets. He
stared at the floor. "Order the *Winston-Salem* to launch
immediately," he said quietly.

"Yes, sir," Rebeck said.

# 00:31

THE CONTROL CENTER SPEAKER BLASTED OUT, "CONN, Radio. Incoming EAM, Captain."

Vantrease felt a slight warmth caress his right ear. "Conn, aye. Bring it forward."

A moment later, the radio officer brought the decode and handed it to Vantrease. He read it. It consisted of three three-letter groupings. Still staring at it, he said, "XO, retrieve the authenticator."

"Aye, sir."

Delannis and the navigational officer, an ensign named Parisi, moved to a safe on the starboard bulkhead of the CIC. Both carried keys to open it. Delannis took out two red plastic cards, each the size of a small envelope. He handed one to Parisi. They moved back to the plotting table where they tore their cards open.

Parisi read his aloud: "Delta-charlie-tango . . . mike-charlie-india . . . kilo-quebec-alfa."

Delannis said, "Mine concurs, sir."

Vantrease nodded. "We have a properly formulated launch message."

349

The dive officer called, "Sir, we have achieved six-zero feet, zero bubble."

"Very well," Vantrease said. "Officer of the deck, achieve and maintain launch position designated delta-one-three."

"Achieve and maintain delta-one-three, aye."

Orders and acknowledgments echoed throughout the control area as final engine settings were issued to bring the *Winston-Salem* to hover at the firing position of delta-one-three.

"Weapons, Conn, you have permission to activate circuits."

"Circuits activated. White lights on."

Vantrease turned slightly to Delannis. "Executive officer, break out the CIP key."

"Aye, sir."

The CIP key was kept in a separate safe. Delannis retrieved it and handed it to the captain, who immediately inserted it into a small box beside the navigational panels. When aligned, it completed the sub's firing circuits.

A second later: "Conn, Weapons. We have green lights."

Vantrease took one of the loudspeaker mikes. "This is the captain. We are in Condition 1-SQ. This is a Missile combat launch."

He then handed the mike to Delannis, who identified himself and repeated the status. The entire ship's crew had to recognize the voices of both senior officers before a launch.

Vantrease said, "Officer of the deck, recommend position for hover."

"Captain, recommend hover commence in forty-five seconds."

"Make it so."

"Aye, sir. Helm, achieve hover in forty-four seconds."

"Forty-four seconds, aye."

"All stop."

"Tracking party, insert existant CCS-2 mission plan into

missiles three and five," the captain ordered. The warmth in his right ear increased. He fought off the urge to touch it.

Three seconds later: "Captain, MP insert complete on three and five."

"Stand by Fire Order."

"Stand by Fire Order, aye."

"Fire Order will be simultaneous."

The command was relayed and acknowledged by the fire control officer. In the weapons bay, all the firing grid lights went off except those of missiles designated three and five.

"Weapons, Conn. Open outer doors."

"Open outer doors, aye." A moment later. "Outer doors open and locked."

"Sir," the dive officer called. "Permission to initiate hover."

"All stop and commence hovering."

"All stop. Hover has been initiated."

Vantrease looked at the chronometer above the CCS-2 console. Twenty seconds to launch.

"Pressurize tubes three and five."

"Pressurize three and five." There were soft hisses as several atmospheres of air were pumped into the Tomahawks' VLS firing tubes. "Tubes three and five on full pressure."

Ten seconds . . .

"Sir, we have full hover on delta-one-three."

Five seconds . . .

Two . . .

"Weapons, Conn. You have permission to fire."

There was a strong jolt as the booster packets on both Tomahawks went off. It was followed by the high-pitched sound of releasing pressure.

"Conn, Weapons. Numbers three and five away on simultaneous firing. Approximate time to target will be fourteen minutes, eight seconds."

Vantrease said, "Very well. Chief of the Boat, log firing

time. Helm, all ahead one-third. Stand by to run up antennae.''

''Ahead one-third. Stand by to run up antennas.''

''Radio, Conn. Notify COMSUBLANT that missiles are away. TOT fourteen minutes plus.''

''Away missiles, fourteen minutes plus on TOT, aye.''

Vantrease glanced over at Delannis, met his dark eyes. They exchanged a long look.

Ashdown had loosened four turnbuckles on the number-three hold hatch. Behind him, the wind had already torn out two boards. The others were slipping and sliding under the battens, water flooding down into the hold.

He jumped from the hatch and worked his way to the number-one hold. Crawling onto it, he started on the first batten turnbuckle. From below, he caught the squeal of cable tension and that deadly humming between gusts of wind.

The Cuban chopper was still up there. He didn't look at it, maybe not wanting to see its closeness, which was yet so far away. Didn't want to think of his salvation hanging by a small harness whipping in the wind.

As he worked, he got an oblique thought. The son of a bitch flying that thing sure as hell had some balls on him. If he had any real sense, he'd be long gone by now, driven downwind and away.

He started on the second turnbuckle. A new squall of rain lashed into him, the drops smoking off the deck. With it came the stark realization that he'd probably have to go into the sea, whatever that helo did. Damned soon, too. And with only dunnage strips to hang onto since all the rafts had been swept away.

He glanced out at the gray tumult of the ocean. Without a vest, a man wouldn't last long out there. And if a missile hit while he was in the water, its concussion could crush his ribs, immobilize his muscles, even at three hundred yards out. Closer in, the ship would suck him under when she went down.

He swung his mind around and homed it to the wrench, the turnbuckle, the pain in his body to distract himself. He had to consciously let his body feel the pain since it was clothed in adrenaline immunity. Muscles, bones, skin all felt hot and raw from the collisions of the rain.

Through the hatch boards, he felt deep impacts rumbling within the ship. The flooding from her engine room had obviously spread into the upper midhouse and was now tearing it apart. Then he sensed another huge wave coming; he looked up. There it was, rising like a moving building.

The *Bengal*'s stern was now under so much water that her bow had lifted high into the wind, which turned her slightly, pivoting the hull. When the wave struck, it came into the port bow.

Jack had already hurled himself off the hatch and was scrambling for the foremast table. He reached it as the wave exploded against the hull and slanted deck. The avalanche of white water came crashing and roaring toward him.

He grabbed the base of the jumbo boom and held on. The tidal surge boomed and slurred and hissed all around him, made his eardrums hurt. Then his arms and fingers were torn off the boom. He felt himself go tumbling crazily backward, skidding over objects like a bodysurfer over rocks. Then there was a solid slam into something, and he was jetted into comparatively calm water.

It was gray-black dark. He instantly realized that he was in the tween-deck space of the number-two hold. But the tumbling had disoriented him. Where in Christ was the surface?

He thrashed around, caught in the same whirling terror he'd experienced that night in the Singapore Strait. His adrenaline-laced blood was like molecular blue static in his tissues.

He finally saw stronger light, a shapeless, faded gray. He kicked toward it and popped through the surface near the hold's after coaming.

He heard a deep rumbling close by. The timbers in number three were loose and shifting. Frantically, he swam for-

ward, crossed the hold and pulled himself out near the base
of the foremast's jumbo boom. Grabbing boltheads and
deck machinery, he made his way to the windlass and cow-
ered there. Nearby, the ship's bell clanged, a discordant,
sorrowful sound barely heard above the scream of the wind.

Timbers began blowing through the number-three hold
hatch along with shattered boards and twisted cross battens,
everything flying upward and back against the face of the
midhouse. Then the main body of logs erupted through the
breached hold, twisting and rolling as if they were in a mill
sluice.

Above the midhouse, Jack saw the chopper hanging directly over the flying bridge deck. It juked and trembled,
the downwash furring water off the deck and railings. He
saw the two pilots looking out at him, their helmets giving
them the look of large insects.

A flash of lightning burst off to his right, the thunder
quick and volcanic. Another squall crossed over the ship,
the hurtling raindrops actually pinging off metal. Shielding
his eyes, Jack tried to keep the helicopter in sight. But it
had disappeared in the rain.

The burst of lightning had been so close, Ana was
blinded for a few seconds. In reaction, she lifted the Helix.
It immediately was caught by a wind gust and swept past
the starboard side of the ship and overrun by a dark, almost
black downpour.

*Mierda!* she kept moaning in her head. Shit!

She was suddenly conscious of the fatigue in her arms
and shoulders, her hand, fingers. It seemed as if she had
been fighting the controls for hours and hours, her sweat-
soaked flight suit sticking to the seat, the musky odor of
her fear and exertion lingering in the air.

Jesse swung around and looked at her. "Did you see
him?"

"Yes."

"I thought he was gone in that wave. The other must be
dead."

She nodded.

"Can we approach with those masts?" Perez said. "The bow's lifting fast."

"We might get one try."

Jesse stared. Those same girl-pretty eyes squeezed with anxiety. He said nothing.

Ana moved her head slowly this way, that, scanning. Nothing below but rain-misty ocean. She glanced at the radar screen. The blob of the *Bengal* appeared. The ship lay off about a half mile behind them at 104 degrees. She eased around and headed back, dropping altitude.

Once more, the thought of the incoming missiles assailed her. Her eyes slid to the MRP lights. Both off. She frowned. Why hadn't the missiles already come? Perhaps they wouldn't come at all. That hopeful thought evaporated. No, they were out there all right, already drilling fire holes in the storm.

She experienced a moment of hopelessness. I can't do this anymore, she thought. I won't. She glanced at Perez, searching for that fear in his eyes. If it was really there, she would swing around and head back for clear weather.

He was staring out his window. She closed her own eyes, drew in a lungful of air. Anger came with it. I *will* do this. Her fingers gripped the stick anew.

At 150 feet, they crossed over the *Bengal* again. It lay below them, still so huge, yet so pitiful. Her afterdecks were fully under now, the outline of her hull shadowy beneath the water. The midhouse was hard over to port, the bulwarks submerged. Whole and splintered logs were scattered on the forward deck and out in the ocean.

The sight of the bow touched Ana's heart. It rose upward, tilted sharply, exposing the rusted starboard waterline, the faded Plimsoll marks. It was as if the ship were desperately holding its head above the ocean in one final gasp for life.

She and Perez spotted the man at the same time. He was squatting near some forward machinery, his yellow T-shirt an incongruous swatch of color in all the gray.

She keyed the intercom. "Escalera, do you see him?"
"Yes."

"Start lowering. Be damn sharp. We get maybe one pass
before that ship goes under."

She took the Helix past the ship, directly into the pre-
dominant wind. Then, slowly, tightly, she began to lower,
synchronizing her power setting so that the wind would
drift the aircraft right over the bow.

Escalera began calling up position reports.

Two minutes after launch, the two Tomahawks entered
the outer storm wall.

Their launch had been perfect, both missiles blowing
through the surface of the ocean cleanly. Instantly, their
rocket boosters fired off, lifting them in an oddly tilted way
into the sky.

Five seconds later, at two hundred feet above the sea,
the boosters dropped off along with engine inlet covers.
The missiles' small turbojet engines ignited.

Their GPS transmitters immediately sent request pulses
to the NavSat satellite for position and altitude fixes to
which their inertial navigation units keyed. Then, responding to the *Winston-Salem*'s TMA presets, they turned
slightly to a heading of 271 degrees.

Both were now traveling at five hundred miles per hour,
approximately eighty feet apart. Two thousand yards down-
range, their 488-pound high-explosive warheads automatically armed for contact detonation.

Since no two missiles will maintain an absolutely identical speed regime due to tiny differences in power and
aerodynamic characteristics, the number-three Tomahawk
slowly began to pull ahead of its mate. Two minutes, thirty
seconds after entering the storm wall, it was a full hundred
yards beyond number five.

Suddenly, it crossed through a narrow, spiral gravita-
tional force field. These aberrant bursts are millisecond distortions of the normal gravity created by photon frequency

oscillations within the vast magnetic energy complex of a hurricane.

Instantly, number three's MGU system began to decay. The continuous position updates quickly lost accuracy. Twenty seconds later, the missile veered slightly to the left. The position errors had confused the inertial guidance computer. It now attempted to reacquire the proper preset command.

Altitude readings also skidded upward, indicating the missile's altitude at a false height of 357 feet above the ocean. Once more, the guidance system attempted to realign, canting the steering vanes slightly in order to descend. Ten seconds later, the missile went into the sea, exploding with a powerful, fiery outthrow that hurled water two hundred feet up into the rain.

A quarter mile to the right, Tomahawk number five hurtled past, still dead on course.

*WHITE HOUSE*
*2:15 P.M.*
On the conference room plotting board, the positions of the Tomahawk missiles were displayed by tiny orange lights. Beside the moving lights was the digital readout of the time to target, put there by the Situation Room computer, which ingested hot tracking data directly off the mainframes of COMSUBLANT in Norfolk.

The president had experienced a sickening sense of despairing irretrievability when Rebeck informed him that both missiles had been launched. Then their lights appeared on the board, drawing from him a fleeting memory. College years. Late-night poker games in the frat house. *He'd always lost against the odds.*

Then one orange light went out.

He blinked. "What the hell's wrong?" he barked. "One of the missile lights just went out."

Ever since the launch, Rebeck had been holding direct

conversations with Norfolk by phone. Now he lowered his head, listened, then said, ''God*damn* it.'' He looked up. ''One of the Tomahawks malfunctioned and exploded. SO-SUS picked up the detonation.''

Shit! the president thought. The odds had just doubled.

He looked back up at the single orange light, shot his gaze back and forth between it and the *Bengal*'s. ''Where's Anholt?'' he snapped. ''Who the hell's got Anholt?''

''I have him on-line, sir,'' Colonel Trautloff answered.

''What are the pressure readings at the *Bengal?*''

The colonel talked for a few moments, put down the receiver. ''Anholt says they can only estimate, sir. But they think it should be in the range of 28.80. But they're very anxious. Indications are that the pressure is dropping much faster than expected in that segment of the storm.''

The president felt his bowels grip. He had a sudden, painful urge to urinate. Couldn't remember the last time he had. His eyes shifted to the time-to-target readout. It was in seconds and tenths of seconds.

480.3 . . . 480.2 . . . 480.1 . . .

**Eight minutes to go.**

He whirled and headed for the bathroom.

The *Bengal* began disgorging her life's blood.

As the engine room settling tanks and fuel piping burst open and timbers ruptured the deep tanks below the number-four hold, great pools and globs of Bunker C crude started surfacing along her port side.

Each time a sea came into the midhouse, it smeared a coating of it over the metal. The stanchions and railings and deck machinery all looked as if they had been dipped in tar.

Like any oil, the crude quickly smoothed out the ocean surface to a hundred yards beyond the port and forward side. Now, as wave fronts came in, they were bare of storm spume, their faces instead dark and ripply like moving walls of black silk.

As each one crashed over Ashdown behind the windlass,

he had to bury his head into the crook of his elbow and hold his eyes tightly shut. Still, the fuel stung his eyes, clogged his mouth and throat. His entire body was covered with it.

Whenever he could, he glanced up to search out the position of the helicopter. Now it was coming back for him. He studied the fo'c'sle deck, the towering foremast. Could they get at him? In time?

From where he was, he could see all the way down the length of the ship. Seas were already washing cleanly over the *Bengal*'s boat and bridge decks on the port side. He knew she'd begin her final plunge in minutes.

Another wave smashed into the bow. When it washed past, Jack saw the belly of the chopper fifty feet above and back of him. Its powerful downwash fumed oily spray off the deck. The cable and harness trailed out, blown toward him by the wind.

The harness weight struck the windlass drum. Instantly, he leapt for it. His shoes slipped on the oily deck. He missed it, the yellow harness so close that he could see the weave of its dense nylon. Like the straps on an ALICE H-pack in the army.

The harness weight struck the bow chock, bounced, dragged over a bulwark wing bracket and then was gone. Overhead, the helo dipped slightly and then went sliding off down the wind. In seconds, it was swallowed by the slanted, gray-black curtain of an incoming squall line.

Jack put his head down, cursing helplessly as the shrapnel of the rain swept over him.

Ana was also cursing. She knew they'd missed the pickup. No weight had come onto the rescue cable. Now they were sliding wildly downwind, and beside her Perez pounded his fist against his right thigh in frustration.

She keyed. "How close was he?"

"He almost had it," Escalera answered.

"One more time."

"Jesus!" Perez said.

"One more time, I said. Escalera, stand by. I'm going to make the approach against the wind this time."

She got the Helix around and they began the slow, driving fight back to the ship. The downwash of rain was so heavy that there were only split seconds when she was able to see ahead. The gray ocean was so close down there. Then the black pooling of oil and the huge, darkly opaque shape of the *Bengal*'s bow were dead ahead.

"Ready back there?" she cried. "Here we go."

Beside her, Jesse metronomed his head back and forth in time with the windshield wipers, catching the little moments of clear vision just behind the sweeping blades.

She lifted slightly. The dark trianglar bow image dropped and finally went out of sight beyond the bottom of the windshield. She glanced out the side. There it was again, so close it seemed that she could step right out onto it, the metal oil-black.

"Up ten feet," Escalera called. "Up, up, God dammit, Lieutenant."

Ana powered. The dark image slid under the helicopter's left wheel strut. Now ahead was the indistinct mass of the tilted midhouse and stack. And somewhere in between, she knew, the foremast and cross braces.

"Where's the mast?" she yelled. "I can't see it."

"Down and to the right," Jesse came back. "We're clear, we're clear."

"Steady up," Escalera called. "Hold . . . right there."

Ana closed her eyes, fixed her hands so strongly onto the stick that they became it, holding, holding. . . .

Sixty-three feet below the Helix, the accumulated water in the forepeak trunk had receded from the bomb due to the sharp lift of the bow. Now it was gathered against the collision bulkhead, partway up the ladder.

The tiny trigger unit light still glowed: **28.52**

Over the past hour, the ambient storm pressure had dropped drastically—all the way down to 28.64, where it stabilized momentarily. Then, thirty minutes earlier, at the same time that Jack was making his final inspection of the boilers, it began another downward slide.

28.62 . . .

28.59 . . .

Down it continued, the average drop approximately one-hundredth of an inch every four minutes. Now the aneroid barometer within the trigger unit clicked off another hundredth of an inch. To 28.54.

**Eight minutes to detonation. . . .**

Huge bubbles of frothy black water began belching out of the *Bengal*'s partially submerged midhouse as trapped air pockets flooded. On the forward deck, more water and oil erupted out of the breached holds. The deep fuel and ballast tanks below the hold floors were shearing open from the massive torsion effect in the ship's hull created by the increasing flooding.

Under the roar of the wind and the rapping crack of the Helix's props, Jack heard the gushing discharges from the holds. They sounded like a sub blowing ballast.

The ship was now heeled over at least fifty degrees. Every few seconds, she'd tremble, an odd metallic flutter in her decks and hull plating. Like the quiver in the skin of a terrified horse.

Protecting his eyes against the whirling maelstrom of flying oil from the helo's downwash, Jack watched as the whipping rescue cable came slowly, erratically toward him. The Helix was right above him, shaking violently in the countering updraft wind off the bow.

His entire body throbbed with intense excitement. He could feel, sense the *Bengal*'s final plunge coming. Not minutes now, but seconds. He had a sudden wild urge to hurl himself over the bulwarks, to go into the sea.

He didn't. It was too late. He'd never be able to swim far enough away to escape the powerful suction of the ship. He saw the harness weight slam into one of the catheads, drag for a second along the starboard anchor chain, then lift slightly and flail away from him.

\*   \*   \*

Twenty-five miles from the ship, Tomahawk number five entered its end-game search pattern quadrant.

Instantly, the ESM or electronic support measures seeker system within the guidance packet clicked on its active radar. Since a ship, under normal conditions, is a moving object, no absolute preset target data can be input at firing. The search pattern allows the missile to locate and home to its target by itself.

Now it began a series of back-and-forth jogs, hurling radar pulses. A search pattern is laid out in a series of ever-smaller electronic boxes. Finding nothing in the largest box, the ESM moved to the next. Then the next.

In the fourth box, it picked up a rebound signal off the ship. Instantly, the guidance computer fixed the heading, and the missile homed to it. Since the sub's fire control technicians had preset for a waterline hit, it also began a slow descent.

The *Bengal* began her plunge.

Her stern started down first, sucking a long trough into the sea as its mass gathered momentum. Slowly at first, then faster and faster, the ship rolled to port until she was on her beam ends. Abruptly, the bow drove upward, lunging, rising high out of the water as the stern pulled the ship toward the vertical.

Jack felt the deck heave violently into the roll. In a frenzy, he grabbed for anything to hold onto, finally got his fingers around the windlass's wildcat wheel. His legs were whipped out from under him. He hung there, slanted across the huge windlass gear, staring wild-eyed down the long drop to the midhouse.

All around him, powerful sounds overrode the wind's noise: deep rumblings, the moaning scream of twisting steel, splinterings, rendings, air blowing hollowly, whomping through passageways. Debris came popping to the surface—barrels, clothing, cork vests, wooden furniture, a tin washbasin.

The three bridge windows suddenly blew out, followed by three streams of water shooting through the empty sills. Then the ocean reached the stack and poured into it. There were muffled explosions as the water hit still-hot vents and baffles. The ship ponderously twisted itself as it approached near-vertical.

Jack was aware that he groaned, deep in his throat. A babbling, his terror become sound. With a vicious jolt, he felt as if the bottom had just dropped out as the ship started down, sliding into the sea.

Frantically, he looked up. There was nothing there but the swift-moving gray-blackness of the storm clouds and the massive triangle of the bow. Then the curved blur of rotor blades appeared; behind them, the round white nose and radar dome and then the wheel struts of the helicopter.

It went into hover forty feet above him.

"I'm here," he screamed. "I'm here."

He swung his legs up, locked them around the wildcat engage bar. Pulling himself up and over it, he took hold of the starboard anchor chain. He climbed it hand over hand, oil-slippery, the toes of his shoes fitting into the spaces between the huge links.

The quiver in the deck and machinery had become a powerful shudder, a quaking from way down through the fundaments of the ship, in her cross frames and longitudinals and bulkheads. Higher and still higher went the tip of the bow as it became more vertical, the helo up there moving upward to get out of its way.

Jack reached the stopper chock where the chain reaved down through the hawsepipe. He braced his feet against it and leapt upward to the ship's bell stanchion. From there to the lookout's platform.

Blood rushed through his body in streams of super heat, gave his muscles an unusual strength as he pulled himself to the bow bulwark and took hold of one of the stays on the jackstaff. He lifted himself and stood up on the very tip of the bow, his hands around the jackstaff. The storm wind and downwash from the Helix scourged him.

He glanced down. The sea had reached the number-two hold. The *Bengal*'s plunge was speeding up now as the increasing weight of her submerged sections pulled her deeper.

He lifted his head to look at the chopper. There was a flash of color to his right. It was the rescue harness, above him and out about twenty feet, spinning like a whirligig.

Three seconds later, it hit him in the chest.

Through the soft, quick jerk of the control stick and the slight shift of the aircraft within all the other shiftings and lungings, Ana's body received the transmission of Ashdown's weight as it came onto the rescue line.

Then it was gone.

"Is he on?" she screamed into the mike. "Is he still on?"

"Wait, wait," Escalera called. His voice was deep in the wind sound as he leaned out to see the man on the bow. "There, he's got it now. Up, pull up!"

Ana gave the engines more power, slowly, equalizing pitch so she would lift straight up. Up it went, rocking as the man's weight distorted its precarious stability. Perez had his head cranked around, staring down and back.

The sound of the MRP warning alarm cut through the other noises like a stiletto, the red light suddenly flashing.

*Incoming missile!*

Ana's heart jumped. Perez's head snapped around. They both stared at the light for a nanosecond, then exchanged terrified looks. But her body was already moving, slamming the throttles to the firewall, throwing pitch, the helicopter responding instantly as it pulled up and away.

Fifteen seconds later, the second warning buzzer went off, its light flashing. *The missile had just locked onto the Helix.*

Jack had almost lost it. When the harness struck him, he rammed his right arm through it and clamped it tightly into the crook of his elbow. Instantly, he was lifted off the bow.

The wind caught his body and blew him away from the jackstaff, right into the face of a wave. It engulfed him. He held on desperately. A second later, the wave slammed him into the jackstaff.

A numbing surge shot through his left leg, spread across his groin. In reflex, he snapped forward at the waist. His arm slipped back through the harness, then down his forearm to his wrist.

Just before it went completely, he grabbed hold and shoved his other arm through. He dangled, his leg beginning to throb hotly. The cable, twanging in the wind, lifted him clear of the bow once more.

Directly below him, the ocean had reached the ship's number-one hold. Another wave peeled a slab of cement off the starboard gun pit. Water sucked and swirled around the twin hood vents, then surged up and over the windlass housing.

At last, with a final blowing, hissing boil of crude-black water, the *Bengal's* bow slipped under. The shadow of her held for a moment like a reef below the surface, the thin, curved jackstaff trembling in the streaming plunge.

Then the shadow was gone, and there was only ocean.

Jack watched her go and felt his heart ache. Then the harness began to jump and jerk as the cable started reeling in. His body, slanted to the side by the wind, spun and careened, the rain jolting him with hot blows. From somewhere deep in the storm, he heard a keening sound, a soughing ululation like the wails of mourning women.

Suddenly, the cable line snapped him violently upward. The motion was so abrupt, it nearly tore the harness from his grasp. The helicopter moved sharply to the side, still going up, dragging him with it.

Forty seconds earlier, Tomahawk five, five miles out, had suddenly lost its huge metallic target. It had simply disappeared.

The missile had already reached its optimum attack height and now hurtled just above the surface, so close that

at times wave crests nearly washed along its underside, the
bottom steering vane slicing through water.

Instantly, the ESM seeker tightened its radar frequency
and began lashing the target zone to reacquire a fix. Rebound immediately picked up a metallic object above the
original fix. The seeker homed to it.

The new target suddenly began rising with great speed.
For a moment, the guidance computer was confused, its
program unable to track the velocity of such a target. Trying to counter it, the computer sent a command to the steering vanes for full ascension deployment.

The Tomahawk lifted away from the surface, angled upward and began to chase the new target.

For Jack Ashdown, the next two minutes seemed caught
in some web of aborted time. It was as if his mind had
absorbed so much high-speed input, it now decelerated itself, everything suddenly appearing in slow motion. All except the thudding pound of his heart, which hammered
against his inner ears.

He looked up. He was fifteen feet below the aircraft.
Through the contrails of the rain, he saw the chopper's
winchman leaning out the open door, a safety harness
around his shoulders, his helmet shield down. And the underside of the helicopter. He could actually see the rivets
in its sheeting, saw the twin gray missiles, the wobble and
spin of its wheels with their crisscross tread.

There was a small, sharp explosion, and a stream of silvery strips like magnetic tape blew out of a hole in the
helicopter's fuselage forward of the after wheel struts. The
strips were instantly swept away by the wind, twirling and
unraveling.

Jack's whole body went cold. Radar chaff! That meant
a missile had locked onto the chopper and the Cuban pilot
was flying break maneuvers, laying a false radar trail.

The cable continued reeling in. He heard the sound of
the turning drum traveling down through the steel. Time
still moved with agonizing sluggishness as he spun a con-

tinuous 360, the ocean skidding past without horizon, giving no sense of altitude.

Eight feet to go . . .

He heard it before he saw it: an odd buzzing that rippled through the helo's roaring engines. And there it was, the missile, coming upward, shafting through the rain. The rounded nose and stubby wings, the long gray-white body like a telephone pole in flight, the four steering vanes and, behind them, a trail of engine heat that left a tube of shimmering air like glass.

Oh, Jesus almighty, his mind screamed. Terrified, he tried to climb the harness strapping.

The Tomahawk flashed past twenty feet below him with an air-shattering jet-whine rush. He felt its turbulence wash over him. It went boring off into the rain, the orange oval of its exhaust like the glow from a boiler viewing window. He saw it begin to turn. A second later, the orange fire of its exhaust disappeared back into the storm.

The winch stopped reeling. Jack shot a glance upward. Nearly within reach was the Helix's left rear wheel. Above that, he saw the winchman yelling into his mike. Then he was yelling soundlessly at him, indicating something. He hugged his arms to his chest and then pointed down.

He was still shouting as the helicopter suddenly dropped into a steep dive. Jack was thrown back and up against the wheel. A knife-sharp shock of pain went through his leg. He hung on and looked down as the gray, roiling plain of the ocean began to come up to him.

Just above it, the chopper pulled level again and skimmed above the waves. The crests zipped past right below Jack's oil-soaked shoes. In contrast, the seconds passed in an elongated motionless motion.

He caught the peculiar buzz of the missile's engine again. His head swiveled around. Oh, shit, where is it? In a groin-dropping surge, the Helix pulled up in a pure vertical, its engines screaming like banshees.

Up it went, the ocean falling away faster and faster. Then

the Tomahawk was down there where they had been. Jack saw it cross from rain wall to rain wall.

Four seconds later, there was a brilliant flash. The light illuminated the storm clouds like orange lightning. A concussion wave swept past Jack. The energy of it impacted and enfolded him like a comber across a reef. Above him, it made the helicopter rock. He heard metal things clanking together.

The winch started again.

Five feet . . .

Three . . .

The winchman grabbed for him, got one hand under his armpit, then the other on the harness. He was lifted and hauled across the door foot, dragged over decking. His leg quivered with pain. He smelled the acrylic odor of flight instruments and felt the solid tremble of the engines.

The winchman's helmeted face loomed into his vision. He was shouting something in Spanish. He couldn't understand it. It didn't matter.

Jack grinned up at him and took his hand in a reverse handshake. The man smiled back, nodding. They broke the grip, and the Cuban slipped a safety harness around Jack's shoulders and began to probe at his leg.

The leg felt hot and swollen. The winchman's fingers were cool and moved with slow, gentle pressure. Jack closed his eyes and listened to the steady, whomping chop of the rotors.

# AFTERMATH

THE GROWING WAVE OF HYSTERIA IN THE GULF AND southeastern states never peaked.

At 2:37 P.M., the president held his news conference. He was already at the podium when Santia brought him a note from the Situation Room. The *Bengal* was on the bottom.

He laid out the entire scenario for the gathered journalists and television cameras. The conference took an hour and a half. The following day, the story blew everything off the newspapers and TV channels around the world.

The hurricane came ashore at St. Augustine, Florida, precisely twenty-two minutes before the NHC model predictions said it would. It swept north and finally returned to the sea near Cape Hatteras. Millions of dollars in damage resulted. But because of the evacuation, not a single life was lost.

Within hours after it passed the Bahamas, Navy divers were sent down to search the *Bengal* for the Red Bomb. She was in forty-six fathoms of ocean. Her stern had struck first, the impact shearing it off to the number-four hold. Sea bacteria had already begun bubbling her plates.

It took the divers two days to probe her before they found the bomb. The trigger mechanism was still alive, but the water pressure had gone beyond its calibration span and the unit had shut down. The readout window showed 00.00.

Subsequent deep intelligence investigations were never able to produce an absolute link between Libya and the *Bengal* affair. Still, the president condemned Gadhafi and terrorists in general. The UN squabbled over sanctions. Eventually, it all just faded into the background as other, more pressing issues arose.

But the U.S. media never forgave the president for keeping them in the dark for so long. Congressional members in opposition, focusing on his abrogation of the states' constitutional rights, created a firestorm against his administration. Two years later, he was not reelected.

But that lay in the future. . . .

SACRED HEART HOSPITAL
MONTECRISTI, DOMINICAN REPUBLIC
OCTOBER 4

Ashdown could walk in his cast, with a steel bar down across his instep and the cast up to his mid thigh. It didn't hurt to walk, but now and then there would come a little stab of pain, even when he was sitting.

He walked all the way down to the main veranda of the hospital. It was hot-sunny outside, the light white through the screen door. He stepped out, went to the rail and looked out over the hospital's huge lawn, which slanted down gradually to a stone wall.

The lawn was filled with jacaranda trees. All their leaves had been whipped away by Emma's edge, and the hibiscus and bougainvillea and ginger shrubs around the edge of the hospital were uprooted and torn apart. Pools of standing water glistened in the potholes of the hospital driveway.

A half mile away was the ocean. It was milky white from the storm flood, all the way out to where the sun made it impossible to see its color. Tree trunks and floating debris and dead birds were everywhere, and there were deep drain-off channels in the beach. A few small boats were out there, gathering up things still usable.

He made his way around the corner of the veranda. Just

below the porch railing, a nun pushed an old woman in a wheelchair along the pathway beside the torn flower shrubs.

Jack looked at the sea again. He could smell it, the thick, salty, tropical fragrance of it overlaid with the slightly rancid smell of rotting vegetation.

He allowed himself to think of Carol and Jamie then. They came gently. He watched them with his mind's eye, walking with him down to the chalk-white beach and sea and laughing together.

It suddenly occurred to him that something had changed. His guilt was gone. He wondered about that. Why? How? Perhaps it would take time for him to fully understand the dynamics. But for now, in this moment, he knew only that it wasn't there and that he was damned glad he was alive.

"Ashdown?" a woman said behind him.

He turned. She was lovely, dark-haired, with skin the color of a model in a suntan lotion ad. She wore a cleanly washed green flight suit with a yellow Cuban navy patch on her left sleeve.

He tilted his head. "You're the pilot," he said.

Back in the helicopter, he had not seen Ana. After the winchman gave him a shot of morphine, his exhaustion had plunged him into a sleep from which he had not awakened until he was in the ambulance.

She came forward, stood close. "Yes. Lieutenant Ana Castile."

They looked at each other, then silently put their arms around each other and hugged tightly. Jack smelled her hair, a light carnation scent.

They pulled apart. He saw that she had deep, lovely eyes. "Thank you," he said.

"And thank *you*," she said. "A lot of people thank you."

He looked at her face, absorbing it. "You're beautiful."

She flushed slightly. *"Gracias."*

"This morning I got a call from the president. Quite an honor."

Ana nodded. "Yes, he called me, too. He offered my

crew and me political asylum. Also my daughter, Pilar. We have accepted.''

Then a slight frown creased her forehead. She turned away and looked wistfully out toward the ocean.

"I'm glad for you," he said.

"Yes."

"Where is your daughter now?"

"In the British Grand Caymans. She will fly to Miami tomorrow. Then she and I will stay with relatives there." She turned back. "And what of you? You will go back to sea?"

He chuckled. "Maybe. If I don't get my license pulled by the Maritime Commission."

She looked shocked. "They would do such a thing? After what you did?"

His smile faded. "I was a mutinous officer."

Ana's gaze focused on his eyes. "So was I."

They looked at each other for a long moment, some unspoken thing passing between them.

He finally broke it, spoke. "I'd like to meet your daughter sometime."

"I'd like her to meet you, too."

"Tell you what—when you're settled in Miami, I'll take you both out to dinner."

She smiled then, a quick, clean smile that lit her face. "That would be nice."

"How will I reach you?"

"My relative's name is Fernando Zamora. He lives on Pico Street in South Miami."

"I'll find you."

She touched his hand lightly. "Until then."

"Until then."

He watched her walk away and turn the corner of the veranda. He could still smell the scent of her. He walked over and leaned on the rail and thought about that.